Countdown to Destruction

Sergeant Adams warned, "We've got less than ten seconds before the missile is out of range for good."

Lance answered "We're almost there. . . ."

"Eight seconds."

"The MiGs are firing," Critter said. "Air-to-air missiles."

"Six seconds."

"The ICBM is at thirty thousand feet."

"Four seconds."

Lance's eyes were glued to the screen. This was it.

"Two seconds."

The blip on the screen was almost imperceptible. "I've got it! Firing!"

Twelve seconds with the laser should do it, Lance thought. And at that instant, the nose of the plane lurched violently down.

Then he heard Sergeant Adams's desperate voice. "No! No! I'm losing the target! I'm losing it. . . ."

SILENT SALVO

Joe L. Gribble

AN ONYX BOOK

ONYX
Published by New American Library, a division of
Penguin Putnam Inc., 375 Hudson Street,
New York, New York 10014, U.S.A.
Penguin Books Ltd, 27 Wrights Lane,
London W8 5TZ, England
Penguin Books Australia Ltd, Ringwood,
Victoria, Australia
Penguin Books Canada Ltd, 10 Alcorn Avenue,
Toronto, Ontario, Canada M4V 3B2
Penguin Books (N.Z.) Ltd, 182–190 Wairau Road,
Auckland 10, New Zealand

Penguin Books Ltd, Registered Offices:
Harmondsworth, Middlesex, England

First published by Onyx, an imprint of New American Library,
a division of Penguin Putnam Inc.

First Printing, December 2000
10 9 8 7 6 5 4 3 2 1

BOOKS ARE AVAILABLE AT QUANTITY DISCOUNTS WHEN USED TO PROMOTE PRODUCTS OR SERVICES. FOR INFORMATION PLEASE WRITE TO PREMIUM MARKETING DIVISION, PENGUIN PUTNAM INC., 375 HUDSON STREET, NEW YORK, NEW YORK 10014.

Prologue

Undergraduate Pilot Training—1978

"But I'm the top pilot in this class!"

"No. You were ranked second." The captain's face was getting red.

"That's crap, and you know it. I can outfly, outgun, and outsmart Lieutenant Warner any day of the week. The only reason you picked him as top pilot is so you could avoid this . . . this situation." Lieutenant Billie Powers was getting the shaft, and she wasn't going to sit still for it. "I'm the best pilot here and I've got the right to fly fighters. Even if I am number two—which, frankly, is ludicrous—I should still get my pick of planes. And I pick fighters."

"Lieutenant, my hands are tied. This isn't about you, and it isn't about who's the best pilot. Congress has mandated that women are not to be allowed to fill combat roles in the military. I'm not saying that won't change one of these days, but as of today you may have your pick of any noncombat aircraft. No fighters."

Billie knew she couldn't win this battle—not here. The captain was right; it was Congress that was preventing her from achieving her goals. She would have to bide her time, position herself so she would be prepared when the lawmakers finally relaxed their archaic mind-set and allowed women to compete fairly with men. "What about my second selection?"

"Test pilot school? Get real, Lieutenant. You can't even volunteer for test pilot school until you've got a lot of hours under your belt."

"Then let me get the hours, sir. Let me get them here." Powers continued to stand stiffly at attention.

"You want to be an instructor pilot? No one picks this job. Dealing with some of these amateur fliers is pretty tricky. You're a ninety-day wonder, too. You don't have the military background to connect with the Academy grads."

"Sir, I've been all over the world, following my father's career. I'd bet my next paycheck that I've been on more Air Force bases than you have, which gives me a particularly good view of military life. I also worked well with the men in my flight."

The captain relaxed and leaned back in his chair. "Your dad was well liked. Any of his friends would have weighed in if you had asked. My phone would be ringing off the hook with calls from the Pentagon, 'suggestions' that I try and do right by you and the Air Force and give you your pick of jobs, short of congressional limitations. But you didn't do that. I respect that you're trying to make your own mark, without any help. You'd be surprised how many graduates threaten me with calls from this colonel or that colonel if I don't give them the plane they want. I can't give you fighters, but I can gladly make you one of my instructors. Welcome aboard."

Undergraduate Pilot Training, Randolph Air Force Base, Texas—1982

Second Lieutenant Tom Driscoll banked the T-38 Talon hard to the right, focusing his entire being on perfectly executing every maneuver. It all boiled down to this check ride. They hadn't told him, of course, but it was common knowledge that the final check ride was one of the most important considerations when assignments were issued. And Driscoll knew what he wanted. Fighters.

Driscoll considered himself lucky even to be offered a chance to go to flight school. He was a quarter of an inch too tall to pass the flight physical, and without his uncle's intervention, and the subsequent waiver, he wouldn't be here.

The assignment to fighters was critical. Almost all the high fliers—the U-2 and SR-71 pilots like his uncle—started out in fighters. That was the track he had dreamed of following ever since visiting the Air Force base in California when he was thirteen. That was where his uncle, now a full colonel, had begun flying the SR-71s. Tom's plans were even more ambitious than his uncle's, though—he wanted to be an astronaut, to fly in that newest and most dangerous frontier of space.

Driscoll rolled out and pulled into a steep climb, listening, waiting for his IP, instructor pilot, in the backseat to say something. Anything. Thus far he had been totally silent, not giving a clue as to how he thought Driscoll was doing. Tom was beginning to wonder if he was even awake.

Rolling inverted, Tom checked his route map. It showed his simulated attack ingress route to the target area. He was right on course, the bright Texas sun glinting off the top of Shamu's dome at Sea World, visible about twelve miles dead ahead. He rolled again, dropping to the treetops, searching for the simulated runway at the old Marine Corps training facility. He spotted it off to the left, just where it was supposed to be. He started into his attack climb.

"Engine one—flameout!" the IP warned him, throwing a major glitch into the entire attack scenario.

Driscoll pulled the throttle back to simulate the engine problem, added rudder to compensate for the asymmetric thrust, and trimmed the nose up for maximum rate of climb for one engine.

"Engine two—flameout!" called the IP.

Driscoll pulled back the throttle and trimmed the nose back down to go to maximum glide ratio. The rules called for him to turn back to the base in order to save the aircraft. Instead, he turned for the target.

"Where the hell are you going?" the IP screamed into the interphone.

"Preparing to drop ordnance," Driscoll replied, trying to sound as calm as possible. He dropped the nose to pick up airspeed. Then, using his higher speed, he pulled up and called a lofting shot.

"BOMBS . . . BOMBS . . . BOMBS!" he yelled, simulating the release of the munitions, then dropped the nose and turned to search for a spot to set her down. There was a road in the distance. He knew it would be close. They might not make it.

"Okay, simulated engine out emergency is over," the instructor pilot said, calmer now. "You've got some explaining to do, Lieutenant."

Driscoll pushed the throttles forward. "I had to get rid of the weight, figured I might as well put it where it could do some good. My orders were to strike the target."

Driscoll waited for the instructor to say something. It was quiet for what seemed a long time. Driscoll began to wonder if he had totally blown it.

Finally the instructor spoke up. "Correct answer. You've learned that flexibility is the key to airpower. A lot of our students don't figure that out until someone is shooting at them. Good job."

Driscoll smiled. Fighters it was.

Orientation Flight—1985

The three senior cadets sat on the jump seats in the KC-135 as it bounced through the turbulent air. "Maybe we should have warned them before the flight," Cadet Skeeter Aziz told his two companions as the plane hit another swell of air and seemed to lift hundreds of feet. "They look pretty green."

"Naw, would've spoiled it for 'em," Cadet Turbo Miller said as the airplane lost the altitude it had just gained, in the same brief amount of time. "They need to see what recycled tacos look like before they decide they want to be pilots."

"Plebe Killeen doesn't look too good," Cadet Critter Warren said from the other side of Skeeter. "I think he's going to hurl first."

"My bet is on the gorilla next to him," Skeeter said.

"That's my nose-guard," Turbo said. "He sure as heck better not puke or I'll make sure he stays on the second string."

"Question is, how many of them were issued the modified barf bags?" Skeeter asked.

"What do you mean?" Critter asked.

"Well, while you guys were asleep last night, I made some special 'plebe' mods to a few barf bags."

"Don't you ever sleep? What'd you do, anyway?"

"You'll see. I think Killeen is going to win the prize. See? He's already looking for his bag."

The cadet's face was taking on the same hue as his flight suit—washed-out green. They watched him pull the yellow envelope from the zippered calf pocket of his flight suit. The plane lurched, and he quickly pulled the small plastic bag out of the envelope and shoved it up to his face. In moments the smell of bile saturated the hot air inside the cargo area of the refueling aircraft as the liquid poured from a hole clipped in the bottom of the plastic bag, covering the cadet and splashing onto the cargo floor.

"Bingo! We have a winner!" Skeeter said. The plane banked, and the liquid flowed across the floor of the plane. Several more of the new plebes grabbed for their own bags as the pungent smell reached them. Only one of them had the foresight to check his bag before filling it. He held the hole shut with one hand. The other cadets got in on the act, and soon more streams of recycled Mexican food laced the floor of the aircraft.

"No, you don't, Critter," Turbo said as the upperclassman reached for his own emergency envelope. "You better not let a plebe catch you hurling."

"Just checking for any modifications," Critter said as he unfurled the bag from the envelope and examined it.

"Don't worry, Brainiac, I only modified the plebes' barf bags." Skeeter took Critter's bag and blew it up, then popped it. "Upperclassmen don't need such things."

"I don't know, Skeeter." Turbo was pulling his own bag out. "That smell is pretty bad."

Southern Indiana—1986

"It's your responsibility!"

"Yeah, Marv. You have to do something."

"Why?"

"Those FAA boys won't leave us alone until they find out who did it. One of 'em threatened to start pulling extra inspections on my plane if I didn't tell him."

"And he said he might just have to monitor the airfield pretty closely for a while. Thought he might find enough little violations to shut us down."

The conversation paused as the old Pitts Special dipped low at the north end of the little grass strip. It popped up and slipped sideways in the crosswind, then settled in for a clean three-point landing.

"That kid is going to ground-roll that tail dragger if he keeps pulling that nonsense. You taught him to do that, didn't you, Marv?"

"Yeah, I guess I did. He's pretty good, isn't he?"

"Good? Crazy is what I'd say. You gonna talk to him?"

"I suppose."

"When?"

"Soon."

"What's wrong with right now?"

The Pitts taxied into parking position close to where they stood. They waited for the noisy engine to shut down.

"Right now?"

"Nothing to be gained by waiting, Marv. The feds aren't going to cool off none too soon."

The pilot climbed out of the open-air cockpit and waved at the men. "Hi, guys. Did you see that landing? Bet you wished you could pull that off in this stiff crosswind."

"Most pilots got better sense than to even try it, kid. See ya, Marv."

"What's with those two?" the young flier asked.

"FAA is still on our case about that little stunt you pulled."

"That was over three weeks ago. I wish I knew who turned me in."

They headed for the little building that served as the gathering place for all the pilots and wanna-bes that frequented the little grass strip.

"That doesn't really matter, does it?"

"What are you getting at, Marv?"

"You have to turn yourself in."

"What? Why?"

"Because the FAA is going to make life miserable for all the guys who fly out of this little airfield. Most of us just do it for fun, and we're more than happy to tell the feds to screw off, but those two guys make part of their living out here. This is the busy season for crop dusters. If the FAA shuts either of them down, even for a few days, their kids could well go without winter coats."

"That's life."

Marv stopped and grabbed the young man's arm, spun him around, and stifled the urge to shake the arrogance out of him. He took a deep breath to get his temper under control. Even though Marv's 180 pounds gave him at least an 80-pound advantage over the young pilot, there was no fear in the young man's eyes. Never was.

"It's life, all right—serious life when your livelihood is on the line and you've got kids to clothe and feed. You're too young to understand that now, but someday you will. Take the Chieftain and get down there. Now!" Marv spun him around and pushed him toward the plane that was Marv's pride and joy.

He had never been there before, but he knew the FAA building was on the north side of the field, so he asked ground control for permission to park nearby. He grabbed his flight log and climbed out of the plane. It was a short walk.

The receptionist was courteous—until he told her who he was and why he was there. She led him down the short hallway to a small room.

"Have a seat in here. I'll get Mr. Montgomery."

He thought he saw the hint of a smile as she left, closing the door behind her.

The room was austere, furnished only with a metal table and three matching chairs. He sat in one of them.

He had been waiting for more than twenty minutes when the door finally opened again.

The man who entered closed the door behind him. He put his hands on his hips and stared for a moment before speaking. "I'm John Montgomery, and son, you're in some deep trouble."

"Why is that, sir?"

He didn't answer, just shook his head. "This your logbook?"

"Yes, sir."

Montgomery took a chair and opened the small black notebook. "Jack Williams. That your name?"

"Everyone calls me Jake."

Montgomery began turning the pages. His expression slowly changed as he continued to flip through the flight log. He was halfway through the book before he stopped and looked up. "You've got over three hundred hours logged, looks like about half of them in aerobatic planes, and two trips to the Oshkosh Air Show."

"Three hundred seventy-two hours total. Two hundred fifty-seven in aerobatic aircraft."

"Just how old are you, son?"

"Almost sixteen."

"When did you start flying?"

"I was twelve. Friend of my dad's took me up to pay off a bill. Guess I got hooked. Been flying since then every chance I get. When I can afford it, that is."

"And when did you decide to start flying recklessly?"

"I've never flown recklessly."

Montgomery leaned forward and rested his weight on the table. It creaked under the load. "You don't consider flying under a bridge reckless?"

"Not the way I did it."

"You may be a good pilot, but anyone who flies under a bridge on a whim is reckless. I don't care how many hours he has."

"Sir, what I did wasn't reckless, and I didn't do it on a whim. It was perfectly planned. Before I made the flight I measured the bridge—the lateral span and height—and the height and width of the plane. There was so much clearance that a rotten pilot could have flown through there half drunk."

Montgomery didn't answer, just rested there while his knuckles turned white. "You broke the rules, son."

"My dad always said rules are a barrier to creative thought."

Montgomery dropped his head and shook it from side to side. Jake couldn't see his face very well, but he thought he detected a slight smile. When Montgomery looked back up, there was nothing but a deep frown.

"I'm going to have to suspend your license for ninety days. Let's have it." Montgomery stood up and held out his hand.

"I don't have a license, sir."

Montgomery's mouth dropped open, his hand frozen in midair.

"You mean it's already been revoked?"

"No, sir. Never had one."

Montgomery placed his fists on his hips. His face started to turn red. "How come?"

"Never really saw the need to get a license."

"Never saw the need?" He turned around and stormed out of the office, slamming the door behind him.

Jake was sure he was screwed now—wasn't sure what kind of trouble he had managed to get into. He had to wait only a few minutes before Montgomery came back in.

Montgomery left the door open this time. "How did you get here?"

"I flew the Chieftain parked on the ramp."

Montgomery shook his head, but the anger wasn't there anymore. "Son, this is a controlled airfield. You have to have a license to fly into here. You gonna tell me you didn't know that?"

Jake sat silently, knowing there were no words that could get him out of this.

"How are your grades? You doin' good in school?"

"Mostly A's. A few B's."

"Do any sports?"

"I run cross-country. I'm a little too small for football."

Montgomery slid a business card across the table. Jake picked it up.

"I want you to call this guy. He's the Air Force ROTC recruiter at Notre Dame. That's the Reserve Officer Training Corps. You like to fly so bad you might as well get paid for it. Keep your grades up and your nose clean, and you'll have no problem getting into the program. Now, there are two things you have to do. First, don't ever fly under a bridge again. Second, get your license. Next time I see you, you better have it—and I'm coming up to Weatherford soon. If you don't have it I'm gonna pull Marvin Walker's license. He's the one who taught you to fly, isn't he?"

"Yes, sir. But why pull his license?"

"I gotta pull someone's, and you ain't got one. Now get out of here."

Montgomery followed the young pilot past the receptionist, then watched him walk toward his plane.

"He's the one?" the receptionist asked.

"Yeah."

"What'd you do to him?"

"Nothing. I sure as heck wanted to, but I called the guy who owns that plane out there. He taught him to fly—says the kid's a genius, a natural flier. Just needs a little discipline."

"Why don't you call in his parents? That usually works when kids his age get out of hand."

"I tried. Found out they were killed a couple of years ago. He's an orphan."

They watched silently as the teenager started his plane and taxied away.

Stanford University—1992—3:00 A.M.

Sweat dripped down Zhen Rhongi's back, even in the damp coolness of the nuclear physics building's basement. He crept quietly along the darkened hallway, the emergency lights providing the only illumination. Somewhere in the darkness he heard a noise and stopped quickly, holding his hand up to warn Wu Li. She stopped close behind him.

"What is it?" Her whisper sounded much too loud in the quiet confines of the hallway.

Rhongi waited several moments, listening intently. Nothing. "Probably just a mouse," he replied. "Let's keep going. The safe is in the office just ahead."

They continued their silent journey toward the office. As graduate students they had both spent many hours down in the research labs, but neither had ever been allowed access to the research the university did in support of the American National Laboratory at Livermore. Their nationality had precluded any such collaboration. That didn't matter now.

Rhongi produced a key and opened the heavy metal door to the office. It was dark inside, but he knew his way around well. With the aid of a small flashlight he quickly made his way around desks piled high with documents to the row of safes standing against the far wall.

"Are you sure you know the code?" Wu Li asked.

"I have seen them opened many times, when the

stupid American students didn't know they were being observed." He spun the dial as he had seen the others do, then stopped on the first number.

In just seconds he had the first safe open. "Look for the blue folder in the top drawer. It will be labeled 'M-88 Fuse.' "

Wu Li quickly thumbed through the drawer as Rhongi went to the third safe and worked the combination.

"I have it," Wu Li said.

"Take the pictures, quickly."

Wu Li cleared a spot in the center of one of the desks and switched on the table lamp. She laid the folder beneath the bright glow of the bulb and took a small camera from her purse. She clicked and flipped to the next page as quickly as she could. Worried her shaking hands might blur the data, she sat in the chair and rested her elbows on the desk, steadying the image she saw through the miniature lens.

"The file on the trigger isn't here. The American pigs have moved it." Rhongi quickly closed the last drawer.

"You're sure?" Wu Li stopped clicking the camera. "The trigger is critical."

"I know it. But the file is not here. We'll have to find out what happened to it—we might have to come back. Finish taking your pictures. Hurry."

Zhen Rhongi closed the safe and repositioned the dial just as he had found it. Then he went to where Wu Li sat. He turned the pages as she took the pictures, accelerating the process.

"Done." Rhongi let Wu Li replace the file just as she had found it, then closed the safe and returned the dial to its original setting.

Rhongi quickly clicked off the light over the desk and they retreated to the hallway, closing and locking the door behind them.

"I truly can't believe this," the dean told the two students sitting in front of his desk. "We have not had an event as embarrassing as this in more than fifty years. Do you have anything to say for yourselves?"

The students sat silently. Finally the woman spoke quietly. "There must be a mistake. We are not guilty of this crime."

The dean clenched his fists, could feel his face flush. "Miss Wu Li, there are videotapes of you and Mr. Rhongi in the lab, surveillance tapes. We have been suspicious of your activities for some time now and had the cameras installed only last week. By using the lamp on the desk to take your pictures you allowed your image to be perfectly captured. We have absolute proof that you made copies of classified information. We haven't figured out how you got the combination to the safes, though. An accessory, I suspect. Things will go much easier for you if you tell me who helped you. Would you care to enlighten me?"

A long, tense silence was his only answer.

"If you are not inclined to cooperate, I'm afraid we have no choice but to turn you over to the authorities. The diplomatic immunity you enjoy as the daughter of an ambassador may save you, but it will not help your friend. He will surely go to prison for this."

"Very sorry, sir, but Zhen Rhongi is my husband."

"What? That's not in our records."

"We just married one month ago. We have not reported our marriage to the university."

"Oh, for Christ's sake. Well, at least you'll both

spend the night in jail before you're deported. I've already called the police."

The door to the dean's office opened, and a man strode quickly inside. "I think not, sir," he said.

"Who the hell are you? Don't you know how to knock?"

"I'm John Engles, counselor to the deputy ambassador of North Korea. I understand there is an issue with his daughter and son-in-law?"

"Issue? Hell, these two have been caught stealing classified government records—they are spies and must be treated as such."

"I beg to differ. They are covered by immunity granted to dignitaries of foreign governments. I suggest you release them into my custody and avoid an embarrassment to the school."

"I will do no such thing. I'm going to have these two arrested. You may get them out of jail if that is your employer's wish."

The dean's intercom buzzed. "I am not to be interrupted," he scolded his secretary.

"I'm sorry, Dean, but it's President Williams."

"Very well." As the dean picked up the phone, he couldn't help but notice the lawyer's ludicrous grin.

"Good mo—" He didn't even get the greeting out before the university president began screaming. The message was clear. He was not to embarrass the university by making a federal case out of two students apparently caught pilfering low-level classified information. It made no difference that they were caught red-handed. They were to be released immediately to the deputy ambassador's counsel. There was no use in arguing. "Yes, sir."

The dean dropped the phone into its cradle. He

looked up at the communist spies sitting in his office and the lowlife attorney who had somehow gotten to his boss. He realized there was nothing he could do, so he walked over to the door and opened it. "Please leave before I become sick."

Wu Li quickly jumped to her feet and grabbed her husband's hand. She hurried him out the door before the dean could change his mind. They had been caught, and that was unfortunate, but they were now saved from the American prison. "I told you all would be okay."

"I am saddened we did not complete our mission. We still don't have the information for the trigger."

"Be quiet." She pulled Zhen Rhongi into the backseat of her father's limousine. He was waiting for them there.

"That was close, Father." The limousine pulled away from the curb.

"It is unfortunate the Americans caught you when you were so close to achieving your goal," the Korean dignitary said. "However, you have done well. The engineers have sent word that your other discoveries have rapidly advanced our weapon development program."

"But we lack the drawings for the trigger," Zhen Rhongi said. "Without them we will not be able to finish the design."

"Do not worry yourself. The trigger is being developed at Los Alamos, a laboratory in New Mexico. We have friends there. It is time for the two of you to return home."

"Home? To Korea?" Wu Li asked.

"Yes. I have arranged for you to supervise the completion of this design. You will jointly manage the engineers at the institute."

"This is a great honor, Father."

"We will do our very best to develop this weapon at the greatest possible speed," Zhen Rhongi said, "before the American warmongers can fully enslave our brothers in the South."

Over the Mediterranean—1998

It had been a quick trip. Lance had left California only twenty-eight hours earlier and was already on his way back, unaccustomed to the trappings of his first-class surroundings. His visit to Tel Aviv had lasted only fourteen hours. Barely enough time to take care of his business and get a few hours of sleep. Fortunately the Israelis had been the most gracious of hosts, treating him like a VIP everywhere he went. He wasn't sure that accepting all these perks was within regulations—all expenses paid, staying in a five-star suite, luxury accommodations all the way, all at the invitation of a foreign government.

Lance had voiced his concern when the representative from the Israeli embassy phoned with the details of the trip. His benefactor had quickly come up with a splendid idea and modified the formal invitation. Lance had "officially" been asked to present a lecture on space structure control at the University of Tel Aviv. And while he was in Israel would he mind attending a reception that was the real reason for the trip—to be awarded the Etour HaMofet, the highest decoration Israel gave to noncitizens? Of course, that meant he would have to bring two sets of clothes—a suit for the lecture and his uniform, a brand-new dress uniform he'd bought last month when he joined the reserves as Colonel Kirk had asked. Colonel Kirk. Too bad he couldn't have been there to accept the award.

Initially Lance hadn't wanted to accept Israel's kind gesture, but then he'd thought about Kirk and the rest of the Airborne Laser Lab crew, remembered watching the mighty bird fall into the sea as he hung below the canopy of his parachute. Kirk, Jones, Red, and the Chief . . . all dead. A war averted, but at a huge personal cost. Lance had decided to accept the award on their behalf, a final tribute. He looked out the cabin window, gazing at the sparkling water of the Mediterranean as the setting sun painted it vivid orange. The plane was down there somewhere, along with her crew. Lance raised his glass. "To fallen heroes," he said quietly.

Chapter 1

The Pentagon

"I can't believe you're even proposing this. You know it's the Air Force's top priority. The commander of Air Combat Command will crap when he hears what you're doing."

"That just shows what kind of predicament we're in. Besides, since when does the Army care about Air Force priorities?"

"I just don't want you backing down after we commit to this. I don't want to hear that you had to re-insert the Airborne Laser program funding line after we'd already given up the Comanche."

"Don't worry. That won't happen. Now what about the Navy? Do you agree? We zero out the Arsenal ship production funds?"

The admiral shifted in his chair. He looked down at his coffee, somehow not able to look the vice chairman in the eye. "Agreed." Now he looked up. "But the three test articles continue in development. Right?"

The room was quiet. Finally the vice chairman of the Joint Chiefs of Staff, an Air Force general, spoke up. "That's correct. Let me summarize what we've discussed. The Army drops the Comanche production

funds and retains ten divisions. The Navy drops the
Arsenal ship production funds to retain the current
fleet, and the Air Force drops the Airborne Laser production funding in exchange for a guarantee that we'll
complete production of the F-22 at the planned fleet
size of four hundred thirty-eight aircraft. Is that what
we've all decided?"

The three officers glanced at each other, then each
nodded.

"It's a shame we have to go this route, gentlemen,
but I know you all agree there was no other way.
Inflation is killing us. Our budget was based on last
year's miniscule inflation numbers. How were we to
know the economy would stall as hard as it did? Our
only hope of retaining our current force level is to
pillage the modernization accounts, and the SECDEF
agrees. With North Korea ready to blow up and Hussein in serious negotiation with Iran, it looks like the
two-medium regional conflict scenario we've always
tried to prepare for may actually become a reality. We
cannot afford to downsize any further. At least not
right now."

"You two are really going to make some enemies
down at Langley," the admiral said.

"Can't be helped. There's just not enough money.
Not nearly enough."

"How do we advertise this?" the Army general
asked.

"You don't," the vice chairman said. "Our agreement
is not to be discussed outside this room. The ABIDES
database closes on Friday, day after tomorrow. None
of the budget information can be changed after that.
I have permission from the SECDEF to reopen the
database on Saturday morning and make the deletions

we've agreed to here. Be ready for a lot of howling on Monday when everyone gets back to work and takes a look at what happened."

"And how do you propose we stop the howling?"

"Send them to the field. All those training and deployment dollars you've been missing are going to be back into the accounts. Send the ships, planes, and tanks out. Get 'em ready to fight. I don't know who we'll have to hit first, the Arabs or the Koreans. Unless something unexpected happens, my guess would put us in the desert, but both situations are so volatile it could go either way. Tell your men that. They'd better be spending their time honing their war-fighting skills, not bemoaning the loss of their precious modernization money."

The soldier and the sailor excused themselves. The airman remained.

"There's only one big problem. In cutting the Airborne Laser you leave us with no missile defense. It was our linchpin, our only viable missile defense system."

"But it's far from ready," the vice chairman replied. "And even if I was in a position to allow you to offer up an offset, how many fighter squadrons do you think it would cost to stand up the laser force?"

"We both know the answer to that. One and a half wings. I know it's painful, but we really don't have a choice. The commander of Air Combat Command wants this weapon bad. And he is our top war fighter— Congress listens to him."

"Congress won't listen this time—they know what's about to happen. Besides, he just *thinks* he wants the laser force. Hell, he wants everything these nickel-and-dime contractors brief him on. Fiscal reality says he

can't have the ABL—or anything else right now, for
that matter. The only way we can save the air wings
is to give up some of the new stuff. We're about to
go to war, and that's not just some feeling I have. It's
a fact. We can't go in and win it with a bunch of laser
planes, even if they were ready to fight. We have to
go in with fighters and bombers, or else the enemy
will walk all over our butts. Not to mention the Army
and the Navy. Hell, I may even have to cut the research and development money for the laser program."

Air Force Research Lab, Directed Energy
Directorate Kirtland Air Force Base, New Mexico

Lance Brandon stared at the printout in disbelief. He
followed the thin, computer-generated line with his
pencil again. Even in the low-power laser test, the
beam control system was still too unstable by a factor
of ten. Jitter levels were much too high to provide
enough stability for the laser to track even a slow-
moving target. What had gone wrong?

"The plane's here, sir," Staff Sergeant Adams told
him over the headset.

"Okay. Let's call it a day," Lance answered over
the intercom, an exact replica of what they would wear
in the airplane when the laser was installed. *If* they
ever got the stabilization problems isolated and repaired. "Go ahead and shut down the power supply
to the YAG. I don't want to run the laser any more
than we have to. From the looks of things, we're going
to need quite a few more test runs. Don't forget to
turn off the coolant to the lithium niobate crystal. If
it cracks we'll be another six weeks getting a replace-

ment. We can't afford that kind of schedule slip. You need any help?"

"No, thanks, sir. I'll have it cleaned up in just a few minutes. I'll join you in the hangar. Don't forget our bet."

"Not a chance, Bryan. Honestly, I don't believe you've ever even seen a 747. If you had, you'd be as certain as I am that the thing won't fit in this hangar."

"It's your dinner money, sir. If it's all right with you, though, I'll take dinner some other night. I'm kind of beat, and I'm sure Debbie would like some company for what's left of the evening."

"Don't count your chickens before they're hatched. But if they can squeeze that plane in here, I'll treat you and Debbie both to dinner."

"Deal."

Lance pulled off his headset and shut off the power to the computer he had been working on. His faithful sergeant was busily taking the necessary safety precautions and shutting down the test laser and cooling systems. Lance had been working very long hours trying to get this system up and running, and the sergeant had been there every night, usually arriving before Lance and often staying later than he did to clean up and secure the test equipment.

Lance had tried to compensate where he could. He had taken Bryan and his new wife, Debbie, out to dinner a couple of times. They had even had him over for a cookout a couple of weeks back. They were a very nice young couple, and he was disappointed when he saw the kind of housing the Air Force had provided them. Kirtland was an old base, one that had been spared the chopping block only through some heavy

lobbying by one New Mexico senator, and its housing
showed its age.

Lance put on his flight jacket and left the beam
control lab. He stepped through the door into the
large hangar bay. On the north side of the hangar, the
aircraft doors were open wide, and Lance could see a
few stars beginning to sparkle in the clear evening sky.
A looming Boeing 747 was creeping toward the hangar doors from the Albuquerque International Airport
runway. It had crossed the road, with the assistance
of security police who stopped traffic on both sides,
and was entering the fenced-in "secure" area near the
hangar. He could already tell it was going to be a
tight fit. Lance had been assured that the hangar could
handle the plane's wingspan quite easily, but its height
was another matter.

The aircraft came to a halt short of the hangar doors
as airmen closed the fence behind it. The engines
wound slowly to a stop as the Boeing pilots shut down
all the systems. They would tow the massive beast into
the hangar. That was safer. It was an expensive plane.

"She'll fit, easy," Sergeant Adams said as he came
up beside Lance.

"I really do hope you're right. If it doesn't, we'll
have to work on it outside, and I bet it'll soak up this
desert heat like a sponge."

"Check out the nose art," Adams said.

A large drawing on the nose of the plane showed a
coiled rattlesnake with laser beams spouting from its
eyes. Those beams were attacking a missile. YAL-1A
was written along the circular edge at the top. AIR-
BORNE LASER circled the bottom, and PEACE THROUGH
LIGHT was a subtitle below it. Very similar to the old
Airborne Laser Lab crest.

It didn't take long for the ground crew, a detachment of the 4950th Test Wing, now stationed at Edwards Air Force Base in California, to connect the big tow tug to the nose of the plane and begin the process of dragging the huge machine into the hangar. Lance and Sergeant Adams watched silently as men and women surrounded the plane while it was towed inside. These "wingwalkers" were charged with signaling the tug pilot to stop if any part of the plane got too close to the hangar.

The wings fit easily through the hangar door, with at least ten feet of clearance on either side. The vertical stabilizer was another story. It barely cleared the top of the hangar entrance, with only inches to spare. But that was enough.

"I guess that'll be one dinner on you," Sergeant Adams said.

"But not by much. I think the tail scraped the paint off the top of the hangar door when they pulled it in."

"Close enough. I'll hit you up for the dinner some other night, though. I'm going home to see Deb. Everything is locked up in the lab."

"Okay. Thanks for staying late again. And thank Debbie for putting up with the late hours. You can tell her I owe both of you."

"How about tomorrow?"

"Sounds good. Ask Debbie if six o'clock is okay."

"Eighteen hundred hours. Roger."

Even though Sergeant Adams excused himself and went home, Lance decided to stick around for a while. There wasn't much to do back in the visiting officers' quarters, the VOQ. Might as well hang around and maybe get a look inside the plane.

He watched the Test Wing crew push portable stairs

up to the side of the plane near its nose. A door opened and the flight crew began to disembark. Six men came out, two wearing standard Air Force flight suits, the other four in a similar-looking uniform, but deep blue in color. Lance went to meet them at the foot of the steps.

"Welcome to Kirtland. I'm Lance Brandon," he greeted the men gathered there.

A man in a green flight suit held out his hand first. Lance figured he was at least six three.

"Hi, Lance. I'm Bud Davis."

Lance shook his hand and checked out his name tag. It was decorated with master-pilot wings and the name Scarecrow Davis. He also wore the rank of lieutenant colonel.

"Nice to meet you, Colonel," Lance said as he shook hands.

"This is Burbank Gifford." Scarecrow introduced the other man in Air Force issue.

Lance greeted him and noted his rank of major.

"My pleasure," the major said. Then he turned to his boss. "I'm going to go check on our ride and VOQ reservations."

The colonel nodded, and Burbank walked toward one of the offices along the side of the hangar. "We're both assigned to the Test Wing. These other guys are high-paid Boeing test pilots. Captain Powers will be down shortly."

"It's good to meet all of you," Lance said. "Why the name Scarecrow?" he asked the senior airman.

"Bad knees. Before my surgery I walked like I was headed for the Land of Oz."

"And Burbank?"

"He couldn't quite make it in Hollywood."

"Oh, I get it. What about you guys—don't Boeing pilots have nicknames?"

"Sure we do," O'Malley said. "We just aren't allowed to tell the customer what they are."

"Wrong, O'Malley," a female voice came from the door of the plane. The woman continued talking as she walked down the steps. She had short brown hair and green eyes and also wore the blue flight suit of a Boeing pilot. "The reason we don't give you a nickname is that you wouldn't be able to remember it," she said.

"Billie Powers," she introduced herself as she met Lance at the bottom of the steps.

"Pleased to meet you. I'm Lance Brandon. You're a test pilot?" he asked.

He felt her grip tighten, and her deep green eyes seemed to harden. He realized the question had come out wrong.

"Captain Powers is our chief test pilot," O'Malley said.

"I didn't mean . . ."

"It's okay. I'm used to it," Billie said as her grip softened and her eyes lost their edge.

"You guys figured out where we're going to stay tonight?" she asked her pilots.

"We're all scheduled to stay together in the VOQ," Colonel Scarecrow answered. "Team integrity. We'll have to move downtown tomorrow night, though. Some kind of big conference starting here. Burbank is checking on our transportation."

"Great. Downtown usually means some low bidder. I just hope the bugs aren't too hungry."

"I'm going to check in with the Test Wing detachment. Hey, you guys remember Garvey, don't you?

Crew chief on AGAR 35? He's supposed to be around here somewhere."

"He's usually in the Detachment office if he's around," Lance said.

"Yeah," O'Malley said. "He still owes us that beer, doesn't he?"

"I think it was a six-pack," the other Boeing pilot corrected him.

"We better go with Scarecrow to make sure Garvey doesn't get away."

"Go ahead," Billie told them. "Check in with me before you leave."

Lance had been staring up at the plane. It looked even bigger up close.

"She's a monster, isn't she?" Billie asked.

"Huge."

"Care for a tour?"

"I'd love it," Lance said, then followed her up the stairs.

"It's actually a close copy to one of the old NAOC birds," she told him as they stepped through the plane's door.

"NAOC?" Lance wasn't familiar with that term. He sucked in his breath as he looked toward the tail of the plane. It was like a massive tunnel, half filled with the prototype laser device, with still enough room to walk down the center passageway easily.

"Yeah. You know, the National Airborne Operations Center. This was the original NAOC airframe."

"I guess I'm not familiar with that operation," Lance said.

The look she gave him made him slightly uncomfortable.

"How long have you been in the Air Force?" she asked.

Lance thought momentarily. "About five and a half years if you add it all up."

"And you're a major? You must have pulled a few strings."

"Not really. I went through a compressed Reserve Officer Training Corps program at MIT, then spent four years as a lieutenant here at the lab. After that I got out. About two years ago I got a call from my original boss, and they pulled me back into the reserves to work on a special project. Promoted me to major for some reason."

"Must have been some project."

"Worked out pretty well, except for our losses. A couple of very good men didn't come back from the"—Lance looked at her, remembering the details hadn't been fully declassified—"test flight."

Billie stared at him momentarily. "A mission . . . like this one?" she asked with a lowered voice.

"Similar," Lance answered. "But it was much more urgent."

"I guess you haven't heard," she said.

Lance looked at her. What was she talking about? It couldn't be another mission like the last one. Not again! "Heard what?"

"I'm not supposed to say much, but suffice it to say we had to pay for a lot of overtime to get this laser in place for the flight. We were originally supposed to fly down here, install the beam control system, and then head to TRW to install the laser. When someone decides to foot the bill for that much overtime, you can guess something is up. Been watching the news lately?"

"Not much. I've been under the gun to get some bugs worked out of the autotracker. Another compressed schedule. I thought it was a congressional oversight thing, you know, how the lab is always under the gun to show results in order to protect future funding."

"I don't think this is a show-and-tell for the budget cutters. Tell you what. Let me give you the tour, then you can join me for dinner. We'll talk about it there. I'm afraid the rest of the crew is going to meet up with Tech Sergeant Garvey. I worked with him a few years ago. If that crowd gets together they'll be lucky to stay out of jail. I've got too much paperwork to finish up to deal with their antics."

"Deal."

"I'll show you what we've done. As I mentioned, this is one of the original NAOC airframes. We stripped out all the communications equipment and practically rebuilt the plane from the landing gear up as the initial test bed for the Airborne Laser."

Inside the cavernous beast, Lance noticed that a majority of the plane's space already seemed packed full of gear, and half of the beam control equipment wasn't even installed yet.

"On the other side of this bulkhead"—Billie patted a wall just to their left—"in the nose section, is the beam control system. The telescope is already installed, along with most of the optical systems. I understand there are a few components that still need to be installed by your people?"

"Only a few. Mostly we just need to load some software patches and run some control tests."

"Good." Billie turned right and headed toward the

rear of the plane. "This is the straphanger section and crew rest area."

There were two short rows of seats and a few bunks attached to the walls of the plane. They seemed cramped, stacked on top of each other, yet they provided enough room to sleep. Lance had never been very good at sleeping on an airplane, though. "Straphanger?"

"You know, the folks that just come along for the ride, who want to help take credit for all your hard work."

"Oh, you mean Congress?"

"Yeah, them too. Then here's where the real work is done. It's the battle management section."

Two rows of seats, each facing a console, were set along the side of the plane.

"This first row is the beam control and laser control section, as well as the mission commander's position. The second row is for the future installation of communications gear and intelligence support systems. It's not installed yet—that would make the plane a classified asset. We thought it'd be better to hold off until we finished your integration tests."

"Good idea. You say the mission commander sits here? He's not in the cockpit?"

"Again with the 'he'?"

"Whoops, sorry."

"Yes, you're right. He or she would sit down here. That was one of the big challenges, as I understand it, in getting Air Combat Command to buy in to the program—they wanted the pilot to control the actual battle, of fighting the laser. From what I hear, the commander was finally convinced there was simply way too much information to assimilate and control for the pilot to be able to take care of all of it while also flying the plane. So the mission commander, probably a rated officer anyway, will sit back here.

"Beyond the battle management consoles is another bulkhead. Behind that are the laser modules, fourteen of them. I don't think you need all fourteen lasers to kill the missiles."

"That's right, the design calls for graceful degradation," Lance said. "We learned that lesson on another project. Modularize the laser generators and optically couple their beams. That way you have spares to bring on-line in case there's a problem with any of the primaries."

"The fuel cells are also back there," Billie continued, "at the very rear of the compartment. There will be enough in the mission aircraft for about two hundred engagements, but since this is a prototype and test aircraft we only have enough for about fifty shots."

"That wasn't very smart," Lance said. "Why not make this bird fully mission-capable, just in case? The laser fuel modules couldn't be that expensive."

"You'll have to take that up with Colonel DeMarco, the program manager. From what I understand, it was a schedule trade-off. The fuel cells aren't that expensive, but they're made of a special material and are built essentially by hand. It was going to take another year before the supplier automated his construction process, and the schedule couldn't take the slip. If we have to, we can always go back and install more fuel cells. I know Boeing would gladly accept more government money to continue to improve the fleet."

"Isn't this one of the biggest Defense Department jobs around already?"

"It's one of the only Defense Department jobs of any magnitude. Come on, let me show you the flight deck."

Lance followed the test pilot back the way they had come, to a steep ladder that led upward. "Isn't this kind of dangerous? Someone could fall off of this thing."

"We won't be flying this like a fighter. The mission is just to stand off outside the enemy air defenses and shoot down the missiles as they're launched. There shouldn't be any safety concern." Billie grabbed a rung and began to climb.

"All the 747s I've been on had a stairwell." Lance followed her up.

"Those were all airliners. This is a military plane."

The flight deck was sparser than Lance had expected—seats for the pilot and copilot, with another seat behind them. At least there was a latrine just to the left of the ladder.

"Obviously the pilot and copilot sit up front, and there's room for a trainee here in the jump seat. It's a standard 747 flight deck. But with mostly digital controls and triply redundant computers for all the major systems."

"It looks pretty spartan," Lance said.

"Don't need much while you're up here. Maps are all digitally stored on the computer, navigation is by GPS, Global Positioning System—basically all the pilot needs to do is get it in the air and point it in the right direction. The computers take care of the rest, unless there's a problem. Oh, the pilot does most of the landings, too. We weren't able to install the autoland systems that we built for the 777. Too expensive. Go ahead, have a seat."

Lance climbed into the right-hand seat. It was comfortable. The windows seemed too high, though, not at all like the little Cessna he used to fly. "I can't see very well."

"Not much to see when you're flying this thing. Like I said, the computers do most of the work. The crew is basically here for emergencies."

Lance stepped out of the seat and followed Billie back down the ladder to the landing near the entrance to the plane.

"I'm guessing you know that the laser beam travels through a tube along the upper spine of the plane, then into the beam director in the front. You can get a look at the optical systems through a window up here."

The bulkhead had a window, but no access panel. Lance looked into the dark recess of the big plane's nose.

Billie flipped a circuit breaker, and the compartment suddenly filled with light.

"Wow!"

"Chock-full of stuff, huh?"

Lance was astonished to see the primary beam director's one-and-a-half-meter mirror staring back at him. It was a beautiful piece of optics. And Billie was right—the front compartment was filled with a variety of mirrors and sensors, all brilliantly reflecting the lights like so many prisms. "The telescope points in this direction when it's stowed?"

"Yes. When it's turned this way there is a positive seal with the exit aperture in the nose. We pump argon gas through there all the time to keep positive pressure, and it also helps keep the mirrors clean. When the system is powered up and brought into standby mode, the telescope points forward and we continue to keep positive gas pressure on the system. It's all sealed. Breaking the seal requires a twenty-four-hour process to clean and reseal the compartment. It's not fun."

Lance backed away from the window. "Let's hope we won't have to go inside there to work on anything."

"Shouldn't need to." Billie led him back to the door in the side of the plane. "It's all supposed to be working fine."

"If the data I've been provided on the control parameters are correct, we won't have any problems. If they aren't, we may have to go in and modify the antivibration weights on some of the components. We'll find out during the initial low-power tests."

"Here we are."

"Thanks for the tour," Lance said as they stepped out the door to the top of the stairs. "I've got a pretty good idea what we've got in front of us now. This is sure going to be a lot easier than the last time I had to characterize a beam control system on a flying platform."

"You mean the Airborne Laser Lab?"

Lance looked at her before answering. Again she was hinting that she knew what happened aboard the laser lab, what happened to Colonel Kirk and Colonel Jones. But that mission was still classified. "No. But that one was a challenge as well."

"Then what were you talking about?"

"It was a space-imaging system, much like the Hubble telescope. You can imagine how difficult a system like that is to build."

"Is it still flying?"

Lance checked the date on his watch. "It should be coming back soon. But I can't say much more about it."

"I understand. Hey, we've still got dinner to take care of."

"I'm ready if you are. What about your crew?"

"Looks like they've already gone. That's my bag down there."

They went down the steps to get her bag. They found a note attached to it.

"It's from O'Malley. They hooked up with Garvey and headed out. I'm on my own."

"Well, I guess you might as well join me for dinner, Captain."

"Call me Billie, please. Titles and ranks never have done much for me."

"Works for me. I prefer to go by Lance, too. I'm still not very comfortable with this military protocol."

"Then Lance it is. Over dinner you can tell me what really happened to my old friend Colonel Jones."

Lance grabbed one bag and Billie took the large chart case and her briefcase. "My car is just outside the fence," he said, wondering how he was going to get through the meal without revealing anything he shouldn't. "Mexican okay?"

"Is there anything else down here?"

"Not much."

"Mexican is fine."

They loaded the gear in the back of the car Lance had been assigned. Billie took her briefcase into the front.

"Issue?" she asked.

"The car? Yeah. I'm actually only on an extended reserve tour, and they figured assigning me a car out of the motor pool would be cheaper than letting me rent one. How could you tell?"

"Well, the license plate really gave it away, but motor pool cars haven't changed much. Still the simple little AM radio. No one buys cars with just an AM radio anymore. No one except the government. At least they don't still paint them all Air Force blue."

"Another cost-saving measure, I understand. It used to cost an extra eight hundred dollars to get the special paint from the car builders. Actually the only thing special was the color. It was nonstandard."

"I'm going to call in," Billie said, pulling a small cellular phone out of her briefcase.

"Go ahead. I'll stop by the VOQ if you want to change before we eat."

"Don't bother," Billie said as she selected a speed dial number from the phone's memory. "I don't mind wearing this flight suit to dinner, as long as it's not a formal place."

"Good. I'm starved. And no, it's far from formal."

"Hi, Bernard," Billie said, turning her attention to the phone. "We got the plane stored in the hangar. No problems to report. The crew . . ."

Lance pulled through the base gate and headed west to a restaurant he'd been to a couple of times before. His passenger was still intently listening to some instructions from her boss.

"We could," she said. "We haven't been through all the maintenance checks yet, but the plane flew fine on the way down. Does our customer know this?"

Know what? Lance wondered as he turned back north.

"Can you stall for a day? At least give these guys time to make a few phone calls."

Billie waited.

"Fine. Do what you can. We may find something wrong with the plane, anyway. Something that might delay our return flight for a couple of days. Understand?"

Lance didn't know what was going on, but it didn't sound pleasant, at least not for the Airborne Laser program.

"Okay. I'll check in with you in the morning. Are you going to call DeMarco or do you want me to?"

DeMarco? Colonel DeMarco? Lance wondered what the program manager had to do with this.

"Okay. About noon tomorrow. 'Bye."

Lance didn't say anything as he pulled into the parking lot. It wasn't crowded, for a change—probably because it was a weeknight.

"What happened to Marsha?" Billie asked as she put away her phone.

"Who?"

"Marsha. This place used to be called 'Ron Y Marsha.' Now the sign just says 'Ron's.' "

"I don't know," Lance answered. "You could ask inside if you want."

"Probably not something I want to know. As long as the food is still good."

"I think it is," Lance said as they got out of the car. "You've been here before, then?"

"Long time ago. Boeing used to support a test program down here called Big Crow. I used to fly it for them sometimes."

"Two. Nonsmoking," Lance told the host.

"How about over there?" Billie asked as they passed through an unoccupied room of the converted house.

The host seated them at one of the four empty tables.

"It's quiet here. We can talk," Billie said. She paused as a young man delivered a basket of chips and a bowl of salsa.

"I'd wait until he brings some water," Lance warned Billie as she dipped a chip into the fiery hot sauce. "Talk about what?"

She ignored his warning and dropped the chip into her mouth. "That call I made was to the vice president for research and development at Boeing. He's been running the Airborne Laser aircraft modification program for the Air Force. He told me I was to turn around and bring the plane back. Someone at the Air Force has told us to cancel the project. Promised to pay contract termination costs and everything. I don't think that's a good idea. Neither does Bernie. Particularly with what we've been hearing about the Koreans."

"I'm lost," Lance said as the young man delivered two plastic glasses of ice and a large plastic decanter of water.

"You say you're a reservist?"

"Yes. Actually this is only the second time I've been on active duty since I came back in. I work for Santa Barbara Electro-Optics most of the time."

"I'm going to guess Santa Barbara Electro-Optics does mostly commercial work?"

"Almost all commercial. A little work for NASA now and then."

"Boeing does a fair amount of commercial work, but we also do quite a bit of work for the military. Since we do so much military work, we have a lot of—shall I say 'interest'—in both the budget status as well as the current world situation. The bottom line is that the Air Force is being pressured to salvage as many conventional air wings as they can. Pressured from the top, from both Congress and the Joint Chiefs of Staff. Conventional air wings keep money flowing into constituencies. That's where the congressional pressure comes from. The chairman of the Joint Chiefs doesn't care much for technology. Warriors on the ground and in the air are what he thinks will win the next war.

"Unfortunately, there isn't enough money to go around. Without identifying additional funding, at least one air wing, possibly two, will have to be moth-balled. That's fiscal reality. That's why we got the call to terminate the program. We don't agree with that move—and not just because it's our program. Contrary to widespread belief, military contractors aren't just a bunch of moneygrubbing thieves. At least not at Boeing. We're actually at least as interested in doing what's right to protect the country and the men and women who serve."

"Okay, I understand the money issue. And I don't hold the belief that contractors are thieves," Lance said. "But what do the Koreans have to do with this?"

"It's the corporate position at Boeing—" Billie started, but she stopped talking when the server came by to take their order.

Lance noticed she didn't say anything until he was gone, and when she did start to explain again, she talked very quietly.

"We think there's a very strong chance the North Koreans will launch a war against South Korea within three to six months. And if they do, the United States will be knee-deep in it."

"I'm sorry, Billie, but I've heard that same forecast for years now."

"I know. I've heard it, too. This time it's different, though. Believe me—I've seen the intelligence data. You didn't hear this from me, but we've broken one of their tactical communications codes. The North Koreans are moving troops into position as we speak."

"But why now?"

"This is their fourth straight year of drought. We thought they might decide to pick a fight last year because of food shortages, but they didn't. China bailed them out. Unfortunately, China hasn't fared much better the last two years. Through their diplomatic communications, we know the Chinese refused them this year and will not furnish food. They will, however, provide troops if the North Koreans decide to pick a fight with the South. We've even seen more than two divisions of Chinese light infantry moving toward North Korea. Training exercises, they claim."

"That does sound bad. Surely the U.S. military isn't standing around doing nothing?"

"We've protested the Chinese troop movement within the United Nations. Actually, we fed the information to South Korea and let them lodge the complaint. The Navy has moved part of one Carrier Battle Group into the area. One squadron of F-16s has been moved to Osan Air Force Base in South Korea. But we're strapped—we don't have the fighting power we had in the past. Plus, we're committed to too many contingencies across the world. The last Quadrennial Defense Review limited us to a single MRC, a single major regional conflict. We downsized our forces to meet that task. They didn't take into account the need to fight one MRC while having so many forces committed to policeman status across the globe.

"But that's not even the biggest problem. Have you ever heard of the WoDong II?"

"I'll guess that's not the name of a new kung fu movie."

"Not even close. It's North Korea's new missile. China provided some guidance technology that the North Koreans fitted to their Taepo-Dong II missile. It has such better capability, the intel guys gave it a new name. WoDong."

"How good is it?"

"As far as range, it can reach anywhere in South Korea and most of Japan. Good precision, two-hundred-fifty-meter CEP."

"CEP?"

"Circular error probability—how close it can come to the designated target. Two hundred fifty meters is pretty good. Especially with nuclear warheads."

Billie stopped talking again as the server brought their food. They were still the only ones in that section of the restaurant.

Lance poked at his burrito as the waiter left. He had all but lost his appetite. "I thought we had always estimated the North Koreans didn't have a nuclear capability."

"We did, until Hwang Jang Yop. He is—was—a high-level member of the North Korean Communist Party until he defected to the South in '97. He tipped us off on the North's nuclear capability, and about some of the assistance the Chinese were providing them."

"You sure that wasn't just some political ploy, either by Yop or by the South Korean government?"

"Actually we thought so at first, and we took his comments with a large grain of salt. But he also tipped us off on where to look. We looked. He was telling the truth."

Lance twiddled his fork. "You seem to have some pretty good information. Are you sure it's accurate?"

"Positive. You see, I'm a reservist, too. Not as a flier, though. I work for the Deputy Chief of Staff for Operations, Intelligence Directorate. I just came off a six-week special assignment. Just in time, too, it looks like."

"That's where the ABL comes in."

"It's designed to take out ballistic missiles."

"Yes, but it's not ready."

"We've got to get it ready. Fast."

"Range control has you seventy-five miles down-range, altitude fifty-three thousand feet."

"What a ride!" the mission specialist exclaimed for the dozenth time in the last ten minutes.

Driscoll smiled beneath his helmet. It was indeed quite a ride, his first in command of the Shuttle. He had waited four years for this. From his initial astronaut training he had been detailed to a special classified three-year tour. Three years of fantastic flying, but it hadn't been quite like being an official astronaut. Although he had been qualified to wear astronaut wings during his first tour, he hadn't been allowed to wear them in public.

"Welcome to space, gentlemen," Driscoll called over the intercom.

"Welcome to you as well," the mission specialist from Northrup/Grumman answered.

"No one lost their breakfast, I hope," Driscoll asked.

"I'm fine back here."

"How about you, Johnny?"

Driscoll's copilot gave him the thumbs-up as he adjusted the controls for the cabin air pressure.

Johnny Walker, his copilot, was good. Former Navy aviator and now a test pilot for Lockheed. Driscoll had been warned that his copilot was upset he hadn't been selected to command the flight—didn't understand why an Air Force officer with zero time in space would be selected over him. Walker already had two missions in space under his belt, one as a mission specialist and one as copilot. Driscoll understood. He would have felt the same way. Unfortunately there was no way to tell his copilot that his feelings shouldn't be hurt, that Driscoll was really no stranger to this flying environment.

They had to put their differences behind them. The mission was all that mattered for the next four days. Their job was to deploy their payload and retrieve a space experiment that had been launched on a mission two years earlier, the second of the long-endurance space experiments that would pave the way for the planned trip to Mars.

The satellite in their cargo bay was critically important, with the Koreans' actions becoming ever more blatant. The classified military satellite would provide the U.S. government decision makers with valuable insight into the real intent of the Koreans, beyond the rhetoric at which they so excelled.

"One hundred miles downrange, seventy thousand feet."

"We copy, Range Control," Driscoll answered.

"I'll begin checking out the satellite systems," the mission specialist said. "Let's hope she took the launch stresses without any prob— Hey, did you guys feel something?"

Driscoll was already in action, checking sensors and scrolling through the flight data display. "Hold off on the satellite checkout. We've got a slight yaw, two tenths of a degree per minute. Initiating control-motor burn to correct."

"Are you thinking what I am?" Walker asked.

Driscoll nodded his head, then got on the radio: "CAPCOM, we may have a problem. About ten seconds ago we felt a slight bump, then the shuttle began a slight yaw. We initiated a booster control function and have corrected the drift."

"Debris?" asked the controllers back at Johnson space center.

"That would be my guess. One of those small pieces of space junk. You know, the ones under a foot in diameter that we don't bother to track."

"There shouldn't have been anything in your path. No satellite we know of has jettisoned a piece of material of any significant size into your orbit."

"Comforting thought," Driscoll said to his copilot without keying the mike. He didn't want the ground control folks at Houston to hear him. "What about all those Russian and Chinese satellites we don't know about?"

"How bad is it?" the mission specialist asked.

"Can't tell," the copilot answered. "We can't see if there is any damage from here. More than likely the left wing was hit, since we were yawing in that direction. We probably lost some thermal tiles."

"And that's not good," Driscoll answered, glad

there were no more people aboard than there were. He knew they might not make it back if too many of the thermal tiles were missing. The heat from reentry couldn't be dissipated and the part of the wing that lost its tiles could easily melt away. It all depended on how bad the damage was, and they couldn't tell from where they were. He keyed the microphone. "CAPCOM, recommend we go ahead and deploy the satellite, then use the camera on the robotic arm to examine our situation."

"We'll talk it over down here, but that sounds like a good idea. Be advised you may have to make an EVA if the camera can't find a problem."

"Copy, Houston." Driscoll released the mike switch, then turned to his copilot. "How well were you paying attention during the space-walk classes, Johnny?"

"I guess we'll see."

The satellite launch went without a hitch, not that anyone was particularly concerned about that part of their mission. Everyone's mind was on the other part—the getting-home part.

"Looks like we peeled back about eight tiles, right near the junction of the wing and the fuselage. But they're toward the bottom side of the wing. Are you guys getting a good picture down there?" Driscoll asked.

"Great picture here. We confirm what you see. Looks like you lost eight or nine tiles. We'll digitize the picture to see exactly how bad it is, then we'll run the thermal reentry model against a modified Shuttle, with the tiles removed. That'll tell us how bad the problem is. It'll take a couple of hours, at least. You guys try and stay calm up there. We'll get back to you as soon as we can."

For the first time, Driscoll wished they'd brought up some of those little science experiments just so they'd have something to do. They could only wait, circling Earth at more than seventeen hundred miles per hour.

Chapter 2

"If it isn't so bad, why are you going to have to fly that attitude on the approach?" Driscoll's copilot asked desperately. "This machine wasn't designed to fly sideways. And why are we landing at Edwards?"

"Just a precaution, I'm sure," Driscoll answered. NASA didn't like to land at Edwards simply because of the cost of mounting the Shuttle on the modified 747 to transport it back to Florida. But it was safer there—more room to recover if there was a problem. And fewer civilians on the ground if there was a major problem. He keyed the mike: "Let's go over that maneuver one more time."

Driscoll leaned hard on the rudder, keeping most of the slipstream flowing over the outside end of the left wing. The maneuver, worked out during the thermal model runs at the computer center, was supposed to protect the bare metal exposed on the left wing. Easier said than done.

A red light flashed on the instrument panel. "Warning," a feminine electronic voice came over the intercom. "A12 thermocouple high temperature: 400 degrees."

Driscoll gritted his teeth. He had already trimmed the rudder as far as he could, working the pedals to give it more or less pressure to keep from losing control of the spacecraft. The ride was getting bumpy as the smooth airflow was disturbed by the mass of the Shuttle's fuselage.

"The wing's only tested to 900 degrees. The contractor says they won't be responsible if it goes higher than that," the copilot said.

The mission specialist, an employee of the contractor that built the Shuttle, shrank in his seat, sweat dripping from his forehead.

"A12 temperature 500 degrees."

"She can get pretty annoying," the copilot said. He wanted to help, but there was little he could do.

Driscoll continued to fight the rudder, hoping he could keep the monstrous craft under control.

"A12 temperature 600 degrees. Approaching safety limit."

"650 is the safety limit," the copilot warned. "Beyond that we're in the statistical regime. She should hold together, but there's a possibility she won't."

"Safety limit exceeded," warned the computer in its unhurried voice.

"We're on our own now." Driscoll glanced at the digital display. They were still picking up speed, the metal rapidly continuing to heat.

"A12 temperature 700 degrees."

"Can't you begin to level out?" the copilot asked. "That'll slow us down, and the temperature should fall."

"Can't yet," Driscoll answered as he pushed the rudder even harder. "We'll overshoot the runway if I level out now . . ."

"A12 temperature 750 degrees."

"And if we overshoot we won't be able to get back

in time to land. That happens in a glider. I sure would like to have at least a little motor on this beast right now."

"A12 temperature 770 degrees. Thirty degrees to predicted failure."

The temperature inside the cabin was rising sharply, reflecting the thermal load on the exterior of the Shuttle. The air temperature management system couldn't keep pace with the increase. The big glider was being buffeted as well, forcing its way sideways through the smooth air.

"A12 temperature 780 degrees. Twenty degrees to predicted failure."

The buffeting increased. Driscoll knew he was at the control limit. He couldn't push the Shuttle sideways any more than he had without stalling it. Driscoll realized they weren't going to make it. Airspeed was still increasing and they were still too far uprange to begin the flare. There was only one choice. He banked the huge falling rock and rolled it over.

Their airspeed catapulted as the Shuttle entered an inverted dive.

"What the hell are you doing?" the copilot screamed.

"Trying to cool it off," Driscoll answered calmly, intently monitoring the airspeed as well as the thermocouple temperature. "There's less air flowing over the bare metal at this attitude. As soon as the thermocouple temperature drops to 760, I'll flip it back over and begin the landing rollout. That should put us in a lower speed regime and still get us far enough to hit the runway."

"*If* the thermal load hasn't weakened any of the wing components. If any of the struts has lost its strength in the heat it'll snap off during the pullout.

You're nuts." The copilot held the sides of his seat, waiting for Driscoll to roll out of the dive and pull back on the stick.

"A12 temperature 760."

Driscoll rolled the big glider back upright and gently pulled back, watching his airspeed and altitude. They were right on the mark. Now if the wing would just hold together . . .

"A12 temperature 770 degrees. Thirty degrees to predicted failure."

"See, it's heating up again," the copilot said, with a death grip on his seat now.

Driscoll wished he were alone and didn't have to listen to the frightened voice of his copilot. At least the feminine voice was emotionless—designed that way. "Take it easy. We're already slowing down. That should help the wing cool off. The temperature will climb a little more until the thermal inertia slows down, but we're going to be okay." *I think.* He pulled back on the yoke to flare out for the impending touchdown.

"A12 temperature 780 degrees. Twenty degrees to predicted failure."

Driscoll could hear the contractor in the back taking short, rapid breaths. He pulled back on the yoke a little more, trimming the elevator to take the load off the controls. The airspeed continued to drop. They just might make it.

"A12 temperature 760 degrees."

The copilot let out a long, slow breath. Driscoll adjusted the trajectory to line up with the thick black line painted on the dry lakebed before them. He could just begin to make out the emergency vehicles gathered at the midline of the runway, arrayed in their efficient arrival formation.

"A12 temperature 650 degrees. Now at safety limit."

Driscoll glanced down as the red warning light dimmed, then went out as the structural member continued to cool. He caught himself letting out his breath, relaxed, and concentrated on landing the big glider.

It had been a quick transition, from Shuttle pilot back to his old operational unit. That was unusual, and while Driscoll knew not to question his orders he sure wondered why they had been cut so quickly. Only days earlier he was busy flying an emergency landing in California; now he was heading for his old unit in the backwoods of Michigan.

Driscoll would have preferred to show up unannounced. That would have given him an opportunity to get a feel for what things were really like before he announced that he was the new boss. That wasn't possible. The facility was so tightly controlled for security reasons that no one showed up without prior clearance.

The guard who met him at the security checkpoint, a small passageway in the thickly wooded area, wore the clothes of a civilian security officer. ARCORE INDUSTRIES was embroidered on his black nylon jacket. He carried some type of automatic rifle, not the standard M-16.

The guard's combat boots were highly polished, and he wore his hair cropped close on the sides, maybe a quarter of an inch on top. This guy was military through and through—not a civilian drop of blood in his body. Driscoll waited in his rented Jeep while the guard checked his ID, a special card that Driscoll had been sent via registered mail.

It had been more than four years since he'd last been here, and he wondered if the place had changed much. He tried to make out what it was like beyond the single barbed-wire-topped fence that extended into the nearly leafless trees in both directions from the guard station. It was hard to see very far. Even without the leaves, the trees were so dense he couldn't tell what lay past them. The road beyond the fence curved sharply to the left, and with the shadows generated by the early-morning sun it was impossible to see much of anything. An old Chevy Suburban pulled up on the far side of the gate. It was Air Force blue, but ARCORE INDUSTRIES was stenciled on the doors. A man wearing a brown hunting coat, blue jeans, and boots stepped out from the passenger side, and then the driver turned the muddy car around and immediately headed back to wherever he had come from. The hunter approached the guard, swiped a credit card through a security device, and a personnel gate opened to let him through. The man consulted briefly with the guard, then approached the Jeep. Driscoll rolled the window back down.

"Welcome to LaLa Land, Colonel Driscoll. I'm Major Warren; I go by Critter. Excuse me for not saluting, but we don't do that out here."

Driscoll shook Critter's hand through the open window.

"I know. This isn't my first time out here."

"That's right, sir, I forgot. Mind if I ride with you to the facility?" Critter asked.

"You mean the base?"

"We don't call it a base," Critter answered.

Driscoll smiled. That hadn't changed either. He nodded. Critter walked around and hopped into the passenger seat.

The guard activated a motor and the chain-link gate rolled to the side to let them through.

Driscoll pulled through the opening and made the turn in the trees.

"You'll want to take it a little slow right through here," Critter said.

"No kidding," Driscoll said as the road in front of them suddenly stopped at a creek crossing. The pavement dropped eight or nine inches into the muddy creek bank. Deep tire ruts in the mud on the other side marked where the road appeared again. "What happened? The road wash out?"

"All the better to fool you with, my dear," Critter answered. "Actually, it's just a security measure I thought up. The road is buried right below the mud, so just ease into it and take it slow. You'll make it across fine. Need four-wheel drive to get back up onto the road on the other side, though."

"Well, that won't keep many people out."

"Not intended to. Just need to slow folks down so our camera"—Critter pointed into the trees ahead of them—"can get a good look. I'll bet half the squadron is in the security office, trying to see what our new boss looks like."

"I suppose I could moon 'em," Driscoll said as he slid the Jeep down into the creek.

"Probably not a good idea—about half of our staff is female."

Driscoll pulled forward into the mud. The Jeep slid down into the thick slop and slipped sideways as they plowed toward the other side. He slowly eased up onto the far side of the obstacle. "So, how busy have you been here lately?"

"We always have something going on. Keep along the road, about three miles farther. We're down to two pieces of equipment now, and that keeps us pretty busy."

"You mean two planes? What happened to the other two?"

"I guess I'd rather wait until we get into the facility to discuss that. No telling where this Jeep's been lately."

"Good point. So how's the fishing up in Lake Marquette?"

They made small talk until they reached the next checkpoint. The guard post was situated inside a ten-foot chain-link fence with strips of opaque material inserted in the weave of the fabric. It effectively blocked any view of what went on within. Critter passed his badge over for examination by another supposed ArCore Industries security official with close-cropped hair. He opened the gate, then waved the Jeep through.

Driscoll took a look around. It didn't look much different than it had when he'd spent his first tour here as a pilot. Astronaut, really. But they weren't allowed to wear the wings on their uniforms. The only reference to their high-flying skills was a highly classified report filed in a separate personnel folder secreted away in a safe on the fourth floor of the Pentagon. The facility looked older, though, worn out.

"Looks like your maintenance funds have been in short supply."

"More like nonexistent. Our funds will barely cover

the flying mission. There's a move to eliminate what's left of the squadron and close down the shop. Word is there's something better on the horizon."

"Better than the Aurora?"

"Pull in here. Your slot's right up front. It's not marked as such, but it's the commander's reserved parking spot. We can talk about the funding—or should I say lack of funding—when we get inside."

Driscoll pulled into the slot and they got out. The building in front of them wasn't large. Its sheet metal and concrete structure wasn't really old either, but it showed extreme signs of age and weather. Driscoll shook his head as he stepped over a crumbling hole in the sidewalk.

He followed Critter up several steps and into the building. Though weathered, the building was clean, the carpet frayed but not dirty.

"Your office is this way," Critter led him up another flight of stairs, then through the only solid-oak door on the floor.

"It hasn't changed much," Driscoll said, scanning the room, then stopping to gaze at the large U.S. map hanging on the wall behind the desk. Small telltale holes punctured the map in dozens of places. Driscoll pointed at the map. "Our old commander, Lieutenant Colonel Bill Porter, used to mark all his fishing victories with pushpins. See this little lake? We flew up there in an old DeHavilland Beaver. The pilot had a hissy fit when Porter commandeered the stick and started flying 'touch-and-gos' on the lake. Did you know him?"

"Yeah." Critter plopped down in one of the leather-covered chairs that surrounded the small wooden table butting up against the desk.

"Where'd he end up?" Driscoll asked as he sat in the chair behind the desk, running his fingers along the edge of the top.

"You didn't hear?"

Theirs was a tight-knit community, but Driscoll had been away for several years with NASA. Critter's tone of voice implied something ominous. "Hear what?"

Critter looked his new boss right in the eye and gave him the news point-blank. "He went down in number six. He didn't make it."

If Driscoll had been holding a drink he'd have dropped it. "When? What caused it?"

"It was about three years ago, right after you left. We never really got a good idea of what happened— you know, it's not too easy to call in an accident investigation team in this environment. But it appears he overextended on recovery, tried to pull out of hypersonic flight without fully transitioning to the flying wing configuration. He lost control and never recovered. Pilot error."

"Pilot error, my butt. Porter could outfly me any day of the week, and I can fly that transition with my eyes closed. How fast was he going when he tried the transition?"

"Well, that's a tough question. It isn't entirely clear."

"What do you mean it isn't clear? Who was his control?" What the hell was going on here? Driscoll felt like he was getting the slow-roll from his new second-in-command. Every flight had someone on control, another pilot with nearly instantaneous access to the exact same flight data the pilot was faced with.

There was a brief pause. Critter's eyes jumped back

and forth a couple of times before they landed
squarely back on Driscoll.

"Major Killeen was his control. I was there for part
of the mission."

"Killeen? He related to . . . ?"

"His son. Lot, of pressure on that young man. I was
with him at the Academy. His old man was always
stopping in to see how his boy was doing."

"Is he a good pilot? A good control for the other
pilots?"

"Okay, I guess. I'd rather let you make your own
assessment."

Something was fishy here. Driscoll couldn't lay his
finger on it, but Critter was holding back about Killeen. Being the son of the chief of staff probably put
everyone on the cautious side. No telling what effect
it might have had on young Killeen himself. "Then
what airspeed was he at when he attempted the
transition?"

Critter gave another pause, shorter than the first.
"Two thousand eighty knots."

"Two thousand eighty? That's marginal, but he
should have been able to recover into flat profile at
that speed. What went wrong?"

"I think it would be better if you took a look at
the tape."

Driscoll couldn't tell what was going on. Either
there had been a major screwup and his old commander had made a blundering, deadly error, or something had gone wrong with the plane. "I want to do
that as soon as possible."

"Of course. How about tonight? I think you should
get a quick tour of the place, say hello to the troops
and let them see you; then I'll get the tape and we

can play it back in the simulator after everyone else has gone for the day."

Driscoll looked suspiciously at his deputy, wondering what kind of drama he'd gotten himself involved in. "Okay, sure. Why don't we take a quick walk over to the hangar? I'd like to see what's left of this little squadron."

Critter stood up and Driscoll followed, stopping momentarily at the door to glance back at the map, remembering a better time when multicolored pins protruded from almost every lake and stream in a five-hundred-mile radius. He'd accompanied his old boss on a few of the fishing trips, remembered frying up the northern pike they'd pulled out of that little lake up in Canada. He felt a deep sorrow, then turned and followed Critter, resolved to find out what had happened.

"Lance, this is Lieutenant General Walter Morris. He's the commander of the Space and Missile Systems Center. My boss." Colonel DeMarco introduced the newcomer.

Quite a way to end a short summer tour, Lance thought. First he'd been invited to Israel to receive the award, then fixed a couple of problems on the pointer/tracker for the new Airborne Laser. Now he'd been ordered to meet with a three-star general.

"I'm pleased to meet you, sir," Lance said as the tall officer strolled into the room.

The general shook Lance's hand, then said, "Colonel, if you'll excuse us?"

The colonel, director of the Airborne Laser System Program Office and its twenty-million-dollar budget, was dumbfounded. He hadn't expected to be asked to leave. He stumbled back toward the door. "Just let me know if you need anything, General . . ."

The general waved him out. "Sit down, Lance," the general offered as the colonel closed the door to his own office.

Lance took a chair while the general walked behind the desk to look out the window at the Sandia Mountains rising up east of the city.

"Beautiful, aren't they?" the general asked.

"Quite." Lance wasn't sure what was going on, but he decided not to volunteer anything until he found out.

"You see that mountain? It was the predecessor to our emergency command center in Colorado. It's a fascinating place. There were even quarters for President Eisenhower. The lab uses some of the facilities for testing now. You should try and get a tour of it sometime."

"I'll do that, sir." Lance still wasn't sure what was up, but he was certain he was about to find out when the general turned and looked directly at him.

"Jim Kirk took me through it, right before he launched off to get the Airborne Laser Lab flying again."

"Colonel Kirk was a good man."

"The best. It was his vision that not only rejuvenated the Airborne Laser Lab but also got the smart folks thinking about operationalizing it for real. The Airborne Laser is his brainchild."

"I kind of figured he had something to do with getting this program started."

"More than just had something to do with it—he nurtured it, sold it, birthed it. I'm just glad he isn't here to see what's happening to it now."

"What do you mean, General? We're making very good progress. If I had another few weeks on my tour I'm sure we could have the tracker ready to fly."

"No, son. It's not you. You're doing some fine work. I get reports shipped in to me every week. You've been here, what? Four weeks?"

"Three, actually. I slipped a few individual mobilization days onto my normal two-week tour."

"Well, from what I've seen, the progress has increased exponentially in the little bit of time you've been here. What concerns me is what my fellow officers are doing back in that five-sided nuthouse. I've been told to cut back on the developmental engineering, that the production funds have been cut to ensure we retain our current fighter strength."

"What does that have to do with me, sir?"

"Don't you see, son? Don't you share Colonel Kirk's vision? Fighters can't do diddly against missiles. The only thing we have that can kill a missile right now is another missile, and then only if our target stays put. And if he stays put, he usually does it in a hardened silo and it takes a nuclear warhead to dig him out. And we can't use nukes—not first, anyway. You see the dilemma?"

Lance nodded his head as the image sank in. "So we need a laser to kill the missile after it leaves the silo. That's what we're working on."

"Exactly. It's our only choice. Of course, the fighter mafia don't think so. They're running amok all over the Pentagon, bemoaning the potential loss of one of their wings, clueless as to the big picture. They've gotten those Rand head-bangers convinced that if push comes to shove we'll have unequivocal aerial supremacy, as we had against that idiot Hussein, and that they can then swoop in with some of the bunker-busters they've finally got in the pipeline and knock out anything. Hell, they don't have a clue what they're up against."

"Surely they've thought it through?"

"They've modeled it. And they've simulated it. And they've convinced themselves they can kill a Dong Feng Five, China's longest-range ballistic missile. But I ran a test last year out in the desert, a test they don't want to admit even occurred. I threw together a silo with some spare parts. Damn bunker-buster barely dented it."

"So we're building a false sense of security with respect to our ability to defeat these missiles?"

"We're sticking our friggin' heads in the sand, is what we're doing! Don't get me wrong—we need fighters and we need fighter pilots, but the next war isn't going to be anything like what happened in the Gulf. We're going to have to kill a whole load of missiles to get through this one."

"Again, sir, I don't exactly see how this has anything to do with me. I'm just a reservist doing my summer tour. I don't play in the politics of the budget or the war planning."

"I know that, but you're a bigger player in this than you can imagine. You're one of the few people alive who's fought a laser in battle. You're the only one who can bring our new system on-line in time to show these idiots what the weapon can do."

"I'd be glad to help wherever I can. What exactly do you need from me?"

"I need you full time in uniform."

"What do you mean? Back on active duty?"

"No, I can't do that to you. I'd have to bring you in at a lower rank, and that wouldn't be fair. What I need is for you to come back as a reservist on extended active duty."

"For how long?"

"How long would it take to get the Airborne Laser up and running?"

"That's a loaded question, General. With sufficient support, I think we could have it ready for a demonstration in two to three months, but there are a lot of ifs."

"Like what?"

"We could do it if the laser works. I don't mess with the photon generator that much. I'd need quite a bit of technical support on the airplane, the diagnostics, the instrumentation. And we'd need something to shoot at. A target."

The general finally sat down across from Lance, his eyes boring down hard. Lance shifted in his chair.

"And if you had all these things, what is your estimate of our probability of success?"

"I'd say sixty to seventy percent."

"That's all?"

"General, most of the technologies going into this program are mature, but they've never been integrated. That's certainly one of my major concerns—we don't know with much certainty how they'll work together. That was one of the big surprises on the Airborne Laser Lab program. Things we didn't dream might cause trouble on their own became almost insurmountable when we tried to put them together. On top of that, there are a few technologies that haven't been tried. For instance, we've simulated part of the sensor suite by mounting surrogates on North Oscura Peak down at White Sands Missile Range and used them to identify and track missile launches. But that's only at twelve thousand feet, not the thirty-five thousand feet the Airborne Laser will operate at. There's also the lack of windflow over the sensor head . . ."

"Okay, I think I get it. I'm willing to take the chance if I've got you running the show. What do you say?"

"You need an answer right now?"

"Yes. I'm going to kill a program this afternoon and move the money here. Fifty-two million dollars directed at this program to set up the plane, test objects, range time . . . the whole enchilada. But only if you agree to help."

Lance could dream up a dozen reasons not to get on board with this. Not the least of which were Mandy and the girls back home. But even that argument didn't hold water. It was almost time for summer break and he could bring them all here, maybe rent an apartment west of town near all the riding stables. The kids would love it. But how would Mandy react if she knew he was about to repeat the nearly fatal mission he'd attempted just a few short years ago? And what about his work? "I'll have to discuss this with Dr. Alexander. I can't risk losing my job."

"Bull! You know exactly what he'll say."

The general was right. Alexander would be all for it. There was really no choice. "All right. I'm in."

"All the way?"

"All the way."

"What do you need to do first?"

"Unpack my bags and call my wife." He knew that wasn't what the general wanted to hear. "Then we need to get some very specific expertise out here to put some of these pieces together. We'll probably need to hire some contractors. It'll take some time to let the contract."

"You don't worry with the paperwork end of things. Just tell Colonel DeMarco who or what you need, and he'll get it here in record time. He may not be a technical genius, but he can move mountains of paperwork when called upon. And he'll have the funds. I'm fixing to drop a ton of money on him."

"That's great, General. That'll help a lot. Maybe we can pull this off."

"No 'maybes.' This is our chance to help democracy survive in some of the most tenuous places in this world, perhaps even in our own country as well. 'Maybes' won't do it. Results will. Don't forget that."

The general stood and reached out to shake Lance's hand. "Get busy, son. Here's my card—call me anytime, day or night. I'll keep the Pentagon clowns at bay. You just get those photons out of that beast and put 'em on the target."

"You'll have photons on demand, General."

The general followed Lance to the door. As Lance stepped through, the general's voice boomed over his shoulder. "Colonel DeMarco, get in here. I've got a job for you."

Lance wondered how the colonel would feel, taking direction from a major . . . from a reservist, at that.

"Good flight, Captain?" asked the technical sergeant manning the weather desk at base operations.

"JFW. Just friggin' wonderful. Fourteen hours in the air practicing for something we'll never need to do." Captain Jake Williams dropped his helmet bag on the floor beside the counter.

"We hope we'll never have to," the sergeant replied. "At least you had good weather. By the way, there's a note here for you. It's from Colonel Bastrop. He wants to see you ASAP."

"What's this about?" Jake took the message, scrawled on a standard yellow Post-it.

"Don't know, sir. The colonel's exec dropped it off about an hour ago."

"Bull. You guys in ops always know what's going on."

"Well, maybe. You didn't hear it from me, but I'm guessing you're getting a little tired of the great weather I keep providing you here in Omaha."

Jake caught himself crushing the small yellow slip of paper in his hand. "It can't be." He snatched up his helmet bag and spun around, jogging toward the exit, intent on seeing the squadron commander as soon as possible. "They can't do this to me."

"Colonel Bastrop will be right with you," the secretary said. "Please have a seat."

Jake couldn't sit. He couldn't relax. His mind was racing. He stood impatiently by the window, looking out into the brightly lit sky. He could see his beat-up old Camaro in the parking lot across the street. He could afford something better, but spending his money on a nice car would put him behind schedule. His dream of starting his own private flying business was going to cost plenty. Start-up capital was tough to get these days, even though he'd come up with the perfect niche business. Flying for the small companies that couldn't afford their own jets, ferrying their top executives to important meetings in his "air taxi," could be immensely profitable, but he needed more than two hundred thousand dollars for the down payment on the plane—a fast, sleek jet. Yeah, his goal was going to cost plenty, and he'd already figured out the only way to get there was to quit the Air Force and take the job he'd been offered at American Airlines. A 747 pilot made quite a bit. And he lived frugally. It would only take a couple of years, and he'd have the money he needed. He didn't really want to quit the Air Force, but even with the new pilot bonus program he'd still be a decade away if he stayed in. At American he'd have enough to launch his business in less than three years, and he would get more than fifty thousand dollars in severance when the promotion board passed him over. But that was before this.

"Colonel Bastrop will see you now," the secretary announced.

Jake knocked twice on the doorframe and stepped inside. Colonel Bastrop's desk, normally uncluttered, was piled high with folders. The colonel closed the folder he was studying and looked up.

"Hi, Jake. Take a seat," he said, motioning to the well-used oak conference table. "I'm afraid I've got some good news and I've got some bad news."

Jake waited without saying anything. He had already figured out what the bad news was, and he hoped the good news could make up for some of it.

"First the bad news. I'm going to lose one of my best pilots—that's you."

That wasn't what Jake expected.

"Good news is that you get to move on to one of the hottest jobs around for a heavy driver."

"Move on? Sir, I put in a request to separate two months ago. I can't take on a new job now."

"Look, Jake, I know all about your request to separate. I had to sign it, remember? I told you it was a mistake at the time, and I still think so. You don't want out of the Air Force as much as you think you do."

"Sir, with all due respect, you don't have any idea how bad I want out."

Colonel Bastrop propped his elbows on his desk, steepling his fingers. "It's that damn sky taxi service you keep talking about, isn't it? You're an Air Force pilot, Captain. Not a taxi driver!"

"Sir, I just spent ten hours in the sky, carting a bunch of guys around, not going anywhere or doing anything but burning fuel. I'd call that a taxi driver."

The colonel shook his head and reached over to a pile of folders, tapping the top of the stack with his index finger. "You know what these are?"

Jake didn't answer.

"They're personnel folders on every eligible captain in the squadron. You're in the zone for the upcoming promotion board, eligible for major."

"Sir, I'm two years below the zone. My chances are nil."

"Nil? Not exactly. I've taken a long, hard look at every folder. I know every one of these guys, but you stand out above all of them. Hard worker, and an excellent officer—when you aren't wasting your time dreaming about that private business garbage. You're the best pilot I've ever seen. I can submit only two Definitely Promotes to this board for seven officers, all of whom deserve to be promoted."

The colonel slid a form across to Jake. He picked it up, seeing that it was a promotion recommendation form. The DP square, Definitely Promote, was neatly *X*'d.

"I appreciate the thought, sir, but why don't you

save your DP for someone who really wants to make the Air Force a career?"

"Damn it, Jake, don't tell me how to do my job!"

Jake had never seen his colonel upset, at least not to the point where the veins on his balding forehead were pulsating like they were now.

"It is my job," the colonel continued, "to identify the most capable officers in my unit and recommend them for promotion. You are the top officer, whether you recognize that fact or not."

Jake contemplated his options while he pretended to examine the narrative on the form. "My top best," the first line started; "Brilliant," stated the second; "The best of the best," started the phrase on the third line. The words didn't phase him. They were vague, cookie-cutter descriptions that had no substance. All the pilots probably had similar descriptions. But not all had a DP, which almost guaranteed a promotion. And a promotion meant no severance pay under the new rules. There was one way out, but the colonel wasn't going to like it: "I could write the promotion board, tell them I don't intend to accept the promotion." He could see the colonel clench his teeth, the bulge at his temples now ready to erupt.

It seemed like several minutes before the colonel said anything. Jake pretended to examine the form, settling in for the outburst.

"You have the right to send a letter to the president of the convened promotion board. You don't have to tell them anything—just decline the promotion when it is offered. A lot of pilots did that two years ago, wanting to take the separation pay and get out. Of course, that option is gone now."

"What do you mean it's gone?" Jake's head snapped

up from the promotion form. "I thought you were authorized to receive separation pay the first time you were passed over under the new drawdown rules."

"Oh, *now* I get it." The colonel's fingers resumed their thoughtful steeple. "You were planning on a 'take-the-money-and-run' strategy. Hoping to get passed over because someone saw the separation request and figured you weren't in it for a career. Then you'd be qualified for the separation pay. How much is it now? Forty thousand?"

"Closer to fifty."

"Too bad your active duty service commitment doesn't expire until about a week after the board results are due out. That means you will meet the board, whether you want to or not. That's tough, especially with a DP."

Now Jake was really confused. He could write the board, tell them he wasn't going to accept the promotion offer, and they'd just shelve his paperwork, giving the promotion to the next guy. "I still have the option to write the board."

"You had better look into the rules, Jake. I'm not going to tell you what to do, but you better give this letter idea some serious thought. I guarantee you it will not be in your best interest. That's your copy of the promotion recommendation form. Oh, here's something else you need to take a look at."

Another form slid across the desk. What now?

"Congratulations. All kinds of good news for you today."

Jake picked up the paper and looked at it. It was a much different kind of form, but he knew what it meant instantly—orders. Permanent change of station. "What is this?"

"You get a new job. Sorry for the short notice, but orders came from the top. They need my best 747 pilot as quick as they can get him. And that's you, just like it says on the promotion recommendation. You're due in Albuquerque in ten days."

"But, sir, my separation papers are in."

"As long as you have an active duty service commitment, you're subject to reassignment."

"But I'll get another two-year commitment when I'm reassigned."

"Again, check the rules. It's a two-year commitment if the Air Force moves your goods. If you move them yourself, it's only a one-year contract. I think that'll be long enough."

Jake glanced up from the form. "Long enough for what?"

"Long enough for you to realize why you're in the Air Force, and why you'd never be happy on the outside."

The colonel had calmed down now, the veins on his scalp no longer pounding with anger. Jake, though, was extremely agitated. He started to tell the colonel just what he thought, but the colonel stopped him with a raised hand. "Don't say anything, Jake. There's no reason to burn any bridges at this point. Go walk it off, think about it, and figure out how you can best use this opportunity. You're not stupid. This may slow down your fanciful dreams for a few months, but go figure out how you can use it to your best advantage. Dismissed."

The colonel motioned toward the door, and Jake stood to leave, clenching the paperwork in his fist.

"And Jake—hold off on your letter to the promotion board. You've got two months to get it in, so take as much time as you can afford to think about what you want to do and what you can do for the Air Force."

"Hi, Mandy." Lance hadn't even changed out of his newly issued flight suit. It had been another long day, already ten o'clock in Albuquerque. Fortunately it was only nine in Santa Barbara, and he wanted to talk to the girls before they went to bed. "How're things back home?"

"Great, but lonely. We're all looking forward to seeing you tomorrow. The girls really miss you."

Lance searched for the right words to tell her he wouldn't be back for a while. "I miss the girls, too. And you. There's been a small problem out here, though. I'm afraid I won't be back for another couple of weeks."

"What kind of problem? Can't you come back at least for the weekend? The girls are going to be terribly disappointed."

"I know. I'm sorry, but they brought a three-star general out here to ask me to stay on to get the optical system checked out on this project. It's awfully important for the Air Force."

"The girls won't understand. Or care."

"I know. Let me tell them." Lance suddenly had an idea. "Hey, why don't you guys come out here? I'm going to be really busy, but Albuquerque is beautiful, and you'd have tons of stuff to do."

"But I've got that final interview up in Palo Alto in a couple of weeks. I can't miss it. You were going up with me, remember?"

"Yeah. I doubt I'll be able to make it. But you guys

can still come out for the week. It'd be great to see you. Please?"

"All right. As long as I'm back in time for my interview."

"Great. And don't worry about the job. You're a shoo-in. No one has the geology credentials you have."

"I know. Still, it's nerve-racking. It's not every day a big-name school comes looking for you to fill a vacant professorship. By the way, what does your company think about this little extension?"

"You know Dr. Alexander. As long as I'm doing something for the Air Force I have his total support."

"And the move up here? If I get the job?"

"You mean *when* you get the job. I talked to him about that a couple of days ago. He's already landed a research contract with Stanford. I'll be assigned to the project. I'll probably even be working on campus. We can commute together."

"That's terrific, Lance! This is going to be a big change in our lives, but I'm looking forward to it. I hope you are, too."

"Absolutely. I've always liked the Bay Area."

"The twins want to ride the trolleys again. That's all they've been talking about."

"Are they there? I'd really like to talk to them."

"No, they're spending the night with their friend Jessica. They miss you, though."

"Tell them I miss them, too." Lance tried to stifle a yawn.

"You're tired. You better get to bed."

"Yeah. Listen, call the hangar when you get your flights nailed down. I'll pick you up at the airport."

"Okay. I love you."

"Love you, too. 'Bye. "

Lance dropped the handset into the cradle and fell back onto the bed. The VOQ was small, with only one full-size bed. He wondered if the base had any other accommodations. If not, he'd just foot the bill for a hotel downtown. It'd be worth it to get to see his family, if only for a few days.

Chapter 3

Driscoll settled back into the seat. It felt strange not to be wearing the standard pressurized suit. He pulled the shoulder harness tight, even though he knew it wasn't necessary. The Aurora simulator wouldn't throw him around very much, even in the most demanding maneuvers. Still, the safety harness made him feel more like it was a real mission. He pulled the checklist from the thigh pocket of his flight suit.

Critter stuck his head inside the door, centered in the dome to Driscoll's right. "All settled in, sir?"

"Yeah. You sure no one is going to stumble in here while we run through this?"

"Positive. Door to the hangar is locked, and I had security send a man around to stand guard."

"Won't that make someone suspicious?"

"I doubt it. We store a lot of classified stuff in here, and sometimes we have to add the additional guard just to meet our customers' requirements. I don't think anyone will think anything of it."

"Okay. I think I'm ready."

"You won't be able to see me, but we can communicate over the net, just as if I was the controller for the mission. I'll play the mission tape from the colonel's last flight. Since we record all the avionics signals as well as the voice, the simulator will move and act as if Colonel Porter's Aurora mission was real. You'll feel just like you were in his place. Do you want me to fast-forward to the accident?"

"No, I want the entire flight. We've got all night, so there's no hurry."

"Roger. I'll be on-line in about five minutes."

Critter closed the door, dousing the entire dome in blackness. Driscoll's eyes quickly accommodated, but he could still barely make out any of his surroundings. He reached up, grabbed the canopy, and pulled it down. No need for the automatic canopy servo system in the simulator. He reached forward and slid his hands into the gloves, and felt the familiar actuators that gave him control of the flight computer, which in turn adjusted the control surfaces on the aircraft. It felt good to be back in the seat of this amazing aircraft. Then he remembered it was just a simulator. Still, it sure felt like the real thing.

"Colonel Driscoll." A speaker near his right shoulder crackled to life. "Colonel Porter's call sign for the mission was Trout Three Six. Major Killeen is Control One Niner."

The instruments began to come to life, glowing with a familiar faint red hue.

"I reviewed the preflight logs," Critter said. "The only discrepancy reported before that mission was a slowly rising fuel flow sensor reading. That particular sensor is a flow gauge on the secondary fuel pump for the starboard engine. No limits were breached, so the sensor problem was not a showstopper."

Driscoll keyed the microphone switch with his right thumb. "Copy. I'll keep the discrepancy in mind."

"No need to key the mike switch, sir. The simulator cockpit is always on hot mike."

Driscoll nodded, knowing also that the cockpit video camera would record his every move while he was in the simulator. "Okay. Are you about ready?"

"Affirmative. Tape's rolling, beginning at engine start-up."

Driscoll actually felt the simulator shake slightly as the instruments indicated the port engine was being spun up to ignition speed by the simulated ground starter. He listened intently to the audio that was being piped into the cockpit. Colonel Porter's voice was calm—no sign of strain or concern. It was eerie, hearing his old commander go through the steps that would inevitably lead to his death.

He waited, listening intently. Eventually both engines were running smoothly, and he heard Colonel Porter attempt to contact Major Killeen. The controller was supposed to be in the command center as soon as the pilot arrived at the plane, but for some reason Killeen hadn't yet shown up. Critter's voice came online, not from his current post in the simulator but on the tape.

"Hold here," Driscoll said. The static from the audio stopped, and all the signals on the instruments froze in place.

"What is it, sir?" Critter asked.

"Where was Killeen?"

There was a brief pause before Critter replied, "He showed up just as the colonel was about to launch."

"I didn't ask that. I asked where he was."

Another pause, slightly longer than the first. "He said he'd been stopped by the Admin office on his way over. Something about his flight physical."

"The inquiry confirmed that?"

"No, sir. The sergeant running the office retired before the board could talk to him."

"The board could have recalled him to duty if necessary. What happened?"

"As I understand it, the sergeant had a job lined up down in South America. He was gone before the board convened. They considered bringing him back, but didn't think it was warranted."

"That's crap. They just didn't want to make waves around the chief's son, didn't want it to look like there was anything out of the ordinary. How was he acting when he finally arrived?"

"Seemed okay, sir. I didn't notice anything unusual, except for maybe one little thing."

"What?"

"It's probably nothing, but his name tape was kind of crooked."

"That doesn't sound like much of anything."

"On most people it wouldn't be. But Killeen is different—he's a stickler. Never a hair out of place, never a loose thread on his uniform, even centers his security badge squarely under the V of his pocket flap when he wears his blues. I always figured he got it from being the four-star's son. You know—he needed to walk the walk. I don't even know why I noticed his name tape being crooked."

Driscoll thought it over. It was probably nothing. "Let's continue."

He felt the actuators under his fingers move as the aircraft began to taxi to the single, dark runway. Just as he was about to take off, he heard Major Killeen's voice for the first time.

"Trout Three Six, Control. You are clear for departure. After climbing to six thousand feet turn to heading . . . one seven five."

There was a delay in Killeen's direction. One seven five was always the departure heading. He had almost sounded undecided, unsure. And was there a slight lisp to his words? Or was that just an artifact of the recording system as it played back audio from the secure communication circuit?

An hour later Driscoll was reentering the atmosphere, following closely as Colonel Porter bled his Aurora's airspeed to below two thousand knots for the transition from space flight to aerial flight. He was over the western Pacific at seventy-two thousand feet—standard flight altitude for a high-speed photo reconnaissance pass under supercruise conditions. So far there had been no problems.

"Trout Three Six, Control One Niner," blared through the silence. That was unusual, too. Normally control is there only for assistance, not to interrupt things.

"Go, Control."

"We have a mission change. New mission data being passed via data link."

"Stop," ordered Driscoll.

"What is it, sir?" Critter asked.

"Tell me about this mission change before we fly it out."

"Well, sir, as you know from the pre-mission brief, this was to be a routine intelligence-gathering mission over the eastern Siberian landmass. We had to keep tabs on the missile fields to see if there had been any changes. We had been getting these missions fairly routinely during the winter months, and it seems our other systems were having a problem with that piece of the world.

"The mission change was pretty unusual, but it came from DV-1, so you know it took precedence over everything else."

That was true enough. DV-1 signified the president or the vice president.

"The new mission was a low-altitude pass—twenty-five thousand feet—over the eastern half of Mainland China with a return pass over the western half."

"Twenty-five thousand feet? That's awfully low for this bird to be running at hypersonic speeds. It uses up a lot of fuel."

"Affirmative. We had already dispatched a tanker out of Andersen Air Force Base in Guam as soon as we got the change, figuring the colonel would have to refuel before returning to base."

"And the objective of the mission?"

"It was never really stated. In fact, when we first got the orders, they didn't even ask for photos."

"No pictures?"

"That's right. I was in the communications center when we got the flash message to change the mission. I asked if they wanted photo reconnaissance for the entire pass or just pieces of it. They seemed surprised—didn't seem to have thought it through. They just came back and said they wanted it all."

"Any idea what they did with the data?"

"I don't think they ever looked at it. We transferred the file to the analysis site. I checked on it last month as part of our routine review to see which customers are requesting our data. That data file has never left the site."

"If they didn't want the data, that leaves only one explanation."

"Well, I'd sure like to hear what it is."

"I've only had to do it one other time. This mother leaves one whale of a sonic boom flying at twenty-five thousand feet and two thousand knots. We used to refer to it as a calling card. Obviously someone needed to leave a message with the Chinese. Okay, now I know what's coming up. Let's keep going."

Driscoll heard Colonel Porter voice similar concerns as he watched the new mission profile play out across the heads-up display. Nevertheless, it was a profile Porter had flown before, and the aircraft soon began a rapid descent. Driscoll rode the mission through the first pass, noticing nothing unusual. During the second pass, however, a warning light flashed on the radar warning display. A Straight Flush target-tracking radar had painted the plane with a fairly strong signal. That was unusual. There would normally have been a search radar indication long before the tracking radar came up. Worse, the tracking radar seemed to be keeping up with Porter's Aurora—that was very bad news.

Unexpectedly, the simulator threw Driscoll over on his side as Colonel Porter pitched hard over and raced for the ground. Driscoll hadn't even noticed the warning indicator light up, signaling the approach of an SA-6 missile.

Was the Aurora susceptible? It was only a matter of time before some engineer discovered a way to use traditional radar to track stealthy aircraft like the F-117, which had its development roots in the same Skunkworks back room shared by the Aurora engineers. Had the Chinese done it?

The missile warning light faded and the simulator leveled off at three thousand feet, flying fast and low. Colonel Porter was now on a course that would put him back over the Pacific in less than three minutes. "I need a heading," the speaker screamed.

There was a brief pause, probably caused by the time it took for the comm signals to make their way across the satellite links back to the command post. Then: "Come to heading zero eight niner."

That was strange. "Play back the last ten seconds," Driscoll ordered.

Critter rewound the tape and played it over.

Driscoll stared at the instruments, glowing faintly in the darkness. Something was wrong, but he couldn't put his finger on it. He let the tape roll on. The heading indicator, fed from signals from the highly accurate Global Positioning System, settled on a heading of zero nine eight. Nine eight? That wasn't the heading Killeen had given Porter.

"Hold it there," Driscoll said. "Can you feed your threat display through so I can see it?"

"Sure, sir. Hang on a second while I swap a cable on the patch panel."

After a few seconds a small grid map replaced the flight instrument readout on the larger display in the cockpit. Driscoll traced a straight flight path from the plane's current position through a bearing of zero nine eight. The path took the Aurora directly over a small gulf of water, then over an SA-6 battery. "Okay, let's finish it up." He already knew how the rest of the flight was going to turn out—it was more than obvious now. Question was, why?

The Aurora used its high-tech materials and sophisticated design to reduce the amount of radar energy it reflected. Coupled with the natural tendency of radar energy to dissipate with range and the machine was nearly invulnerable. But if you flew too close to any radar, the cloak of invisibility was incapable of masking the plane's presence, and Colonel Porter was about to fly directly over one of the most dangerous radars in the world—the kind with a colocated battery of surface-to-air missiles.

The hair on the back of Driscoll's neck stood up as the radar warning indicator lit up, then the missile warning display flashed almost instantly from orange to red. The plane pitched sharply to the right, then the marginal fuel pump sealed the colonel's fate. He couldn't accelerate through the turn, and the flying dart was buffeted, losing lift on the trailing edge of the flying wing. The Aurora stalled and slipped into a modified spin. This wasn't unusual—they practiced recovering from this flight attitude in training—but Driscoll's former commander never had a chance. The instruments went blank as the SA-6 slammed into the airframe.

He sat there somberly, wondering what Colonel Porter must have been thinking during those last few minutes. They had been conditioned to think they were invulnerable in the Aurora, trained to go places and fly profiles that no sane pilot would have dared in a conventional aircraft. Now they were no longer invulnerable.

"That's it, sir. End of the tape. Would you care to run through it again?"

Driscoll pulled his hands out of the gloves and stared at them. They were trembling—not from the physical effort, but from the tension. He had just simulated death.

"No. I'm done here. Come let me out of this thing. We'll debrief in my office."

"Killeen gave Colonel Porter a heading of zero eight nine, according to the tape," Driscoll relayed what he had experienced for Critter as they sat in Driscoll's office. "That would have taken him along a perfect course, clear of any threats. Instead, Porter flew a course of zero nine eight, which brought him right over the SAM battery. That doesn't make any sense."

Critter didn't say anything, didn't offer any explanation.

"The findings of the accident review board," Driscoll continued as he paced behind his desk, "are that 'according to the tape,' Colonel Porter flew an incorrect course, and that's what got him killed.

"Point one"—Driscoll raised a finger—"is that the flight instruments are frozen for about three seconds during Killeen's order to take the zero eight niner course. Why would that be?

"Point two," Driscoll said, raising a second finger, "is that Killeen's words were slightly slurred during much of the mission. But Killeen's words were clear as a bell when he gave Colonel Porter the zero eight niner heading. Why?"

"And finally point three"—Driscoll raised a third finger—"is Killeen's name tape was crooked. How come?"

Driscoll ripped his own Velcro-attached name tape off his flight suit and slapped it against the material covering the bulletin board that Colonel Porter had used to post the flight roster. It held tightly, upside down.

"I think you see what I'm getting at." Driscoll leaned over his desk and eyed Critter.

"I'm afraid I don't."

"He'd been drinking. That's why his name badge was crooked—he'd turned it over to signify he was off duty, out of habit. He had a few, then didn't get it back on quite straight when he realized he was late and had to hurry over."

"I'm afraid that's speculation, Colonel Driscoll."

"Perhaps. Unfortunately, we don't require alcohol tests of our controllers after mission accidents. Perhaps we should."

"But still, the tape shows he gave Colonel Porter the right vector."

"The tape has been tampered with." Driscoll stood at his window and stared out into the nighttime blackness.

"What makes you think so?"

"The digital power readout on the number two engine. It had been wavering between ninety-eight and ninety-nine percent for the entire flight. It cycled about every second, wavering between numbers. Then, while Killeen gave the new heading, the engine reading stopped changing and settled rock-solid on ninety-nine. It isn't obvious, but it's there. Someone has modified the mission tape, voiced over Killeen's original heading instructions to make it look like Porter misunderstood where he was supposed to fly. They probably sat right in the Aurora simulator, plugged in the tape, and made the modification there. But they didn't modify the engine settings when they changed the tape—just used the simulator's inputs. They probably assumed that since it was straight and level flight there would be no need to worry about the instrumentation signals.

"And, throughout the rest of the tape, there was no challenge from Killeen. He had the same data as Colonel Porter, and could see he wasn't flying the right heading, but he never questioned him. He should have been all over Porter, ensuring that he changed back to the proper course. He wasn't. Killeen looked at the threat map, accidentally transposed the numbers, and ordered Porter to his death. Then they tried to cover it up, tried to make it look like pilot error."

"But who could have modified the tape?" Critter asked. "Whoever it was would have to sound just like Killeen."

"Killeen sounds just like Killeen," Driscoll said.

"But how could he modify the tape? It was sealed as soon as the accident board convened. They were the only ones who had access to it."

"Don't forget, Killeen is the chief's son. This isn't the rose-colored world we would all like it to be. Such small 'transgressions' for the chief's son could probably be forgiven, even covered up if necessary, for the benefit of the service. Can you imagine what it would look like if the chief of staff's son had been found to be the cause of an accident? And worse, if it was because he'd been drinking?"

"I guess I see your point. Frankly I had my suspicions all along. Killeen isn't that great a pilot. I haven't let him go up since I took over for Colonel Porter. He hasn't seemed to mind, either."

"So I guess that puts the two of us in some kind of pickle, doesn't it? What do we do now?"

"I haven't a clue."

"We have no real proof. And the accident investigation board has already made its recommendations."

"And like you say, he is the chief's son."

"Yeah. That doesn't leave us a lot of choice." Driscoll sat down in his leather chair. "We can keep him grounded. That will be no problem."

"And maybe just watch him for a while, see what he does."

"Yeah, this kind of pressure has to grate on a guy, knowing he's responsible but not being able to make reparations."

"What do you mean it's our last test?" Lance asked incredulously. How could they expect him to fix all the problems without the right data collection tests?

"You know what we're up against," Colonel DeMarco said. "The Pentagon wants this project killed. General Morris is throwing up smoke screen after smoke screen. He's even laundered some project money through Air Combat Command to throw them off. But General Killeen, in his last act as chief of staff, has demanded that we curtail this program. Sooner or later the bean counters in the Pentagon are going to figure out what we're doing."

"Listen, I appreciate all you've done to keep this project going," Lance said, "but I don't think I can reasonably guarantee that either the laser or the pointer/tracker will work without gathering the right ground test data. I still need to determine what the Strehl ratio will be with the new adaptive optics algorithm, what the normalized beam power is, and how much jitter is left on the beam. That'll take at least three more tests."

"You really mean you need at least that much beam time, don't you?"

Lance had to think about that. "I could get the data if I moved the beam between different downrange targets during the firing time. But since I only have one downrange target site, that won't work."

"You aren't thinking out of the box, Lance. Time and money are resources. We have enough money, but not enough time. We'll build you three more downrange sites, and collect all the data you need at once."

"People are resources, too. And I don't have enough."

"I thought about that. I've convinced the department head at the Air Force Institute of Technology to send me thirty of his top students. They'll be here this evening. You'll have the Air Force's brightest physics, electro-optics, and electrical engineering graduate students here for two weeks. At the end of the second week you'll shoot that laser for the full duration, sampling the beam at each downrange site so you'll have all the data you need. After that, we'll tune up what needs to be fixed and start flying this thing. Questions?"

Lance was flabbergasted. How was he going to keep thirty officers working together effectively, particularly under such a time crunch? "I'm not sure how to get all this to come together."

"Simple. You've got about four hours yet. Get out of your lab coat and find a desk. Write down what you need to get the job done and don't overindulge in the details—we'll let the engineers figure out how to do it when they get here. That's what supervision is all about."

"You said four downrange sites, but I only need three. What's the other site for?"

"What's the beam run time for the laser?"

"It should go for about sixty seconds. After that we have to recycle the coolant for the mirrors."

"Okay. You take whatever run time you need for your three experiments, and give me what's left over. I'm going to run a real test." The colonel turned and walked away without further explanation.

Lance looked up at the airplane. It was inside the hanger, its nose pushed up almost against a roll-up door in the back of the building. The door was closed, but could be opened enough so that the laser could be fired from the beam director in the nose toward the downrange targets. There were about ten engineers working on the laser, preparing it for its first test. The system had worked in the test cell before installation, but it hadn't been tested from inside the airplane. Would it work? Would there be unforeseen problems? That's what Lance intended to answer during the three planned ground tests. Now he wondered if he would have enough time.

Colonel DeMarco was right, though—Lance needed to spend more time figuring out what needed to be done instead of trying to do it all himself. He climbed up the steps to find Staff Sergeant Adams. Sergeant Adams had worked more than a few miracles during the last two weeks, ensuring that the subsystems they'd been working on went into the airplane as quickly as humanly possible. He even built some mechanical parts himself when the designed part didn't fit where it should have. Lance found Adams in the plane, straightening out some software problem. He told Adams where he'd be, then headed for an office

on the top floor of the hangar. It was seldom used
and would provide a quiet atmosphere where he could
figure out what needed to be done.

The AFIT students arrived from Wright-Patterson
Air Force Base aboard a T-43 late that evening, just
as the sun was dropping below the western horizon.
The old navigator trainer, a Boeing 737, had suffered
the trip with hydraulic problems and nearly skidded
off the end of the runway when a tire blew on landing.
The students, all young Air Force officers, were un-
fazed and ready to get busy. Even though it was late
and they'd already had a long day, they met in the
hangar conference room to lay out their plans.

Lance spent about an hour briefing them en masse,
then the students took over. They were mostly captains, with two majors and a few lieutenants rounding
out the team. Lance found out they had been told that
they were going to Albuquerque only that morning,
each roused by an early-morning phone call from their
class leaders. Those leaders, the two majors and one
of the captains, took charge now. They split the students into three teams, then broke each team into
two twelve-hour shifts. Colonel DeMarco arranged for
food to be sent out as needed from the base cafeteria
and shuttles to run members back and forth to the
visiting officers' quarters. Colonel DeMarco peeled
out four of the officers from the group to work on
what he called his special test. Lance wouldn't see
those officers again for several days.

The next week went by in a blur. The thirty officers
spent their time running all over the three target sites
that had been established approximately two and a

half kilometers across a dry desert ravine from the hangar. A fourth site, Colonel DeMarco's special target site, was more than six kilometers away, across the shallow valley southeast of the hangar. Colonel DeMarco told Lance he wasn't even allowed down there until the day before the test. It didn't matter much to Lance—he was much too busy with his other work.

The students were extremely efficient. Not only did they prepare the downrange target sites with the necessary diagnostic equipment, they also prepared computer programs to analyze the large mass of data that would be collected. Toward the end of the week, they didn't even go back to the visiting officers' quarters, instead catnapping in the empty hangar offices and showering in the old Test Wing support facilities.

Finally, two days before the test, a lieutenant who had been working on Colonel DeMarco's special test asked Lance to accompany him to the secret target site.

It took fifteen minutes to cover the six kilometers to the site, riding slowly over washed-out dirt roads in an old Air Force four-wheel-drive pickup.

The lieutenant eventually stopped in front of a concrete-block building that was about twenty feet square and almost as tall. One wall had been roughly demolished, then covered with several large pieces of black plastic. A sheet-metal roof topped the structure.

Colonel DeMarco, now sporting the same camouflage battle dress uniform the students wore, stepped out from a small door in the side of the building.

"So, what's the big secret, Colonel?" Lance asked.

The lieutenant was grinning from ear to ear.

"Come on in and we'll show you." The colonel gestured to the small door.

Once inside, Lance found his gaze drawn upward by the smooth surface of the sleek cylinder. It was over a dozen feet in diameter, painted white with strange Oriental markings on the surface. It was encased at the bottom with a steel band. The band was bolted to the concrete floor in more than a dozen places around the cylinder's circumference.

"What in the world is it?" Lance asked.

"I'm sure you know," the colonel answered. "The bottom stage of a missile. What you probably don't know is that it's the bottom stage of a No Dong II."

"A No Dong II—the Korean missile? Where in the heck did you get one of these things?" Lance asked.

The colonel looked at him and a slight smile formed on his lips. "Those are the kinds of questions we don't ask. We're just glad it's here. And you get to shoot at it."

"It'll be pretty easy to hit at this range," Lance said.

"I don't doubt that. I'm more interested in the failure mechanisms. You can turn down the power of the laser, can't you? Wouldn't that simulate a longer range?"

"Yes, sir. We can shut down some of the modules to reduce the power. Unfortunately we won't be able to simulate the other parameters, like the actual range for the tracking algorithms and the missile motion."

"At least we can simulate the range for the laser weapon," Colonel DeMarco said. "I don't know what you'll be doing during the first three phases of the test, but for this last one I want you to turn down the power to simulate a nominal range of one hundred kilometers. The kill mechanism is dependent on the missile being in simulated flight with longitudinal loads on the casing—that's why we have this beast bolted to the concrete. I'm going to ignite the motor just before you hit it with the laser. With the proper range simulation we'll get a good idea of how long the laser must illuminate the missile before it is destroyed. I have a feeling that information might come in handy."

"You're probably right. I'll give you a ten-second warning before we bring the laser on the target. That'll give you time to fire the motor."

"Perfect. It should be a good show."

"You want to meet the copilot?" Billie Powers asked.

"I might as well take a little break." Lance tossed the graph down on the makeshift workbench.

"Problem?"

"Problems. A lot of them. Sensor readings go haywire when we try to adjust the phase of the deformable mirror. Probably just a ground loop."

"Huh?"

Lance pointed at the hiccup in the wobbly line on the graph paper and started to explain, but quickly realized it wouldn't do much good. Billie Powers ate, slept, and drank airplanes, but she hadn't taken much more than a polite interest in the inner workings of the laser—or any other part of the weapon system, for that matter.

"Where is he?" Lance asked.

"What makes you think the copilot's a man?"

That shocked Lance. He always considered himself to be fairly liberated, in tune with the world. But every now and then he would make an assumption that was steeped in the traditional male-chauvinistic mind-set. "I don't know why I . . ."

Billie smiled at him. "He's down in the office. I haven't met him yet—thought you'd like to tag along."

"Glad to. And sorry."

"Don't sweat it. I'll get you trained soon enough. Let's cut across the hangar floor to the Test Wing offices. I just got back from Seattle. Who are all these young officers I see running around?"

"These are the guys . . . and gals . . . who are going to save my tail. Colonel DeMarco brought them down from AFIT. They're all graduate students, getting a little real-world design and test experience. They're really quite remarkable and have done some amazing things in the last three days. We've only got two days left before our first, and apparently only, ground test. Without the help of these folks, and the rest of the engineers working at the four downrange test sites, I'd never have the necessary data to feed the beam control systems."

"Only one ground test? Sounds like someone has turned up the heat again." Billie opened the door and let Lance enter first. "You can tell us both about it."

They walked past a tall partition, then into a small, open bay office with several old gray metal desks. The room was empty with the exception of one officer, a captain wearing a flight suit. He was working at a computer and didn't even notice them enter.

"Hi. I'm Billie Powers." Billie interrupted his concentration.

Jake Williams stood without saying anything, looking over Billie's blue flight suit, then glancing at Lance's battle dress uniform.

"I'm the Boeing test pilot. This is Major Lance Brandon, the project engineer."

"Jake Williams."

He seemed distracted. Lance tried to be courteous. "Welcome to Kirtland. Did you just arrive?"

"Yeah."

Lance glanced at the computer screen and saw what looked like a personal letter. Jake followed his eyes to the screen, then reached down and turned the monitor off. It quickly went black.

"What can I do for you two?"

Their new pilot was obviously irritated, even somewhat rude. Lance glanced at Billie, but she shrugged her shoulders.

"Just wanted to say hello. I've got to get back to work," Lance said.

"Same here," Billie added. "Let me know when you get settled in and I'll give you a quick tour of the plane. It's probably unlike anything you've ever flown."

"Fine. I just need to finish this letter to the board and I'll be ready."

"The promotion board?" she asked.

"Yeah. You must be former Air Force."

"Eight years active duty, now in the reserves. If you're up for major, good luck."

"You don't understand. I don't want the promotion."

Lance could see Billie's eyes narrow. She seemed very disturbed by what Jake had said.

"You're right," she said. "I don't understand. Every officer I've ever been associated with worked hard to be competitive for promotion. The step to major is a big one, an important milestone in your career. Maybe you can explain this to me."

"I don't understand it either, but I really do need to get down to the target site," Lance said.

He hoped this wasn't going to cause too much tension between the two pilots. It was a bit disheartening, he realized as he stepped out the door and saw three of the AFIT students coming down the stairs from the plane. He had worked with these officers closely, knew they hadn't even been back to the visiting officers' quarters for more than forty-eight hours. They were dedicated, striving tirelessly for results. Lance knew that in the back of their minds they were concerned about the limited promotion possibilities for nonrated officers—for nonpilots. Yet he had just met a pilot who didn't even want to be promoted. Why? He'd have to ask Billie what the deal was later. He couldn't worry about it now. He had a test to run.

Chapter 4

Driscoll strolled down the hall, heading for the ready room. On his way he stopped in his office to check on some paperwork. Acting as both the squadron commander and the lead pilot was becoming a very time-consuming job, particularly with the whole Killeen problem hanging over his head. He had grounded the chief of staff's son, unofficially, to avoid a potentially sticky political situation. With only two planes left, there weren't enough flying hours to go around, so it was simple to eliminate Killeen from the flight schedule for the next two weeks. After that, it might be tougher to hide.

Driscoll opened the door and stepped inside, glancing up at the wall where Colonel Porter's fishing map used to be. Porter was one of the last SR-71 pilots—the original Habu, a nickname given to the old SR-71 reconnaissance aircraft by the natives of Okinawa, who thought the plane looked like a local poisonous snake. Eventually the pilots themselves took the same nickname. Driscoll owed his old boss a lot, and he intended to make sure that what had happened was not permanently recorded as pilot error.

Driscoll reviewed the planning folder during the hour before the flight. It was going to be a tough

mission, but fortunately Major Warren—Critter—was
going to be his controller. Going aloft in the Aurora
was more like a space mission than a normal flight.
No one ever went up without being in constant contact
with ground control, via a series of secure satellite
links. The pilots took turns acting as controllers for
the other flights. Warren had become Driscoll's regu-
lar controller.

The mission called for an overflight of North Korea.
That was somewhat unusual. Normally, these missions
were left to the R/F-117s stationed out of Japan. The
reconnaissance version of the stealth fighter was well
equipped for the flight, and it was cheaper to fly than
the Aurora.

Driscoll was going to have to stay buttoned up while
over Korean airspace. Some kind of laser had been
detected, probably by the R/F-117s. He had read that
the Koreans had grabbed some of the same laser technology that was rapidly propagating in many of the
rogue Third World countries—lasers that didn't shoot
down aircraft but instead blinded their pilots. That
meant that as long as he was in North Korean airspace, he was going to have to keep the screens up to
protect his eyes and rely on the aircraft sensors to
guide the flight. Later in the report Driscoll learned
one of the R/F-117 pilots had received some bad eye
damage while flying the same track he was slated to
run. Without some kind of protection, like the screens
prototyped in the Aurora, the R/F-117s were unable
to fly their reconnaissance missions.

To gather the data that the R/F-117s normally collected, Driscoll would be going tactical—minimum altitude for hypersonic flight. Twenty-five thousand feet
was pretty low for these birds. He would have to

watch his fuel closely. At such a low altitude, once the Aurora converted to hypersonic configuration, flying like a dart through the air, it would be sucking down fuel pretty fast.

In the life-support room, Driscoll stripped out of his conventional flight suit and hung it in his locker.

A staff sergeant and a technical sergeant helped him into the bulky pressurized flight suit. The run to Korea would take him to the upper reaches of the atmosphere, and without the pressurized suit nitrogen bubbles could form in his blood, subjecting him to the dreaded "bends." Early flight tests of the hypersonic Aurora had shown that simply breathing oxygen at high pressure wasn't sufficient. The pressurized space suit was uncomfortable but vital.

They finally got him into the cumbersome equipment, but left the helmet off until later. The two sergeants escorted him into the hangar, supporting him on either side.

The Aurora hangar was probably the cleanest aircraft hangar in the world. It had to be. These aircraft were half spaceship, requiring clean room procedures at the same exacting standards as any NASA facility. Even the technicians—the lowest rank held among the group was that of staff sergeant—wore smocks instead of the usual fatigues. The floor of the hangar was painted a gleaming white, which made the reflections of the overhead lights almost unbearably bright.

The other Aurora had already left on a mission to South America. It had been gone for about thirty minutes and wouldn't be back for two more hours. The portable lift was waiting next to aircraft number two, the oldest flying Aurora. Number one had crashed on its initial flight because of an undiscovered flaw in the computer program that adjusted the surface of the flying wing. A fatal flaw.

With the exception of Colonel Porter's crash, they'd had little trouble with the Auroras. They looked like miniature versions of the B-2 bomber—the flying wing. This radical design had applications beyond that of the now-famous bomber. Its ability to transition into a dartlike configuration that was able to sustain hypersonic flight made it the perfect platform for a strategic intelligence collection aircraft. Driscoll still laughed whenever he read the letters in the back of *Aviation Week and Space Technology* from readers lamenting the second and final retirement of the SR-71, the Air Force's long-standing strategic reconnaissance aircraft. The letter writers all worried that the United States had lost a strategic capability when the fleet was mothballed. They should have realized the Air Force would never give up a capability unless it had something better. And the Aurora was better. Much better. It combined speeds the SR-71 couldn't approach and cutting-edge stealth technology. It was fast. And it was invisible.

Driscoll and the sergeants stepped onto the hydraulic lift for the short ride to the cockpit, near the left tip of the wing. Driscoll climbed down into the specially designed cockpit, glancing back at the liquid oxygen system filling the special oxidizer tank. An eerie vapor wafted about near the end of the connecting hose. Two technicians wearing safety gloves and face masks were disconnecting the line from the airplane. Once seated, Driscoll waited for the sergeants to strap him in. He always imagined himself at the Indy 500 when they went through this procedure.

"Ready to check the mike, sir?" the technical sergeant asked.

"Yeah." Driscoll put his helmet on and adjusted the radio, flipping the switch to activate the "hot" mike. "Aurora Two Three to Control. Radio check," he said into the helmet before letting the sergeants tighten the collar and connect the umbilical from his suit to the ECU, the environmental conditioning unit. It would keep him cool here on the ground and warm in outer space.

"Copy, Aurora. Control reads you five by five."

Driscoll pointed at the radio and gave the thumbs-up to the technical sergeant. The sergeant nodded and proceeded to tighten the collar.

Once the helmet was fastened and the umbilical was in place, the sergeant closed the canopy and the two men rode the lift back down. Driscoll called up a checklist on one of the computer screens and started going through it while he waited to be towed out of the hangar.

Eventually one of the sergeants came up on the intercom, having hooked into the receptacle in the wheel well.

"Ready to tow, Colonel?"

"Ready. Brakes off."

Driscoll felt a small bump as the tow bar jerked the plane forward. Once outside the hangar, the tow bar was released and a start cart was hooked up to provide high-pressure air for the Scramjet engines. It took less than two minutes to get all four engines running.

The sergeant called one final time on the intercom. "I just took one last walk around the plane, Colonel. Everything looks good."

"Copy, Sergeant. Thanks."

"Have a good flight, sir."

Driscoll looked out the window and watched the sergeant step back into the beam of one of the landing lights. The sergeant held the end of the disconnected intercom cord in his left hand, then saluted with his right.

"Aurora to Control. Ready to taxi." Unlike other types of aircraft launches, this one had Driscoll talking only to control. Critter would be his interface with air traffic control and the rest of the world. He would intercept all the bothersome questions from curious FAA personnel and others, freeing Driscoll to concentrate on flying the mission.

"Aurora is clear to taxi to the active runway."

Of course he was, Driscoll thought, smiling. The Auroras were the only aircraft cleared to use the restricted airspace over the special airport, and his Aurora was the only one waiting to launch.

Driscoll pulled onto the runway, the flying wing extending outward to his left. It was an unusual way to fly, with the bulk of the airplane sticking out to the side, but Driscoll had gotten used to it fairly quickly during his initial training. Now it was second nature. Besides, once he entered hyperflight, most of the airplane would be behind him.

One last check of the information on his three data displays and he contacted his controller again.

"Aurora ready for launch."

"Aurora clear to launch. On departure turn to heading one zero five and maintain this frequency."

Driscoll nudged the digitally coupled throttle forward, watching the reading run to full thrust. The tapered inlets on the engine nacelles opened wide, allowing as much air as possible into the specially designed Scramjets, saving the precious liquid oxygen oxidizer, the LOX, for the space portion of the flight. The Aurora raced forward, more like a streamlined fighter than the broad-nosed wing that it was. Driscoll checked his airspeed as the plane accelerated down the runway. It never failed to amaze him how responsive the Aurora was, even on the ground. It was surprisingly quiet—and amazingly fast.

In less than seven seconds he was moving at takeoff speed, 160 knots. A slight tug on the stick and the wing pitched up into a phenomenally steep angle of attack, beyond the normally "stable" flight envelope. This angle of attack was attainable only with the Aurora's unique deformable skin concept. The wing itself changed shape as thousands of small actuators responded to one of the two onboard computers. The process allowed the wing to adapt to the constantly changing atmospheric environment it encountered. The plane was even able to compensate for a significant amount of the low-level atmospheric turbulence that often threw similarly designed aircraft into unrecoverable spins.

Even while he was still in the steep angle of climb Driscoll nudged the stick to the right, pointing the wing toward the one zero five heading he'd been given. The digital heading display slowed, then stopped on one zero five as he pulled out of the turn, continuing to climb.

"Aurora climbing through eight thousand five, heading one zero five."

"Roger, Aurora. Maintain heading and climb to flight level two five zero. At altitude, call up preprogrammed flight plan and proceed to refueling point. Mama's already in the air."

"Aurora, wilco."

Driscoll relaxed, knowing the KC-10 was already airborne. He hated having to wait on those guys. Out of habit he checked the airspeed—180 knots. There was really no need to worry about any of the flight parameters, as the computer took care of almost everything on this bird—all the routine stuff, anyhow. His job was the nonroutine, to handle problems when they came up. And they would come up—they always did on this kind of mission.

At twenty-five thousand feet he touched the video screen with his gloved hand. The screen sensed the input from a light wand embedded in the finger of the glove, bringing up the flight plan and directing him to turn to course zero three zero. Instead of pushing the stick, he let the autopilot take control. The plane wheeled left, turning to the computer's preselected heading. Driscoll let the plane fly itself while he reviewed the orbit initiation sequence.

Driscoll switched frequencies as soon as he was clear of the tanker.

"Control, Aurora. I'm full of gas and ready to go. Over."

"Roger, Aurora. Turn to heading zero seven five and configure for insertion. Contact when ready. I just checked with the folks at NASA. They confirmed the Air Force assessment. The solar storm we've been expecting shouldn't interfere with satellite communication for a few more days, so communications shouldn't be a problem during this mission."

"Wilco." Driscoll called up the classified flight plan and let the autopilot bring him onto the right course. He debated momentarily on whether to let the computer initiate the configuration change or to do it manually.

He decided to do it himself. Configuration change involved the trickiest flying he'd ever tackled, and he was constantly trying to do it better, to make the transition more smoothly. Of course, it wasn't totally manual; the computer still maintained control of many of the flight surfaces to make sure the wing didn't stall.

Driscoll took the stick in his right hand and put his left in the holster at his side. The holster was a glove-shaped device containing dozens of sensors that would react to the slightest motion of his fingers. With his thumb, Driscoll disengaged the autopilot. Immediately the nose of the plane pitched slightly upward.

A sensor beneath the index finger of his gloved hand registered his finger's pressure, and the nose came down as elevator trim was applied. With the plane trimmed correctly, Driscoll took a deep breath and pulled his thumb inward. Small spoilers on the right tip of the wing popped up, increasing the drag on that side of the plane. The throttle on the left side engines automatically increased as the right side of the wing fell further behind. Driscoll's gyro-stabilized seat began rotating to the left, keeping him facing forward as the wing moved toward its hypersonic configuration. The engines also pivoted to stay aligned with the direction of flight. Turbulence hit when the wing was moving through the air at about a forty-five-degree angle; air split from the forward edge of the wing that had been recombining in empty space now found the right side of the wing in the low-pressure area. Driscoll was sweating, making short, rapid corrections to the plane's pitch and roll as the wing passed through the most unstable flight regime that had ever been successfully negotiated by man.

At fifty degrees the automatic actuators began to change the wing's shape, forcing the air to remain separated longer, recombining further behind the tail. The turbulence dropped substantially and the wing continued to reconfigure, the right side dropping further and further behind as Driscoll retracted the spoilers.

The plane flew through the air like a dart. What had once been the left edge of the wing was now the nose, its tip of black metal leading the rest of the dagger. Simply making the transformation had added more than 100 knots of airspeed, as the drag from the wing was now substantially reduced. And it was smooth. Driscoll had to make only minor corrections to the plane's heading before letting the computer take control again. Not a bad transition, he told himself, pulling his left hand out of the holster and relaxing. He keyed the mike.

"Control, Aurora. Transition successful, ready for insertion."

"Copy, Aurora. Begin procedure and maintain current heading."

Leaving the autopilot on, Driscoll hit the illuminated switch on the front display. The acceleration to hypersonic speeds required no great deal of effort on his part. Entering low Earth orbit required precision that no human could master, so he gladly let the computer do its job.

Driscoll felt a slight shudder as the plane passed smoothly through Mach 1, breaking the sound barrier somewhere over Pennsylvania. He was still amazed that the Aurora—or any plane, for that matter—could go so fast without its afterburners lit. And as far as the Aurora's top speed was concerned, it was still barely moving.

The nose of the pointed vehicle pitched up sharply, still accelerating. The airspeed indicator had already passed Mach 1.5. Driscoll looked up at the beautiful night sky, the silvery moon now full, brighter and clearer than he had ever seen it. He made a quick check of the oxygen system when he remembered the reason it was so clear. A glance at the altimeter showed he was at seventy-two thousand feet—far above most of the earth's protective atmosphere, his speed at Mach 3.3.

Now the moon seemed within reach. He was passing through the ballistic portion of the flight, more than eighty miles high, effectively in outer space. The moon was huge, looming right in front of him. He could distinctly see a few of the larger craters on its surface, craters he had studied in books as a child. The moon began moving rapidly upward as the Aurora tipped nose down to reenter the atmosphere. Driscoll checked the running clock at the top of the computer console. It had been only twenty minutes since he achieved the transition to hypersonic flight. The entire flight to the Far East would take only about forty minutes, not counting the time to refuel.

He kept a watchful eye on the LOX levels as well. It wouldn't do to use up too much of the precious oxidizer. There was no way to refuel those tanks without landing first.

Earth moved up to fill his view as small booster rockets located all over the Aurora began to burn in short bursts, orienting the craft for the upcoming reentry. Driscoll could feel them pop and could soon see the lights of the burning jets outside his canopy.

The front of the plane began to heat up as the Aurora reentered the upper levels of the atmosphere, the thermal sensors beneath the plane's special skin registering close to 300 degrees Celsius. At twelve miles high the plane began to level off, its speed decreasing to just over Mach 3. Driscoll felt the special flight suit squeeze his legs and arms to force the blood back to his head, keeping him from passing out during the sustained seven-G load. He strained to keep from becoming disoriented.

Finally the rollout was complete and Driscoll was flying over the Indian Ocean at more than a thousand miles per hour, his altitude just above fifty thousand feet.

"Control, Aurora," he called.

"Copy, Aurora." The answer from Critter at control came after the half second delay required for the satellite to relay the transmission back to the base. "Come about to preprogrammed flight plan. Nice flight so far."

Driscoll watched the computer display, letting the autopilot take care of the workload. He flew in total confidence. No radar had ever been designed that could pick up a plane with such a small radar signature.

The plane began a turn to intercept its programmed heading, dropping as it banked. The mission would consist of a high-speed, low-altitude photo reconnaissance pass over the upper half of Korea. It took less than three minutes to get into position for the run.

Driscoll had already engaged the electro-optical shutters, bathing the inside of the canopy in darkness. It would not have been standard procedure during a normal mission, but it was necessary for this one—the lasers the R/F-117s reported could be extremely harmful to his eyes. He was already in Korean airspace and would stay there less than five minutes. Then he would let the computer take him back to the States, via outer space. He sat with his hand on the stick, his thumb ready to abort the computer-controlled flight as soon as he detected any problem. He continuously scanned the instruments, paying particularly close attention to the displays from the closed-circuit video—his only visible link to the outside world.

A yellow warning light suddenly flashed on the left side of the computer display—LASER DETECTED.

Driscoll didn't worry. He was always picking up some alerts during these missions, although he'd never seen the laser warning sensor go off before. Usually it was just some surveillance radar whose beam he had accidentally flown through.

Then the TV video bloomed, a bright flash saturating the black-and-white display. As the screen slowly returned to normal, a tone went off in his left ear, accompanied by the smooth, almost seductive voice of a young woman: "Missile warning," she said. "Surface-to-air missile launch detected." A bright red light on the left side of the display accompanied the aural warning.

Driscoll took over control of the plane from the computer, just in case. It might be some Korean missile test the sensors picked up. He punched up the sensor output just to be sure. The display showed his airplane in the center and a tiny line arcing up toward him. Now he started to get worried. This was something more than a random missile—it was definitely heading in his direction. A quick check of the camera status showed that the reconnaissance system was con-

tinuing to gather data. Driscoll wondered if he could
hold out long enough to get all the data he was supposed to collect.

Driscoll hit the red switch on the throttle, automatically sending a digital command to the two engines,
pushing them to full power. He called control as the
TV screen bloomed again.

"Control, Aurora."

"Aurora, this is Control."

Critter was sitting in a booth that looked a lot like
the Aurora cockpit. The important information was
being telemetered to the station via satellite link to
keep Critter informed of what was going on miles
above the Korean landmass. Driscoll's radio call
meant he was looking for ideas on what to do. "Recommend using rear aspect illumination radar and set
automatic impact countdown."

Good idea, Driscoll thought. He engaged the rear
aspect missile warning radar—no need to be stealthy
now, since whoever had fired the missile already
seemed to know where he was. The radar would give
him more accurate data on the missile's position than
the passive infrared system was providing. The display
changed when the radar was activated. His plane was
still in the middle and the small white line was still
arcing toward him, but now the range and time to
intercept were displayed at the top of the screen.

"Twenty-five seconds to impact." The sexy female
voice generated by the computer didn't show any
concern.

Driscoll felt the pull as his airspeed increased to
Mach 4.2. He knew some of the camera data would
be harder to analyze at this speed, but he had no
choice—he had to try to outrun the missile. He pulled

a hard left turn, hoping to outfly the deadly javelin. The Aurora's computers continually reshaped the wing's surface. Driscoll felt the blood drain from his head as he pulled seven, then eight G's. The pressure suit inflated around his legs and abdomen, forcing the blood back to his head.

At first he appeared to be succeeding, as the range to the threat increased, the missile trying to correct its flight path.

"Thirty seconds to impact."

Driscoll knew better than to relax yet. The Aurora was gulping fuel at an alarming rate. The engines were designed for hypersonic flight, flight at supersonic speeds without the use of their afterburners. But his afterburners were lit now, pushing the plane ahead of the pursuing missile. Driscoll yanked back to the right, feeling the space suit squeeze his body once again.

"Twenty-five seconds to impact." It was catching up again. Only this time it was dead on his tail. No more of its flight would be wasted maneuvering for the intercept.

Driscoll mentally reviewed his ejection procedures, wondering what it would feel like if he had to pop the ejection capsule at this speed. It would be a first— no one had ever ejected until the plane was trimmed back to sub-Mach velocity.

"Twenty seconds to impact."

Even in the environmentally controlled suit, sweat started to trickle down Driscoll's back.

"Fifteen seconds to impact."

He was already over the Yellow Sea, still heading west. He noticed the camera had automatically turned itself off. Fortunately the data had been relayed back to control along with the avionics signals. Even if he didn't make it back, the mission wouldn't be a total failure. Driscoll shook his head. He had to stop thinking so negatively.

"Ten seconds to impact."

That sexy voice would update him every second now. She was starting to get on his nerves.

"Nine seconds to impact."

"Control?" Driscoll desperately need to hear a human voice, some reassurance that he'd done everything he could.

"Eight seconds to impact."

"Your only option is to bail out, Aurora. It's never been done at that speed before. Don't wait past five seconds to impact before you eject."

"Seven seconds to impact."

"What I wouldn't give for a flare dispenser or an onboard jammer," Driscoll told control, thinking back to his F-15 days. He didn't know if either would work against this type of missile, but it would have given him something to do.

"Eight seconds to impact."

What? Driscoll looked at the display. He was still at Mach 4.2, yet the missile seemed to be trailing further behind. Had it run out of propellant? He switched to the infrared missile warning display. It was dark. Good. That meant the missile was no longer burning, no longer generating the infrared signature of a hot motor. Driscoll flipped back to the tail aspect radar.

"Ten seconds to impact." Driscoll switched off the automatic impact countdown. He could tell the range to the missile was increasing now.

"Aurora, this is Control. You still with me?"

"Roger, Control. Breathing easier now."

"You aren't out of it yet, Aurora. Fuel is below

minimum. You have less than ten minutes of flight at this rate of consumption. Shut it down, fast."

Driscoll was already doing it, backing off the throttle and climbing to reduce airspeed. He would reorient to takeoff configuration as soon as his airspeed was slow enough.

"Aurora, Control. Bad news. You've overflown the preplanned tanking point. I've vectored the alternate tanker to intercept you at alternate refueling point Bravo. Maintain your present heading and reconfigure for refueling. It's going to be close."

"Copy, Control. I'm reconfiguring now."

Driscoll felt the turbulence that accompanied the transition to sub-Mach flight. The knifing plane started to drop rapidly, the hypersonic configuration extremely inefficient at this slow speed, the engines running at only 50 percent. Driscoll pushed the port engine to full throttle and retarded the starboard engine, letting the asymmetric thrust force the tail of the plane forward. In seconds he was flying the conventional wing again.

"Control, Aurora. I have the tanker in sight."

"Copy, Aurora. Maintain standard flight profile and contact control when ready for return flight."

"Wilco, Control. Go ahead and pull down the data from the mission. I want to know how I got picked up by the Koreans." If the Aurora was now susceptible to some new laser radar, it might very well spell the end of the Aurora program.

Lance made one last trip up the aircraft's center aisle, stepping around a couple of the engineers. There were more people onboard than necessary to run the test, but that was okay. He needed to give the AFIT students an opportunity to witness firsthand the results of their work. If it hadn't been for them, he'd still be weeks away from being ready for this. Besides, since this was a ground test there was little danger to anyone aboard. The only real potential for safety problems was in the laser fuel. If there were a major leak into the operator's compartment they would all be asphyxiated.

"Test crew, go to one hundred percent oxygen." Lance ordered them all to don their masks, much as he remembered Colonel Kirk giving the same order only a couple of years earlier aboard the Airborne Laser Lab.

"Air crew to one hundred percent oxygen." Lance heard Billie Powers order over the interphone. She was up in the cockpit with their newest officer, a captain who apparently wished to stay in that rank. She hadn't given Lance all the details, but she had obviously taken it as her own personal mission to convince him of the error of his judgment, even calling his old boss at the NAOC to find out what had gone on there.

The aircrew up front would have a good view of the test, sitting just above the nose of the aircraft, just above the output aperture for the laser beam. It wasn't even really necessary for the aircrew to be onboard for the test. There was a special switch in the cockpit, a consent-to-fire switch, that had to be held down for the laser to fire, but Lance could have overridden the switch if he'd had enough time. Billie had wanted to be there, though, to get a sense of what it would be like when the laser fired.

Lance rolled up the slack headset wire and held it in his hands as he stopped behind Sergeant Adams. "How's it look?"

"Picture-perfect, sir. All of the parameter settings the AFIT engineers recommended are in, and the whole beam control system is stable as a rock."

"Good. They've done some fine work," Lance said, certain that the three officers sitting around the beam control operator heard the compliment. They had indeed done an excellent job, running hundreds of tests over the last few days to determine to most accurate optimization for the jitter reduction parameters, then modifying the software to incorporate the new data. The cold-fire test results had been superb. Now if only their luck would hold.

Lance began walking through his checklist, broadcasting his announcement to all personnel involved over the interphone that had been installed at each test position:

"Downrange sites, confirm ready for test."

"Alpha site ready."

Good. The closest site had been having the toughest luck getting things set up properly, and it was the most critical part of the test. At just less than one kilometer away they would be the first to see the beam, albeit at the lowest power they would send downrange.

"Bravo site ready."

The rest of the laser modules would be engaged when they delivered the beam to the Bravo site, almost two kilometers away. There they would make the first real measurement of the beam's power.

"Charlie site ready."

Charlie site would also take the brunt of the beam, but whereas Bravo site would simply measure the energy in the beam, Charlie would measure beam jitter, one of the most important parameters necessary to keep it under control.

"Delta site ready."

Lance recognized Colonel DeMarco's voice. The colonel had taken personal responsibility for the final target site. Though targeting a real missile wasn't really very scientific—too many variables weren't under control—it would make good public relations for the program. As long as no one got killed.

"Instrumentation?"

"Instrumentation ready." The captain from AFIT had patched all the signals from the laser and beam director diagnostic instruments into a single computer. This enabled them to monitor any test parameter they wanted and would allow them to reconstruct any problems after the test.

"Range safety?"

"Range is clear." The safety officer in the short tower attached to the hangar had a good view of the arroyo between the hangar and all four of the target sites. He would call a test abort it anyone crossed into the test range.

"Device?"

"Device is ready," answered the Lockheed engineer monitoring the parameters of the chemical oxygen-iodine laser. One of the AFIT students, Captain Hawkins, watched closely over his shoulder.

Lance guessed the contractor was annoyed at Hawkins's presence, but Colonel DeMarco had mandated it. He wanted a military crew that was capable of operating the entire system.

Lance took a deep breath. There was only one more system to check.

"Beam control?"

"Ready to fire." Sergeant Adams was at the stick,

a very similar system to what Lance had used in the Airborne Laser Lab during that last fateful mission.

Everything was ready. It was now or never. Time to light this thing up and see how good it really was.

"Request air crew consent."

The consent-to-fire light went green on Lance's console.

"Device on."

The monstrous plane wobbled slightly as the exhaust from the lasers was pumped out of the belly of the plane and into catchment tanks, simulating operation at forty-five thousand feet.

"Beam control, do you have the target?"

"Tallyho on target Alpha."

"Beam on."

Pneumatically driven shutters slammed out of the way, releasing the stick of light from six of the laser modules.

Lance was closely watching the signal from the integrating sphere at the closest test site. His display showed a red line, indicating the level of power they expected to achieve at the target. Using the integrating sphere allowed them to get a good idea of all the other parameters as well. If the beam jittered too much, if the phase was wrong, if one of the laser modules wasn't operating at optimum performance, or if they simply missed the target, the integrating sphere data would let them know.

"On target," the downrange test crew called.

Lance watched a thin white line climb rapidly toward the red marker on his display. Within a few tenths of a second the white line crossed above the red target and settled into a steady, level indication. Perfect.

"Autotrack," Lance ordered, satisfied with the first phase of the test.

Sergeant Adams fingered the trigger on the stick, allowing the computer to take control. The computer had been preprogrammed to engage each of the down-range targets in a precise sequence.

Shutters slammed into the beam, diverting the lethal energy into specially designed beam dumps that could absorb the heat for a few seconds without melting. This was a safety precaution for the ground tests. It wouldn't be prudent to wave the lethal stick of light all over the New Mexico desert while the beam director searched for its target. Safer to kill the beam briefly while the beam director found its prey, then let it back out. The computer ordered the other laser modules to come on-line in standby mode while the beam director quickly slewed to the next target. When the target was centered, the beam shutters slid back out of the way.

"Target Bravo engaged." Sergeant Adams rested his hand near the stick, ready to take control if anything went wrong.

This time all the laser energy was thrust through the optical system and directed at the water-cooled calorimeter two kilometers away.

Lance watched a digital readout, indicating the relative temperature of the water in the target. He had no way of knowing exactly how much energy was going downrange. He would have to use the classified calibration factors to calculate the beam power after the test was complete. But his indication did show a steady value after about a second and a half, signaling that the beam had reached peak power. After two and a half seconds the shutters again engaged to kill the beam, allowing the beam director to safely slew to the next target—downrange site Charlie.

Once again the beam director settled quickly on target and the full, lethal energy of the beam was hurled downrange. This time Lance had a pictorial image of what the beam was doing. A dancing, circling line marched across a video display that had been hastily added to the test director's console. The line circled briefly as the conical scan algorithm allowed the beam to scan the target, searching for its center. Once on target, the algorithm gave up to the fine-track process and the dance stopped. No movement, at least none that Lance could see on his own monitor. Perfect.

"Delta site initiating motor ignition."

Colonel DeMarco was getting ready for the last portion of the test.

After two full seconds, the shutters killed the beam again so the beam director could find its final enemy.

So far the test had gone perfectly. Lance couldn't have asked for a better test run.

The beam director settled on the final target, nearly five kilometers downrange. The secondary mirror in the telescope shifted on command of the computer, spreading the beam. Captain Hawkins had come up the idea, and it turned out to be the easiest way of decreasing the energy density at the target, simulating an operational range of more than 100 kilometers.

Lance settled back into the test director's seat, watching the infrared camera mounted within the beam director. The gain on the camera was turned down as much as possible, and an additional filter was mounted in front of the lens, again a way to simulate the planned range to an actual target. Even with the filters in place, Lance could easily see the harsh glow of the fire from the rocket as its motors pushed against the concrete floor of the building that housed the missile.

"Problem," came a call over the net from the specially built revetment about one kilometer from test site Delta.

"What?" asked Colonel DeMarco.

"Strain gauges on north side of missile are showing excessive load."

"Will the mounting brackets hold?"

"I doubt it."

"Ready to fire." Sergeant Adams held the trigger, waiting for consent from the test director. They had allowed the automatic control system to point the beam at the final target, but he had manual control of the shutters just in case anything went wrong.

"Hold one." Lance was undecided. Should he go for it or wait until they were sure the missile would stay put? There was no way to turn the motor off once it was lit. Only when it ran out of fuel would it shut down.

"Shit!" It was the colonel's voice.

Lance saw the missile move in the video. Surprisingly, it was moving vertically. Must have sheared off the hold-down clamps. There was only one possible solution: "Fire!"

Adams pulled the trigger, and the shutters exploded outward again, releasing the beam from the laser.

The missile ripped through the sheet metal that covered the top of the building and accelerated upward as the beam heated the thick outer shell of the rocket.

Lance watched the target-tracking camera as the blurry image of the rocket's exterior began to lift away from the pad. How much room was there before the beam impinged on the hangar door? Probably not much. The laser had to work, and work quickly.

The system safety officer in the tower was near panic. Lance heard him ordering the control tower at the Albuquerque airport to clear all air traffic in the area. And that wasn't the worst of the problems. If they didn't kill the missile quickly, it could well end up showering fragments of itself all over southern Albuquerque and the small towns south of the city.

Lance leaned forward in his seat, urging the laser on as the missile slowly climbed. He stood to look over Sergeant Adams's shoulder, watching as the missile lumbered into the air, already almost twenty feet up. Without any guidance system it would go unstable within seconds, shooting off to God knew where.

Captain Hawkins moved from behind the Lockheed engineer and began hammering at the keyboard beside Sergeant Adams. "I'm overriding the secondary mirror defocus command," he told them as he instructed the telescope to bring the beam into a tight focus on the target.

The blurry image in the target-tracking camera snapped into focus, and almost instantly a flaming hole the size of a soccer ball erupted in the side of the missile as the laser burned through its casing. In the next instant the rocket exploded violently, saturating the tracking camera with a burst of white light.

"Holy cow!" The range safety officer summed it up quite succinctly.

"Beam off." Sergeant Adams released the trigger. The shutters slammed back into place, blocking the laser beam from the input to the beam director.

"Begin system shutdown," Lance ordered the laser device operator.

The rumble of the laser settled to a stop as the various subsystems shut off its fuel.

"Status check: test site Alpha?" Lance wondered if everyone was all right.

"Shut down."

"Beta?"

"Shut down."

"Charlie?"

"We're okay here. Systems shutting down."

"Delta?"

There was no answer.

"Range Safety, can you see test site Delta?"

"Affirmative. The explosion tossed fragments over a large area. Test stand is gone. Instrumentation site is heavily damaged. Hold one."

Everyone in the plane held their breath as they waited for range safety to try and contact Colonel DeMarco and the other AFIT engineers.

"Test Director, this is Range Safety. Everyone's okay," the safety officer called over the intercom. "Looks like the explosion knocked out their intercom land line. I just talked with Colonel DeMarco over the backup radio. They're all fine. Just a little shook up."

"Good," Lance exhaled slowly. "I would like everyone to come to the conference room in about an hour. Ask Colonel DeMarco if he can get back here by then."

"Wilco. I have a few small brushfires in the distance, but it looks like most of the fuel burned up in the explosion. I've already got the fire department on the way out to clean up."

"Okay, but they know not to ask any questions, right?"

"Sure do. Colonel DeMarco clued in the fire chief before his little 'experiment.' "

J-2, COMUSFORKOREA

"Sir, we have a launch indication from DSP satellite two."

"Get me a track." Colonel Bradford, the officer in charge of the watch, dropped into the watch commander's chair in the center of the room and picked up the red telephone. The other end, connected to the commander's stateroom two doors down, started ringing immediately. "Sir, sorry to bother you this early, but we have a situation. DSP indicates a launch. We're confirming right now and working the trajectory. . . . Yes, sir. Wilco."

"We are at Threatcon Charlie," Bradford said as soon as he replaced the phone in its cradle, his voice echoing ominously within the confines of the war room. The room's occupants, wearing the uniforms of all the U.S. services as well as the Korean Army, leaped into action to relay the situation to all units within the Korean theater. "This is not an exercise. Repeat. This is not an exercise."

Bradford watched as the display on the large screen shifted to highlight the central portion of North Korea. A small, silvery track was superimposed on the map. The silver line started in the northeastern region, well away from the known missile fields. Fortunately, the track was headed out to sea. Unfortunately, Japan was right in line with the indicated trajectory.

"What've we got?" Bradford asked, standing to move behind a Navy lieutenant with telephone handsets at each ear.

The lieutenant put one of the phones down on his small desk, examining the screen in front of him. He pointed at the smaller but more detailed replica of the image playing out on the large display at the front of the room.

"My guess is it's a Taepo-Dong. Probably a test missile. It's not coming out of the known missile fields, and we've had suspicions of a test site near this launch area," the lieutenant said as he tapped his screen.

"Attention on deck," the marine at the door shouted above the din of the busy war room.

"Carry on," General Montgomery said as he entered the room and made his way to his chair.

"I want CNN here, leave the track, and missile defense status," he commanded, sequentially pointing at the three sections of the screen at the front of the room.

Instantly, the CNN news program appeared on the left screen, and a map of South Korea with many green, yellow, and two red markers came up on the right-hand screen. The CNN program was still focused on the embattled chief of the Joint Staff as he fought for an expanded military budget, even after killing many of Congress's pork projects.

"Kill the audio on CNN." The general flopped down in his chair. "What've you got, Colonel?"

"Probably an experimental launch, General." The colonel reiterated what the lieutenant had told him. "It's heading out to sea, but not on a standard test trajectory. It looks as if it might pass over the Japanese islands before impacting."

"It's not armed?"

"I doubt it, sir. It's not coming out of an operational missile battery."

"Then why toward Japan?" The general picked up

the phone handset. "Patch me into NORAD," he said into the phone. "Why Japan?" he repeated while he waited.

"Don't know, sir."

"If it's armed, it's a show of force, meant to indicate they could attack Japan at will," the general said. "If it's not armed, it's just to demonstrate that they have the capability of reaching Japan."

"What've you got?" the general asked into the phone. The general listened to NORAD, the North American Air Defense Command, provide their analysis of the data. It mimicked what his own staff had already told him. "Alert CINCNORAD. Tell him I want all available surveillance on the peninsula."

"All right." The general's voice boomed across the room as soon as he put down the phone. "Stay on this one and be alert. I'm going to be getting a call from the Japanese Air Self-Defense Force any moment now, and I want to be able to reassure him he's not under attack."

The general sat back and watched his men spring into action. They were good, dedicated officers, experts at what they did. He admired them, was proud that he had trained them so well. Hell of a time to be going home, but the Army hadn't really given him a choice. His replacement was due in just a few short hours, and after a minimal transition he would be heading back to the States. He absentmindedly rubbed his stomach. Too bad the prostate test had come up positive, ending his tour much earlier than he would have liked.

"Beta test site results are overlaid here."

Lance listened from the head of the table. Everyone

was quiet in the crowded conference room. All the engineers were there except the crew that had been at Delta site—the chaos caused by the errant missile had kept them downrange longer than expected. Billie Powers, the Boeing test pilot, had already told them the test had no ill effect on the aircraft. She was interested in the results and had asked to remain through the briefing. The Air Force pilot, Captain Jake Williams, hadn't even bothered to come to the meeting. He had left the hangar as soon as the test was over.

The major heading the team dedicated to conducting quick-look analysis of the data stood by the diffuse glow of the overhead projector. He flipped a second acetate sheet over the first, allowing easy comparison of data between the Alpha and Beta test sites.

"As you can see, the power levels at both sites have a fair amount of fluctuation. We believe this was caused by beam wander as the tracker tried to close the loop on the simulated target. As you know, we had a difficult time building an accurate simulation of the target at that close range. The fluctuation rate is a constant forty hertz in both instances, same as the forty-hertz fine-track loop correction frequency. In spite of this fluctuation, nominal power levels were achieved at both targets as indicated by the peaks in each of the two charts."

Lance made notes in his test log, wondering if that really was the reason for the beam oscillation. It could just as easily have been an unknown resonance in any one of the mirror mounts—he had been haunted by that very problem for years during the Airborne Laser Lab test series.

"The beam jitter measurements at the Charlie test site also show a predominant forty-hertz component.

If you assume the forty-hertz jitter will not be there during an actual test shot, then we can mathematically remove it to arrive at a real beam spread number." The major used his pencil to point at yet another chart. "Around one hundred nano-radians, right at the extreme end of the requirements."

"If the forty-hertz component is included, what level of jitter does that give us?" Lance asked.

"With the forty-hertz component we have another hundred nano-radians."

"Twice what we predicted." Lance made another note in his log. "That will effectively reduce our power density on target by a factor of four. Very marginal."

"Correct; however, we have much better beam quality than we had expected." The major pulled out his last chart.

The room came to attention as Colonel DeMarco entered. Lance thought a small piece of the colonel's camouflage trousers looked singed, but it was hard to tell in the darkened room.

"Take your seats and please continue." The colonel took a chair vacated by a captain at Lance's right.

The colonel might have barely escaped injury, but the smile splashed across his face was unmistakable, even in the darkness.

The major used his pencil again to point out two different curves on the acetate. "This is the predicted beam quality, and this is what we measured. At least ten percent better."

"That's good news," Lance said, though he had always felt the contractors were overly cautious when estimating the actual beam quality that could be expected. "Unfortunately, that's only a linear phenomenon, so it won't offset the degradation of the beam due to the jitter. I'm afraid I'm not convinced the forty hertz is a product of the tracker interaction with the simulated target. The target at Charlie site should have been far enough away to appear accurate to the tracker, yet the jitter is still there. That means we have a marginal system, very marginal."

"Maybe from where you sit, Major Brandon, but from the perspective at test site Delta, I think we have a phenomenal weapon. Did you see how the laser punched through that casing? Like a knife through butter! This thing is unstoppable!"

"Hold on, Colonel," Lance said. "The missile was only six kilometers away. A real target will be at least twenty times that far away, and that means the laser's energy at the real target range will be lower by at least a factor of four hundred. I wouldn't count on this system being able to do what we saw today, not at all."

"But you had compensated for the range difference, changed the focus or something."

"We did initially, but when the missile broke loose Captain Hawkins overrode the focus the computer had impressed on the beam. That put the entire beam right at the target."

"Not exactly, Major Brandon." Captain Hawkins, who had been quiet in the back of the room until now, spoke up. "If you examine the prescription for the telescope, you'll find it has a hyperfocal distance of at least twenty-five kilometers. When I overrode the autofocus patch we had installed, the telescope automatically focused as close as it could—to twenty-five kilometers. So the beam still had a fair amount of defocus to it."

"So what does all that mean?" The colonel looked confused.

"Boiled down? It means we have quite a few unknowns. I wouldn't bet either way whether this laser can kill a missile at operational range." Lance wondered if maybe the test hadn't generated more questions than it had answered.

"Welcome to Korea, General Killeen. How're things at the Pentagon?" the outgoing commander greeted his replacement.

"Hosed up, but hopefully better than they were when I got there," General Killeen answered. He looked over the screens in front of him and at the officers scurrying around in the command post. "Have things calmed down at all?"

"Mostly back to normal. You were briefed?"

"Yeah, en route from the flight line."

"Good. I would rather have greeted you myself, but I thought it might be inappropriate if I was gone in case war did actually break out."

"Were we that close?"

"Closest I've ever seen it."

"General Montgomery, Major General Nakano is on the line," an aide interrupted.

"I was expecting him. Ask him to hold for a couple of minutes while I get back down to my office. I need to introduce him to my replacement, anyway. Please join me, General Killeen."

The outgoing COMUSFORKOREA headed for the door and down the short hallway to his main office. His replacement followed. "So, tell me, Killeen, how does a former vice chief of the Joint Staff get a plum little assignment like this? You could have gone any-where you wanted. Why pick Korea?"

"You're right, I could have picked any major com-mand I wanted. And this is it. There are only two places we might actually have to fight—here and in the desert. I never liked the heat."

You don't fool me, General Montgomery thought to himself as he led the airman down the hall. No Air Force officer has ever held this post, and you just used your leverage to muscle your way in, to get another four-star billet for the Air Force.

The phone was ringing as they walked into the mea-gerly adorned office. Metal desk, a small conference table with clean but uncomfortable-looking chairs, and a small sofa.

General Montgomery punched the speaker button on the handset. "Good morning, General Nakano. I hope you've not been too inconvenienced this morning?"

After a few seconds of waiting for the encryption circuit to engage, the Japanese general replied with a long litany in his native tongue, none of which Kil-leen understood.

At the end of the dissertation, General Montgomery roared in laughter. General Killeen shrugged his shoulders.

"One moment, General Nakano. I must introduce you to my replacement, General Killeen, United States Air Force. I'm afraid he doesn't understand Japanese. Would it be possible to continue in English?"

"Of course," came the reply. "What can you tell me of this missile that came from the dark side of Korea toward my homeland?"

"I'm afraid not a lot at this point. It didn't come

from any known operational launch site, so we believe it was a test missile. Fortunately it fell short of Japan."

"Not exactly." The box spoke again. "I have word that portions of the missile did fall short of Japan, probably one of the rocket stages, but that the payload passed over Japan and landed in the water. That puts us within range of their rocketry."

General Killeen nodded, admiring the army officer's trickery in getting his counterpart to confirm what U.S. sensors had already told them.

"This is not a good sign," Montgomery continued. "Perhaps the payload was only simulated, not heavy enough to test the range of a real weapon."

"Perhaps. We are attempting to recover the payload now, but I do not hold much hope. I'm afraid I must err on the side of caution, however. I must assume the North Koreans now have sufficient technology to launch a missile attack upon Japan. And you know we have no defense against a capability such as that. Only your Patriot system has shown an ability to defend against missiles such as this. Unfortunately, to deploy a system such as that would be prohibitively expensive for Japan. And the systems you have deployed in South Korea would provide little defense for any missile that isn't fired toward the south."

"The Patriots would probably provide some level of defense, even if the targets were fired away from the batteries." General Montgomery wondered just how much the Japanese knew about the shortcomings of the Patriot system. "The only other thing that might be of use is a laser plane I've read about in the aviation press."

General Killeen knew that wasn't a credible idea. After all, he had just killed the funding for it. "I'm afraid that particular Air Force system is only developmental in nature, wouldn't even provide as much defense as the Patriots."

"I have heard of this new weapon." Nakano seemed to ignore the newcomer. "I am sure any help you could provide would be greatly appreciated. I anticipate my government will formally request such assistance."

"We'll certainly do what we can," General Montgomery answered, knowing full well there was little an experimental plane could do beyond providing some political goodwill. "Please stay in touch. We'd love to take a look at the missile warhead or any other parts you might be able to recover."

General Killeen listened as the soldier said something in Japanese. Montgomery then killed the connection.

"I suggest you go pay our friend in Japan a little visit as soon as things settle down here," Montgomery said. "He's a good ally to have. Knows a hell of a lot about what goes on in North Korea, probably more than the South Koreans do. The Japanese have a fantastic human intelligence apparatus laid in up there."

"I'll do that, just as soon as possible."

"Wouldn't hurt to learn a few phrases in Japanese before you go—that always makes a good impression."

"Okay. Why'd you bring up the laser plane?"

"No particular reason. Seemed Nakano was grasping at straws. He'll have to report to his government shortly, let them know what happened and what he intends to do about it. If he has nothing to offer as a countermeasure he'll suffer embarrassment. You've heard of 'losing face'? If he can tell them he's working on getting an experimental defensive weapon from the Americans, it'll certainly make him look better. Then he'll owe us a favor, and I guarantee he'll pay up when the time comes. He can't afford to lose face with us, either."

"The package has arrived, my husband." Wu Li addressed Zhen Rhongi in such an affectionate tone only when they were secluded in his tiny office at the research center.

"It's finally here?" Zhen Rhongi looked up from the financial sheets. "When? Where?"

"Just now, at the loading docks."

Zhen Rhongi carefully closed the ledger and locked the discouraging figures in his lower desk drawer. While the future of the institute was certain, many critical engineers would soon be sent to the fields to help with the harvest. There was no money left to pay for the equipment needed to keep them efficiently occupied. Such was the poor state of the Korean economy. He grabbed his light jacket to ward off the chill of the hallways. It would be good to take a break from these depressing numbers.

"I can tell you have been studying the budget again," Wu Li said.

Zhen Rhongi seldom discussed the financial situation with his wife, who was the codirector of the research center. He preferred to retain that burden himself and leave her free to concentrate on the engineering aspects of their pursuits. Somehow, though, she could always tell when the funding looked grim. "Yes. It's those filthy American dogs again. We've had to send more troops to the front lines, siphoning off money for the center. Don't worry, though—we'll make it. And if the package is as advertised, it will advance our program at least two years and will save us much money in the process."

They left his office and headed toward the loading docks. The workers they passed in the hallway each paused to greet the two heads of the research center. Zhen Rhongi and Wu Li didn't stop to converse—they were too interested in seeing the new arrival.

"I'm sure the trigger will be fully functional, as promised by the engineering center. Remember, I've been there twice to ensure that all the critical specifications are properly considered."

"Yes, I'm confident all is correct. It is our good fortune to have such good friends in the Los Alamos, isn't it?"

"Quietly," she whispered. "That is still our secret."

"You haven't heard? Our friend has been arrested. Our enemy will surely put this great hero to death for his work to support our cause."

"I didn't know. That is unfortunate. He could have provided much more information. Perhaps our friends to the north can help our hero avoid execution? They have much influence with the American president, I understand."

"It is doubtful. Besides, there are other heroes in place. We will not lack for information."

At the loading dock a small crate was being removed from a truck under heavy guard by Korean Army soldiers.

"If the trigger checks out and is fully operational, how long will it take to integrate it with the rest of the nuclear weapon?"

"Only a matter of days. Three at the most."

They followed silently as the box was transported

down a short hallway. It was moved into a secure engineering room guarded by special army troops, each of whom held the most prized security clearances.

"I only hope we will never have to use this device," Wu Li said as they followed the box into the room.

The guards scrutinized their badges before letting them enter.

"It is a terrible thought," Zhen Rhongi answered. "But we must be prepared to do what is necessary to defend our people from the Americans. With this American-designed lightweight warhead, and the missile so kindly provided by our friends in China, we now have the might to strike at the heart of the enemy."

"But it would be senseless to exchange nuclear missiles with their military. We would surely lose a conflict such as that."

"You are correct. We could not send our special missile against a military target and expect to win concessions."

The new package was placed on one of the tables in the large engineering room. There were several other small tables there, and on one sat the parts that made up an M-88 warhead, designed by the engineers at Los Alamos National Laboratory.

"When we install the trigger into our weapon we will target a civilian population center. The reasoning for this is that the swell of American sentiment after such an attack, and their fear of further bombings, will force the American military to withdraw from our shores. Our communist brothers in Vietnam showed the way."

"We will target American civilians? I had no idea."

"It is for the security of our nation, Wu Li. There

is no other option. And I have already nominated my preferred target to our leaders."

"I know of your hatred of those who captured us at Stanford. But my father is still in California!"

"I guess I'll tell you a little surprise I was saving to give you tonight. Your father is coming home. He will be back in only one week. Isn't that exciting?"

Wu Li's eyes lit up. With her father out of danger, she was suddenly enchanted with the idea of bringing the American warmongers to their knees.

Chapter 5

The alarm seemed out of place, surreal. Then Killeen realized it wasn't the alarm but the special alert phone that had been installed in his quarters. He glanced at the clock. It was 0530.

He grabbed the handset. "Killeen."

"Good morning, General. Major Deeds at the watch. We have no significant activity to report this A.M. All's quiet along the DMZ. We've not seen any significant troop movement north of the line."

Killeen swung his legs over the side of the bed and sat up. "What about the missile fields?"

"Nothing to report. The test preparations at Yon River have continued, but we still assess they're at least thirty days out from any kind of launch."

"How good was your assessment prior to the last test?"

"Unfortunately, not very good. They caught us with our drawers around our ankles."

"That won't happen again, will it?"

"No, sir, General."

"Any changes to my schedule?"

"One, sir. General Kang has asked to join you on your TDY today."

"Why the hell does he want to go to Japan with me?"

"The message doesn't say, sir."

"Very well. I'll see you in an hour for the standup."

"Yes, sir!"

Killeen dropped the handset into its cradle, then lay back on the bed. The mattress on his small cot felt like a series of cotton knots loosely bound together. He flipped the switch on the wall, and the small lamp on the nightstand burst into life. The light drenched the wretched little room in its dull glow. Killeen examined his meager surroundings. The small bedroom was connected to an even more cramped sitting room. A miniscule kitchen was on his left and a tiny bathroom on his right. Still, it was better than the billeting he'd had when he was first assigned to Korea almost fifteen years ago. He was only a major then. Killeen sat up and looked at the nightstand with his clock and the two phones. The high-tech red phone he had just used to talk with the ops officer in the command center over the encrypted link looked out of place against the ancient black contraption that sat next to it. He picked up the black phone and spun its rotary dial.

"Captain Walsh, sir."

"Looks like we're okay for the flight over to Misawa. We'll have a passenger, though—General Kang. Bring me the dossier on him so I can look over it this morning while I'm eating."

"It's already in your morning mail, General."

Efficient. "And where might I find my morning mail, Captain?"

There was a short rap at the door. Killeen pulled the phone with him as he waited on the captain's answer.

"It should be there any second now, General."

Killeen opened the door to a young soldier dressed in his camouflage uniform, carrying a very large briefcase.

"Good morning, General. I have your morning mail."

Killeen waved the corporal in.

"I believe my mail just showed up."

"Anything in particular for breakfast, sir?"

"Eggs. Lots of 'em. Over easy. And wheat toast."

"On its way, sir. It'll be there by the time you get out of the shower."

"I can't wait." Killeen hung up the phone and replaced it on his nightstand. He glanced back at the corporal in the sitting room. He had opened the briefcase and was arranging folders on the coffee table. Many of the documents were labeled as classified.

The corporal finished with the folders and looked up to see the general watching.

"How do you like your coffee, General?"

"Black and strong."

"Yes, sir. I'll get it started."

Killeen headed for the tiny bathroom, confident the corporal would keep an eye on the folders until he was ready to look at them.

When Killeen stepped out of the bathroom, the aroma of a freshly brewed pot greeted him. He spotted his service dress uniform hanging neatly from the back of his closet door and noticed his bed was already made. He slipped into his trousers and a T-shirt but decided to wait until after breakfast to don his shirt and tie.

Just as he pulled on his shoes he heard another

rap at the door. The corporal answered it quickly and
supervised the delivery of two steaming plates covered
by shiny steel covers.

In the kitchen, the corporal had laid out his table
with breakfast, coffee, and the priority mail folder.
Killeen sat down to eat and begin his long day of
work.

The folder contained several messages from his Korean counterparts, intelligence summaries, for the
most part. While the U.S. had the most sophisticated
technical intelligence collection systems that had ever
been developed, the Koreans excelled at the only kind
of system that could clearly reveal the enemy's inten-
tions—human intelligence. Spies.

Unfortunately, while it was extremely difficult to
confuse or deceive the technical intelligence systems,
humans were another story. Killeen had learned long
ago that human intelligence must be taken for what it
was—usually confusing and often wrong.

Beyond the intelligence summaries were operational
status reports, and a special folder that Killeen had
requested. He was going to have to watch the missile
developments closely, and he had ordered his intelligence staff, his G-2, to provide a detailed briefing
every day. He scanned the documents quickly and
noted nothing that would change his plans for the day.
As he closed the folder the corporal replaced it with
another, this one unclassified. The corporal laid a standard government issue pen on the table as Killeen
stabbed at his eggs with a fork. It was the dreaded
signature folder.

Killeen bore down, mechanically signing the various
decorations and routine correspondence after glancing
at the staff summary sheet accompanying each one.

"Any idea when my signature wheel will be ready?"

"It's on order, sir. I'll try to find out when it's supposed to be here."

"The sooner the better. I like my signature to look perfect each and every time, and the machine can do a hell of a better job than I can."

"Yes, sir, General. We should have had it before you got here, but your arrival was a bit of a surprise to us, and it takes a while to get specialized equipment like that out here in the sticks."

"I'm not used to waiting on things, Corporal. Get on it. See what you can do."

"Yes, sir!"

"Is that it?" Killeen closed the signature folder.

"This is your schedule for today, sir." The corporal handed him a small blue card.

Killeen glanced over it. "Where will the staff car pick me up?"

"Right here, sir, in fifteen minutes or so. The driver will knock when he arrives. This is the folder on General Kang. He'll be traveling with you to Misawa."

"What do you know about Kang?"

"Haven't really met him, General. Most of the Korean officers don't associate with the enlisted types. Seen him around, though. Short guy. Real intense-looking."

"That will be all." Killeen kept the folder on Kang while the corporal put everything else back in the satchel, fastened the latch, and locked it to his wrist. "I'll look this over until the driver gets here."

"Have a good trip, sir." The corporal picked up the satchel and left.

Killeen flipped open the folder to get a look at the eight-by-ten black-and-white picture of his Korean

counterpart. He was already suspicious of the man
who had invited himself along on Killeen's trip to
meet with General Nakano of the Japanese Air Self-
Defense Force. Killeen wondered why Kang hadn't
even bothered to ask to go. Probably a little power
play going on early in Killeen's watch. Killeen smiled.
He'd never lost a power play like this before. He
would make sure Kang coordinated with him next
time. He grabbed the phone and dialed the direct line
to his exec.

"Sir." The phone was answered before the first
ring ended.

"We're going to Japan in a C-21, executive configuration, I believe. Anyone else going along?"

"I'll be accompanying you. Other than that, it's just
you and General Kang. I don't believe General Kang
is taking his exec."

"If you and I sit in the forward seats to discuss
business, General Kang will have the bench seat in
the back to himself. Correct?"

"Yes, sir. He'll probably prefer to sit up front
with you."

"If he had coordinated with me earlier, that might
have been possible. I want two guards to accompany
us. Find me a couple of men fresh out of the field, if
possible. They can keep General Kang company in
the back."

"Right away, sir."

Killeen hung up the phone. He tapped the picture
of General Kang. "Next time you'll ask me before
inviting yourself along."

Killeen headed for the bathroom, carrying the
folder with him. He intended to be prepared for anything Kang might throw at him.

*   *   *

Killeen sat in one of the two forward seats in the specially configured C-21, the military version of Lear's famous business jet. He worked closely with his executive officer, laying out for his aide how he liked things to get done. It wasn't really necessary to get this mundane work done during the flight, but Killeen had an ulterior motive for having his exec sit in the other seat in the forward part of the cabin. The only other seat in the plane was the rear bench seat, and it was barely wide enough for three people.

Killeen glanced back. General Kang was sitting in the middle, flanked by two burly privates. Even though he hid it well, Killeen knew Kang was furious. He wasn't used to being relegated to the back of the bus, much less being forced to sit with lowly enlisted personnel.

Killeen turned back to his exec and went through a few final details about how he liked his correspondence prepared. Finally they were done. The captain gathered the documents into the chart case he had brought them in while Killeen checked the little blue card that held his itinerary. Killeen glanced at his watch. They were about ten minutes out.

"Swap out with the general." Killeen turned back and waved Kang forward.

Killeen's exec moved to the rear as Kang moved up to take his place.

"Sorry to have to make you sit back there," Killeen said as Kang buckled in. "I had already planned to use this time to break my exec in; I do things a little differently than my predecessor. I didn't know you planned to come along until just before we left."

Kang said nothing, simply nodded.

"I presume you already know General Nakano?" Killeen asked.

Kang nodded again.

"I haven't met him yet. In fact, that's the reason for this trip. No big deal. Why did you decide to join us?"

Kang paused before speaking. "This is a very important meeting, General. The three of us must work as a team. The security of Korea depends upon this. The security of the entire region—even of Japan. Also, I have some new information on the missile test that should be shared with General Nakano."

The small jet banked to the right, and Kang turned away to look out the side window. The green fields of the Japanese islands were visible below.

Killeen let him alone. Let him stew at having been made to sit in the back with the privates. Kang hadn't been too forthcoming, but that didn't surprise Killeen. Kang's dossier had said he was quiet, more a man of action than a man of words. He would have never made it to his two-star rank in the U.S. military that way. You had to be able to play the political game as deftly as you planned your wars. Still, Killeen wondered what Kang was up to. He had said this was an important meeting, but how so? All Killeen wanted to do was make the face-to-face with Nakano and get the formalities over with. In fact, Killeen would have postponed the meeting if his predecessor hadn't insisted, even going so far as to arrange the meeting before he left.

Maybe that was it. Maybe the former COMUS-FORKOREA, General Montgomery, had urged Kang to come along. Made sense. The former U.S. commander was really into this make-nice garbage. All Killeen wanted to do was make sure everyone in the theater knew he was in charge, and that included both the Koreans and the Japanese. He intended to turn this chance gathering of all three leaders to his advantage. Killeen would ensure that the other two generals understood they were to answer to him.

The base commander, a colonel, met them at Ops. He greeted them there as protocol dictated, then provided his own staff car to take the high-ranking officers to his headquarters, where General Nakano was already waiting. During the ten-minute ride the colonel explained his base's mission, mainly for the Korean general's benefit.

"All of the aircraft here are assigned to PACAF, Pacific Air Forces, headquartered at Hickam Air Force Base in Hawaii."

"But they chop over to me if the balloon goes up in Korea," Killeen said.

"That's correct, General."

The staff car pulled up in front of the base headquarters. The colonel rushed forward to get the door, then led the men to his personal conference room.

As they stepped inside, the colonel made the introductions. Kang and Nakano bowed slightly to each other. Then Nakano turned to Killeen.

Nakano bowed again. "It is my pleasure to meet you, General."

Killeen thrust his hand forward, ignoring the bow. The U.S. had fought too many wars to ensure that they didn't have to bow to anyone. "The pleasure is mine."

Nakano straightened quickly and shook Killeen's hand. Kang and the base commander were taken aback at the severe breach of formal courtesies.

Nakano hid his own injury and became very diplomatic. "Welcome to Japan, General."

"Unfortunately I don't have a lot of time. Why don't we get down to business?" Killeen sat down at the head of the table. "You're excused, Colonel."

"Yes, sir. I'll be right outside if you need anything." The colonel closed the door behind himself.

Kang and Nakano sat near Killeen along both sides of the table. They each left a seat between themselves and the American.

"I know this was supposed to be an informal meeting for us to get acquainted, General Nakano, but I have a bit of business I'd like to get out of the way first."

Nakano nodded.

"First, I believe General Kang has some information he would like to provide you on the recent North Korean missile test."

Kang reached inside his uniform coat and retrieved a small envelope. From it he took two copies of a photograph. He passed one to Nakano and the other to Killeen.

"The two men you see in the picture are Kim Jong Il, leader of the communists of the North, and Zhen Rhongi, the man who recently took over the ballistic missile program."

"Zhen Rhongi? The spy who was kicked out of the United States?" Both men glanced at Killeen. Nakano was visibly disturbed. "We thought he was running North Korea's nuclear weapons program."

Kang nodded his head. "This is the same man. My sources in North Korea have confirmed that the recent missile test was undertaken to verify guidance and reentry technology that would allow the North Koreans to target Japan with their weapons. The test was approved by Kim Jong Il himself—in fact, he attended the test at the launch site. That is where this photograph was taken."

"And your sources are reliable?" asked General Nakano.

"Extremely," Kang said.

Nakano simply nodded. He seemed to believe Kang, didn't request any additional proof. But that wasn't sufficient for Killeen. "How reliable? How can we be sure your information is accurate?"

Kang glanced at Nakano, then focused a steely glare on Killeen. "General, while you utilize your sophisticated network of spy satellites and technical marvels that can only tell you what has already happened, my intelligence organization has worked for fifty years to ensure that we have the means to determine both the capability and the intent of the communists in the North. The reliability of my sources is my concern alone. If I say the source is reliable, you may rest assured he is."

"I seem to have offended you," Killeen said. "My apologies. It has been my experience, however, that spies are seldom accurate and must never be taken at face value unless their information is corroborated by some other means. That is why I must ask the question."

Kang was visibly angered. "You have my assurance that the information is reliable, General Killeen. That is all I will say."

Killeen let the quiet linger without answering. Instead he flipped open his notebook and jotted something down, leaving his companions with the sense he was writing down what had just occurred, perhaps that the Korean general did not trust the Americans

enough to share the source or the bona fides of his information.

"Very well. Is there anything you would like to add
to your information, General Kang?" Killeen put
down his pen.

Kang's jaw was clenched and his temples were
throbbing. He shook his head.

"That brings us to the point I am here to make,"
Killeen continued. "The annual U.S./Korean staff exercise, Ulchi Focus Lens, is scheduled to begin later
in the year, in August, just as it has in the past. General Nakano, the Japanese have never participated in
this command post exercise, since it is not held on
Japanese soil, but you have as much at stake as anyone. That's particularly true given North Korea's recent
missile tests, tests that could well be in preparation of
targeting your homeland.

"That's why I'm telling you this. August has always
been a stupid time to hold our exercise. Our replacement personnel usually arrive in August with little experience, and our skilled personnel rotate back to the
United States right after the exercise is over. Lots of
wasted effort, very little effective training accomplished. Meanwhile, the communists know exactly
what we're going to do and when we're going to do
it. Even though the exercise involves only the staff
and no additional forces are brought in, they've convinced the politicians to call off the last two actual
exercises by turning on their propaganda machine well
before the exercises are supposed to begin. If things
continue as they have in the past, the communists will
work to have our exercise canceled again this year.
This is unacceptable. I have received permission to
accelerate the schedule for this year's Ulchi Focus

Lens. We'll be starting in a little over two weeks. The communists won't have time to shut us down, and we'll be sure to make enough noise so they'll know not to threaten us in the foreseeable future. I would like your support, General Nakano, in ensuring that the communists' pleas to halt the exercise and their propaganda claiming that this will cause instability in the peninsula are ignored. I don't expect that will be too difficult, given the recent missile test and the information General Kang has provided you today."

"I agree," Nakano said. "There may very well be pressure to cancel or limit the exercise. And you are correct, the North Koreans do lobby my government to support them. I do not believe the North Koreans will receive a sympathetic ear on this occasion. I will support the acceleration of your test schedule."

"Good." Killeen closed his folder. He was about to adjourn the formal portion of the meeting when Kang began speaking to Nakano in Korean, or Japanese, Killeen wasn't sure which. The report on Kang had mentioned he was fluent in Japanese as well as his native tongue.

Nakano nodded and replied.

Killeen cleared his throat.

Kang looked in his direction. "I am sorry, General Killeen. I was asked to relay a greeting from my president. Unfortunately, it does not translate well into English. The second part of his message is easily translated."

Kang turned back to Nakano. "The Republic of Korea invites our trusted friends from Japan to participate in the Ulchi Focus Lens, scheduled to begin on March 18."

Though his expression showed no sign, Killeen was

absolutely stunned. How in the hell did Kang know he had planed to start the exercise on the eighteenth? And where did Kang get off inviting Nakano without clearing it through him first?

"On behalf of my emperor, I am pleased to accept your invitation," Nakano answered.

Killeen had just been tossed a political hot potato. Nakano couldn't accept that kind of invitation without getting approval first. That meant he had already gotten it, that Kang and Nakano had planned this whole thing ahead of time. Then this was just a formal act to inform the American. Or to embarrass him. Killeen wasn't going to give Kang that pleasure.

"Great. Fantastic." Killeen rose from his chair to shake Nakano's hand. "We're delighted you can join us in this exercise. This will be the best exercise ever, a true joint endeavor with all our forces in full cooperation and coordination." Killeen spent the rest of the meeting espousing the great things that would come out of the joint exercise, all the while growing angrier and angrier at the way Kang had played him and wondering how the politicians in Washington were going to react. That wasn't really too hard to figure out. The politicians were going to hit the ceiling. And half the Pentagon would join them up there. Involving the Japanese in Ulchi Focus Lens would infuriate the North Koreans and might even drive them to the brink of the war that they routinely threatened. And Killeen knew he would be the point of blame. He'd catch all the flak for not intervening, for not killing the Korean's idea. His only chance now was to convince them back home of the truth—that he didn't know about the Korean's invitation until it was already a done deal.

The communists were another story. They wouldn't care whose idea it was. This could be enough to tip their maniacal scales. But then, if the Koreans invaded from the north, well . . . maybe that wouldn't be all that bad, either. The stalemate had gone on long enough. Perhaps it was time to finish it, once and for all. Killeen would be more than happy to provide the leadership for democracy's final, decisive victory over communism.

The mission had come straight from COMUS-FORKOREA himself, indicating the urgency of the need. Driscoll couldn't help but remember his nearly disastrous recent flight over the northern half of the peninsula. Somehow the Koreans had figured out how to acquire, track, and target the Aurora, turning what would have normally been a relatively easy mission into a real nail-biter.

"Control, this is Aurora. Initiating turn to final vector." Driscoll rode the bird through the turn. "Heading zero seven zero, altitude forty thousand, speed Mach two point six."

"Copy, Aurora. One pass is all you need. Will provide feed from Joint STARS for threat awareness."

"Copy." Great. The Joint STARS bird would be a big help. The Joint Surveillance Target Attack Radar System was the star of the Gulf War, second only to the stealthy jets. It used its radar to pinpoint any movement on the ground that might become a threat to his mission.

Driscoll watched his nearly blank threat display as he leveled out on his final vector. At least he needed only one pass. The requirement was extremely precise for a change—take a look at the missile field and make sure the North Koreans weren't getting ready to lob another "test" missile toward Japan. That was easy enough, compared to the more recent missions when he had had to map a significant portion of the country.

"Aurora, this is Control. Bad news. Looks like you're going to hit some clouds over the target area. You might have to drop to thirty thousand feet to get under them."

Crap. Driscoll keyed in the new altitude, and the plane began responding by tipping downward. Dropping to thirty thousand would eat up his safety margin. At forty thousand he'd have enough warning to maneuver out of range if the Koreans lobbed an SA-6 at him. At thirty thousand he might not be able to dodge it, depending on where they fired from. If they shot from off to the side, it wouldn't be a problem. But if they shot from just in front of his flight path, the missile could cover the distance between them before he could maneuver and get under it.

"Copy the bad news. Let's maneuver between the known shooters. That'll give me a little more negotiating room. Give me a vector."

"Wilco, Aurora. Unfortunately they're pretty thick near the target zone. And they've been maneuvering quite a bit lately. I can optimize your route to take you through the last known reported positions—but that's the best I can do."

"I'll take it."

"Turn left to zero six three. I'll telemeter the rest of the flight path to you as soon as the computer crunches it."

Driscoll keyed in the new heading as the plane leveled off. "Rolling out at thirty thousand. Turning to heading zero six three." He felt the bird buffet as he slipped through the wake of a jetliner that had passed nearby minutes earlier. The display brightened as the satellite relayed data into his avionics computer. The thin yellow line that indicated his flight path showed he would need to make five minor course corrections, and one major one. Surface-to-air missile sites were scattered along his flight path, but nothing much to be concerned about. "I've got the course."

"Copy, Aurora. Unfortunately the threat data is pretty stale. I'm checking the national database to get the latest info. I should have an update momentarily. Meanwhile, I'm getting data from Joint STARS and another reconnaissance asset in the air near the border."

"Good. It looks like I'm ten minutes from the major target area. Initiating camera sequence." Driscoll watched as the infrared camera system began to pan the ground directly beneath him, capturing high-resolution images of the North Korean landmass. The data was displayed on his secondary monitor, in addition to being telemetered via another satellite to a ground station south of the border.

"Possible problem, Aurora."

"Go."

"Latest imagery shows significant change in positions of SAM systems. Tactical reconnaissance in the area is now collecting signals representative of systems on the move. Other information indicates a missile test may be imminent. My guess is the SAMs are moving to provide better cover for the test. No guarantee where they are now. You may end up flying right over one of them."

Great. "Okay, keep me posted. Pipe the Joint STARS data my way as soon as you can. I may need some real-time information pretty quick. Five minutes out."

Driscoll waited. The Aurora passed between the two small dots on the screen and automatically made a gentle roll to the left. The computer had recommended a five-degree course change, a modification of his flight path designed to keep him as far as possible from the last known position of the threat missiles.

At two minutes from the target control called again. "Got the Joint STARS info. I'm passing it to you, correlated with the moving map. You should have it now."

The threat display, with the postulated positions of the defensive missiles, changed abruptly. Not only were there more missiles now, but they had also moved. Two of the deadly weapons lay right between Driscoll and the target. And it was too late to change the flight path without screwing up the camera coverage.

"Recommend evasive maneuvers," Control said.

"Negative. I'm almost over the target now. Can't chance blowing the camera angle and coming up empty-handed."

Driscoll held tight. This was going to be a true test of the Aurora's stealthiness. If the Koreans had indeed come up with a way to see America's most invisible aircraft, he'd know soon enough.

The pilot waited patiently as his plane passed over the first dot on his way to the target. The ballistic missile test site lay only thirty seconds in front of him. He checked the camera. It was working flawlessly.

Then the voice came back, that seductive yet ominous female voice. "Tracking radar detected."

"They've got you," Control warned.

Chapter 6

Lance gritted his teeth while he waited for his ride to show up. In the hangar behind him, final preparations were being made for the first, and most probably last, flight test of the ABL. He knew he should be in there with them. Instead, an urgent call from the site commander's executive officer had instructed him to wait at the gate by the hangar, saying that some big wheel wanted to see him. Lance was a little surprised when the car that arrived to pick him up was the base commander's own personal staff car. He was even more surprised to see Colonel DeMarco, the Airborne Laser System program director, sitting at the wheel.

"Hop in, Lance," the colonel said through the window as it was powered down.

"Yes, sir." Lance got into the front seat.

The colonel was pulling away before Lance could even get his door closed.

"I know you're getting ready for your flight, but General Morris is here. He wants to see you posthaste. He's over at the site commander's office."

"Any idea what this is about?"

"Nothing certain. I've gotten word that the fighter mafia in the Pentagon has somehow gotten wind of your flight test. They found out someone has been funneling test money to the range at White Sands for a missile test and tracked down the rest of the details. I've answered a few calls myself. So far I've been slow-rolling them. That could very well be what the general wants to see us about."

"I hope this doesn't take too long. We're launching in just over an hour and a half, and if we miss the window we won't get another shot at this. The range is booked solid for the next four weeks for testing of Israel's Arrow missile defense system."

"Don't I know it. General Morris had to place two calls to the Israeli Ministry of Defense to get clearance for us to fly today."

The colonel pulled into a parking space right in front of the lab headquarters. The sign posted at the spot ensured no one but General Morris parked there.

Lance followed the colonel up to the second floor. The conference room door was shut, so the colonel knocked twice.

"Enter," someone shouted from inside.

Lance followed the colonel in. The general sat at the head of the table. Several other officers sat around him, and a captain was standing at the front of the room, pointer at the ready.

The general rose to meet them. "Good to see you again, Lance. Colonel DeMarco has been keeping me informed—says you are doing a fantastic job."

"The colonel has been a great help. I couldn't have asked for better support. And that little missile test he set up, well, I never would have thought of it. It gave us better data than all the other tests combined."

"Even though the missile went a little crazy," the colonel said.

"I saw the video. Scared the hell out of me all the

way over in L.A. when I watched it. But it proved
to me our system can handle anything that's thrown
at it."

"On the ground, I'd agree. We still have to shake
it out in the air." Lance glanced at his watch.

"I know you've got a deadline, Lance. But it's
important that you hear what the captain is about to
say. It'll only take five minutes; then you can get back
to the plane."

Lance nodded and took the chair next to the general as some full colonel Lance had never seen retreated to one of the gallery seats.

The captain began his briefing as a summary slide
came up automatically.

"This morning's intelligence summary is classified
TOP SECRET. The topics I will be covering include the
North Korean response to Japanese participation in
Ulchi Focus Lens, as well as North Korean missile test
preparation activity. Additionally, the Defense Intelli-
gence Agency has just established a North Korean
Ballistic Missile Order of Battle."

Even though Lance worried about making it back
in time for the flight, the briefing topics were certainly intriguing.

A photograph of an Oriental man standing behind
a podium flashed up on the screen as the intelligence
officer began his presentation. "North Korean president Kim Jong Il has stated that the deliberate actions
taken by the United States in inviting the Japanese to
participate in the upcoming exercise are clearly an act
of open hostility."

Another image, this one of much lower quality,
showed a reconnaissance photograph of some part of
the Korean landmass. Red boxes marked several items

in the photograph, and arrows indicated that the items were headed south. "The North Korean Army has already begun moving the 4th and 15th Divisions, normally held in reserve, forward. Additionally, there has been an increased number of AN-2 flights occurring just after dark. AN-2 aircraft are often used to transport squads of North Korean special operations forces into the South. It is clear that the North Koreans are taking the participation of the Japanese seriously, and the Chinese are fully behind them. This has all the likelihood of developing into a serious confrontation if the Japanese participation is not curtailed."

"I think we get the idea," General Morris interrupted. "Let's hear about the missile test preparations."

"Yes, sir."

Behind the screen a technician advanced the Power-Point presentation to the next major topic. A title slide called it "Imminent No-Dong Missile Test."

Lance studied the next slide. It was unusual but familiar. He couldn't put his finger on it right away.

"This image shows the missile test field just east of P'yŏngyang."

Suddenly Lance remembered. The image was very similar to the picture he'd been shown in the hangar on Cyprus before they'd launched the old Airborne Laser Lab on its fateful mission. The yellow tint of a haze filter was obvious, but the extremely high resolution meant the image had to have come from an aircraft. Were they flying spy planes over Korea?

The captain used his laser pointer to identify some particularly interesting details. "The vehicles located here near the missiles marked A, B, and C have been identified as part of North Korea's classified nuclear weapon test program."

"That's the program we found out about when that high-level defector came over in 1997?" the general asked.

"Exactly, sir. The defector, Hwang Jang Yop, was one of twelve members of North Korea's highest decision-making body, and a tutor to Kim Jong Il. Information that he provided to the South Koreans allowed us to find the weapons program test facilities, among other things. From that point on we have used technical sensors as well as South Korean sources to maintain a very close watch on their program. These vehicles"—the captain tapped the screen with his pointer—"were tracked coming from a final nuclear assembly plant. They moved to the missile site less than thirty-six hours before this image was taken.

"The rest of these vehicles are standard for the missile test site. They are currently in the same configuration they were in just before the test missile was fired at Japan. Our assessment is that they could launch another missile within forty-eight hours. Three within seventy-two hours."

The slide changed to show a larger region of the test facility.

"The entire missile field, eighteen missiles in all, could be ready for launch in under four days."

Colonel DeMarco asked the question that Lance was scared to ask: "Are you saying the North Koreans are now capable of launching nuclear weapons with these missiles?"

"That's correct, sir. Not only are they capable of launching nuclear weapons, but they have the range to reach anywhere in South Korea, as well as all but the northernmost part of Japan. Including Tokyo.

"This chart shows the Defense Intelligence Agency's new missile order-of-battle assessment. As you can see, North Korea has three nuclear-capable missiles with the range I just mentioned. In addition, the other missiles have almost reached operational capability, but with their shorter range they cannot reach Japan and can only carry the lighter high-explosive and chemical weapons warheads into South Korea.

"Furthermore," the captain said as he pointed at the last entry on the slide, "component parts of a Chinese Dong Feng Five missile have been delivered to the main assembly area. With this long-range ballistic missile, the Koreans have the ability to reach portions of the United States—the northern states and western seaboard are at risk."

The seaboard? California? A cold shiver ran down Lance's spine.

"Thank you for the briefing, Captain," General Morris cut the presentation short. "Lance, you can see why I wanted you to hear this. This is exactly what I have been dreading, but we all knew it was going to happen. It was only a matter of time before the North Koreans completed mating their nuclear weapons program with their ballistic missile effort. Ever since Hwang told us their plans, we knew the entire region was headed toward a disaster. That's why the tests you're about to perform, and the Airborne Laser, are so critical. Air Combat Command still wants the project killed—still thinks they can use their fighters to kill the missiles before they get off the ground. I believe that's crap. What you didn't see on the slides was the extremely heavy air defense network the

North has laid in around that missile field. A sparrow couldn't get within fifty kilometers of that place, much less a Strike Eagle. No, the only way to stop those missiles is by standing off and using a long-range weapon—a laser—and you've got the only one around that can do it. That's your job, and it has to take precedence over everything else in your life right now."

"I appreciate your confidence, General. I've got a top-notch team. If anyone can make this system work, they can."

"We don't have much time, Lance. Ulchi Focus Lens begins in eight days. If the North is going to blow their stack they'll do it during the exercise. All the evidence indicates that's when they'll go ballistic . . . pardon the expression."

Lance swallowed hard. He was about to begin the initial flight test of a planned four-month series. The general wanted a weapon ready in just a few days. "Sir, there is no way we can be ready to support the exercise that soon. It's just impossible."

"Nothing's impossible if you put your mind to it. Now that you know the schedule, I think you might find a few ways to get creative. Now, I know you've got to get back to the plane, and I've got to leave for the Pentagon in about an hour to see if I can salvage the rest of the test program, but I want a full report on the test as soon as you get back. Colonel DeMarco has my personal number. Call me. You're dismissed."

Lance stood to leave. The general stood too. "Good luck, son," he said.

Lance shook his head, then turned and left the room.

*   *   *

Things were hectic back at the hangar. The plane had already been towed outside, and the ground crew was scurrying about, completing the myriad tasks that remained before the behemoth of a plane could be launched.

Lance took one last walk around the bird. There wasn't much that interested him about most of the plane, except for the beam control system in the nose. He watched as the ground crew, hoisted into the air on a powered scaffold, removed the protective covers from the high-optical-quality windows that would allow the infrared laser beam to escape. It was an amazing piece of workmanship that had taken two years to construct. There were no spares, and development of the system for the second weapon had been put on hold because of the funding cuts. One bird strike and they were out of the game. Permanently.

As he walked around to the side of the plane and started up the steps to go inside, Lance considered the placement of the beam steering components. They had been designed to give the ABL the greatest angle of fire possible. But physics was physics, and they would only be able to shoot forward up to a maximum of thirty degrees off the nose of the plane. Any more of an angle and, the analytical studies showed, the beam quality would be so severely degraded that the weapon couldn't kill its target. They would need to be flying directly toward the target to be effective.

Inside the plane it was relatively quiet. Lance climbed the stairs to check on the flight crew.

Billie Powers and Captain Jake Williams were already strapped in. Powers had been a tremendous help. While Lance had been completely engulfed in preparing the laser and beam control system, she had quietly and efficiently prepared the plane for flight. Lance had forgotten just how difficult it was to get equipment installed on an airplane—the necessary crash load testing, electrical interface documentation and analysis, weight and balance calculations. Powers had taken that load off his engineers. If something needed to be installed, all his engineers had to do was show her where. She took care of the rest. Even though she wasn't in charge of the maintenance crew, they all looked to her as their boss. She had obviously earned their respect. Everyone, including Lance's engineers, had begun calling her by her military rank even though she wasn't on active duty.

Even with all her other work, Powers hadn't forgotten her first priority—making sure that the man sitting in the copilot's seat on her left understood that getting out of the Air Force was the worst decision he would ever make. She had talked with Lance about it several times when her frustration seemed about to get the best of her. Once she had said she just wanted to take Williams out behind the hangar and thrash him. But she held off, patiently trying to answer all his arguments, showing him the good and bad sides of each option.

"How's everything up here?" Lance stepped up behind them.

"Finishing the checklist now," Colonel Powers answered. "Only problem so far has been the fire consent switch. Your guys in the back had to reboot the master computer to get it to work. It's fine now."

"GPS is calibrated and set. Mission plan confirmed," Captain Williams said. "Checklist complete. We're good to go. Everything's set up here. Haven't even had any of those little gremlins you usually get in such a new plane. If the folks in the back ever get ready, we'll get this bird in the air."

"I'll go see what I can do." Lance backed out of the cockpit and carefully climbed down the ladder to the main deck. He couldn't help but marvel again at how much more room there was in this plane than there had been in the old Airborne Laser Lab. He took a deep breath and pulled the final preflight checklist out of a zippered pocket in the leg of his flight suit.

This was it—the first flight test he would be in charge of. It was a fantastic opportunity, but also a tremendous responsibility. He wondered if Colonel Kirk had felt this much pressure when he was in charge of the old Airborne Laser Lab flight tests. Lance touched the vest pocket of his flight suit to make sure the medal the Israelis had given him was still there. It was.

He made his way back to the laser device compartment in the rear of the plane. He glanced down at the checklist, then slid the safety catches back from the bulkhead door. He stepped through and began examining the laser. He couldn't possibly tell if every piece of the complex laser weapon was in working order. He had to leave that up to the device and beam control engineers. He was looking for anything obviously out of place—stray equipment, broken wiring, that kind of thing. Everything seemed to be ready for the test. For his final checklist item, he visually traced the path the laser beam would follow, imagining it as it left the laser modules and traversed the water-cooled mirrors on its way to the argon-filled tube that would deliver it to the telescope in the nose of the plane. All the optics were clear, no covers accidentally left on. They were good to go here, too.

Lance stepped back through the bulkhead door and closed it securely behind him. The rest of the test crew were already in place. Both of them. Amazing. During the Airborne Laser Lab test series there had been more than a dozen people on the test crew, not counting all the engineers that flew alongside in the escort aircraft. Here there were only two. On the one hand it was a tribute to the exponential increase in computing power that had been achieved over the last twenty years, but on the other, it was more of a tribute to the two men assisting him.

Staff Sergeant Adams was manning the beam control system. No one knew more about how it worked and what its quirks were than Adams did. He had patched more software errors in the last two weeks than Lance could count. Lance would be surprised if Adams hadn't rewritten the entire code by now. He was entirely confident that the system would find the target and put the laser beam on it.

The other crew member, Captain Jeff Hawkins, had agreed to stay on after the other graduate engineering students had returned to their studies at the Air Force Institute of Technology. Lance had asked Hawkins to stay, though he knew the captain was well on his way to becoming the top student in his class. By agreeing to stay, Hawkins had sacrificed that honor. Lance had talked to the head of the electrical engineering department and explained the situation before he even asked Hawkins if he would be interested. Hawkins's advisor had explained that the brilliant engineer would have no problem graduating and that the department had already decided to offer him an opportunity to continue at the Institute to work on his doctorate. Though staying to help on the laser flight test project would set him back a quarter, he would be able to make up his studies. But as far as his class rank was concerned, that would be forfeited. There was no way around it.

Lance knew that Hawkins had sacrificed an important opportunity, and wouldn't have asked him to stay if he hadn't been so good. Hawkins had led the team that worked out all of the laser device issues and had made several innovative changes that boosted power and increased beam quality. All within only a few weeks of arriving. Within days he had outclassed and replaced the contractor who had been chosen to run the laser during the tests.

Hawkins didn't hesitate to accept when Lance offered him the job.

Lance picked up his old headset, the kind they had used during the old Airborne Laser Lab tests. He preferred its big ear cups and their ability to reduce external noise to the newer, "McDonald's drive-through" kind that the others wore. "You guys ready?"

"Affirmative, sir," Sergeant Adams answered. "Checklist is complete and all systems are nominal."

"Laser is a go, sir." Hawkins reached up to touch one of the display enunciators on the touch screen panel. "Checklist is automated and continuous. I'll get a warning on this panel if any of the sensor outputs exceeds the preset parameters."

"Colonel Powers said her consent-to-fire switch failed during the early check. Any idea what caused it?"

"No, sir," Sergeant Adams answered. "We couldn't get it to reset through software, so we had to recycle the hardware. It reset fine and the problem hasn't recurred."

"All right. We'll keep that little item in mind. I guess we had better settle in for launch."

Lance sat down at the test director's console located between the two men. He pulled his seat restraint over his shoulders and fastened it tightly. The two engineers shut their systems down, as per procedure. It became hauntingly quiet in the rear of the big airplane. He pulled the switch that allowed him to listen in on the aircrew net.

"Air crew, this is Test. Comm check." Lance began his own checklist.

"Copy, Test. We're preparing to start engines."

"All systems are shut down, ready to transfer power."

"Copy. By the way, the annoyance factor may have just gone up a notch," Billie Powers told him.

"How's that?"

"We're going to have a straphanger. Someone from Langley, Air Combat Command. He says he's been ordered to monitor the test."

"Where are you going to put him?" Lance was surprised they hadn't sent a spy out sooner.

"Unless you have a burning desire to have him back there with your crew, I think it'd be best to put him in the jump seat up here with us. He won't be in your way, and my guess is he's a pilot, so we can probably answer any questions he has better than you guys can."

"Works for me. Let me know when he's aboard."

"Wilco."

Lance could hear the first of the engines spin up. A moment later the lights inside the plane flickered on, and the instrument panel in front of him came to life. He then continued down his checklist, moving quickly through the sequence, following the instructions to call up certain laser, beam control, and safety parameters to verify they were within limits. They were. He had written the final item on his list with a pencil so he wouldn't forget. He pulled out the medal the Israelis had given him and pinned it to a spot in the insulating fabric just above the overhead console.

"What's that?" Sergeant Adams asked over the test crew net.

"Kind of a tribute." Lance hadn't been cleared to tell anyone about the previous mission—it was still classified. "Maybe I can fill you guys in on it later."

"Our passenger is on board," Colonel Powers called over the net. "Lieutenant Colonel Aziz."

"I go by Skeeter. Strike pilot."

"Welcome aboard, Skeeter," Lance said. "I'm sure you're going to be quite impressed."

"We'll see. I'm from ACC/DR, the requirements shop. Apparently someone didn't get the word that the chief wanted this program killed. My boss couldn't believe it when he heard there was a flight test in the works that was bumping some of his own test resources. I'm to report back on what's happening. I guess I should be considered a hostile witness."

The second engine began to spin up in the background. "I still think you'll be impressed. If you have any questions, just let Colonel Powers know and she'll try to answer them. If it's technical, we'll help you out here in the back. Obviously it will get pretty hectic during the test, so I'll ask you to hold any questions during that phase of the mission."

"I probably won't have any technical questions. All

that science stuff makes my head hurt. I'll just watch the flight performance of the plane . . . and the pilots."

This Skeeter guy was obviously not here to provide his support to the flight test. Lance wondered how to make the best of the situation.

Soon the rest of the engines were running, and they rolled to the runway. They held at the edge of the active runway, a few minutes early for their planned departure time.

Lance punched in on the aircrew net, knowing that everyone was listening on that channel. "I thought I'd let you all know why I was called over to headquarters this morning. I can't go into details because the intelligence briefing I saw was classified. Suffice it to say there is a belligerent nation, one we've been toe-to-toe with for the last forty years, which has finally succeeded in mating its nuclear weapons program with its new ballistic missile program. It may even have the capability to reach parts of the United States with its missiles, as well as most of its closer enemies. All indications are that the leadership of this rogue nation is on the brink of insanity and may use these weapons at the slightest provocation.

"There are a variety of views in the Pentagon about how to deal with such a problem. Within the Air Force there are two generally opposing views. One is that aircraft with highly accurate weaponry can penetrate the foreign airspace and destroy the missiles on the ground. The other view is that a long-range stand-off weapon like this laser is the only viable option. While many are confident that some of our stealthier aircraft could fight their way in and take out some nuclear armed missiles, few actually believe they could destroy an entire missile field before at least some of the missiles could be launched.

"Our laser, on the other hand, could theoretically destroy all the missiles as they break free from the ground."

"I believe 'theoretically' is the operative word here," Skeeter said.

"Exactly," Lance continued. "That's why we're here today. To show that these theories have been turned into a viable weapon system. We're all going to have to be on our toes for this test. Our targets—and there will be several—are simulated missiles of the same type we would face with that belligerent country. Same launch profile and signature. No warheads, though. The upper stages have been fitted with telemetry packages that will monitor missile performance and relay that information to a ground data-reduction station. The data will provide truth in testing—we can't cheat the test.

"The mission profile has us standing off at a distance, which will reflect our positioning under an actual scenario. This is do or die. If any of the missiles get through, we will have failed."

"We're cleared to the active," Colonel Powers said. "Prepare for takeoff."

Lance hoped the message had gotten through. If they failed here today, the program was certainly dead. And that not only would kill the dreams of the true visionaries but also would put millions of people around the globe under the threat of a new nuclear menace. Cold War II would be at hand.

The flight to the White Sands Missile Range would take just under an hour. During the first part of it

Sergeant Adams practiced going through the system fire command sequence in detail.

The system was working beautifully.

Then Lance had an idea. He made his way up to the cockpit and found their passenger, introducing himself personally.

Lieutenant Colonel Aziz tapped Lance's name tape. "What kind of wings are those?"

Lance glanced down. It wasn't the first time he'd been asked that question. "Nonrated officer aircrew. There aren't many of us around."

"You're not a pilot, then?"

"No," Lance answered.

"Academy grad?"

"No. MIT." What the heck was this guy after? Lance wasn't about to tell him he was only a reservist on extended active duty. "How about coming back to the test compartment for a little demonstration of the fire control system? You can even stay back with us to observe the test firsthand."

"I'd rather stay up here where all the action is. I need to see what really happens during the test to make my report."

"I agree, but the real action will be in the back with the fire control system."

"You mean the pilot doesn't have control of the weapons? Whose brilliant idea was that?"

Uh-oh. "All the pilot has to do is flip a switch providing consent to fire, but once that occurs the fire mission will be controlled from the back. We have all the sensor and weapon data back there, which leaves the pilot free to fly the plane."

Aziz shook his head in disapproval, then released

his seat restraints. "All right. Let's take a look at what you and your science buddies have come up with."

This had become a political test as well as a techno-logical test. That worried Lance. He could handle ex-plaining the technical aspects to Aziz, but trying to butter up some staff officer who already seemed to have his mind made up wasn't something he was really prepared to do.

Lance led him down the steep steps, passing the laser crew on the way. Once through the bulkhead doors, he began explaining the various pieces of equipment that made up the laser weapon. Aziz didn't seem all that impressed. Lance led him forward again and closed the bulkhead door securely behind them.

"Captain Hawkins is manning the laser system con-sole and Staff Sergeant Adams is running the fire con-trol system."

"Wouldn't an officer be more appropriate for such a great responsibility?" Aziz removed a small black notebook from one of his pockets and began to write something.

Lance bit his tongue. Sergeant Adams had made more personal sacrifices to get the system ready to fly than anyone in the program. He didn't deserve Aziz's comments. "Frankly, I don't know of an officer who could handle this system. Sergeant Adams, why don't you run through the canned demo so our friend from ACC can get a better idea of what is going to happen during the test?"

"Yes, sir."

Sergeant Adams began a demonstration that simu-lated what would happen during the test sequence. Lance watched Aziz throughout the short demo. He had hoped a pretest demonstration of the fire control sequence would pique Aziz's interest, and perhaps influence his report to headquarters. Unfortunately, the pilot's eyes had glazed over fairly quickly during the demonstration. He didn't have a clue what was going on.

"Very interesting." Aziz wasn't even looking at the demo. He was writing in his notebook again.

Lance patted Sergeant Adams on the shoulder, then continued the tour for Aziz. "Normally we would have someone sitting at this station, interfacing with the Airborne Warning and Control System—AWACS—but for this test it isn't necessary."

"I see." Aziz made another note.

"Do you have any questions?" Originally Lance had hoped Aziz would decide to sit back there with them during the mission, but after his comments about having a lowly sergeant man the fire controls, Lance just wanted the jerk out of his sight.

"No. I think I've seen quite enough. I imagine we're almost over the range by now, so I better get back up front."

"All right. I'll escort you."

"No need. I can make it fine."

Lance watched Aziz make his way forward, then returned to his own seat between the other two men.

"What a weenie," he said before plugging in his headset. He didn't want to adversely influence the spy's report by broadcasting what he really thought of Aziz over the plane's intercom system.

Sergeant Adams put his hand over the microphone portion of his own headset, "Typical officer."

Lance, alarmed, turned to look at Adams.

Adams was grinning from ear to ear. He leaned toward Lance, hand still covering his microphone.

"Don't sweat it, sir. Officers don't have a lock on the jerk population. They come in all sizes, colors, and backgrounds, from airman basic to four-star general. We just drew the short straw today, and our jerk happens to wear silver oak leaves and pilot wings."

"I just don't want you to take his comments personally. His opinions are way off base."

"Don't worry about that, Major. I've seen his type before. Idea is to avoid 'em when you can, screw 'em when you can't. I have a friend who's a crew chief over with the Tacos, the National Guard wing. He's got a pilot like that. Poor pilot, seems every training weekend the plane he draws has something wrong with it. He has a heck of a time getting any flying hours. My guess is our friend up front often runs into the same kind of problems. Fortunately his problems aren't ours. Our problem is to make this test work."

"You're right. And a hell of a lot smarter than I have given you credit for so far. Let's check the master consent sequence one more time. That problem with the pilot's consent-to-fire switch worries me."

"Here we go." Adams typed a short string of commands.

"Pilot to Test. Fifteen minutes to the initial point on the range."

"Copy fifteen minutes. We're going to exercise the test sequence one more time."

The monitors over all three consoles reset. A red digital clock over the top of the each console read three minutes, then began to count down.

Lance consulted his own checklist spread on the narrow table in front of him. He would request pilot consent to fire at T minus one minute, thirty seconds. Sergeant Adams's and Captain Hawkins's fingers flew over their respective keyboards and intermittently reached up to touch indicators on the sensitive screens embedded in their consoles.

The clock read T minus two minutes, thirty seconds.

Test Director: "Missile launch detector status?"

Adams: "Launch detector coolant green. Launch detector bias voltage green."

T minus two minutes, fifteen seconds.

Test Director: "Switch to aircrew net."

All three men reached forward and turned the dials on their communications panels to the master position.

The clock reached T minus two.

Test Director: "Pressurize laser modules one through six."

Hawkins: "Modules one through six pressurized. Simulated fuel flow nominal. Diffuser doors open."

T minus one minute, thirty seconds.

Test Director: "Pilot, this is Test. Request consent-to-fire."

Pilot: "Consent-to-fire granted."

The red light on Lance's console changed to green as the pilot enabled the consent-to-fire switch.

Test Director: "Consent-to-fire test complete. You may release."

Pilot: "Copy."

The light switched back to red. The system seemed to be working okay.

T minus one minute.

Test Director: "Final system check."

Adams: "All green."

Hawkins: "All green."

Pilot: "All systems go."

Lance made one final check of his own systems status. All the lights, reflecting duplicate sensors of the ones monitored by the laser device operator and the beam control operator, glowed green. They were good to go.

T minus thirty seconds.

Test Director: "Pressurize laser modules seven through twelve for reserve."

Hawkins: "Modules seven through twelve pressurized and set to standby. Simulated fuel flow nominal."

Lance reached up to engage the final system. "Beam control enabled. All systems nominal and we're set to fight."

Sergeant Adams placed his hand gently around the joystick. He thumbed the slide switch on the side of the control, opening the protective cover over the nose of the plane. The highly sensitive infrared missile warning system was now able to look through the laser beam director to scan for threats. "Negative returns on radar. Negative returns on missile warning. Negative infrared."

Lance looked over at the two master displays in front of Sergeant Adams. The display on the right showed only the falsetto of a multicolored terrain. That was the infrared imaging system. It was optimized to operate in the near infrared portion of the spectrum, the area where a missile plume would show up most prominently. The other screen had the traditional sweep of a radarscope as the fire control radar scanned the region in front of them, looking for any airborne moving target. There were none, so far.

"Okay folks, that was an excellent run-up," the test director said. "No system problems. Let's run a quick check on fuel status. Give me the temperature on the laser modules and run the missile warning system through its self-test."

Lance sat back as the men on either side of him accomplished their assigned tasks. It didn't take long.

Hawkins: "Fuel system at ninety-eight percent, effective thirty-two rounds. Laser module five is running within ten percent of the high temperature safety limit."

Test Director: "Shut down module five and bring module seven on-line as replacement. Divert fuel flow as necessary to shut down module five."

It was just a precaution. Lance didn't want an overheated laser module screwing up their only shot at this.

Adams: "Missile warning self-test complete. Operating within all system parameter limits."

Test Director: "Excellent. Pilot, system is operational and ready for test."

Pilot: "Copy. We are three minutes out. Switching to Range Control frequency.

"Range Control, this is Eagle Three Three. We are turning inbound to the top of the box. All systems are ready for test."

"Copy, Eagle Three Three. Come to a heading of zero niner five. Range is hot. Repeat. Range is hot."

Test Director: "Okay, crew, we'll hit the threat envelope in just under two minutes. Give me a final status check."

Adams: "Beam control ready."

Hawkins: "Laser ready."

Test Director: "Pilot, all systems are go."

Pilot: "Confirm. We're about a minute out. As soon as we enter the box we'll be given an unknown vector, probably about a twenty-degree left turn. Somewhere down there, somewhere in all that desert, three ballistic missiles are waiting to be launched. Hope you guys can find 'em. From up here I can't seen anything but a whole bunch of sand and dirt."

Ground Control came on-line again. "Eagle Three Three, you are in the box, come to a heading of one two one and maintain altitude. Confirm when on heading."

Lance felt the big plane turn slowly to the left. It quickly rolled out of the turn and leveled off.

"Ground Control, Eagle Three Three is on heading," the pilot announced.

"Copy, Three Three. All systems come to operational frequency. All systems report status."

"Troll One ready."

"Troll Two ready."

"Troll Three ready."

"Ground telemetry up and ready."

"All systems up and ready," Ground Control reported. "Eagle Three Three, you are now in the box. Weapons free. Repeat. Weapons free."

"Test Director, this is Pilot. We are in the box and weapons are free. Better start looking for those ballistic missiles."

"Copy. Radar is searching. All systems are go."

"I need consent-to-fire," Sergeant Adams said.

Lance mentally kicked himself. How could he forget such an important item? "Pilot, this is Test. Request consent-to-fire." Lance quickly reviewed his checklist to see if he'd missed anything else.

"Consent-to-fire engaged."

The red light on Lance's console didn't waver.

"Pilot, this is Test. Consent did not clear. Request you repeat consent-to-fire."

"Test. Pilot. Consent-to-fire granted. I don't think I can push this switch any harder."

The red light continued to burn.

Sergeant Adams keyed in a short command. Various numbers marched up his screen. "Sir, we have a software problem. The pilot is keying the switch, but the software isn't recognizing it in both memory addresses."

"Can you fix it?"

"Sort of. But it'll take a couple of minutes."

Lance had to decide quickly. "Pilot, this is Test. Abort the run. We have a malfunction."

"Copy, Test. Ground Control, this is Eagle Three Three. Request a reset. We have a small problem."

Ground Control confirmed the request. "All Troll shooters. Hold fire. Repeat—hold fire. Range is still hot. Eagle Three Three, how long do you need?"

"Test, how long?" Powers asked.

Lance watched Adams pull up a software routine. He wasn't too familiar with the particular flavor of operating system the computer used, but he did recognize what the sergeant was doing. "You 'remarked out' all the code?"

"Yes, sir. A quick patch. I just need to write a little code snippet to simulate the consent switch. Maybe five minutes to write and test the code."

"Pilot, we need five minutes," Lance said.

"Ground Control, Eagle Three Three. Request five-minute delay," Powers relayed to ground control.

"Copy, Three Three. Five-minute delay. Orbit to right and enter the box in five minutes. All Troll systems maintain ready posture. Test will resume in five minutes."

"Test, this is Powers. Colonel Aziz requests permission to come back to the test compartment."

Damn. Lance had forgotten about Air Combat

Command's spy. Bet he's got a lot of interesting notes in his little book by now. "Fine, send him down."

"You write the code, Sergeant Adams, and I'll debug for you," Captain Hawkins said.

"You know SimScript?" Adams asked.

"Yeah, I helped build the original compiler."

Adams's fingers were flying over the keys. "But I heard a contractor for the Information Directorate up in Rome developed the original software."

"Right. The contractor wrote the documentation. I was a three-striper at the time, working for a captain. We wrote the shell for the development environment."

"Cool. Here's the first snippet." As soon as Adams loaded the code onto the main computer, it showed up on Hawkins's display. "Just check for syntax errors while I write the other two pieces."

"What about testing the code?" Lance asked.

"That red light over your console is the only test we'll need, sir," Adams said.

Aziz stepped up behind the three men. "I suppose we would have asked the enemy for a time-out, too?"

Crap. Here we go. Lance was about to reply when Sergeant Adams weighed in.

"Negative, sir. This was a nuisance abort. We should have deleted the pilot consent switch in the original software, but our customer—your command—wanted it left in."

"What do you mean, Sergeant?"

"Sir, the need to have a pilot in the loop is a hold-over from the dark ages, back when you could see your enemy before you could ever shoot him. Now we can reach out and kill our enemy well beyond visual range. We don't need to eyeball him. You were up front; they can't see anything up there."

Aziz didn't argue.

"Here's the second snippet," Sergeant Adams said to Captain Hawkins.

Lance wondered how the heck he was managing it—justifying the laser program and writing code at the same time. The younger generation had grown up with computers, not helped develop them like his own generation. There was a phenomenal difference.

"Anyway," Adams continued, "there's really no reason to require a pilot consent to fire the laser. We'll see the target back here before the pilot has an inkling it's been launched. Assuming he'll see the thing at all."

"Just how far away is the target?" Aziz turned to Lance.

"For this test the missiles will be somewhere between eighty and a hundred kilometers from us when they're launched. That's restricted by the range size. In a real scenario like the one I talked about earlier, the range might increase to about a hundred and twenty kilometers, depending on a variety of factors."

"You can see a missile launch from that far out?"

For the first time Lance detected a sense of wonder in their baby-sitter's voice. "Yeah. Easily. Our sensors are better than anything you've probably ever seen."

"There's the third piece of code," Sergeant Adams said.

"I give you a ninety-eight," Hawkins said after he quickly scanned the code. "You forgot to capitalize one of the variables."

"But the code isn't case-sensitive."

"I know. But I never give perfect scores."

Lance knew the code was perfect. Hawkins had just given sergeant Adams a big pat on the back.

"I've connected the code snippets. Where do we need to load them?"

Adams moved the cursor on his other screen to a spot just below where he had disabled all the original code. "Right here."

Two keystrokes and the code was appended to the fire control program.

"Now to recompile and reinitialize." Adams's fingers flew again. "Cross your fingers."

"What will happen?" Aziz directed his question at Sergeant Adams.

"With any luck, we'll go through the setup sequence again and that annoying little red light on the test director's console will go out."

"We're two minutes to the box. How's it going back there?" Powers asked from the cockpit.

"We'll know in just a few seconds." Lance prepared to run down his short checklist, but his two crewmen were already halfway down the sequence, running from memory.

"This is where you'd ask for consent-to-fire," Sergeant Adams said. "But don't bother."

They all watched as the amber fire consent light changed to green.

"Cool," Hawkins said.

"Pilot, we've cleaned up the problem. Let's try it again," said Lance.

"Copy, Test. Do you want to send Colonel Aziz back up here?"

"If it's okay with you, I think I'd like to stay back here," Aziz said to Lance.

Lance noticed he hadn't been writing in his little

notebook since coming back this time. "Fine with me. Have a seat here in the gallery."

Aziz sat down in the observer's seat just behind the three men.

"Colonel Aziz has asked to stay back here," Lance informed Powers.

"Copy. You guys better strap in, we're about a minute out. Everything working this time?"

"Status check," Lance said.

Adams: "Beam control ready."

Hawkins: "Laser ready."

"Pilot, all systems are go," announced Lance.

Pilot: "Ground Control, this is Eagle Three Three. All systems operational."

Ground Control: "Eagle Three Three, you are in the box. Come to a heading of one three five and maintain altitude. Confirm when on heading."

Pilot: "Ground Control, Eagle Three Three is on heading."

Ground Control: "Copy, Three Three. All systems come to operational frequency. All systems report status."

"Troll One ready."

"Troll Two ready."

"Troll Three ready."

"Telemetry up and ready. "

Ground Control: "All systems up and ready. The range is hot. Repeat. The range is hot. Weapons free. Repeat. Weapons free."

Pilot: "Test Director, this is Powers. We are in the box and weapons are free. Let's go find and kill some missiles."

"Where will they come from?" Aziz asked.

Lance pointed at the radar display. "Somewhere out

there. We don't know where they're hidden. The operational test guys wanted to give us a little more realism than a simple experiment would have provided. I would have preferred to set up a test for a single missile. But there was no time. So they hid three missiles out there in the desert and we're supposed to find them when they're launched."

A piercing squeal sounded the first alarm. Sergeant Adams reached over and flipped a switch to kill the noise. "Missile launch detect."

"I don't see anything," Aziz said, his eyes growing wide.

Lance held up his hand to quiet the observer. He flipped his checklist over and started to tick off the steps. "Reset missile warning audio. Arm laser. Select narrow-band filter . . ."

"Request weapons free," Sergeant Adams said.

Lance realized his crew was once again already several steps ahead of him. "Weapons free."

A battery of lights flashed green on the laser control console as each of the primary laser modules began pumping their poisonous gas through the individual resonators. Only pneumatically actuated shutters kept the lethal light energy confined within the modules.

"Laser up," Hawkins said.

Aziz was leaning forward in his seat, his restraints loosened so he could get a better view. "Where is it?"

Lance pointed at the center screen on Sergeant Adams's console. "There. The narrow-band sensor has picked it up."

"Beam on," Sergeant Adams said.

As he keyed the finger switch on the joystick the most powerful laser beam ever generated in an airplane leaped from the beam director in the nose. It sliced through the turbulent desert air and pounced on the burning missile. The missile itself was still moving relatively slowly, but accelerating. A small amount of the laser energy reflected back to the airplane.

Sergeant Adams: "Range eighty-nine kilometers. Autofocus is closing the loop."

Another light flashed green.

Sergeant Adams: "Autotrack is solid."

Hawkins: "Power is up."

Sergeant Adams: "We have thermal signature. Missile is cooking."

A bright flash saturated the infrared monitor.

"Yes! Got it!" Sergeant Adams said, louder than necessary.

Ground Control: "Solid kill on Troll One. Telemetry confirms we have missile destruction at six thousand feet."

Pilot: "Copy, we have a kill."

Powers relayed the information and congratulations to the test director over the intercom. "Outstanding! I never saw the target, but I sure saw what happened when it blew up."

"You should have seen the infrared video," Lance said into his mike. "It was beautiful. Let's stay on top of things, though. There are two more targets out there."

Ground Control: "Eagle Three Three, come right to one one zero."

Pilot: "Eagle Three Three wilco."

"So what exactly happened?" Aziz asked.

The big plane banked quickly to find the new heading.

Lance checked his weapon's status, then turned to Aziz. "The moving target indicator algorithm in our on-board radar identified a possible missile launch and targeted the sector where the missile appeared to be coming from. In other words, it steered the beam control system in the right general direction. Our infrared imaging system looks right through the beam control optics and shares the same beam path. As it detected the infrared signature of a missile plume, we sent a very broad laser beam at the target area. We used the reflected laser light to track and eventually focus the laser on the missile casing. Once we set the focus, the laser cut through the outer missile casing and set the fuel on fire. That's all it takes."

"But I didn't see you guys do anything."

"The computer controlled most of the events. There's not enough time to let a human get very involved in the process."

Aziz nodded, putting his little pad in his pocket. "That's pretty dang slick."

The plane leveled off.

Pilot: "Ground Control, Eagle Three Three is on course at one one zero."

Ground Control: "Copy, Three Three. Troll Two and Troll Three, you are cleared hot."

"Get ready, test crew," warned Powers.

Lance watched intently, while Aziz strained to see over his shoulder. The radar screen, with the exception of the rapidly circling beam line indicator, remained blank.

Suddenly the missile warning receiver blared in their ears again.

"We've got a target." Adams reached up and hit the switch to kill the warning speaker. A small green dot appeared on the display.

The missile warning receiver blared again.

"I thought I shut that thing off," Adams said, reaching up and slapping the switch again.

"Two targets," Hawkins said and pointed to the radar screen. "Repeat—two of them."

Lance saw it too, two separate blips very close together. The targets were just beginning to appear as dusty orange spots on the infrared screen, so close together they were almost inseparable. Suddenly the image began a rapid oscillation.

"We've got a break lock. Uncontrollable oscillations," Adams said.

"Go manual. Max magnification," Lance ordered.

Adams reached over to grab the joystick. He thumbed a switch and the rapid oscillation of the image stopped. Unfortunately, the missiles appeared to be well off the center of the crosshairs. Lance reached up to boost the magnification.

Then the images disappeared from the screen entirely.

"Too much," Adams said as he moved the stick to the left in a futile search for the missing targets.

Lance backed off the magnification, and two barely separated blobs of orange infrared energy reappeared at the bottom left of the screen. The display indicated the missiles were already at fifteen thousand feet and accelerating rapidly.

"Give me module one only," Adams requested.

Hawkins reached up to hit three switches, blocking most of the laser energy before hitting the master fire switch. "Module one."

"When I tell you, give me all you've got." Adams deftly moved the crosshairs over the brightest area of the blurry connected spot on the screen. "Now!"

Hawkins reached up and enabled all of the laser switches.

The screen bloomed red as the missile was destroyed.

Ground Control: "We have a kill. Telemetry confirms a single kill at eighteen thousand feet. Troll Three is approaching safety altitude. Preparing for autodestruct of Troll Three at twenty thousand feet."

"Should I reset for automatic track?" Adams asked.

"Negative," Lance replied. "Maintain manual track. Module one only."

Hawkins reset the switches. "Module one."

Sergeant Adams reduced the gain on the infrared display, but the entire screen went blank. "Dang it!" He switched back to the highest setting.

Hawkins called, "Target altitude at nineteen thousand feet."

"Come on, come on," Lance urged.

Finally the image condensed to a smaller spot. Adams quickly settled the crosshairs on the target.

"Fire!" Lance yelled.

Hawkins enabled the master switch again.

They waited silently as the laser beam cooked the missile shell. In less than two seconds the image bloomed brilliant red and filled the screen.

"Got it!" Adams said.

Ground Control piped in, "We have a kill. Telemetry confirms a kill at nineteen thousand five hundred feet. Good shooting, Eagle Three Three."

"Copy, Ground Control. Attaboys all around back there, Test Director. I was beginning to wonder if you were going to get that last one or not," said Powers.

"Frankly, so was I," Lance answered. What the heck had happened?

"We barely made it," Aziz said. "Look at the altitude."

Lance and the other crewmen saw that the altitude Ground Control had reported as nineteen thousand five hundred feet was actually closer to nineteen thousand nine hundred. Very close.

"What caused the break lock?" Lance asked.

"Not sure," Adams said. "My first guess is that with the two missiles so close together, they were both within the tracker's field of view and it couldn't tell them apart. That drove it into an unstable oscillation as it tried to pick the hottest target."

"I never expected them to fire two at once," Lance said.

"Why not?" Aziz was intensely curious now. "That would be standard surface-to-air missile doctrine for most air defense systems. Why wouldn't a ballistic missile unit work the same way?"

"I guess we don't know the operational issues involved in implementing this weapon," Lance said. He could build the system, but putting it into action required a different kind of knowledge and experience. The kind of a background a war fighter would have, not a scientist. What little he did know he had learned over the Syrian Desert, and Colonel Jones had taken care of all the operational issues there. Too bad he was gone now—he could have been a big help in this program.

"The operational flavor is what this program is lacking. One of the reasons my boss wants it canceled."

"Mind if I ask what you're going to report back to him?"

Powers chimed in just then. "We are clear of the range. Estimated time to land is just over half an hour. Do you have the systems shut down?"

Lance had been too busy discussing the test with Aziz. He glanced back at Hawkins's console. All the laser modules were shut down and safely stored. Sergeant Adams was working with the beam director before shutting it down. That wouldn't affect the rest of the flight. "We're all set back here. Laser system is shut down. Give me a ten-minute hack and I'll have our laser jock shut down the beam control system."

"All right," Powers said. "My congrats to your laser jock. Good shooting. You might want to remind him he just entered the record books."

Lance smacked Sergeant Adams on the back.

Adams had heard the pilot's comments and was grinning like a kid with a new Nintendo.

"What does she mean?" Aziz asked.

"This is the first time a ballistic missile has been destroyed during launch by a laser fired from an aircraft." Lance was proud of the accomplishment, though bothered by the near failure caused by the multiple launches.

"By *any* kind of weapon fired from an airplane," Sergeant Adams reminded Lance.

"Hey, that's right." Aziz loosened his seat restraint so he could lean forward and get a better look at the console. "I don't think we have any other kind of weapon that can do what you've just done."

"Not even your F-15s?" Lance asked.

"Couldn't even come close. Best we can do is try to find the launcher and kill it before it shoots. Frankly, that's a tough job. Assuming one of our intelligence systems can find it, it's either mobile or fixed. If it's mobile, it's usually gone before we get close enough with a plane to kill it. If it's fixed, it usually comes with a slew of air defenses that we have to slug

our way through. That gives the missile crew enough
time to launch if they have all their ducks lined up."

"Is that what you're going to report?"

"I'll report what I saw: that your system had one
problem that almost let a missile get through. But that
problem was solved in time to kill one hundred percent of the targets. I'll also mention that this is a
first—that nothing else in the inventory has the capability I've just witnessed. As far as shortcomings, there
is a lack of operational experience on the development
team. That experience might have saved you from
being surprised at the tandem launch. If it's all right
with you, I'd like to volunteer to join your team."

"I think that'd be great," Lance said. He had a convert. "I've got to admit, I'm kind of surprised, though.
Won't you miss flying your fighters?"

"I'm on staff now. Don't get to fly a lot anyway.
Besides, your pilot said it all. This is the wave of the
future."

"Bad news, gentlemen." Powers broke into their excitement. "The tower just relayed a message from the
Pentagon. We are to set this bird down, unload all
unnecessary equipment, and return to Seattle for the
removal of the laser. Looks like the program has been
officially killed."

An elephant couldn't have weighed more heavily on
Lance's chest. He looked back at Aziz. "If you really
want to be a laser jock, you might want to hurry with
that report of yours."

Then Lance keyed his mike. "This is Test. Copy the
bad news. Can you patch me through to General Morris's cell phone? I owe him a report on the test and
should probably tell him about this latest development."

Chapter 7

"It is all in place, Comrade," Wu Li informed the leader of the rocket forces.

"Very well done. My compliments to the daughter of our newest member of the Central Committee. Would you and your husband care to join me in the command center?"

"What is the command center?" Zhen Rhongi asked.

"It is the nerve center for this entire operation, the place from which all launch commands are given."

"We would be most humbly grateful for your hospitality," Wu Li answered.

They returned to the car specifically provided for use by the administrator of Korea's newest weapons. The driver took them to a slight rise on a hill overlooking the field where the missiles waited.

Inside the building, the leader guided the engineers to a large room. More than a dozen Korean soldiers were monitoring every facet of the weaponry deployed in the valley below. A large map covered the entire front wall.

"As you can see, most of our weapons are targeted at the American forces in the South. Some weapons are presently targeted at the Japanese, in the event they decide to assist the Americans. And, of course, your most special gift to the Korean people is targeted at the city of San Francisco in California, just as your father has advised."

"Have you seen this morning's news?" Hawkins tossed his copy of *USA Today* on the table. The officers' club was almost empty, so he put his tray on the adjacent table after setting his plate of fried eggs across from Lance.

"Yeah, I caught a little on the TV this morning. Four armored divisions and another four infantry. You believe it?"

"What's not to believe? Starving populace, Japanese Army playing war games on the southern border, Americans threatening to cut off aid if you don't capitulate—it's a pretty traditional response."

"Mind if I join you gentlemen?" Aziz set his coffee between the two officers.

"Not at all," Lance answered as he poked at his bacon. "In fact, since you're the alleged warrior, you might have better insight into this. You think the Koreans will invade?"

Aziz plopped down in the chair and glanced around them, making sure there was no one within earshot. "Word I got before I left Langley was that we were expecting this. The intel toads have been briefing that the North Koreans are at their wits' end. Of course, they've said that for over a year now. All they needed was a gentle push to put them over the edge. The Japanese on their border was more like a big shove."

"How's that?" Lance asked.

"They're traditional enemies," Aziz said.

"I heard there's no love lost between the Koreans and the Japanese."

"I was stationed in Japan for a couple of years. The Koreans and Japanese are like the blacks and whites of the Old South—they have bitter hatred toward each other," Aziz said. "Stems from World War II and the fact that Japan has prospered so much more than Korea, at least than North Korea. The Koreans helped China defeat Japan, yet Japan is now wealthy and prosperous while North Korea is starving. And now the Japanese are back, right on the 38th Parallel."

"But it's not like there's a whole Japanese Army down there. It's just a command post exercise," Hawkins said around a mouthful of eggs. "How many people did they bring? Five hundred? A thousand? And they're all staff officers."

"Not quite. They brought a wing of F-16s," Aziz said.

"I didn't know that. Why'd they bring fighters?"

"Shake out the logistics, make sure they could all play together if necessary. You know, the new commander of U.S. Forces is an Air Force four-star. A fighter pilot. I heard he specifically invited the Japanese planes over."

"Not to speak poorly of my superiors, but that was sure dumb," Hawkins said.

"And considering the briefing I was shown before yesterday's test, it looks to me like this whole thing could get pretty dicey," Lance said.

"It could blow up at any second," Hawkins said.

"Speaking of the test, did you get through to General Morris?" Aziz asked.

"Yeah. He was glad to hear about the results, but couldn't offer any encouragement on being able to cancel the orders to gut the plane." Lance poured some more coffee.

"I figured if anyone could short-circuit Langley, he could," Hawkins said.

"When the commander of Air Combat Command gets his mind made up, it's tough to get him to do an about-face," Aziz said. "I did what I could last night. I was up until about three trying to get the words in my report right. It was an amazing piece of prose, glowing in its praise for this new weapon. I E-mailed it straight to the director of requirements with a copy to the director of ops. Those two guys were very interested in the test, mainly since the commander was so anxious about it. They're both early risers, and since they're two hours ahead of us I'll bet they've already read my message. If they take my recommendation, they'll convince the four-star to cancel his previous order and reinstate the test series. Then again, they may just walk the party line and ignore my recommendations. It's all politics up there."

Hawkins aimed his fork at the door. "There's Colonel DeMarco."

The colonel spotted them and headed toward their table. He swung by the buffet line and grabbed a coffee mug before joining them. Aziz poured from the urn on their table as the colonel sat down.

"Morning. You guys have as rotten of a night as I've had?"

"What happened, sir?"

"You've heard about the Koreans?"

"Only what's in the news."

The colonel lowered his voice and leaned toward the others. "That's not the half of it. Last night they launched another 'test' rocket. Lobbed it right over the top of Tokyo. They command-detonated it, blew it up before it even reached its apogee. They just wanted to prove a point. Trajectory analysis says it could have landed anywhere in Japan. We've also confirmed that their Chinese missile is up and operational. Could reach as far as Los Angeles."

"Impossible," Aziz said.

"Used to be impossible. Not only have the Koreans joined the nuclear club, they've also joined the intercontinental ballistic missile club now. Most of that info is being closely held, but it won't be long before the press gets hold of it."

"That should raise some eyebrows at the Pentagon."

"Already has. Kim Jong Il is supposed to make a statement to the world press tomorrow morning their time. Probably the routine 'we're not going to take this anymore' crap. Anyhow, the Pentagon is stirred up because the Koreans have put their missile field on full alert."

"But from what we were briefed yesterday they only had the one long-range missile, and it wasn't fully ready for launch." Lance said, absentmindedly tapping his plate with his fork.

"Well, it's ready now. Any educated guess would put a nuke on its tip. If all this data is accurate, the United Stated is now at risk from North Korea. And the Japanese are scared to death. Guess who they've asked to help."

"The United States, of course." Aziz was rapidly stirring his coffee, splashing the hot liquid out of the cup.

"Not just the United States, but specifically the Airborne Laser."

Lance stopped tapping on his plate. "What?"

"The Japanese know about the plane. We haven't exactly been keeping it much of a secret. They've asked specifically for support from the ABL until this crisis blows over."

"What does our government say?"

"Are you kidding? Since when have we turned down the Japanese for anything? The president has personally weighed in. He had the chairman of the Joint Chiefs over early this morning. The Air Combat Command commander was in town, so the chairman dragged him along. You know how the two of them have been trying to kill this program. Sending it on an operational mission will devastate their plans. But your test yesterday showed the viability of the system. When the secretary of state offered up a test report from one of our Air Combat Command's own officers who personally witnessed the test, they ran out of arguments."

"My report?" Aziz's mouth was hanging open. "How did the secretary of state get a copy of my report? I'm doomed."

"My guess is your career as a fighter pilot is over, so long as your commander remembers this. Don't know how the secretary of state got your report. You sent it by E-mail?"

"Yeah." Aziz was wiping his hands on his napkin.

"That's probably it. E-mail has this funny way of getting forwarded everywhere, even places you never intended it to go."

"But realistically, our test was nothing more than just that—a test. This plane is certainly not ready for combat." Lance wanted desperately to interject some sanity into what he had just heard.

"Yesterday's test was operationally oriented. General Morris planned it that way. It wasn't a lab experiment. The system may not be optimal, but it's close enough. Besides, you're combat-tested in a similar arena."

"That was totally different."

"I don't think that will matter." Colonel DeMarco pulled a yellow envelope from his briefcase. "Here are your orders."

Lance and Hawkins read the papers the colonel gave them.

Lance shook his head in disbelief. "When do we leave?"

"Tonight. The plane will go to the Seattle Boeing plant for a quick—and I mean *quick*—checkout. You guys will get some rest and then head for Japan in the morning. You'll stage out of Misawa."

"There are a lot of things that need to be done to the laser. Fuel, water, sensor coolant, that sort of thing," Lance said.

"I'll have a crew get that stuff ready. You'll leave here with a load of fuel and keep it onboard through the mission. I'll try and figure out how to refuel the laser in Japan if we need to."

"What about passports, that sort of thing?" Lance remembered the last time he had gotten into this kind of mess. They'd had almost four weeks to get ready that time. Now they had only a day.

"Your military ID is all you need." Aziz was rubbing his hands together. "You know, you are going to be awfully short of people."

"We'll try and pick up another pilot from Boeing. The test crew is going to be the limiting factor. I've got Sergeant Adams on the orders, as well as Lance and Hawkins. That's it. Don't really know if anyone else would be of any help. No one else knows how to operate any of the systems."

"Got room for me?" Aziz asked.

"You want to go?" Lance asked.

"Like the colonel said, it looks like my fighter pilot days are over, at least for now. Being one of the first laser jocks might be the next best thing."

"How can you help?" Colonel DeMarco asked.

"I've been to Misawa twice, I can help there with logistics and such. That'll free your crew up for the mission-related stuff. I've watched the test crew in action, and I'm a fast learner. I might be able to help back there. If worse comes to worst, I think I could even be convinced to fly the plane, as long as you don't tell anyone I was flying a heavy."

"Lance?"

At least the colonel wanted his opinion on something. "I'd be glad to have Colonel Aziz on board."

"I go by Skeeter," Aziz said. "Although that doesn't sound too high-tech. We may have to change my nickname."

Colonel DeMarco stood up. "Unless you guys are planning to eat all day, we have a lot of work to do."

The others stood and followed him out the door.

It was going to be a long day, Lance thought as he fell in behind. Telling Mandy and the girls he was leaving again was going to be tough. Very tough.

"I know it's a rotten deal. If I'd known I'd be leaving I never would have asked you guys to come out."

Mandy sat on the small sofa, the twins on each side of her. "If you're going to Seattle, why don't we just come along?"

How was he supposed to tell her what was really going on? It was classified that he was taking the plane to Japan and then probably to patrol near Korea. He couldn't help but notice that the newspaper lying open on the coffee table had a headline that read: NEW CRISIS IN KOREA.

"It just won't work, Mandy. It could be that we aren't going to be in Seattle all that long."

"You're doing it again, aren't you?"

"Doing what?"

She tapped the paper. "This."

The girls huddled close. They could sense the tension between their parents.

Lance nodded. She deserved the truth.

"Then I take it you don't have any idea how long you'll be gone?"

"No."

She sat quietly. Lance thought he saw a glimmer of a tear forming in her eye.

He sat on the edge of the coffee table and put his hand on her thigh. "Look, maybe this will all blow over in a few days and they'll send us back home. You guys stay here, go up to the stables on the mesa, take a few rides. Have a good time. If I'm not back in a couple of days, you can head back to Santa Barbara and I'll meet up with you there as soon as I get done."

Mandy looked past him, forcing back the tears. "I really wanted you to come up to Stanford with me. My final interview is in three days."

"I know, honey. If it's at all possible I'll be there with you, but I can't guarantee anything at this point."

Lance poked at Sarah. "Horseback riding in the desert sound good to you, kiddo?"

Sarah nodded silently.

"Rachel?"

"I guess," the other twin said.

"Look, I really wanted to take you guys out there, but I can't this time. I need to take care of this little job first." Should he even send them to California? Was it safe there? Probably about as safe as anywhere else, he reassured himself.

"Can we come out to see you off this evening?"

"I don't know why not. You girls want to see the plane I've been working on?"

Both girls' eyes lit up. "Yeah," they said in unison.

"Okay, then. We leave at about six o'clock tonight. Why don't you come out about five? I'd come back for lunch, but I really don't think I'm going to have any time."

"It's okay. We'll go by and get Debbie on our way. I'm sure she'd like to go, too."

"Great idea. I'll see you guys then."

Lance stood up to leave. Mandy followed him to the door.

She hugged him close, not wanting to let go. He realized it would be their last private moment before he left. He held her tightly in return. Then he picked up his overstuffed suitcase and left his family behind.

It was 1700. 5:00 P.M. Almost time to go. The big plane was parked outside the hangar, ready. At least, as ready as it could be. Lance stood back and watched as the Test Wing's ground crew finished loading all of their equipment. Fortunately there was a lot of room in the big bird for almost everything he thought he might reasonably need. The plan was to drop most of the test equipment in Japan at Misawa Air Force Base. If something broke they'd return there to do repairs, then turn around and be on station as needed. When it was all over with, they would load up the gear and return to the States. If nothing went wrong, that is. A shiver ran down Lance's spine as he remembered the other time he'd deployed with a laser weapon. The plane hadn't made it back, and four good men hadn't come back either. He prayed that this mission wouldn't have the same results.

"That's all the gear, sir." Sergeant Adams stepped up beside him. "I took everything but the kitchen sink, and we've still got room."

"Laser fueled?"

"Yes, sir. We should be good for seven days or so. Much longer than that and liquid nitrogen boil-off might be a problem. The nitrogen is critical—we need it to cool the sensors. I'm sure we can get liquid nitrogen somewhere in Japan."

"Shouldn't be a problem." Aziz joined them. "C-141s use it to cool their brakes. They sell it by the ton there at Misawa."

"All we need is a gallon or so," Sergeant Adams said.

"Like I said, shouldn't be a problem."

Lance checked his watch. "We leave in a little over an hour. If you guys have anything you need to get done, better do it now."

"I gotta go say good-bye to Debbie," Sergeant Adams said. "I think Mandy and your girls are over in the office, too."

"Yeah. Go ahead. I'll be over there in a minute."

Sergeant Adams headed toward the offices at the side of the now empty hangar.

"Your wife?" Aziz asked.

"And my daughters. They wanted to see me off."

"I thought you guys were from California."

"We are. I invited them out here when I found out

my reserve tour was going to last longer than I expected."

"Do they know where we're going?"

"My wife pretty much figured it out."

"But not what we're up against?"

"No, not quite. She's no dummy, though—she knows enough."

"She worried?"

"Yeah."

"That's tough." Aziz thought for a minute, then ripped his Velcro-covered patch loose from the sleeve of his flight suit and handed it to Lance. "All you gotta do is show her this and tell her Mr. Top Gun himself, F-15 fighter pilot Lieutenant Colonel Yoda Aziz is gonna take care of you. That should put her mind at ease."

"Yoda?"

"Yeah. You know, from *Star Wars*. The little guy that showed all the warriors how to fight with a laser sabre."

"That little thing that hummed like electricity when he cut through the air with it?"

"Yeah."

"But ours won't make any noise when we fire it through the air. . . ."

"So, we've got a silent sabre. And Yoda's the silent sabre warrior. That's me, now."

Lance nodded, "Well, Yoda, why don't you come help me put my wife's mind at ease yourself?"

Aziz put his hands in the air and backed away. "No way. I don't do the crying wife thing."

Lance looked at the patch. It showed the skull and crossbones like the flag of a pirate's banner. "Jolly Rogers" was written across the bottom, "F-15" along the top. Typical. Lance unzipped the chest pocket of his flight suit and pulled out a stack of patches, bound with a rubber band. He'd had them designed when he'd first arrived and just hadn't had time to hand them out. Now was probably as good a time as any.

They were black, with a red snake coiled around a white cloud in the center. The top read "ABL." The bottom said "Laser Jocks." After tossing one to Aziz, Lance slapped one on his arm and went to find his family.

Mandy was there with the girls, and Debbie was with Sergeant Adams over by the door. They were locked in an embrace. It wasn't a sad, good-bye type of embrace but more of a passionate "this is so you don't forget me."

Mandy was a little embarrassed, and the girls were pointing and giggling.

"Oh, to be young again," Lance said.

Mandy punched him on the arm, then hugged him.

Lance sat down, and the girls jumped into his lap.

"You guys seem to be in a much better mood this evening."

"They've been making plans all day. It turns out there is a horse-riding camp-out we can go on tomorrow night," Mandy said.

"We get to ride out for hours into the desert, Daddy!" Rachel beamed.

"And camp out under the stars, just like in the old days," Sarah added.

"Wow. That sounds like fun. And Mom agreed to this?"

"Mom is going to ride out in the Jeep with the sleeping bags and tents," Mandy said. "We'll meet up with them at the campsite. There's also a cabin there if the weather turns bad."

"With electricity and running water, I bet," Lance said.

Mandy nodded.

"Well, it sounds like a lot of fun. I wish I could go with you."

"Here, we made this for you, Daddy." Sarah handed him a small trinket on a long chain.

"It's a four-leaf clover. It's for good luck." Rachel said.

"Yes, indeed, and it's beautiful, too." Lance put the chain around his neck and tucked the charm inside his flight suit. "Thank you very much."

Both girls hugged their dad tightly. "We're going to miss you," they said in unison.

"I'm going to miss you, too, but I'll be back as soon as I possibly can."

"Promise?" Mandy asked, her eyes tearing up again.

"Of course I promise." Lance hugged the girls once more and then stood up. He walked over to Mandy and took her into his arms.

"Is this going to be like last time?" she asked.

"No, much easier. And a lot safer." Lance hadn't gone into the details of the last mission, not wanting to mention that he'd had to bail out of the Airborne Laser Lab before it went down. He never told her two of his crewmates had died in the fight, either, or that two others were killed riding the plane down so he and Lieutenant Murphy could get out safely. Still, somehow she'd heard about the crash.

"How is it going to be any safer? The Koreans are crazy."

Lance could tell she needed reassurance. "Well, for

one thing this airplane is brand-new. There's no way it's going to crash. For another, the Koreans won't have a chance to get close to us. This laser is much more powerful and designed to fire from hundreds of miles away. So you see, there's really no danger. None at all."

She squeezed him tightly. "So how come I'm so nervous?"

"Don't be. Like I said, I'll be back home as soon as I can."

"They're waiting for you to board, sir," one of the crewmen interrupted from the door.

"I'd better be going." Lance kissed Mandy deeply.

"If you're more than a week, we'll be back in Santa Barbara," she said. "How can we contact you?"

Lance fished the general's card out of his pocket. "Just call this number. He'll know how to find me. I'll call you tonight." Lance bent down to kiss each of the girls one more time.

" 'Bye, Dad," they said.

"I love you guys," Lance said as he turned toward the door.

Sergeant Adams followed him.

Lance looked back and saw the girls, all of them, crowded into the door. Both men waved to their families, then headed for the plane.

It had been nice having his family with him for the last week, but now it was time to focus on what had to be done.

"I never thought I'd be doing this," Sergeant Adams said.

"Doing what?" They continued toward the plane, walking around the tail to get to the boarding stairs.

"Going off to fight with a laser. I always considered

myself a lab weenie. Figured I'd be nice and safe doing that. The Air Force warriors were always the fighter jocks."

Lance fished one of the patches out of his pocket and handed it to the sergeant. "Well, you're a warrior now. A laser jock."

Sergeant Adams stepped back to let Lance mount the steps first. "Cool!" he said as he slapped the patch onto the vacant Velcro sewed to his sleeve.

Lance paused as Lieutenant Colonel Aziz joined them, then pointed up at the plane. "It's a little different than a fighter. You sure you want in on this?"

"It's just bigger. It's still a war bird—that's all that matters to me."

"A *laser* war bird," Lance corrected him as he climbed the steps.

The flight to Seattle was uneventful. Lance had provided everyone in the crew with their own "Laser Jock" patch. No one was more delighted than Colonel Powers. She was concerned that she would have to leave the crew when they reached Seattle. Her test pilot job didn't include flying into harm's way, and the Boeing management hadn't been receptive to the idea when she had initially suggested that she be allowed to continue supporting the mission.

Lance knew she wanted to fly the mission badly, and he wanted her in the cockpit. No one knew more about the airplane than she did, and it was an insult to her not to let her do it. Lance didn't agree with many of the recent rules about women in combat, but there was no justification in disqualifying Colonel Powers from this mission. She was perfectly qualified.

Besides, she hadn't quite convinced her copilot about the need for him to stay in the Air Force.

Colonel DeMarco had agreed with Lance when he found out Boeing wasn't going to let Colonel Powers fly the mission. He had promised to do whatever he could. They'd find out when they got to Seattle if he'd been successful or not.

Lieutenant Colonel Aziz, their self-proclaimed token fighter pilot, stayed in the back with the test crew for the first half of the flight, then moved forward to see if he could get some "seat-time." Lance and the test crew discussed a great number of issues with him while he was in the back, not the least of which concerned the mode of operations they might expect from the North Koreans, should they actually have to face that threat. While Aziz didn't know much about, nor seem to care about, the intricate details of the laser's operation, he was a fount of knowledge about operations and tactics. Lance was confident he would be a big help during the upcoming mission.

Lance wandered back up from the latrine to check on his test crew. He looked over Captain Hawkins's shoulder. The AFIT student was leaning back in his seat, arms crossed, asleep. The display panel in front of the snoozing engineer showed no signs of problems. Laser fuel levels were still where they had been before the flight started, and pressurization levels were okay, as indicated by seven illuminated green lights.

Sergeant Adams was reading a book. He glanced up to check the beam control display when he saw Lance approach. "Everything's okay, sir."

"Relax, Sergeant Adams. We've got a long way to go before we hit Korea. What're you reading?"

"Just a novel. Thought it might help pass the time."

"Yeah. This is boring, isn't it? I think we're about an hour out of Seattle. You want to fire up the beam control system and wring it out again?"

"I did that earlier, sir. It's working fine."

"Well, we're probably almost over the Rockies. Want to use the video tracker to get a bird's-eye view of some of nature's wonders?"

"Good idea." Sergeant Adams dog-eared the edge of the page he was reading and stuffed the book into a helmet bag next to him, then eagerly powered up the beam control computer.

He ran through a quick checklist from memory, bringing the beam control system into active test mode. The beam-expanding reverse telescope in the nose of the plane came up on-line. The telescope's primary function was to increase the size of the laser beam as it left the airplane and concentrate the laser's energy onto a much smaller spot on the target—making it more lethal. By looking through the beam expander with a high-resolution video camera, the crew was effectively using the reverse telescope as a huge telephoto lens.

Sergeant Adams took manual control of the system and pointed it slightly downward into the clouds. "Not much to see down there today. Looks like a solid cloud deck."

"Maybe not," Lance said. "Go to wide field of view."

Looking through the magnifying telescope was like looking through a soda straw. You couldn't see much of anything outside of a few degrees' width.

Sergeant Adams pushed a simulated button on the touch-sensitive monitor. The clouds on the video screen retreated as the magnification was reduced.

"There," Lance pointed. "See it?"

Sergeant Adams centered the object protruding through the clouds ahead of them and slightly to the left. Then he increased the magnification, and the object quickly grew to fill the screen. "Beautiful."

"It's Mount St. Helens. Remember when it blew its top back in 1980? Looks like we're going to fly right over it. Want to try atmospheric correction? We can probably get the best pictures ever taken of this place."

"We'll have to fire up the IR imager to do that."

"Go ahead."

"I'll give you a hand." Captain Hawkins said, now awake. He reached over and pushed another button. A cartoon of a thermometer appeared on the monitor as the imager's detector was cooled to operating temperature.

"Wow, that's a nice picture." Lieutenant Colonel Aziz had joined them from the front of the plane. "What is it?"

"The peak of Mount St. Helens. Everything else is covered by clouds, so we're going to take a close look at the old volcano. We're engaging the atmospheric turbulence correction system now."

"The atmospheric what?"

"We're going to correct for the wind flowing over the nose of the beam director. It's a compensation system that's critical to the beam control system's effectiveness."

"Can you talk in English for a change?"

The sensor was cooling down quickly. "Okay. Ever look through the exhaust plume of an airplane engine, say one of your F-15s?"

"Yeah. The thermals make it hard to see anything."

"Exactly. Only it's not just the temperature of the air that makes it hard to see through, it's the turbulence. The air is moving in all kinds of jets and circles, acting like tiny lenses. The high temperature of the air adds to the effect. Well, this turbulence problem exists everywhere. Up at the nose of the plane we have a severe problem as the air rushes past the telescope. Even astronomers have trouble with it on mountaintops."

"But you shouldn't have any problem seeing these rockets launch."

"We don't, but the turbulence also affects the laser beam as it goes to the target. It gets defocused and scattered. It's enough of a problem that we have to fix it. A secondary function of the beam control system is to reshape the laser beam itself, compensating for the turbulent atmosphere that would diffuse the beam. The beam director does it by making extremely minute modifications to the shape of the telescope mirrors. We can also use this effect to take some really good pictures."

"I think I understand."

"We're ready, sir," Sergeant Adams said.

The temperature of the sensor detector was now within its nominal operating range. "Just watch this." Lance pointed at the video monitor.

"Let's go to full magnification."

Sergeant Adams touched the control screen, and the image bloomed to fill the video display.

"Infrared imager on."

"I'll put it on this screen." Sergeant Adams's fingers flew across his keyboard, and a multicolored image filled the second screen.

"That's the same image?" Aziz asked.

"Yes, sir," Adams replied, "only it's a thermal image. The colors represent different temperatures. The scale is on the bottom of the screen. We use the traditional blue for colder through red and white as the hottest."

"We should get an interesting view as we get closer. Now watch the visible image." Lance pointed at the original screen. "See how fuzzy it looks, how parts of it seem to come in and out of focus?"

Aziz nodded.

"Okay, engage autocorrection."

Sergeant Adams pushed another part of the control monitor.

"Wow!"

Even Lance was amazed. The image of the mountain snapped into perfect focus. Every corner, facet, and ledge was absolutely clear.

"Autotrack." Sergeant Adams had engaged the algorithm that would stabilize the image in the center of the field of view of the telescope.

"Looks like we're going to fly right over it," Aziz said.

They all watched as the dormant volcano grew closer and closer. Sergeant Adams had to reduce the magnification so they could see the extent of the mountain as it threatened to spill off the video screen.

"That's interesting," Captain Hawkins said.

"What?" Lance asked.

"Check out the infrared. See the sharp increase in temperature as you get closer to the edge of the crater?"

"But then it gets real cold," Aziz said.

"That's probably just water in the center of the crater. But look toward the edge of the water—it's hot. Very hot."

"There's not even any snow near the edge of the water." Sergeant Adams pointed at the video image. "The snow goes right up to the edge of the crater, then stops."

"Let's record this," Lance said.

Captain Hawkins pushed a switch on his own console and a tape recorder in the back of the plane began to spin.

"Just how hot is it?" Aziz asked.

"Can't tell," Hawkins said. "The infrared detector isn't calibrated for this kind of observation, but it's pretty warm. See how the gradient increases so quickly? How the color bands are so narrow toward the edge of the water?"

"I think there's steam coming from the edge of the lake." Sergeant Adams was still watching the video.

"Hey, you're right," Lance said.

"Is it going to blow again?" Aziz asked.

"It's possible," Lance said. "I'm no geologist, but the signs of a great deal of thermal activity are certainly there. We'll give the tape to someone at Boeing, and they can pass it along to whoever is watching the volcano."

The only thing now visible on the screen was the blue sky.

"You can go ahead and shut off the recorder," Lance told Captain Hawkins. He turned to Aziz. "The beam control system reached its travel limits when it was pointed down and back at thirty-five degrees. That's as far aft as we can look. Don't want to be cutting off parts of our own plane with the laser beam, do we?"

"What about the wings? They aren't that far back."

"The travel limits are all programmed into the software. Don't worry, I've checked the limits. We won't be shooting ourselves in the foot—or the wing," Sergeant Adams said.

"You know, this Mount St. Helens thing worries me a little," Aziz said.

"Why is that?" Lance didn't see why it should be of concern. "I don't think anyone's in danger."

"Maybe not, but if that thing blows, it's possible we'd be grounded for days."

"Why?"

"The ash. You can't take off if there's much of it in the air. It can screw up your engines royally. I would suggest we make our stop in Seattle as short as possible."

"Good point. I'll ask Colonel Powers about it."

Lance sat down at one of the workstations and plugged his headset in to the intercom. "Pilot, this is Test."

"Go ahead, Major," Captain Williams answered.

Lance was surprised to hear Williams. He hadn't been very involved thus far, having left the entire interaction up to Colonel Powers. "How long to Seattle?"

"Less than thirty minutes."

"Do you have any idea when we're scheduled to depart again?"

"Twenty-four hours was the plan, last I heard."

"It may take a little longer than that," Colonel Powers added. "I just talked to Boeing. The Air Force has identified a colonel who's current in 747s and they're sending him to Seattle to meet up with us. He's having to come from Europe, though, and he isn't scheduled to arrive until the day after tomorrow."

Great. Lance didn't want to lose his pilot. And it wasn't fair to her. "That stinks."

"Agreed," Colonel Powers said.

"Ditto," voiced Captain Williams.

"Well, we may not be able to wait that long," Lance said as Captain Hawkins brought the reel-to-reel tape forward. "Can you call ahead and see if you can find out what the status of that volcano we just passed over is?"

"Mount St. Helens? That thing's been dormant for years," Williams said.

"Maybe not," Lance replied. "Would the local weather guys be following the mountain's activity?"

"You got me," Colonel Powers answered. "I'll find out, though."

"Let them know we identified some significant thermal activity in the crater. She's getting hot. We copied our data onto a tape."

"I'll get someone to meet us at Boeing. You can show them what you've got."

"Okay."

Lance pulled off his headset. The rest of the test crew had been listening over the intercom.

"I think I know what you're up to," Aziz said. He wagged his finger at Lance, smiling.

"She may not be ready to blow," Lance said. "But there's no sense in taking the chance."

"On the mountain, or on the new pilot?" Aziz asked.

"Either."

"We're turning final. Make sure everyone is buckled up back there," Colonel Powers called over the intercom.

"Shut down the system," Lance said.

"Might as well." Sergeant Adams reached up and executed the shutdown sequence. The nose cover rolled over the beam director to protect it. Once it was in place, Adams pushed the master power switch. "Can't see anything anyhow. You sure they can land in this fog?"

"Positive," Lance said, though he had been wondering the exact same thing. It was as thick as pea soup. He and the others swiveled their seats until they were facing the rear of the airplane. From this vantage point he could see out the single small window in the emergency door in the side of the plane.

"We're all set back here," Lance informed the pilot over the intercom.

They continued to descend. Lance held his breath as the pilot pulled power from the engines and began to flare before touchdown. Fog still obscured the view through the window. It cleared only a second before he heard the wheels screech on the concrete.

"Welcome to Boeing field," Captain Williams called over the intercom. "Good landing. Weather sucks. Temperature is a cool forty-two degrees under cloudy skies."

During the short taxi to the hangar, Lance reviewed what little he knew about what had to be done to the plane. He realized he really didn't know much about the maintenance aspect. According to his short discussion with Colonel Powers, even though it was practically a new plane there were still quite a few checks that had to be completed. They stopped and the engines shut down. The main lights in the back of the plane were turned off; the dim emergency lamps provided the only remaining illumination.

"Keep your seats for a few minutes," the pilot called.

After a small bump they were rolling again. Bright
light replaced the gloom through the window in the
emergency door as the plane rolled into a special hangar. Finally they stopped, and the lights came back on
in the rear of the plane.

"We're here, folks."

Lance released his seat belt, and the others followed
him to the emergency exit. He looked through the
window and saw a large set of rolling stairs being
pushed up to the plane. He opened the door and
swung it carefully out. The air that greeted him was
cool and damp, a refreshing change from the warm,
dry air in the airplane.

The hangar was cavernous, much bigger than the
Air Force hangar they had used in New Mexico. In
fact, there was another 747 in the building, with room
for yet another between the two planes. Lance stepped
out onto the landing. Though it was late evening by
now, there were more than a dozen men and women
moving scaffolding up to each of the engines. They
had obviously been primed for this work.

"I'm going to check the laser and make sure everything's okay." Captain Hawkins turned toward the
laser compartment.

"I'll give you a hand," Sergeant Adams said.

"Looks like you guys made it in one piece," Colonel
Powers said as she came down from the flight deck
and joined Lance at the top of the stairs.

"No problems back here, but I was beginning to
wonder if you'd be able to land in this fog." Lance
pointed past the slowly closing hangar door. The lights
beyond were barely visible through the haze.

"Ten more minutes and it would have been tough.

Captain Williams was a big help. He's really a heck of a pilot. Still haven't brought him around, though."

"He still pushing the paperwork to get out?"

"Yeah. I convinced him to hold off sending the letter to the promotion board until after we get back, but he still plans to ask the board to pass him over."

Lance shook his head. "He just doesn't get it."

"Don't worry. I'm still working on him."

"So what's the plan here? I realized a few minutes ago I don't really know what needs to be done."

"Mostly maintenance checks. They're critical on such a green bird. We need to take lots of fluid samples from the engines and hydraulics, looking mostly for unusual metal content. That would signify we have a problem somewhere. It's unusual to find something, but it does happen every once in a while. And there are some general maintenance checks on the avionics and instruments. That's pretty routine and doesn't take too long. They used to have to bring out trucks full of test equipment, but now they just plug the airplane into a computer and the plane tells it what's wrong, if anything. Usually it's a three-day effort, but we'll be running three shifts to compress the schedule. We should be ready to fly about this time tomorrow if they don't find any problems. Our schedule calls for departure the following morning, as soon as the replacement pilot arrives. I'm going to take a quick walk around the plane to make sure all the parts are still here."

Though he knew Colonel Powers was bitterly disappointed that she wouldn't be flying the mission, it didn't show. That reminded him of the tape of the volcano. Was it possible that a looming natural disaster would provide the excuse to get them out of Seattle quickly, keeping her in the pilot's seat? "Hang on a second and I'll join you."

Lance grabbed the tape of the infrared signature they had captured of the volcano and followed Colonel Powers down the steps.

They met the head of maintenance at the bottom. Colonel Powers briefly introduced Lance to the maintenance chief, then briefed the chief about some minor issues she had discovered in the plane's handling. They started walking slowly around the plane as the chief headed up the ladder.

When they got to the front of the mighty beast, she stopped and looked up. "She's a great plane to fly, but this thing makes her look a little strange."

Clamshell doors made of a transparent yet hard material had closed off the front of the beam director. Just beneath the retractable doors was a clear bubble, made of special optical material that would absorb less than one thousandth of a percent of the laser energy as it passed through the bubble on its way to the target. Just beyond the bubble was the beam director, which looked like a huge, ominous eyeball.

"Looks a little like a snake's eye, the kind that has a clear eyelid to protect it." Lance had always thought it was a strange design. But it seemed to work. "We'll need to open the shell to check on the optics and make sure nothing has been damaged during flight."

"And if something's broken?"

"If anything's broken we're out of luck. It'd take weeks to replace any of the major components. It's doubtful anything's broken, though. These mirrors are made of metal and are as hard as rocks. They might be dirty, though. If so, we'll need to clean them. I'd rather do it here, in a somewhat controlled environment. If we wait until we get to Japan, trying to clean them might do more harm than good."

"That can wait until the morning, can't it? I'd hate to slow down the maintenance for anything that isn't absolutely necessary."

"No problem. I don't feel like tackling that problem right now anyhow."

They continued their walk around the plane.

"Looks like everything is still intact," Colonel Powers said.

"I'd certainly hope so." Lance was still concerned about the new pilot, worrying that they would be taking on someone who didn't have a clue as to what they needed or expected of the person flying the plane. "Any word on the new guy?"

"He's on his way over from Europe, or at least from Germany to England. I think he had a layover in England before the leg this way."

"Do you know anything about him?"

"Not a lot. Former NAOC driver, same as Captain Williams. He's a headquarters guy now, USAFE. U.S. Air Forces Europe. I don't know how long it's been since he's been in the cockpit. Couldn't be much over a year."

"Will he still know what to do?"

"You mean will he still know how to fly this thing?" Colonel Powers kicked the tire. "You never forget. He might be a little rusty at first, but Captain Williams can bring him up to speed in no time. The kid's good. Used to be an instructor at his squadron."

"I know you don't think this is the best way to approach this situation, and I don't think so either. If I had any say at all I wouldn't even consider replacing you."

"Thanks. I appreciate it. I can stand here and give you the company line—that I'm just the test pilot and will do whatever the Air Force wants. But between you and me, this sucks."

"It positively sucks," Lance said.

"But what the heck, at least we've got a laser war bird ready to go. As long as your Air Force pilot, your new laser jock, doesn't screw something up, you won't have any problem." Colonel Powers tapped her badge, the one Lance had sent forward for her on the trip out.

"I hope so. I see you got the patch. You like my design?"

"All except the 'Jock' part. Not very appropriate for a woman."

Lance hadn't even thought about that. Every now and then he found himself drifting back into the old mentality, the kind that said the crew consisted of all guys and that was how it was supposed to be. This time he dearly wished it wouldn't be that way.

"So what are you going to do with that tape? Sleep with it?" she asked.

Lance had almost forgotten about it during the awkward conversation. "I was supposed to give it to someone when we got here. It's the infrared data we collected over Mount St. Helens."

"Oh, that's right. They said someone from the university would be by to pick it up. Let's go drop it at the office and head for the hotel to get some rest."

"That sounds like a good idea."

"The ground crew will bring our bags over."

Lance followed her to an office near the hangar. They dropped off the tape, and a driver took them to a hotel that was essentially contracted out by Boeing.

Lance's bag was already in his room. He thought about calling Mandy, but decided he'd wait until morning. It had been a long day. He flipped on the TV, switching to CNN *Headline News*, and dropped onto the bed. There was something on about Korea, a protest or something. Students. Tear gas. He drifted off to sleep.

Lance reached over to hit the snooze button but found himself waving at empty air. Confusion hit him. Where was he? Then he remembered. The television's grainy image slowly came into focus, accompanied by low-level white noise. The phone rang again.

"Hello." Lance could tell he sounded groggy.

"Mr. Brandon?"

"Yeah." It was all coming back to him. He was in Seattle. The clock read five-thirty. There was no light coming through the thin curtains.

"I hate to bother you so early, but the note I got with the tape said you wanted to be alerted if anything came up."

"What? Who are you?"

"Oh. Sorry. I'm John Dickson. I'm a graduate student here at the University of Washington. Geology Department."

Someone started beating on his door. "Hold on a second," Lance told his caller. He walked over to the door and opened it.

It was Colonel Powers. "Have you heard about Mount St. Helens?"

"No, I just got a call. Hold on a second." Lance went back to the phone.

"Hi. I'm back. What did you want?"

"It's Mount St. Helens. The volcano."

"I know what it is. What about it?"

"You made the infrared tape?"

"Yeah."

"I gotta thank you for that. You probably just helped me finish my dissertation."

"Glad I could help. Now what about the volcano?"

"She's gonna blow. We've got a level six emergency warning out now. Everyone is being evacuated."

"You didn't come to that conclusion based on the infrared, did you?"

"Oh, no. Once I saw the infrared I checked the seismic readings and some of the other sensors we have monitoring the mountain. We didn't have anything twenty-four hours ago, but now it looks like we're going to have a major eruption."

"When?"

"Of course we can't say for sure, but my guess is that it will be in twelve to twenty-four hours. Possibly even sooner. And it's going to be big, probably bigger than last time. What I'd like to do is get some calibration data from you so I can finalize my analysis. . . ."

Lance was no longer thinking about the young doctoral candidate on the other end of the phone as he slid the receiver into its cradle. "We've got to get out of here. Now. Let's get the rest of the guys. Call over to the hangar and tell them to get the plane ready for launch."

"I already did."

"The others are in 182, 183, and 184."

Lance stopped at the door next to his own and banged on it loudly. Colonel Powers did the same at the next door.

Sergeant Adams, bleary-eyed, opened the door.

"We gotta get out of here—quick!"

Sergeant Adams was instantly awake. "The Koreans?"
"No. The mountain."

The sun was barely starting to creep above the horizon as the taxi pulled to the gate. The guard waved them through when Colonel Powers waved her identification at him.

"Take this side road over to that hangar," she instructed the driver. When they pulled to a stop she tossed him a twenty for a five-dollar trip and climbed out. The rest of the team followed her to a man who appeared to be supervising the maintenance team that was pushing the big plane out of the hangar.

"How'd the maintenance checks go?" she asked.

Lance noticed he wasn't the same man who had been leading the maintenance efforts the night before. Must have been a shift change during the night.

"The engines look good, Billie. Oil checked clean. Keep an eye on number four, though. The computer showed some kind of temperature spike about two and a half hours into your last flight. Avionics are good, so are the hydraulics."

A man ran up from one of the offices and handed a fax to the maintenance supervisor. He pulled out a pair of reading glasses and quickly looked it over. "Oh. I don't know if you're going to like this," he said to Powers.

The plane came to a stop, and the crew began pushing a ladder up to the rear entrance.

"What?" she asked.

The maintenance chief looked over his glasses and smiled. "I think you're out of uniform, Colonel."

Colonel Powers snatched the paper out of his hands. "I don't believe it," she said as she scanned it.

"What?" Lance asked.

"Where is he?" she asked the supervisor.

"Over in the office. He's been here most of the night."

Colonel Powers left without explaining, running toward the hangar offices where Lance had dropped off the tape the evening before.

"What was that all about?" he asked the maintenance chief.

He was still smiling. "You know, that's a hell of a lady. Everyone around here has a ton of respect for her."

"Yeah. So do we. But what's going on?"

"The colonel has been recalled to active duty. Ordered by the secretary of defense himself."

"Someone must have pulled some pretty powerful strings," Aziz said.

"That would be the guy she just went to thank. He's the president of Boeing. He got in from a trip about three hours ago and heard the Airborne Laser was back here and might be going on a mission. Needless to say, he was thrilled and came straight out here. As soon as he heard how the Air Force wanted to bring in another pilot he weighed in with both feet. I was in the office when he started making the phone calls. He started at the Pentagon, but it was middle of the night out there. When he couldn't get any support from the Air Force he called the secretary of defense at home. Just happened to have the old boy's phone number. The secretary wrote the orders himself, with a dang pen. Faxed the papers out here from his house."

"That's more than just respect," Lance said.

"You're right. That's confidence. He knows as well

as I do that no one can fly that plane better than Colonel Powers. And she's been screwed out of opportunities like this too many times."

"We'd better go check out the systems and get ready," Captain Williams said.

"Go." Lance watched the three men trot toward the plane.

"Say, Colonel." The maintenance chief grabbed Aziz by the arm before he left with Williams. "We made that one little modification you asked for."

"What modification?" Lance asked. Aziz better not have had the Boeing guys change anything without getting approval first.

Aziz pointed at the nose of the plane.

The logo had been changed. The words "Peace Through Light" had been changed.

"Silent Sabre," Lance read. "Perfect."

Aziz joined Williams making the preflight checks on the plane.

"I need a white pen," Lance said. "Something permanent."

The maintenance chief pulled a pen from the huge selection in his shirt pocket. "Will this work? I use it to write on Polaroids."

"Perfect. Can I borrow your clipboard for a second?"

The man handed it over.

"How long before we can launch?" Lance asked.

"Fifteen minutes, more or less."

Lance ripped the patch from his own sleeve. He placed it on the hard surface of the clipboard and started making careful modifications with the permanent marker.

Colonel Powers came running out of the hangar.

"We've got to go. I just heard the volcano is starting to billow ash. No explosions yet, but the wind is blowing the soot this way. Portland airport is already shut down."

Lance noticed she was wearing a different name tape than she had before. She still wore the blue flight suit, but the name tape didn't say "Boeing." Now it said, "Billie Powers, Col., USAF." She must have kept it for just such emergencies.

"Thanks for the help, Chief," she said as she hurried toward the plane.

Lance handed back the clipboard and ran to catch up with her. "You're still slightly out of uniform, ma'am."

"I know. I'll get a real flight suit when we get to Misawa."

"That's not what I was talking about." Lance ripped off her shoulder patch and slapped his modified patch onto the Velcro. Then he bounded up the stairs.

She twisted her arm around so she could get a look. No longer was she a "Laser Jock." Now she was a "Laser Jockette."

The ground power carts were already in place. Lance had his two men buckle up for takeoff while the Air Force's newest active duty colonel went through the preflight checklist. Lieutenant Colonel Aziz was in the jumpseat up front, learning as quickly as he could what it took to fly the big plane. It was going to be a long mission with only two pilots, neither of whom had been able to get a good night's rest. In only minutes Lance got a call over the intercom.

"Test Director, Pilot. Prepare for taxi."

"We're ready back here. That was a quick pre-flight."

"We just got word the Seattle-Tacoma airport has been closed. It's only about twenty miles southwest of here. That mountain you were so amazed with yesterday is throwing its guts up. Just our luck it's blowing everything this way."

Lance felt the plane begin to move forward quickly. The rising sun crept in through the single window over the door.

"How long will this flight be, and are you guys up to it?" Lance asked.

"Initial plan is to stop over at Hickman Air Force Base in Hawaii. That'd be about six hours. Not a problem. We do have the option of refueling inflight and continuing on to Japan. That'd be a little tougher, maybe fourteen hours total. Not to worry, though. I think we'll spend part of the time training our friend from Air Combat Command to pitch in. Show him how to fly a real airplane."

"I didn't know you could refuel a 747 in flight."

"Most you can't, but this is a war bird. The Pentagon paid for the modifications."

The plane turned onto the Boeing runway, and Lance listened in as the pilot went over the abort checklist. It was a quick review. Soon they were hurtling down the runway.

"We'll have to stay low, below ten thousand feet, for the first hour. It's going to be bumpy, but that'll keep us out of the soot. I don't want to risk trashing our engines. You guys might as well stay buckled in back there. And keep your barf bags handy."

Chapter 8

Lance made his way up to the front of the plane. They had already been in the air for six hours, and they were looking at seven more. For some reason they had been directed to continue on to Japan, and a KC-10 refueling aircraft was about to provide them with enough fuel to complete the journey.

Lance wanted to see the refueling in person. He recalled his ROTC training, an orientation mission in a KC-135, the older version of the bigger KC-10. Most of the cadets had gone forward when they were released from the jump seats, but he had opted to head toward the back of the plane. The boom operator was there, down in the bowels of the aircraft. The crew chief had seemed to appreciate the company. He had let Lance lie down on the little platform and fly the refueling boom. It was a strange experience. The platform was like a weight-lifting bench. You had to lie on your stomach and rest your chin on a padded pole. In that position you could see the refueling boom through a periscope mirror arrangement. The boom operator had guided Lance's efforts, showing him how to release the boom and lower it, flying it in the slipstream behind the airplane. Eventually Lance had to give the boom operator control of the system, and then he watched from the side as a giant C-5 aircraft pulled up behind them, bouncing the KC-135 as the bigger plane interfered with the slipstream. The boom operator, a magician with the controls, guided the giant cargo plane into position and deftly slipped the tube into the fuel portal on the customer. It was ballet in the air. This would be the first time Lance had seen the exchange from the receiver's perspective.

He climbed the stairs to the flight deck. Aziz was there, observing from the jump seat. Lance followed his gaze through the windows in front of the pilots. The big KC-10 was already poised in front of them, its refueling boom lowered. Colonel Powers was easing the 747 upward, positioning it for the boom operator to connect the two birds. Lance could see the boom operator sitting in the tail of the flying gas station, controlling the flight of the boom.

Lance picked up a headset from the adjacent jump-seat and listened in.

"Eagle Three Three hold," the boom operator signaled.

"Three Three," Captain Williams answered.

The planes were in position. The boom operator extended the stinger.

Lance could see the boom pass over the cockpit, headed for the port just behind them on top of the plane.

"Connected," the boom operator called out.

Lance hadn't felt anything.

Captain Williams checked his indicator. "Confirmed."

"Ready to pump."

"Check manifold setting," Captain Williams said.

Colonel Powers glanced at a panel, then hit a switch. "Manifold autocontrol enabled. Begin pumping."

"Pumping."

"Now we wait," Captain Williams said.

After a few minutes, Lance decided he wouldn't be interrupting if he asked a few questions. First he checked to make sure his communications panel was set to intercom, rather than radio. "How long does this take?"

Aziz had noticed him step in. "In an F-15, only about half a minute. I expect this bird will take a little longer."

"A full load would take close to twenty minutes. We're only taking on three hundred eight-five thousand pounds, about seventy-five percent of capacity. So it'll take a little less than fifteen minutes."

"That's a lot of weight," Lance said.

"That's why the computer control of the manifold is so important," Captain Williams said. "It wouldn't be a good idea to fill the left wing tank first, then go to the right wing. The plane's balance would be so screwed up we'd end up totally out of control, and we'd corkscrew into the water below with the heavy wing leading the way. The computer will direct the flow of the fuel, shifting the weight from tank to tank while it balances the load."

"It's also a lot of time. I sure hope we don't have to call time-out while we're flying over Korea to get a load of fuel."

"That is a problem," Colonel Powers said. "With only one aircraft, we won't be able to stay in position forever, waiting for the Koreans to launch their missiles one at a time. Refueling isn't a limitation, so long as we can figure out how to do it without the Koreans shooting while we're busy getting gas. The crew will probably limit our time on station. I doubt we'll be able to pick up another pilot in Japan, and there certainly aren't any replacements for you guys."

"Not to worry," Aziz said. "You've got a fighter pilot on board. I can do anything."

"Yeah, right," Colonel Powers said. "But these missions will last a little longer than your normal six-hour sortie. You'll probably need a nap before we get done."

"I think he's right," Lance said. "We'll need all the help we can get. I'll show him some of the tricks in the back, you guys show him how to fly this big thing on our way over to Japan. Aziz will be our pinch hitter."

"Okay, Lieutenant Colonel Aziz. Your first job is to figure out how we can take a fuel break without the Koreans' launching their missiles while we're busy."

"Already got it figured out."

Lance saw a broad smile break across the fighter pilot's face. He was glad they'd gotten the opportunity to bring Aziz along. Lance had a feeling he was going to be a big asset.

The entire crew was exhausted by the time they reached the U.S. Air Force base at Misawa, Japan. The trip hadn't been all that taxing, just extremely long. Lance could hardly wait until the stairs had been pushed up alongside the big airplane. He opened the door before the steps were ready. What he saw wasn't exactly what he'd expected.

The scene that played out in front of him was enough to cause a great deal of anxiety. There were warplanes everywhere. F-15 Eagles, F-16 Falcons, even a few F-117s were lined up in long rows. Other planes also lined the tarmac. Along with some Navy birds were some aircraft with Japanese markings like the ones Lance remembered from old World War II movies. Maintenance crews were swarming over many of the birds. Nearer to where they had parked the Airborne Laser, a variety of larger planes surrounded them. Again, these weren't your standard fare of passenger flying craft. Small aircraft with huge radomes mounted on top of their fuselage—Airborne Warning and Control planes—sat nearby.

"Looks like a whole lot of pain," Sergeant Adams said as he joined Lance at the door.

"Yeah, I can't imagine this much firepower being unleashed against anyone, not even the North Koreans."

"They'd sure as heck know something hit 'em," Aziz joined them as the stairs arrived.

Colonel Powers and Captain Williams were there as well. "Unless there's something you need to do on the laser right now, I suggest we all go get some rest," she said as a small blue bus pulled up at the bottom of the steps.

"Sounds good to me," Lance said.

Aziz was unbuckling the tie-down that held their bags in place in the back of the plane. They grabbed their own gear and headed down the rusting steps. Lance and Colonel Powers dropped their bags near the bus and took a quick walk around the plane. "I requested a power cart from maintenance. They'll bring it out as soon as they can and hook it up. That way we'll be ready to do any work you need as soon as we get back."

"Good. We wrung out the system pretty well on the

trip over. It seems to be working okay, but Sergeant Adams has come up with a couple of ideas for some modifications we can make to help distinguish between multiple missiles fired simultaneously." They rounded the nose of the plane. "Everything looks good up here."

"One thing you have to keep in mind, Major," she said. "This isn't an experiment anymore. We're getting ready to fight, just like all the other folks around here."

Lance noticed she'd begun calling him by his rank as soon as she'd been ordered back to active duty. "I realize that," Lance said, though he wasn't really sure it had begun to sink in just yet.

"Configuration control is going to be critical. Make sure you don't change anything that will cause the existing system to malfunction." They finished examining the airplane and headed to the bus. "I'm not sure how you're configured back there, tapes or disks or whatever, but make sure you can return to the original software configuration at a moment's notice. We know the system works, at least against single-missile launches, and that we can ferret out double launches. Let's not screw up what we've got just to make it a little better."

"I understand. But I'm worried about something Aziz told me—they might launch multiple missiles at once. If that happens, the system we have now won't be able to knock out more than one or two. We're working on a way to get them all."

"Like I said, just be ready to fight from the initial configuration." The colonel and Lance climbed into the crew bus. The others were already aboard.

"I don't know about you folks, but these guys look

serious." Captain Williams thumbed toward the fighters on the line.

"Yeah," Aziz said. "Most of the fighters are fully armed. You don't load a full munitions complement unless something's up."

"What's going on, Airman?" Colonel Powers asked the driver as the bus lurched forward. "This looks like a lot of activity, even for an exercise."

"Can't really say much, ma'am. All's I know is that as of yesterday I've been called to sixteen-hour shifts, just like the rest of the unit. I'm an ordnance technician, so I get to pull eight hours fitting missiles, then another eight driving this wagon. Oh. I almost forgot. Are you Colonel Powers?"

"Yes."

"This is for you, ma'am." He pulled a large sealed envelope from the center console.

"These aren't organic units, are they?" Aziz moved up by the driver.

"No, sir. The Navy birds, the fighters, came in yesterday. From the markings I think they're from a carrier called the *Saratoga*. The bigger planes came in the day before yesterday from Guam. About half the fighters are ours, local boys. The others are from a variety of units. They've been showing up for a couple of weeks now. Lot of Guard and Reserve units are here, too."

"What've we got, ma'am?" Captain Williams asked.

"A little bit of an update and our orders." Everyone leaned toward her to hear above the noise of the little blue bus and the tumultuous roar of the airfield. "Nothing good, I'm afraid. Ulchi Focus Lens kicked off this morning, right on schedule. Only thing different this year is that a Japanese two-star general was right in the middle of it, along with a squadron of Japanese F-16s. The North Koreans responded by going on full alert and moving two of their armor divisions right up to the border. There have been more than a dozen incursions into the DMZ. An AN-2 was even shot down over South Korean territory, near the border. Unfortunately, it was empty except for the pilot."

"That's not good news," Aziz said.

"Why?" Lance asked. "What's an AN-2?"

"A large twin engine biplane. It flies so slow you could almost get out and push it. Hard as heck to shoot down. The North Koreans use it to ferry special operations forces around. That's always been assessed as phase one of their attack plans—put the saboteurs in place."

"So if it was empty . . . " Sergeant Adams said.

"Yeah. They've already unloaded. No telling how many other missions have been flown."

"What about our orders?" Lance asked.

"Japanese intel is going to meet us tomorrow on the plane to give us the latest. We're to be here at oh seven hundred. After that we're to stand by. If things get dicey, we launch. That's about it." The colonel put the envelope in her helmet bag. "I gotta tell you guys, I feel like we're working on a shoestring here. All our support seems to be coming from the Japanese. First the initial request to bring us into the country, now the intel preps. I have the feeling that COMUSFOR-KOREA is slow-rolling the Japanese to keep us out of the picture."

Lance was sure his confusion registered on his face when the colonel explained.

"Commander, U.S. Forces Korea. He's the American in charge of all our personnel in the Korean Area of Responsibility. For some strange reason they've recently put an Air Force officer into what's traditionally been an Army slot. I got the skinny before we left Seattle. Turns out he's the same general who killed the funding for this project. I don't think we can expect a lot of support from him."

"Shoestring is right," Aziz said as the bus jerked to a stop in front of base ops. "I don't know how we're going to interface with anyone if we do launch. First off, no one knows we're here or what we can do. Second, even if they did, they wouldn't know how to talk to us or use us."

"We need a link to AWACS, at a minimum," Captain Williams said.

"It would be nice to have a battle manager on board." Aziz climbed down from the bus.

"Thanks for the ride," Colonel Powers told the driver.

He waved and pulled away.

"I don't think we'll be able to find a battle manager that can be spared." Colonel Powers followed the others inside the building. "They're in short supply everywhere, and the crews that are deployed here aren't going to give anyone up."

Once inside, the group came upon some kind of disagreement near the ops desk. A lieutenant colonel had his finger stuck square in the middle of a major's chest and was reading him the riot act.

"Look, Major, I don't know who the hell you are or where you came from, but you aren't putting anything on my plane."

"Talk about a small world," Aziz said. He headed

for the two officers locked in heated debate while the others tried to arrange a ride to billeting.

"But, sir, the orders will be here any minute." The major had been backed against the desk and didn't have much more room to maneuver with the colonel's finger still poking him harshly in the chest.

"Stuff it! I'm damn near ready to court-martial your butt for ordering my maintenance crew to install that crap without my approval."

"Didn't have time, sir—you were nowhere to be found."

"Bull! You didn't try hard enough. You should have paged me." The colonel turned and walked away.

"We did page you, sir." The major was talking to the colonel's back.

"You can pick up your gear on the hangar floor. I don't want to see your butt anywhere near my plane or my crew again. Dismissed," the colonel said over his shoulder.

Aziz walked up to the flustered major. "Critter, every time I run into you you've got some colonel ticked off."

"Well, hey, Skeeter. What the heck are you doing in Japan? I thought you were a headquarters puke."

"I am." Aziz lowered his voice. "I'm on a special mission. And I go by Yoda now."

"No kidding?" Critter lowered his voice as well. "What kind of mission? And what the heck is a Yoda?"

"Like you always say, If I tell you I'll have to kill you."

Critter smiled. "You're finally in the spook business? I always swore you'd never pass the polygraph."

"No, this is better than the spook business. Check out the patch."

" 'Laser Jock'? What the heck is that?"

"I'll tell you about it later. What's the colonel so mad about?"

"Long story."

"Yeah. And if you told me you'd have to kill me, right?"

"You got it. Basically, I needed to put some special gear on his plane and catch a ride. Orders are supposed to have cleared by now, but you know how that goes. By the time he finds out I'm legitimate, he'll be flying circles over South Korea. I didn't want to wait, so I asked his crew chief to start putting the gear aboard. We tried to page him, but I think he was 'indisposed.' "

"What kind of ride do you need?"

"Don't really need the ride as much as I need some four hundred cycle power and a clear line of sight. If I'm closer to Korea, that'd be even better."

"Line of sight to what?"

"Let's just say a clear shot at where a satellite might just happen to be."

"We're all set." Lance and Colonel Powers walked over to where Aziz was whispering to the major. "They've got room at the visiting officers' quarters. We can get something decent to eat over there, too."

"Colonel, Lance, this is Major Critter Warren. He may be the solution to some of our problems."

"How's that?" Colonel Powers asked.

"We need an intel guy and a connection to AWACS. Critter here used to be a battle manager."

"Long time ago," Critter said. "But I still know how they work."

"After his hitch in AWACS, he snuck into pilot training. I keep running into him, but I haven't ever been able to figure out what it is he flies. Something to do with the intelligence business."

"I can't really go into details, ma'am."

"Why are you here in Japan? What unit are you with?"

Lance thought the colonel's questions relayed his sentiments as well. This was suspicious.

"Again, I can't really go into the details. I can only say that I'm supporting a special mission. Normally I run it from stateside, but we've had some equipment problems recently. What I need is a SATCOM patch with a close reach over to Korea."

"You can't hook up with the AWACS crowd?"

"That's what I'm supposed to do. The orders are on their way, but there must have been some screwup at the Pentagon. And the AWACS ops officer won't bend at all."

"The Pentagon? Fourth floor?" Colonel Powers asked.

Critter didn't answer.

"These problems you're having—anything to do with the solar storm?"

Again, Critter didn't say anything.

"You know a Tom Driscoll?"

"Yes, ma'am." A wide smile spread across Critter's face.

"This mission of yours is a Boeing special project I worked on about twelve years ago. I still get a look at the operations reports when I do my two-week annual tour. I thought I recognized your name."

"Can I get some support from you, then?"

"Absolutely. Lance, this guy's all right. In spite of the company he appears to keep."

"Aziz is just my cover," Critter said.

"Okay. You need a real cover. You have any more of those patches, Lance?" Colonel Powers asked.

Lance fished the last one out of his pocket and handed it to Critter as Captain Williams, Captain Hawkins, and Sergeant Adams joined them.

"We're all pretty beat," Colonel Powers said to Critter. "And we've got warning orders to be prepared to launch at any moment. What exactly do you need?"

"Access to your plane. That's it. I've got my own crew, and as long as you have standard racks I won't even need to drill any holes."

"We've got a set of three racks that aren't being used," Lance said. "They're configured for a command and control center. SATCOM antenna is already installed. If it's the right configuration I don't see why you can't use it."

"Perfect."

"We'll need the weight and balance charts," Captain Williams reminded them.

"Oh, this is Captain Williams, copilot. Captain Hawkins and Sergeant Adams make up the rest of the crew."

"Good to meet you." Critter exchanged greetings with the others.

"We're running pretty light right now, sir," Captain Williams told Critter, "so the weight won't be a problem unless it's extreme."

"No problem. Four hundred fifty pounds total, without the operator."

"Piece of cake."

"Obviously," Lance said, "we don't want you fooling with the equipment that's already installed."

"We won't touch it," Critter promised.

"Do you need me to stick around and lend a hand?" Sergeant Adams asked.

Lance realized the question was directed at him. He also recognized the inference, knowing that Adams really meant, *Do you want me to keep an eye on our system while these guys screw around?* "No. You're as tired as we are. Why don't we give Critter your pager number, Colonel? If he runs into any problems he can call."

"Good idea." The colonel turned back to the ops desk and jotted down the pager number she'd been assigned by the ops people when they checked in. Since they were on warning orders, the ops desk would have to be able to reach her at any time. She handed the slip of paper to their new command and control officer. "Have at it. We're going to get something to eat, after which I'm going to take a long shower and climb between some sheets."

"Thanks a lot, ma'am. I'm sure Colonel Driscoll will pass word on how much support you've been."

"I hope so. What I really expect is for him to buy the drinks when all this is over."

"Oh, one more thing, ma'am," Critter said as the others started toward the door.

She stopped and turned. "What is it?"

"Exactly which plane is yours?"

Lance wasn't sure if it was the siren or the phone that woke him up first. He grabbed the phone as the siren continued to wail outside. "Major Brandon."

"Good morning, Major. It's showtime." Colonel

Powers told him over the phone. "Dress as quickly as you can and meet me in the lobby downstairs."

"What's going on?"

"I'm not sure, but my pager went off and I called ops. They said we were to man up. Something must be happening in Korea. Maybe we'll find out when we get to the plane. Get Adams and Aziz. I'll get Hawkins. Don't use the phone, it'll take too long to get through. Hear the siren? We're not the only ones being called in. Ten minutes."

The line went dead. Lance had to hit the light on his watch, since it was still dark outside at only five A.M.

Lance quickly pulled on his flight suit and stumbled out into the darkness. He was on the third floor of an apartmentlike building, with access to the rooms provided by an exterior walkway. Turning left, he beat on the door to the next room.

Sergeant Adams came to the door quickly. "What's going on?"

"We've got to get to the plane." Lance had to yell over a new cacophony of sirens that were now blaring over the visiting officers' quarters' own speakers.

"Got it," Adams said and turned back to his room.

"Be in the lobby in ten minutes." Lance was already running to the next door.

"What took you so long?" Aziz asked as Lance approached his already open door.

"We've got to be downstairs in ten minutes." Lance was out of breath. That was unusual for him, as he was in good shape. Must be the excitement. Aziz seemed to notice it, too.

"Chill, Lance. Want a cup of java?"

Lance noticed Aziz was already dressed, even shaved. He was holding a cup of steaming coffee.

"Uh, no. I've gotta get back. Downstairs. Ten minutes."

"Got it already. I'm on my way. I'll see if I can find some coffee for the rest of you guys. By the way, you need a shave."

As he headed back to his room, Lance wondered how the heck Aziz had gotten ready so fast. Men and women were piling out of the doors all around him, hurrying to answer the call of the sirens. Back at his room, Lance grabbed his toothbrush and threw a few essentials into his helmet bag. He was certainly glad he had showered away the remnants of the long Pacific flight the night before. He glanced at his reflection in the mirror, then decided there was no time to shave. He'd have to do it later. He shoved his toothbrush into his mouth, grabbed his helmet bag, and headed for the door.

The lobby was a zoo. A stream of blue Air Force buses took turns at the front door as crews gathered and boarded. But just as each bus pulled away, dozens of other airmen arrived in the lobby from their rooms. They were in extremely high spirits, pumped, which surprised Lance at first. But then he realized these airmen were warriors, and they were about to take up the fight.

Aziz was standing near the hastily erected breakfast stand, talking to a short lieutenant colonel wearing a flight suit. Lance pulled his toothbrush out of his mouth and shoved it into his pocket, then pushed his way through the milling crowd to get to Aziz. Before he reached him, Aziz high-fived his friend and the colonel left for the filling bus.

"Who was that?" Lance asked.

"That was Lieutenant Colonel Turbo Miller. An old

friend of mine. He's also our competition. Want some coffee?" Aziz offered a Styrofoam cup.

"Thanks. What do you mean, competition?"

"He's here with a flight of four modified F-22s. Raptors. Upgraded radar and weapons specifically designed to find and kill missiles."

"I wish him the best of luck," Lance said.

"Seriously?"

"Yeah. I don't really care who gets the missiles at this point. As long as someone gets them."

"You haven't heard, then?"

"Heard what?" Lance had to raise his voice as the doors near them opened and another crowd of airmen hurried toward the waiting bus. They were a noisy bunch, whooping war calls.

"The North Koreans lobbed two missiles this way about three hours ago. One fell short, and the other passed just over the island and landed in the ocean to the East. The communists are gravely worried, and plenty ticked off, that the Japanese joined Ulchi Focus Lens. The exercise kicked into high gear just about the time we got here last night."

"That is not a good sign." Colonel Powers joined them, choosing a sticky bun from the table of sweets nearby. "Where are the rest?"

"Here comes Sergeant Adams." Lance spotted Adams elbowing his way through the crowd. "I don't see Hawkins or Williams."

"I didn't get enough sleep," Adams said as he grabbed a donut, then started shoving another half dozen into a plastic trash bag he pulled from one of his pockets. "For later."

"Don't worry, there'll be food for us out at ops," Colonel Powers said.

"Here comes your copilot," Aziz said.

Captain Williams wandered through the crowd, not seeming to be in much of a hurry. Hawkins pushed past Williams and began working the donut table.

When the team was finally together, Lance repeated what Aziz had told him.

"Yeah," Colonel Powers said, "that's what I heard, too. Let's talk about it on the bus. Anyone that wants some, grab a cup of coffee and let's get on the next ride."

Captain Williams hadn't said anything. He took a couple of donuts and a cup of coffee, then followed the small band toward the doors.

"Where's Major Critter?" Colonel Powers asked Aziz.

"Don't know. Maybe he's still out at the plane."

"I hope they're not right in the middle of installing something. If they are we may have to just rip it out and leave 'em behind."

"You think they may want us in the air pretty quick?" Lance asked as he flopped down on the seat beside his pilot.

"That's entirely possible."

On the short bus ride out to the flight line, Colonel Powers filled them in on what she had been told, which wasn't much more than what Aziz had already said. She did confirm that neither of the two missiles fired at Japan had been armed. "But General Killeen, who's leading the exercise, received a communiqué from the North demanding that he discontinue the exercise. If he doesn't, the next missiles will be armed. He was given twelve hours to decide."

"And has he?" Aziz was smiling. He already knew the answer.

"He's decided all right. He's not going to be pushed around."

Base ops was an even bigger zoo than the hotel had been. As they arrived, flight teams were moving into the small briefing rooms to get their orders.

"JFACC must have been up all night cutting the frags," Aziz said. "I'll go make sure we can get some flight lunches while you check in at the ops desk. I have a feeling this is going to be a long mission."

Colonel Powers nodded. "Be back here in fifteen."

"What's a JFACC?" Suddenly Lance had the feeling he was extremely out of place. The airmen around him knew what they were doing; they had practiced this type of exercise over and over. He didn't have a clue.

"Joint Forces Air Component Commander," Colonel Powers explained as she lined up behind a major waiting patiently at the ops desk. "He's the guy who has to figure out how to get all these planes in the air, make sure they know where they're going, what route they're going to take, what target to hit, what weapon to hit it with, how to get out of there, how much electronic warfare support they need, fuel, and on and on. Once he figures all that out, he cuts the frag—mission order—and gives them to the pilots."

"Sounds complicated."

"Computerized systems help a lot." Colonel Powers stepped up to the counter as the major in front of her moved out of the way. "Eagle Three Three."

The sergeant behind the counter, bleary-eyed, nodded and turned to sort through a stack of envelopes on the desk behind him. He pulled a yellow sticky off the envelope before handing it to the colonel. "Oh, yeah, the base commander is out at your bird, and he's got a Japanese two-star with him. You're supposed to head to the plane as soon as you get here."

"Thanks. Just what we need," Powers said.

"What's that?" Lance asked.

"Japanese officer coming to help us out. I need that like I need a bad engine."

Colonel Powers took the folder and turned to find the rest of her crew. She spotted Captain Hawkins and Sergeant Adams near one of the small rooms, trying to listen in during the packed briefing. She waved them over. "Let's go."

Hawkins and Sergeant Adams stepped in behind them. "What about Aziz?"

Just then Aziz and Williams stepped in from the outside door. They each held paper bags in both arms. White boxes were stacked inside. "Chow. As much as we could carry. It's nuts over there. They're just stacking boxes on tables for people to carry away."

"Glad you're here," the colonel said. "We gotta get out to the plane. The deputy base commander is there with some Japanese two-star."

Lance and Adams each took one of the sacks and they all piled into a blue bus, much like the one that had provided their ride from the plane to base ops less than six hours earlier.

"Why all the attention?" Aziz asked.

"Don't really know." Colonel Powers peeled open the yellow envelope. She passed several charts to Aziz, who shared them with Captain Williams. Powers sorted through the rest of her data. "Maybe this will explain."

Aziz and Williams stopped examining the charts and joined Lance, Hawkins, and Sergeant Adams as they examined several eight-by-ten photographs. They were grainy black and white shots. But what they showed was clear enough.

"Missile fields." Sergeant Adams pointed at one of the more obvious missiles, still lying flat in its erector/launcher.

"Same ones I was shown back at Albuquerque," Lance said. "See the almost linear layout of the sites? But here, and here—the missiles are missing from those launchers."

"The blackened earth shows why," Captain Williams said. "The lunatics launched them. Must be the two that were fired at Japan."

"Undoubtedly," Lance agreed. It appeared their wayward captain finally was accepting the gravity of the situation.

The bus jerked to a stop off the left wingtip of the Airborne Laser. The passengers piled out, thanking the haggard driver for providing the lift. There were several other vehicles near the plane. Two were standard maintenance vans; one was a high-ranking officer's staff car. The other two were nondescript. Lance wondered what they were doing there. He followed Colonel Powers up the steps, carrying his paper sack full of inflight meals.

"I see you've raided my kitchen." A full colonel greeted them just inside the door.

"We thought it might be a good idea. Don't know how long we'll be up. I'm Colonel Powers."

"I suspected as much. I'm Colonel Thomas, Deputy Base Commander. And this is Major General Nakano."

A Japanese officer, the only person not wearing a flight suit or battle dress uniform, extended his hand. He bowed slightly as Colonel Powers shook his hand.

"This is the rest of my crew," Colonel Powers introduced Lance first, then the others as they put down their bags of food.

Lance couldn't help but notice her unusually matter-of-fact attitude toward the Japanese officer. She certainly wasn't being her usual friendly, diplomatic self. Maybe it was the lack of rest.

"We've already met the rest of your group," General Nakano said.

"Who?" Colonel Powers asked.

The general pointed past her toward the rear of the plane. "The maintenance people who've been assisting you. I didn't know you would be able to conduct such an effective electronic warfare campaign with this new weapon."

"Huh?" Colonel Powers seemed confused.

Lance was just as confused. Then he noticed Critter coming forward, leaving five or six other men in the back working on his system.

"I've briefed the general on our EW capabilities, ma'am. I couldn't give him a demonstration of our moving-target-detecting radar, though. We haven't quite finished repairing that high-voltage fluctuation that caused us such a problem on the flight over."

Colonel Powers looked at Critter. She obviously had no idea what he was talking about. She just smiled at him. "I trust you'll be finished by the time we get ready to launch?"

"Absolutely, ma'am. We're just putting the covers back on the racks now."

Lance understood. Critter, aboard when the two officers showed up, had had to pretend he was part of the crew but didn't know what to say about the laser. Instead, he'd made up some lie that had kept the senior officers occupied while he installed his top-secret equipment. Right under the Japanese officer's nose. Lance smiled.

"Your executive officer has been very hospitable."

"Yes." Colonel Powers glanced at Critter as he walked back to his installation crew. "My executive officer is quite good at what he does."

"I suppose you're wondering why we're out here?" the deputy base commander asked.

"Yes, I am."

"It was at my request that Colonel Thomas allowed me to take a look at this fantastic weapon," the Japanese general said. "It was at my request that you are here to begin with. The Koreans have been threatening my country with a weapon we do not have the means to defend against. When I heard of this technology I was not only greatly impressed but also quite jealous. We have a great need for this defensive weapon, as you probably realize from the events of just the last few hours."

"It was fortunate your request came when it did," Lance said. "The program was about to be canceled."

Colonel Powers glared at Lance. He was taken aback. What had he said? He trusted her, though, and shut up.

"Canceled? Why cancel this program?" The general wasn't looking at Lance, but directly at Colonel Powers.

"It wasn't our decision. You'll have to ask the Pentagon for any information on programmatic issues. We just fly it and fight it. And that's what we need to get busy doing. Our orders want us in the air as soon as possible. If there's nothing else?"

"Only one other thing," the general said, picking

up a small box from the beam control work desk. "I realize it took a great effort on your part to bring this weapon to my country's aid. You could easily have turned down our offer, given the developmental nature of this project. We are extremely grateful. As a gesture of gratitude, I would like to present to each of you a gift."

The general handed out six of the boxes.

"Well, aren't you going to open it?" the base vice commander asked.

Lance was curious about what was in the box, but he wasn't certain of the protocol for this situation. He waited.

Aziz, on the other hand, ripped off the thin ribbon holding the box together and pulled out what looked like a handkerchief. It was white, but in the middle was a red circle. "An ascot."

He put the ends of the triangular cloth around his neck and snapped them together. As he stuffed the other corner inside the collar of his flight suit, the red circle remained centered at his neck.

Lance had started to open his own box when Colonel Powers handed her box back to the Japanese general. Shock registered on the general's face as he slowly accepted the return of his gift.

The base vice commander was not pleased. "Colonel, I don't know what you think you are doing, but in this country it is extremely disrespectful to decline the offer of a gift."

Lance had never seen Colonel Powers's face burn as red as it was now.

"I really don't care what your precious protocol calls for in this situation, Colonel." She had stepped forward and was almost nose-to-nose with the base vice commander. "It doesn't apply."

"It appears I have offended you." The Japanese general put the box under his arm. "For that I am sorry." The general was acting contrite, as if he had not been offended himself.

Lance would have tried to defuse the situation and gotten on with business, but Colonel Powers did not want to let it go. "With all due respect, General, we are not here as mercenaries. I will not wear your symbol of imperial power. I am an American, as was my uncle."

"Your uncle? I do not understand."

"Then you haven't done your research as well as you should have."

Colonel Powers had moved and was now facing the Japanese officer. Whereas she'd had to look up slightly at the base vice commander when she confronted him, she was eye-to-eye with the general. "My uncle was with the Thirty-first Infantry, 1942, in the Philippine Islands. Your army captured him there. Sent him on a little walk to a place called Bataan. We call it the Bataan Death March. He survived that forced march, while many other Americans were brutally slain. When you couldn't kill him there you put him on an unmarked Japanese vessel, in direct violation of international law. That ship was attacked by American warplanes. My uncle was killed during that attack."

The Japanese general said nothing, his face blank. Perhaps he knew that anything he could say would be inconsequential, irrelevant. Not even an apology, if that had been possible, would have meant anything.

Aziz jerked the ascot from around his neck and

wadded it up, then stuffed it into the box and closed the lid. He held it out to the general.

Indignantly, the general took the box.

One by one the other men returned their gifts, unopened.

The general looked disappointed. His eyes met Colonel Powers's. "There is no excuse I can make about the past. I respect your opinion. I want you to know that my people are depending on you."

Colonel Powers waited a moment before replying. "Your people have nothing to fear. In this fight we have a common enemy, and in facing that enemy we will fight beside you. But we will not fight with you."

The general bowed, deeply this time. The base commander just stood there, dumbfounded. He hadn't seen such a breach of protocol since being assigned to the base. What would it do to his already tenuous relations? Colonel Powers remained standing staunchly upright. The Japanese general turned to leave, the base commander following him closely. Lance could hear Colonel Thomas apologizing, already making excuses for Colonel Powers's behavior.

At the door the general turned and addressed Colonel Powers. "Godspeed, Colonel. And good luck."

Colonel Powers nodded, and the Japanese officer left with the apologetic base commander hot on his heels.

"I'm sorry ma'am," Aziz said. "I didn't know. I just like free stuff."

"No problem, Aziz. I just didn't want the Japanese to think we were fighting for them. Not for their military, anyway. We both have something to lose here, and if I have anything to say about it we're not going to let the communists force themselves on the people of South Korea. I will defend the Japanese if necessary to be successful."

"I believe you handled yourself quite appropriately, ma'am," Critter said, joining them from the back of the compartment.

"And just what is all this garbage about electronic warfare?" she asked.

"Had to tell 'em something. They came out here while we were installing the SATCOM gear. Just a little white lie to cover up what we were doing. I didn't have time to stop work, so I just let them watch while we installed the crypto gear. They think it's a radar warning receiver. Wouldn't they be surprised to know it was top-secret communications equipment?"

"I suppose." The colonel turned to her copilot, who had been silent through most of the discussions with the Japanese. "Captain Williams, I suggest you go pre-flight this bird. Make sure the flare and chaff canisters are loaded. We launch as soon as possible."

"I'll give you a hand." Aziz followed the captain out.

Lance had been watching Captain Williams through most of the ordeal with the Japanese general. He had seen the captain smile for the first time. Perhaps he was beginning to gain some respect for Colonel Powers. Lance would have to find time to talk with her about that. Maybe he was coming around.

"Are you ready yet?" Powers asked Critter.

"Yes, ma'am. Just cleaning up now."

Two men passed them heading for the door, carrying tools and empty cases. They wore civilian clothes, but their haircuts betrayed their military affiliation.

A third man, also in civilian clothes, stopped to talk to Critter. "You're all set, sir. She's powered up and on-line. We couldn't run an end-to-end check for obvious reasons, but we did verify comm back to home base."

"Great. Thanks, Sergeant. You guys going back to the VOQ?"

"After you launch. Wouldn't want to leave before you got under way."

"Okay. I'll look you up there when we get back. We'll probably have to pull this equipment back off to ship it back to the base."

"Assuming this doesn't take too long, we could probably just give your men a ride back and drop you off at your base." Colonel Powers offered.

"Thanks, ma'am," Critter said. "But that wouldn't work, for security reasons."

"Well, the offer still stands. I sure wish I'd brought some coffee."

"The coffee's on, ma'am," Critter's sergeant said. "And your galley's stocked. We took the liberty last night. The commissary was open, and we were waiting for the ground crews to bring up power carts. You've got a pretty nice setup on board. I don't think you'll need those inflight rations."

"Thanks," Colonel Powers said.

"No problem. My major tends to eat a lot. Just keep an eye on him for me. Remind him his wife has him on a diet. There are half a dozen microwave dinners in your fridge that say 'low calorie' on them. They're for him."

"Gee, thanks a lot," Critter said. "What would I do without my nursemaid?"

The sergeant smiled and went to the door. "Good luck, sir. Say hi to the boss when you talk to him."

"Will do. You guys try to relax a little, but stay on

your toes. Do like I told you and find some chem-bio safety gear before you hit the hay."

"Lance, is your system ready?" Colonel Powers asked.

"We're all set, ma'am." Sergeant Adams handed her and Lance each a Styrofoam cup filled with hot coffee. "I powered up and ran it through the self-test when we got on board. It's working fine."

"Good. And thanks."

Aziz and Captain Williams came back through the door after completing their preflight.

The sky behind them roared as the first flight of warplanes launched into the early-morning air. Williams pulled the door shut behind him, deadening the noise.

Captain Hawkins came out of the forward galley with his own cup of coffee and another donut.

"Gentlemen." Colonel Powers addressed her assembled crew. "We're most likely off to war. Stay on your toes and keep Captain Williams and me informed of any problems, potential or otherwise. If this does turn into a fight, you will no doubt experience the fog of war unlike any you have ever seen. We're bringing a new weapon into the fray, and no one is going to know how to use us. The battle managers will hold us in reserve and will use what they've already practiced with—the F-15Es and F-22s to take out the missiles, assuming they can get through. We'll have to show them what we can do. At first they won't believe what our abilities are. We'll have to show them again. Then they'll believe and will want to use us extensively."

Critter volunteered his services. "Aziz told me you don't have much in the way of communications with the battle managers aboard AWACS. I can do that for you when I'm not busy on my primary mission."

"That'll be helpful. Just keep us in the loop."

"Yes, ma'am."

"Okay, go through your checklists and report in when you're ready." Colonel Powers said, then headed for the front of the plane.

Lance took out his own checklist, and Captain Hawkins made a quick inspection of the laser compartment. Nothing was out of place, so they returned to the console to verify fuel levels. Sergeant Adams was already finished with his checklist and sat back in his seat, a half-eaten sandwich in one hand.

"Good idea." Lance grabbed one of the boxes and pulled out a sandwich and a can of orange juice. He plopped down in his seat and completed his checklist. Outside, one of the huge plane's engines spun to life. It was time.

Chapter 9

"Prepare to taxi," came the call over the intercom.

"Okay, shut down the systems and buckle up." Lance pulled his own seat and shoulder restraints tight as his crew, now with the addition of Critter as their own battle manager, settled in for the takeoff.

"COMUSFORKOREA is broadcasting a message to the theater forces," Colonel Powers said. "I'll patch it through over the intercom."

Lance turned up the volume on his own panel.

The voice that came through was garbled. "Ladies and gentlemen, welcome to Korea. This is General Killeen, and I wish you could have joined me here at a better time. We have a tense situation, as you well know. The North Koreans have spent forty years intimidating the free and democratic people of the South. In spite of the collapse of their economy and the mass starvation of their people, the communists of the North insist on harassing and threatening the peace-loving people of the South.

"By inviting the Japanese to join in the current exercise, the South Koreans are trying to bridge the gap and restore long-stagnant diplomatic, social, and military ties with other countries. North Korea does not understand this concept. Once again this morning, the

North Korean government has demanded both the withdrawal of Japanese forces, of which there are only a few thousand, and the termination of our command post exercise. This will not happen.

"The North Koreans are woefully poor in military equipment, training, and logistical resources. What they lack in matériel, however, they more than make up for in propaganda, misinformation, and blind loyalty from the troops of the line. While I do not expect that we will face them in combat, I want each and every one of you to exercise extreme caution. One mistake could easily induce the communists to use their weapons of mass destruction and invade South Korea as they have constantly threatened to do. Caution is the byword. Exercise it faithfully.

"If, on the other hand, my prognosis is inaccurate, and we do have to face the Koreans in combat, you have my word that we will do so with great force and even greater resolve to bring this event to a swift, decisive, and victorious end.

"God be with you."

Lance sat quietly. He noticed that the continuous noise of launching jets had abated while the speech was being broadcast. Now, in the near distance, the hollow rumbling of jets taking to the skies began anew. It was time to go to work.

"Good speech." Captain Hawkins was eating a sandwich at the laser operator's console.

"Propaganda," Critter replied from the back.

"What do you mean?" Sergeant Adams asked.

"Well, there was no need to make that speech for us. We all know what we're here to do. Normally, if a commander wanted to say something to his troops it would come out in message traffic, not broadcast over the airwaves for everyone in the world to hear. Including the enemy. That your take, Aziz?"

Aziz replied from the front of the plane, where he, too, had been listening over the intercom to both the speech and the subsequent discussion. "Yes. Preemptive?"

"Could be," Critter answered.

"Preemptive what?" Lance asked.

"Preemptive strike."

Even though Lance didn't really believe that was what the military had planned, he certainly realized it was a possibility. If it did happen, his laser system would need to be up to the task.

"We're number one for takeoff," the copilot announced over the intercom.

Lance pulled his seat restraints tight once more. Though he didn't consider himself a very religious man, he bowed his head and said a prayer.

Driscoll felt strange, taking off without a solid telemetry link to control at the target site. In fact, it was flat-out dangerous. Too many unknowns could turn the mission into a disaster if control wasn't sorting out what was important and advising him on what to do. As Driscoll pushed the Aurora into the initial phase of its orbit, he would have to decide whether or not to continue the mission when he got near the target, after he came out of the space portion of the flight. If he didn't have a good connection to Critter in theater, it would be a difficult call to make. "Launch Control, this is Aurora. Thanks for the help. See you in about three hours."

Driscoll tried to relax as much as he could while the speeding aircraft approached fifty miles in altitude and made the transition to spacecraft. This was the part of the flight Driscoll enjoyed most, looking up at the heavens without the intervening atmosphere to blur the view. It was a beautiful night, with the moon behind him rapidly falling into the shadow of Earth, the stars leaping from the sky to invite him into their realm, the realm of peace. It was no less beautiful than it had been on his very first flight.

He briefly became lost in thought, luxuriating in a visual perspective that few humans would ever have the opportunity to see. His sabbatical was short-lived, though, as his mind kept returning to the dangers of the mission he was about to undertake.

The prebrief had been just that—brief. He had made this same journey seven times in the last month, each time learning something new about North Korea's air defense systems and their fledgling, though potentially deadly, missile program. Things were getting hot over there, and COMUSFORKOREA needed this mission urgently, perhaps for a potential surgical strike to take out the missile fields themselves, or maybe even for a full-fledged assault. The general hadn't yet made his plans known, at least not to a lowly lieutenant colonel assigned to a secret air base ten thousand miles from the theater.

All Driscoll knew was that the mission was urgent and had received a wartime priority. Korean intelligence had gotten wind of a Dong Feng Five, a long-range Chinese missile that hadn't been seen in any of the pictures Driscoll had taken previously. That particular weapon had the range to make California, or any of the western states. The intelligence had also indicated there was a nuclear tip to the deadly arrow. It was a single magic bullet that could decisively, catastrophically, affect the course of this potential conflict.

The solar storm had come at a particularly bad time, knocking out several relay satellites, including the ones Driscoll and the Aurora relied on to provide that critical link between the pilot in flight and the person in control, his virtual copilot. In a mission like this one things could happen quickly, and Driscoll desperately needed Critter to back him up. If he couldn't reach Critter when he got in theater, he'd have to decide whether to try the mission on his own or to abort for safety reasons. Driscoll already knew what his decision would be.

Driscoll listened to the small thrusters that were beginning to slow his orbit, allowing him to fall back into the atmosphere. It was time to try to connect with his good friend. He keyed the encrypted radio: "Control, this is Aurora, do you copy?"

"Aurora, this is Control, airborne aboard Eagle Three Three. I read you."

"Copy, Control. Am beginning de-orbit now."

"Verified. All telemetry links are good to this location. Are your onboard recorders functioning?"

"Affirmative."

"I thought Walker was supposed to fly this mission," Critter said.

"The flight surgeon grounded him. Sinus infection. I'm all you've got."

"You could always send young Killeen back in."

"Not a chance," Driscoll answered.

Critter could hear the strain in Driscoll's voice as the acceleration of the de-orbit forced him deep into his seat. It was an all too familiar feeling. "Be advised it is a very densely populated airspace you are about to enter. Your flight over the main landmass should not be a problem, just use caution at the periphery of the border. Lots of our friends are out for this party."

"Copy that. Do you have a good battle picture?"

"That I do, via solid telemetry link to AWACS."

"You aren't aboard AWACS?"

"That's affirmative. I'll explain later. I've got a good view of the traffic. No trouble so far?"

"None. Either the Koreans can't spot me when I'm at Mach six or they know their weapons can't get to me. Either way I'm happy. This is getting to be pretty routine now. Entering left turn to two three zero per flight plan."

Driscoll had made five flights over North Korea, and a couple over South Korea in the last month. Only once had he needed to fly low and slow, and that was safely over South Korean territory. All the other flights had been made over clear skies, allowing him to fly high and fast, far from the searching eyes of the North Korean air defense units.

"Copy. I have you on screen. Nothing in your flight path. Have at it."

"Wilco. I'll check in with you on the other side, unless something comes up."

"Standing by."

Driscoll leveled off at fifty thousand feet and pushed the throttle forward. The cameras came on automatically when he was still fifty miles from the North Korean shoreline. The recorders, a mainstay of the original program, had been reinstalled after the solar storm had made the data relay satellites unpredictable. The data was still being shipped over the secure telemetry link, but if any of the satellites failed he would have a backup copy of the video with him when he returned to base. The current problems with the satellites had also driven the need to execute the Forward Control Contingency Plan, sending Critter into the theater to monitor the operational phase of the mission. Driscoll wasn't quite sure what kind of aircraft Eagle Three Three referred to. He didn't recall it being an AWACS, and Critter had confirmed that. He wondered what had gone wrong.

"Are you gonna let me know what it is you're doing?" Lance said as he walked up behind Critter.

Critter sat back and folded his arms. "I didn't get approval to tell you guys what you really need to know. I did put in the request, but that takes time. I'll tell you what I can, though. You'll be able to figure it out anyway, since we didn't get the additional encryption gear installed in time. It was lower priority than the rest of the equipment."

"You mean what you just said went out in the clear?"

"No. Our external broadcasts go out encrypted. Optimally you wouldn't have been able to listen in over the intercom and understand it either. We would have had an additional set of encryption devices that would hide our communications from the rest of the AWACS crew, or from your crew, in this case. That's what we didn't have time to install. So what have you figured out so far?"

"Sounds like you've got some kind of reconnaissance mission going on, but I didn't understand the talk about de-orbiting."

Critter mulled that over. "You've already heard enough to figure out what we can do, and since you're the mission commander I need to brief you. I'll worry about getting the right clearances to tell you later."

"Or you'll have to kill me, right?" Lance hated that old joke. It was so arrogant.

Aziz joined them.

"No, only fighter pilots," Critter said.

"How is everything up front going?" Lance asked.

"Fine," Aziz said. "We're at a staging point, a race-track pattern about halfway between Japan and our mission location. COMUSFORKOREA, General Killeen, hasn't decided if he wants our help or not. According to Colonel Powers, there are some high-level discussions going on between him and the Japanese two-star we met at Misawa."

"How long can we stay here?" Critter asked.

"You mean here in this orbit or up in the air?"

"In the air. How long before we have to return for fuel?"

"We've got fuel for nine or ten hours. Refueling would give us another dozen hours or so. That's it, though—the engines can't take much more than that. We'll start to hit the MTBF without some maintenance."

"MTBF?" Lance asked.

"Mean time between failures. We'd be pushing the engine's endurance without checking metal content in the oil, stuff like that."

"Okay, so we've got about twenty-four hours, pushing it. But we can't fight while we're taking on fuel. You said you had an idea to get around that. Did you have time to work it out while we were in Japan?" Lance asked Aziz.

"While you guys were all having your beauty sleep, some of us were working. Right, Critter?"

"You mean you didn't sleep at all?" Lance asked.

"I got a couple of hours in. I don't need much."

"I'm not worth a flip if I don't get at least six hours," Lance said.

"You learn to adapt when you need to. I never have needed a lot of sleep anyway."

"That's the truth," Critter said. "When we were at the Academy, Aziz would sleep for two or three hours, then he'd be up doing his assignments by flashlight. He made the academy look like a cakewalk while the rest of us were busting a gut trying to get our assignments and all the other assorted crap done."

"It all comes from living a good life."

"Bull. I've read about weirdos like you who don't need sleep. Wander the house at night. That's why I say I might have to kill him if he finds out what this is all about."

"Critter was just about to fill me in on what he has going on. But first, what about the refueling problem?"

"Don't worry. It's handled, kind of. We'll play that card if we need to. Who knows, maybe Critter's boy will find out all the missiles are gone."

Critter looked at Aziz. "Just what do you know about this already?"

"Nothing. Honest," Aziz answered.

Aziz was smiling, and Lance was pretty certain he knew a lot more than he was letting on. Aziz seemed to know a lot about everything, even the stuff he wasn't supposed to know about, like Critter's mission.

"Well, this is a multipurpose display. Right now I'm getting a feed from a high-speed airplane that's configured for reconnaissance. You were right about that, Lance."

Lance nodded.

"What I'm about to tell you is classified Special Access and I'll have to get you to sign a release form when we get back. What you heard about a de-orbit refers to the fact that our reconnaissance aircraft is partly spacecraft. It is launched from a secret base and actually goes into a low Earth orbit to get to the target zone quickly."

"You're kidding," Lance said.

"No, sir. We built on some of the technology that was to go into the National Aerospace Plane before that program was killed. We've been flying this system for several years now."

"Unbelievable."

"Normally I'd be controlling the mission from our home base, but as you know we've been having a problem with the relay satellite system. Moving forward into theater lets us use a single bounce system off a stationary satellite in geosynchronous orbit. This is also our standby mode in case we have to go to war. We'd normally send a system into the theater anyway as a backup."

"But you had to go into theater this time, because of the satellite relay problem?"

"Exactly. And that's a good thing for you."

Lance watched as Critter used a track ball on the desk to move a cursor over a set of menu items on the right side of the screen. When he clicked one of the items, the image on the screen was replaced by a much different picture.

"This shows all the aircraft in flight in the area being covered by the prime AWACS. The outline shows the North Korean border. You can see we have quite a few aircraft tracks near the border, both over

water and over the South. I can select to display
fighters, tankers, even Japanese forces."

Critter moved the cursor and clicked another menu
item. Almost all the aircraft tracks disappeared, leaving
about six. "It's just like being a battle manager inside
AWACS. These are the Japanese Air Self-Defense
Force aircraft. You can see they are staying well back
from the front line. Probably a political consideration."

"What kind of planes are they flying?" Aziz asked.

Critter moved the cursor over one of the tracks and
clicked on it. A small box with the aircraft type, the
pilot's call sign, and other information popped up beside the cursor. "It's a Mitsubishi F-1. Call sign is Sam
Three Six and he's at twenty-two thousand feet, heading two zero zero, four hundred fifty knots."

Critter, still wearing his headset, moved his hand
quickly up to one ear and held up a finger. "Hold on."

Lance could tell he was listening intently as he
moved the cursor over to the menu and highlighted
an item. A single marker appeared right smack in the
middle of North Korea. Critter ran the cursor over
the top of the blip and clicked on it. The message box
came up as it had before, but this one was called simply Aurora. Aurora was at forty-two thousand feet,
heading due west, and the speed read "M 4.6."

"That doesn't mean Mach four point six, does it?"
Lance asked.

Critter didn't answer. He was busy discussing something over the radio.

Lance had his headset with him, and he plugged
into an available intercom panel.

". . . pings coming from both forward quadrants.
Please advise."

Critter selected another menu item, and a series of

six rings appeared along Aurora's flight path. Two of the rings encircled the tiny blip.

"You've got SA-6s all the way in to the target. Recommend you maintain heading and increase speed to Mach six. The SA-6 false alarm rejection algorithm should dismiss you because of your speed."

"Copy, Control. Accelerating to Mach six point zero."

"I don't believe it," Lance said to Aziz.

Aziz had remained silent while Critter was helping Driscoll figure out how to avoid detection. But now he agreed with Lance: "Nothing can fly that fast, certainly not at that altitude."

Critter was waiting, watching his display. "Heck, the Aurora doesn't even have its afterburners lit. Driscoll's barely moving."

A red light began to flash in the upper left corner of the display.

"I've got a launch detect," Driscoll reported.

"Confirm. They must have disabled the false alarm rejection algorithm. Suggest you push the throttle up to military power."

"Agree. Accelerating to mil power."

Lance watched the number on the display change rapidly from M 6.0 until it steadied at M 8.2.

"Aurora at mil power. Pictures aren't going to be too good at this speed."

Critter split the display until he had a rapidly moving image scanning across the top half of his screen while the air situation remained in the lower half. "The image is still pretty good. Certainly good enough to count missiles. Keep your eyes open. You've got two more bogies after you."

"Copy two more bogies."

Lance had noticed the warning light as it signaled the launch of two additional missiles.

"He doesn't sound too worried," Lance said.

"The SA-6s aren't a problem—they'll never catch him at the speed and altitude he's at. He's just trolling for SAMs at this point. The more missiles they waste firing at him, the fewer they'll have left to fire at the slower crowd if they have to go in. You know, those slow fighters like the F-15s Aziz is always bragging about."

"I still don't believe he's flying at Mach eight." Aziz shook his head.

"Believe it. He's just outrun the first SA-6, and the others are quickly falling back. If he didn't need to get the pictures, he'd punch the afterburners in and get the heck out of there."

"But that's only because he's at such a high altitude, right? If he was at a lower altitude, even Mach eight wouldn't be fast enough."

"That's right. We had some close calls a few weeks ago when we were making similar photo runs. The requirement out of Washington had us running at twenty thousand feet. They wanted some really high-resolution shots of the missile field. We were hoping the stealthy attributes of the bird would keep us safe, but the Koreans have apparently developed a system that can pick the Aurora up. It was a very close call."

"Control, this is Aurora. I am clear of the threat, feet wet and shutting down camera. Preparing for return to base."

"Affirmative, Aurora. I confirm you are clear of the threat. Will monitor transition to low orbit."

"This I gotta see," Aziz said.

The big plane made a hard turn to the right, unlike

the gentle turns they had been making for the last hour while they held well outside North Korean airspace.

Colonel Powers's voice came over the intercom. "We're going in, folks. Better saddle up."

Lance turned to sit down in his chair between the beam control operator and the laser device operator. They had been asleep in their seats before the hard bank, and the call over the intercoms woke them both. "Might as well fire up the systems," Lance told them.

Lance glanced over his shoulder at Critter's station. He could still see some of the display, but he didn't have a very good view. It looked like Critter was reviewing the video data from the Aurora's run. He was stepping through it frame by frame and appeared to be looking for something.

"We've been cleared to standby position about fifty miles off the North Korean coast," Colonel Powers informed them.

"That's still too far out," Lance said. "We need to be at least twenty miles closer for good sensor coverage."

"Understood," Colonel Powers answered. "But for now that's as good as we can get. From our orders it looks like things are heating up, but my guess is COMUSFORKOREA doesn't yet trust us. He's probably only moving us in close enough to appease his Japanese cohorts there at staff."

Aziz climbed back into the jump seat behind the pilot and plugged back into the intercom.

Colonel Powers continued, "We are cleared into position at fifty miles out, but we are on weapons hold. Confirm weapons hold, Mission Director."

So formal. "Stand by." Lance checked the laser sta-

tus panel. All modules were on-line, thanks to Captain
Hawkins's quick work of bringing the system up. "Put
all laser modules on standby. That'll save a little fuel,"
he told the device operator. The status lights changed
from green to yellow on all twelve modules.

"Pilot, this is Mission Director. We are weapons
hold."

"Very well."

Lance wondered how they could even help if they
weren't allowed to fire the laser. Then he had an idea.
"Sergeant Adams, let's do a sensor sweep, see what
we can find out there."

"But we're at weapons hold, sir."

"I know, but that doesn't mean we can't take a look
around, does it?"

"I guess not. You want the fire control radar up
as well?"

"Bring it up, but keep it on standby—no emissions.
I just want to exercise the infrared, see what we can
tell from this far out."

The screen in front of Sergeant Adams lit up with
a false color image that appeared as a slightly curved
horizon. The upper half of the screen was black, with
the edge of the Earth's surface indicated by a slightly
red color. Earth itself showed up as blue. There were
hundreds of small red dots on the left side of the
screen.

Adams pointed at the dots. "We're picking up jet
engines here in the South. There are a few in the
North as well."

Lance hadn't even noticed the dots up North. They
had to be North Korean fighters.

"Lots of planes in the air." Captain Hawkins was

looking over at Adams's screen. With his lasers on standby, there was little for him to do but watch.

"That's probably only a third of them," Adams said. "At this range we can only see their engine signature if they're flying away from us. We can't see them if they're flying toward us or even perpendicular to our track."

"That batch is flying away from us, but heading north," Lance said. "Wonder what's going on there?"

"Our guys have been vectored north. They're about to conduct a strategic attack against the missile fields," Critter informed them.

A huge void settled in Lance's gut. This was it—they were going to war. He punched up the AWACS frequency so he could monitor the activity. The frequency was extremely busy and hard to understand, particularly for someone who wasn't familiar with the jargon or the procedures they were using. Lance switched it off and turned to Critter for a play-by-play. "What's happening?"

Critter held up one finger again, asking for patience. He was busy warning his pilot of the impending action. Lance switched to Critter's frequency.

". . . heating up down here. You might as well get ready for a return visit. I suspect they'll be asking you for another recce pass in short order."

"Copy. Can you get word to the base to let them know we'll need to be ready to turn quickly?" Driscoll asked. He was exhausted already, and didn't look forward to back-to-back flights without the regulation twelve-hour rest. But he was the only qualified pilot now, with the exception of Killeen, and Driscoll was nearly ready to take the information he'd gathered to the inspector general—Killeen, chief of staff's son or not, was never going to fly for the U.S. Air Force again.

"I'll try," Critter said. "But with wartime communications minimize in effect you'll probably be within radio range of the base before I can get word back."

"Understood. Do the best you can."

"You're fading now. Have a safe flight."

Aziz joined them from the front of the plane. "I heard you guys spotted some planes heading north."

"Yeah." Lance pointed back at Sergeant Adams's screen. "The infrared sensor gives us a pretty good look at what's going on. I was trying to find out what Critter had heard from AWACS."

Critter tried to make a radio call to AWACS, asking them to relay a message back to the Pentagon. It was tough for him to get through, but he finally succeeded. The person he finally talked to seemed a bit aggravated. The AWACS battle manager told Critter he didn't have time to relay messages—he was too busy fighting a war.

"At least you tried," Lance said.

"Yeah, about what I expected. That's one of the downsides of working on such secretive programs—no one knows about it, and so they don't care. They'd probably be more interested in helping if they knew the targeting information they just passed to the F-22s was gathered by Aurora."

"F-22s? Aziz said one of his friends was flying some specially modified F-22s, but I didn't think they were in production yet."

"Another classified program that is just now coming out of the closet. I heard you guys talking about the jets you saw heading north." Critter turned to his display and made another menu selection.

Lance watched as the screen changed to show the positions and flight paths of selected aircraft over the Korean Peninsula. There were four jets currently heading north. He pointed at the screen. "That's them?"

"Sure is. These F-22s were developed under an accelerated program and are specially designed to find and take out ballistic missiles. They're called Strike Raptors." Critter put the cursor on the lead plane and pulled up the data. "Recognize the call sign, Aziz?"

"Reno." Aziz's eyes lit up. "That's Turbo's flight."

"The guy you were talking to this morning?" Lance asked.

"The very same. I didn't know he was flying the Strike Raptors until this morning," Aziz said.

"Yeah. He was in on the program from day one. I even heard it was his idea," Critter said.

"But will it work? Are they stealthy enough to get past the air defense?" Lance asked.

"I guess we're about to find out," Aziz said. "This could be a very short war, or it could become very long. Depends on how Turbo's guys make out."

Lieutenant Colonel Turbo Miller hadn't expected to be put into play this quickly in the game, but he was ready. He glanced back to check on the rest of his flight. The first four production F-22 Raptors had been pulled out of the initial production lot and reconfigured for this special strike mission. Turbo was flying one, and the three others were right with him. He checked the mission panel—they were only three minutes from the border. Time for the final mission check. "Reno Flight Status?" he called over the secure short-range radio link. The answers were immediate, in almost a rapid-fire stutter:

"Two."

"Three."

"Four."

He provided a quick report to the battle manager flying safely hundreds of miles away: "Have Hammer is go for prosecution."

"Copy. Have Hammer cleared for prosecution. Good luck."

Luck. At the Academy they taught you never to count on luck. You counted on excellent training, dedicated warriors, and the very best equipment. He had them all. The men in this flight were seasoned Gulf War vets, their skills honed under fire. America's best and most loyal. No Fear was their motto, and they lived it. The equipment was the newest and the best, the stealthiest fighter aircraft ever built. Turbo smiled. This was their coming-out party.

As they crossed the border into North Korea, Turbo knew that by crossing into the North's national airspace he had just fired the first shot in the newest war, one he was certain would be quick and decisive. As soon as he and his men took out the communists' missiles, they would have no strategic weapons with which to threaten Japan or the people of the South. Without missiles, North Korea would have to rely on starved, weary ground forces. It would be a cakewalk for the rest of the Air Force to counter any offensive the North could throw together. That's what made Turbo's mission so critical. To be effective he had to get in quick, kill the missiles, and then get the hell out. That would pave the way for decisive interdiction strikes by the rest of the Air Force and, hopefully, provide a quick conclusion to the fight. They had to do the job quickly, before the Chinese could get involved.

As they approached the first waypoint, Turbo began to receive new target coordinates from AWACS. That wasn't good—another missile target had been identified. It was within the known missile field, but was now the top-priority target. Why hadn't they spotted this target earlier? He didn't like last-minutes changes to the mission, particularly if they were deemed so important as to redirect his weapons.

On the Airborne Laser, Critter noted the change in the F-22s' mission. "I was afraid of that," he said.

"What's wrong?" Lance asked.

"The AWACS battle managers have reprioritized the target set for Turbo's flight."

"Why would they do that?"

"Let me show you."

Critter changed the display again, pulling up the video the Aurora had collected. It was the same imagery Lance had seen him studying earlier.

"See that?"

"Yeah, it's a missile. Looks like all these others to me."

"Not quite. It's hard to tell the difference between the missiles, but you can see the launcher isn't the same."

"What difference does that make?"

"That's a Chinese Dong Feng Five, an inter-continental ballistic missile. It can easily reach halfway down into the United States. Not quite to Washington, D.C., but New York is certainly susceptible, as well as most cities on the northern part of the eastern seaboard."

And California. Mandy and the kids were back home by now. Were they at risk?

"This isn't good news."

"That's not the half of it. Before I left the States I was reading a recent intelligence summary about our little missile field there in Korea. They guy who's running the show is a Chinese national who married a Korean scientist. He's got ties to the Chinese nuclear weapons program. The South Koreans have tracked a series of shipments to the missile site that are similar to the way the Chinese transport their nuclear weapons. It doesn't paint a very good picture."

"What would they do with a nuclear weapon?" The hollow pit in Lance's stomach had now climbed right up into his throat.

"Do you know the last time the continental U.S. was attacked?" Aziz asked.

"I guess during the Civil War?"

"That's right. With the exception of some guy up in the Northwest who was killed by a bomb the Japanese floated over on a balloon during World War II, the Civil War was the last time we've fought in the lower forty-eight. We've already seen the dramatic way that losing American soldiers during a war can sway public support against it. That one was called Vietnam, and its continued legacy almost caused us to bow out of the Gulf conflict. Can you imagine the public uproar if a fight in Korea spread to the U.S. mainland? With nuclear weapons killing thousands of civilians? It would be unthinkable. The president would have no choice but to pull us back, and the North Koreans would have won."

"It's unthinkable to use nuclear weapons against civilians." All Lance could think of was Mandy and the girls. What if they couldn't get the missile before the Koreans launched it? What if it was aimed at California?

"Tell that to the United States government. Remember a little place called Hiroshima? How about Nagasaki? I guarantee you the Japanese and the Koreans remember it."

"But that was necessary," Lance said.

"I agree." Critter joined in the discussion. "And I'll bet you the North Koreans will have no difficulty justifying their use of a nuke, either."

"I hope Turbo and his cats can get through." Aziz said.

"Doesn't look like he's having a lot of luck right now." Critter pointed at his display. Red circles were lighting up all along the flight paths of the four little dots that were now invading North Korean airspace.

Turbo had known things to go to crap in a hurry, but this was a case study. At the optimum altitude of twenty thousand feet, they should've been invisible to the North Korean radar and perfectly positioned to drop their laser-guided bombs. The plan was to completely surprise the Koreans—their first indication that the Americans were even there was supposed to have been the bombs going off in the middle of their missile field. That wasn't going to happen now.

The radar warning receivers had been blaring intermittently ever since they crossed into North Korean airspace. Turbo had led his planes higher in an attempt to reduce the return signal to the radar receivers. That would put them higher than was optimal in order to hit the targets, but if they were shot down before even getting to the targets it wouldn't make a heck of a lot of difference. Then the radar warning receiver went off again.

"I've got radar warning, search mode," called his wingman.

"Affirmative. Stay tight." Turbo led the four ships as he climbed another five thousand feet, the upper limit of their accuracy for a successful bomb run. Any higher and the probability of accurate hits diminished drastically. The warning receiver sounded again, this time using a wavering tone.

"I've got track mode," his wingman warned.

That wasn't good. But what happened next was worse—the missile launch detector went off.

"Tallyho. SA-6s inbound. At least four of them."

Crap. Time to go back to the basics. "Gentlemen, looks like we're flying a billion dollars' worth of useless stealthy garbage. This high-tech stuff has obviously met its match. Let's see if the plane can at least perform as advertised. We're at the final waypoint. Three and Four break off. Head for the deck and see if you can get the missiles above you, make them go ballistic. Meet you at the target zone. Good luck."

Turbo pushed the control stick forward and to the right while simultaneously shoving the throttle full forward. He was pushed back in his seat as the afterburners lit off and he accelerated toward Mach 2. The flight suit inflated around his legs as the G-forces increased, almost causing him to lose consciousness. As he dived forward he rolled the airplane over in a classic "split S" maneuver, hoping his wingman was hot on his tail. The acceleration force pinned him into the custom-molded ejection seat, preventing him from even turning his head to check on his cover.

He rolled out at three hundred feet above the ground, heading in a sweeping curve that would bring him into the missile field from the northeast. The other flight would come in from the southwest, and they would crisscross in the middle of the target zone. They had rehearsed for this eventuality, and he had come up with an innovative tactic to fire on the targets. He hoped it would work—from the looks of things they were only going to get one shot at this.

At optimum altitude they would have "buddy targeted," with one aircraft dropping the laser-guided bombs while his wingman used an onboard laser to guide the ordnance to the target. At this altitude that approach would be impossible. The alternative was to fly a crossing flight path and rely on the aircraft coming toward you to lase the target for your bombs, while you targeted for the other planes. It had worked in practice. Sort of. It had taken three attempts flying against precisely known targets. And of course they weren't under fire at the time.

"Coming up on final waypoint for bomb run," the wingman called.

They were off to the north about ten miles. Turbo pushed his stick to the left to correct their flight path.

"Mark." They passed the waypoint, one minute away from the target zone.

The sky lit up around them as antiaircraft batteries blindly opened fire. The shells were thick as fleas, exploding above them at about five hundred feet. Again, not a good sign—that was the altitude they would have to climb to if they intended to have any chance at all of hitting their targets. The concussions from the bursting shells began to rock the Raptor as Turbo quickly evaluated their options. There was no choice. He pulled slightly on the stick, hoping the defenders wouldn't position their artillery where falling shells would litter the missile fields. He was only partially right.

The radar indicated two high-speed aircraft approaching from thirty miles out. That would be the other Strike Raptors.

"Light 'em up," Turbo called.

Onboard computers on the aircraft evaluated sensor images to identify and mark the missiles in the field below them with pulsed laser beams. Turbo pulled up, climbing to get enough altitude to drop his weapons. He keyed the stick as one of his weapons emitted a tone through his helmet earpiece, indicating that one of the inbound aircraft had marked a target just in front of his plane. Turbo felt the plane tug slightly as the first of his weapons was released from the internal bomb bay.

Turbo watched the targeting display as his own laser bounced quickly from target to target. Ahead of him he saw a flash of light that was too low to be an antiaircraft round. One of the other Raptors had dropped on a target. Things were finally going well.

Then the two Raptors ahead of him dropped off the radar display completely. He looked up just in time to see two fireballs, much brighter and faster than any of the other flashes he'd seen until then. The flames blazed into the earth below.

"Reno THREE, Reno THREE, do you copy?" Turbo knew it was useless. The targeting lasers had disappeared, along with the two high-tech multimillion-dollar airplanes and their brave pilots.

"The flak got 'em," his wingman reported. "I have no targets."

There was now no way to precisely put their weapons on the targets they were assigned to kill. There was only one other thing they could do.

"Reno Two, remember how to carpet bomb?"

"Affirmative."

"Follow my lead." His primary target was still there. He might not hit it, but he sure as hell wasn't going home without trying. Turbo turned the nose of the plane slightly north. There was a glimmer of an extremely bright light off to his right. He hoped it wasn't what he thought it was.

"Things are not going well," Critter said. He'd been continuously giving Lance and the rest of the crew status reports on what was happening, as near as he and the AWACS battle managers could determine. "Looks like we've got a missile launch."

"Another SA-6?" Aziz asked.

"No. Slower. Bigger. They may have launched one of their ballistic missiles."

"I've got a target, sir," Sergeant Adams called. "Now two of them."

Lance contacted Colonel Powers. "See if you can get us approval to fire. There are two missiles being launched now."

"I'll try."

"Bring 'em up on-line," Lance told Captain Hawkins at the laser console. "I don't want to have to wait for the laser to warm up if we get clearance to fire."

Captain Hawkins's fingers flew over the keyboard, and the yellow lights slowly faded to green as the individual modules came up to their normal operating parameters. "We're good to go. Just give the word."

"Trajectory?" Lance asked.

"Looks like we've got one headed south, the other due east."

East? The nuke? "Can you tell what kind of missiles they are?"

"I don't think either one is the Chinese ICBM. The spectrographic data indicates they're standard No Dong variants. Unless the Chinese missile uses exactly the same fuel, it's probably not one of these two. We've only got about twenty seconds before the first missile is out of tracking range, forty-five seconds for the second one."

"Any word?" Lance asked the pilot.

"Nothing. I can't even get through."

"Recommendations?"

Silence. It was Sergeant Adams who finally spoke up. "There's something to be said for asking for forgiveness later. The first missile is ballistic, no signature to fire against. Only twenty seconds left for the second missile."

Adams was right. "Target it!" Lance ordered.

"Sir"—Sergeant Adams had already locked the tracker on the missile—"I have the target."

"Range?"

"Two hundred twenty kilometers."

The beam control display showed the range, right next to the time the computer estimated would be needed to kill the missile—eight point three seconds. There was no time to waste.

"Fire."

The laser rumbled slightly as the photons chased each other through the optical train and sought their target. The beam director pointed the laser in roughly the right direction, guided by the infrared sensors. Then the autotrack algorithm dithered the beam in a spiral pattern as it searched for the missile. When the laser struck the missile, the reflected energy closed the track loop and the beam-pointing telescope focused the beam on the missile's casing. The missile started to cook.

"I have a lock, sir," Sergeant Adams said.

"Parasitic, module two." Captain Hawkins reached up and dropped laser module two off-line before the energy reflected from the missile—the parasitic—could cause an unstable oscillation within the laser itself, causing it to self-destruct before the missile was down. "Bringing reserve module thirteen on-line."

"Three seconds," Sergeant Adams said.

Two clocks were counting on the beam control console, one showing the elapsed time and the other showing the time remaining until the model predicted the missile should be destroyed.

"Six seconds."

"Come on, baby," Captain Hawkins coaxed his laser.

"Nine seconds." The digits on the second clock, the one displaying the estimated time to negation, turned red and began counting upward.

"Come on." Lance closed his eyes and crossed his fingers. What was taking so long?

"Twelve seconds."

Lance gripped the side of his chair. What was going on? The missile should be down by now. He scanned the displays over both consoles. There was nothing that would explain the extensive time it was taking to bring the missile down.

Just then a bright yellow flash saturated Sergeant Adams's beam control panel.

"Got it!" Lance yelled.

"Detonation, fourteen point three seconds of beam time." Sergeant Adams informed everyone.

The excitement in Adams's usually calm voice was hard to miss. "Good job," Lance told him.

"Holy crap!" Captain Williams called from the co-pilot's vantage point. "Blew it to bits! I could see the fireball from here."

"Wonder what kind of warhead it had," Lance said. "Probably not nuclear."

"Doubt it," Critter said. "According to the intelligence reports they've only got one nuke, and it's on the long-range bird. My guess is high explosive. These shots were for PR."

"PR?"

"Public relations. The enemy has shown us that an attack using conventional, or even high-tech stealthy aircraft, is fruitless. The next step in a conventional psychological operation would be to show that not only are his weapons safe from harm but they are also effective. For that I would fire high explosives. Using chemical or biological warheads might provoke an unexpectedly adverse public response. What the North Koreans want to do is show their military superiority."

"But they weren't successful," Lance said.

"I disagree. The first missile got through. They will not admit that they fired two. They probably haven't even figured out what happened to the second one. We can hope they'll think it blew up on its own because of some kind of malfunction."

"We ought to let 'em know it was us," Sergeant Adams said. "Let 'em know the U.S. Air Force is here to shut them down."

"That's the last thing you want," Critter said.

"Why's that?" Lance asked. "If they knew we could blow up their missiles, they might just back off."

"And do what? Wait for the South Koreans to invade? That's what they have been expecting all along. No, what the North Koreans would do if they knew we shot down their missile is come after us, and for now, the guy running our show down there doesn't think much of us and probably wouldn't do much to defend us. That'd take fighter support away from his battle. He can't afford to risk losing his air superiority, such as it is."

"But we have to at least let our command know what we did," Lance said.

"Absolutely. He'll be ticked off that we didn't hold fire as instructed, but he'll have to take into account that we succeeded where his Raptors failed. I've met General Killeen before—his son was in our unit. Still is, actually. No telling which direction the general will lean, but my guess is that he'll leave us up here just in case he can't figure out what else to do. I'll pass the word and try to find out what happened to the missile that got through."

"Sounds good. I'm going to work on the assumption that we're still going to be allowed to fight. We need to find out why the laser took such a long time to kill the missile," Lance said.

"That's for sure. If they launch a bunch of those things at once we won't be able to knock down half of them."

Lance turned back to ask Captain Hawkins about the laser module that went off-line while Critter talked with the battle managers in the AWACS.

"The power level was optimized," Captain Hawkins told Lance. "Even though I had to take module two off-line, I brought a reserve module up almost instantly. I've checked all the calorimetric measurements. This definitely wasn't a power problem."

"Can we bring additional modules on-line?" Lance asked.

"Not if we want to keep the optics in one piece. We're running at the highest peak power load the mirrors can take. Bringing on more power would almost certainly cause one of the optics to blow."

"Was it something in the fire control?" Lance turned his attention to Sergeant Adams's console. "Excessive jitter?"

"I don't think so, sir," Adams replied. "Everything looks good. All the parameters were in line with our earlier test results."

Lance rubbed his chin. Something was wrong, but he didn't see what it might be. "So what does that leave?"

"My guess is the models are wrong," Captain Hawkins said.

"How?"

"The range calculations have been extrapolated from tests at much lower power. Physics is a funny thing—scientific predictions don't always match real-world results."

"So the measurements we made at a hundred kilowatts don't necessarily reflect what might happen if we shoot a beam that's a hundred times more powerful."

"Exactly."

"Or maybe the missiles are different," Sergeant Adams said. "Maybe they aren't even painted. That would make them more reflective, and less energy would be absorbed by the skin of the missile body."

"Another possibility," Captain Hawkins agreed.

"Either situation calls for the same solution," Lance said.

Though everyone nodded in agreement, no one liked the answer. Finally Lance said it for them all: "We've got to get closer."

"I'm getting a report on the fate of the first missile," Critter said over the intercom.

Chapter 10

"Let me patch this into the intercom so the folks up front will know what's going on, too." Critter switched into the aircrew net. "Here's what I've got so far. According to trajectory analysis, the missile we shot down was fired at Tokyo. The missile that got through was aimed at Seoul. Just as I suspected, it was armed with a high-explosive warhead."

"Aren't there Patriot batteries stationed to protect Seoul?" Aziz asked, as he returned from the front of the plane.

"Yeah. They're not very effective, though," Critter continued. "The missile was equipped with several decoys. The Patriots were sucked off and the warhead slammed into the downtown area. Pretty massive damage, hundreds of dead civilians. Not good news.

"As expected, the North Koreans are blaming the United States for an invasion. Somehow they've already got Raptor parts on display for the news crews. They worked fast."

"Any reaction yet?" Lance asked.

"Not much, as far as the AWACS guys can tell. CNN is their best link for that kind of news. Most everyone in the States is still asleep, but a couple of congressmen were interviewed in their nightclothes, wanting the president to justify his actions."

"Well, I'm sure glad we got the other one, at least."

"The Japanese are, too," Critter said. "And that gives us a problem. The Japanese general has made a public statement, thanking the U.S. for allowing the Airborne Laser to defend his homeland."

"Great. Now every North Korean out there is going to be gunning for us. What did Nakano do that for?" Aziz asked.

"I'm not sure, but it was probably self-interest. My guess is that our good friend General Killeen was planning to send us back to Japan, but that would leave the Japanese homeland an easy target. They've seen what little use the Patriots are, and the Raptors couldn't get in. I hate to say it, but it may be that General Killeen didn't want us to steal the limelight. He probably has plans for another airborne assault on the missile fields. Needless to say, we're now a known quantity to the North Koreans."

"What about our status?"

"I don't have anything."

"We got word up here just a minute ago," Colonel Powers said. "We're to stay on station, at least for the time being."

"That won't work. We have to get in closer, even closer than we had planned. If they launch more than a couple of missiles, we won't be able to get them."

"I'll pass that along," Powers said. "But I don't think it'll do any good."

"Hold on to your horses, boys and girls." Critter was holding the earpiece tight to the side of his head. "We've got another problem. AWACS informs me we have a flight of four MiG-29 Fulcrums headed this way. We're at the outer limit of their fuel range, and they're making a beeline straight for us."

"Anyone to intercept?" Colonel Powers asked.

"Negative. No aircraft can be diverted to assist. We're on our own."

"How's that peashooter of yours against MiGs, Mission Commander?"

"I'm not sure, but aircraft are going to be a lot harder to kill than ballistic missiles."

"Well, either we stand and fight or we turn and run."

"If we run, we've lost." Lance was still thinking about the nuclear-tipped Chinese missile and its long-range ability to reach the U.S. "And there will be nothing to stop them from firing their missiles at will. I say we stand and fight."

"If we turn around, we save the plane and live to fight another day," Captain Williams said.

"But there may be no battle left to fight," Sergeant Adams said. "I say we stand."

"We stand," Lance said. He was in charge, and he sensed that with the exception of the copilot, all the others were with him.

"We don't have to decide just yet," Critter said. "AWACS will track the Fulcrums for us. They're still about twenty minutes away from being within missile range."

"That gives us twenty minutes to knock 'em down. Beam control, what've we got to track 'em with?"

"Not a lot. I can use the aircraft radar to get a general fix, but that won't give us a fire solution. We'll have to use the infrared sensors. But they're optimized against missile signatures and haven't even been calibrated against aircraft."

"Try and pick them up on the aircraft radar. Critter, what help can you give us?"

"I can pipe in the AWACS data. You can bet they're going to be watching the show, and they aren't much farther out than we are. If the MiGs come after us, they might pull a kamikaze stunt and head for the AWACS. They wouldn't have enough fuel to get home, but the AWACS would be an easy target and the MiG pilots would go down in Korean history as heroes."

"They could take out the AWACS too?" Sergeant Adams asked.

"It wouldn't be as easy as I made it out to be. The AWACS have some degree of control of the U.S. fighters. They would vector some in to intercept the Koreans before they got close enough to do any damage."

"There they are," Critter said.

Lance checked his display. There were four tiny red blips.

"That's them." Critter pointed at the blips with the end of his pen. "And here we are."

The MiGs were obviously heading for the Airborne Laser, approaching a green arc that seemed to be centered on the ABL. "What's the green line?" Lance asked.

"That's the MiG missile envelope. If they get inside that line we're within range of their missiles. Looks like they'll be in range in about twelve minutes."

"Did you copy that, Pilot?" Lance asked.

"Sure did. This boat's going to be hard to miss, too. I suspect they'll fire radar-guided missiles—we've got a radar cross-section the size of a barn. The only coun-

termeasures we have are some flares and chaff rounds.
I don't think they'll do much good."

"We'll see what we can do to them before they get
within range," Lance said. "Beam Control, can you
get them on the radar?"

"I've got them, I think, along with every other piece
of flying crap out there. Our aircraft radar won't differentiate between bad guys and good guys. Look!"

Lance moved behind Sergeant Adams. His screen
was cluttered, filled to the brim with the blips of all
the targets recognized by the radar's moving target
sensor.

"It's four needles in a huge haystack. Given enough
time, I could modify the radar software to filter out
the targets that aren't coming toward us, but that
could take days and would still only filter about two-
thirds of the targets."

"Not enough time for that. What about using the
AWACS feed Critter is getting?"

"Eight minutes until the MiGs are in missile range,"
Critter warned.

Time was slipping by quickly. They had to do something.

"It might work," Adams said. "I think I saw a digital output on his receiver when I was looking at it a
few minutes ago. Permission to try something?"

"Go, for crying out loud," Lance said.

Adams pulled a long cable out of one of the green
maintenance bags he always carried with him. It had
standard aircraft connectors on each end. Adams
dropped to the floor beneath Critter's feet and connected the cable.

"What's going on?" Critter asked as his screen went
momentarily blank.

"Don't worry, sir, it'll be back on in just a second." Adams was working feverishly beneath the console.

True to Adams's word, Critter's AWACS display came back to life as Adams trailed the cable back to his own station. Once again he dived to the floor to connect the wire.

"That should do it," he said as he climbed back into his seat.

"Seven minutes," announced Critter.

"Fire up the laser." Lance was now standing behind his laser jocks. "We may be cutting this close, and I don't want to have to wait on the device."

Captain Hawkins began to stroke his keyboard, bringing the laser to life and checking on its well-being. Meanwhile, Sergeant Adams was quickly modifying some software to tie the AWACS signal to his own fire control computer.

"Six minutes."

Lance didn't like what he was seeing. "Are you modifying the registry?"

"I have to," Adams answered. "That's the only way to feed the signal directly to the fire control system."

"But that means you'll have to reboot."

"I'm doing it now."

"That'll eat up another minute." Lance glanced back at the AWACS display. The MiGs were getting extremely close to the range marker.

"They should have used Macs instead of Windows machines." Adams was waiting patiently for the machine to reset itself.

Lance wasn't nearly as relaxed. What if the patch didn't work correctly? Then they'd have to recode the registry and reboot again. Assuming that the machine would come up at all after screwing around in the fickle Windows master file.

Adams's fingers flew across the keyboard as soon as the machine came back on-line, short-circuiting several start-up commands to gain a few precious seconds.

"Five minutes."

"I think it worked," Adams said as a replica of Critter's AWACS display filled the screen. "Now I just have to tie them together."

"We have a tone up here," the pilot called.

"What?" Lance was confused.

"Radar is painting us. We're within range of the surveillance mode on the lead MiG. He's not in track mode yet, though."

"Four minutes. Wait, they pickled one off. Missile inbound!" Critter warned.

"But they're not in track mode yet," Lance said.

"Doesn't matter—they have enough time to lob a few our way," Critter said. "Better get ready on the chaff."

"Ready up here," Captain Williams called from the copilot's seat.

"I wish they'd installed the countermeasures controller back here," Lance said. "We've got much better situational awareness than the pilots have."

"Don't worry." Aziz was leaning over Lance's shoulder now. "The chaff and flares are tied into the automatic dispenser, triggered by the missile warning receiver. It's a very good system, the same one we put on the F-15s."

"Three minutes."

"I would still feel better if we were in control back here."

"Now you're starting to sound like a pilot."

Lance realized Aziz was right—he was forgetting to trust the rest of the crew to do the jobs they were trained for.

"Target!" Sergeant Adams had the lead MiG under an electronic set of crosshairs on his display.

"Fire!" Lance ordered.

The laser rumbled, and once again the beam penetrated the dark sky, searching for its quarry. The beam reflected off the leading edge of the wing and provided a good track source for the beam control system.

"I've got track." Sergeant Adams was intently watching the readouts from his sensors while the computer controlled the intricate job of keeping the beam on the target.

"Give it eight seconds and move to the next target," Lance said.

"Why don't you wait until it blows up?" Aziz asked.

"There's only about a fifty percent probability the kill mechanism will result in an explosion. After eight seconds the pilot should be pretty well disabled."

Lance was proved wrong when the infrared sensor bloomed after only five seconds.

"Fried him!" Adams quickly locked on the second MiG. "Target!"

"Fire at will. Eight seconds per target."

"Two minutes." Critter was watching the battle scene, relaying their situation to the AWACS. He was particularly proud to report their defeat of the first MiG.

"Locked on second target."

"Dispensing chaff," came the terse warning from the cockpit.

In the excitement Lance had forgotten about the

inbound missile. He grabbed the back of Adams's chair tightly, waiting for whatever might happen, expecting the worst and hoping for the best. The timer had only reached six seconds when the big plane wobbled in the air.

The plane pitched up sharply as the pilots tried to avoid the flaming fireball and shrapnel generated by the missile's early detonation.

"Countermeasures kicked in when we pitched the chaff," Captain Williams reported from the cockpit. "Hang on, there's a bunch of shrapnel out there."

Lance was still watching the counter, hoping the inbound MiGs were still within the laser's field of fire. The beam director could stand only a thirty-degree upward pitch before the targets could no longer be seen by the sensors. Fortunately, the aircraft's downward pitch didn't exceed the beam director's limits—yet.

"We've got a fire light on number four engine," Lance heard Colonel Powers warn.

"Shutting down four." Captain Williams hit the master switch as per emergency procedure, just in case the engine was really on fire.

"Pulling power on engine one," Colonel Powers announced as she trimmed the power on the opposite engine to control the yaw. The unbalanced thrust was forcing the plane into a sideways attitude that made it difficult to control.

After a full eight seconds the MiG still hadn't blown up, but Adams redirected the beam to the next MiG.

"It hasn't blown up yet," Aziz said.

"Not a problem," Lance said. "He's finished."

"But how?"

"After eight seconds the pilot's eyes are pretty well

destroyed. You don't want to hear the biological details—it's pretty gross."

"Sensor coolant overheat," Captain Hawkins warned.

"I've lost the target," Adams reported at almost the same instant.

"One minute," Critter said. "They're almost within accurate missile range."

There were still two inbound MiGs, and the Airborne Laser was just about out of maneuvering room.

"What happened?" Lance asked.

"We may have taken some shrapnel up front," Adams said. "We've got serious boresight sensor degradation. We need to level out and get the sensor pointed straight ahead again. That should help."

"We need to level out!" Lance was almost screaming into the microphone, trying to get the pilot's attention.

"Not possible. We've got to get under the rest of the fireball or we're likely to suck something into another engine. Our right outboard engine may already be damaged."

"AWACS reports two ballistic missiles fired from the missile field," Critter said. "They're both headed south. They want to know if we can do anything."

"Negative," Lance said. "If that jerk in command down there had given us some support we might have been able to, but we've got our hands full right now. Besides, by the time AWACS finds out that the missiles have been fired, it's too late. They're already beyond our range."

"I'll pass all that on, except for the 'jerk' part."

"You might as well start to turn back and get the hell out of here," Lance warned. "We can't get the other two MiGs flying at this attitude, and by the time you recover it'll be too late."

"Sorry to tell you this, Mission Commander," Captain Williams said as he wrestled with the wounded bird, trying to get it back under control, "but there's no way in hell we can outrun those two jets now."

"We may not have to," Critter said. "Looks like the cavalry is here, and you won't believe who they are."

"What? Who?" Lance asked.

"Holding fire!" Sergeant Adams released the consent switch on the joystick, shutting off the laser beam when he saw four blips pass their own aircraft and surge in front of them.

At the same time, Captain Hawkins shut down the laser modules, saving precious fuel.

The Airborne Laser bobbed again as two jets screamed past each wing, racing with afterburners lit toward the MiGs about to cross into missile-firing range.

"Who in the heck were they?" Colonel Powers asked, as the four streaks passed.

"I don't know," Critter said. "They snuck in using our radar shadow. The MiGs never saw them."

"They'll see 'em now. The MiGs are going to hightail it out of here," Sergeant Adams watched on his own screen as the MiGs turned to escape.

"Too late for them," Critter said.

They all watched the remaining Korean fighters disappear from the screen as their cavalry dispatched the attacking aircraft before they could flee.

"They're coming back." Sergeant Adams pointed at the blips as they arced back to the west.

"Mission Commander, there have been no further

fire indications on engine four. I'm going to try a restart."

Lance was still trying to figure out how they would be able to defend against the remaining ballistic missiles, and he was still curious as to who their benefactors were. He pulled his trailing intercom cable behind him as he moved to the single window in the back of the plane.

"Engine four on-line," Captain Williams reported. "Running at forty percent power with no indication of problems. The fire light may have been a false alarm."

"Let's hope so," Colonel Powers said. "Keep it at forty percent for a while until we're comfortable there's no real damage."

It was extremely dark out now. Lance watched as two aircraft pulled into formation along his side of the big 747, their navigation lights announcing their approach. He could make out the shape of the aircraft, but he couldn't tell much more about them. Finally he heard them announce their presence over the radio.

"Eagle Three Three, this is Sam Zero Six, flight leader."

"Copy, Sam Zero Six," Colonel Powers responded. "Appreciate your assist. A couple of us thought we were goners. You guys with the First Wing?"

"Negative."

Lance was still looking out the window when the lead plane switched on a light that illuminated the tail of his aircraft. A large red circle was clearly displayed.

"Sam is short for Samurai. General Nakano told me personally my country had a debt to repay. I hope you will accept this small gesture."

For what seemed like a very long time there was no answer. Finally Lance heard Colonel Powers respond: "I think I may have been disrespectful to your general at our last meeting. I will correct that when I next see him. Thank you."

"We have another mission," the Samurai radioed. "But we will have someone here if you have need of our help again. Good day, Eagle Three Three."

"Good hunting, Sam Zero Six."

"We are at fuel limits, ma'am," Captain Williams reported to Powers.

"Mission Commander, we are at fuel limits. We need to decide whether to pursue this mission or abort and return home."

"What about the engine?" Lance asked. It would do no good to continue with a degraded laser if the aircraft were wounded as well.

"Looks okay so far," Colonel Powers said.

"The laser is probably okay. We've got some kind of sensor malfunction when there is a steep angle to the target. I think if we can keep the targets pretty much right in front of us we'll be all right."

"That may be easier said than done," Colonel Powers cautioned.

"Understood." Lance pulled the boom mike from in front of his mouth and conferred with his engineers off-line. "What do you guys think?"

"The sensor's pretty severely degraded." Sergeant Adams pointed at one area of his display. "Not only is the field of view obscured, the temperature is rising as well. I'm not sure what's causing it or how long it'll last."

"How's the laser?" Lance asked.

"Seems fine. That parasitic was caused by some chance reflection, so I think module two is okay, but I intend to hold it in reserve."

Lance contacted the front-end crew. "Pilot, this is Mission. We're damaged, but confident we can still pursue the mission. Recommend we refuel and proceed." Then Lance remembered the one issue they had briefly discussed but had forgotten about until now: If they broke out of the pattern to refuel, the Koreans would definitely be able to tell and might use the gap in defensive coverage to launch their missiles. The empty feeling in Lance's gut returned when he thought about the long-range Chinese missile with its nuclear tip. Then he remembered that Aziz was supposed to have taken care of the problem somehow. "How do we break off to refuel without the North Koreans' using the time to fire their missiles?"

"What is that?" Critter was staring at his display.

"What now?" Lance asked.

"A big bird has just flown into this sector. Call sign is Eagle Three Four."

"That would be our stand-in." Aziz was grinning from ear to ear.

"Our what?" Lance asked.

"We need fuel. After you guys got through insulting the Japanese general back at Misawa, I asked him for a favor. That's a Japan Air Lines 747, empty of passengers, of course. It's going to fly our pattern while we break off to get fuel. The North Koreans will think it's our backup. They don't know we're a one-man show."

"The old shell game trick," Colonel Powers said from up front. "Good move, Aziz."

"It's only a good move if it works. You guys need any help up there during the refueling operation?"

"I could sure use a break," Colonel Powers said.

"I'll be right there."

"They're letting you fly this thing?" Lance asked Aziz as he passed by on the way back to the cockpit.

"Yeah, it's not much of a problem. Pitch, power, and trim, same as every other airplane. I'll give Colonel Powers a break while we're not knee-deep in it with the Koreans. Just look at how tired you guys are, and you get to stand up and move around. They've been up there for what, almost ten hours now, and with a new load of fuel we could be at this another eight hours. I suggest you guys take a break, too. Critter will keep an eye on things."

"Good idea," Lance said as Aziz made his way forward. "Why don't you two go up front and lie down for a few minutes? We'll be taking on fuel for at least half an hour."

"Kind of fits with one of my standard rules," Captain Hawkins said as he released his seat belt and stood up. "Eat when you can, sleep when you can. There's no way I could go to sleep, but I could sure use something hot to eat. You guys want something?"

"Sure," Sergeant Adams said. "I didn't know we had anything hot aboard."

"Critter's guys stocked the galley. There's a microwave up there, too. I'll bring some food back."

"I'd give you a hand, but I want to try to figure out what's wrong with the infrared sensor." Sergeant Adams turned back to the computer.

"I'll go with you," Lance said. He definitely needed to walk around for a few minutes, even if it was just to go forward to the galley and back.

"So, what's the latest?" Lance put a steaming microwave dinner in front of Critter.

"Nothing good so far. The missiles both impacted

in Seoul. Mostly civilian casualties. Couple of hundred. That has really worked in their favor. There have been mass demonstrations, mostly by students sympathetic to the North, trying to sway the South Korean government to pull their troops back from the border and to evict the U.S. forces. That's just what the North Koreans want. Without U.S. help, the South would be ill-prepared to defend itself in the face of an all-out invasion.

"There have been a dozen or so skirmishes along the border so far, mostly probing attacks by the North. They're looking for weak spots. We've also shot down a couple of AN-2s carrying Special Forces, but again there's no telling how many have gotten through. The North is really making use of CNN, trying to sway public opinion throughout the world to paint the United States as the aggressor nation and themselves as the innocent target."

"That's pretty much true, isn't it?"

"On the surface it looks that way. But the North has been planning this for several years, and the South Koreans have provided information to show that they have stepped up their invasion plans in earnest over the last couple of months. Their penetration using AN-2s to infiltrate special operations teams is the initial step in their invasion doctrine. They were coming, all right. My guess is it was their missile technology that finally gave them a strong enough hand to execute the plan."

"If we can get in there and take out their missiles, would it convince them otherwise?" Lance asked.

"Possibly. I think that's what our friend General Killeen—you called him 'the jerk,' I believe—was try-

ing to do with the Strike Raptors. Not very successful."

"And we can't get at them unless they launch, which
leaves us as a totally defensive option."

"It's very tough to win a war with a purely defensive
doctrine. I hate to say it, but what we really need is
for the North Koreans to launch all their missiles.
They only have a dozen or so now, and we take out
as many as we can. Once they play that card, it be-
comes a traditional war that we can surely win." Critter turned back to his screen as another report began
to come in.

"My guess is that they already know that," Lance
said, finishing his sandwich.

"The North Korean government has just delivered
an ultimatum: If the South does not capitulate within
one hour and evict all U.S. and Japanese forces from
the country, North Korea will launch all their missiles
at major civilian targets in South Korea and Japan."

"What about the Chinese nuke?"

"They didn't mention that one. Probably don't think
we even know about it and don't want to tip their
hand."

The big plane banked as Lieutenant Colonel Aziz
made an announcement over the intercom. "We've
been called to duty. COMUSFORKOREA has finally
seen the light. Battle stations, everyone."

Lance walked back to his seat behind Sergeant
Adams. A now cold microwave dinner lay untouched
on the workstation next to the sergeant. "How's it
going?"

"Not good. The sensor is still unresponsive beyond
a very limited field of view, and even within that field
there seems to be quite a bit of degradation."

"How much degradation? Can we still track the targets at range?"

"Don't know. I think we can track the missiles, but I'm not sure what our range will be. We may have to get in closer."

"That's not very safe. They came after us once with fighters, so they know we're here. If we get in closer, we may be within range of their surface-to-air missiles."

"We may have to take that risk, unless we can figure out some other way to enhance the target's signature. And I don't know any way to do that." Sergeant Adams continued to query the computer, trying to get a feel for just how badly the target tracking sensor was performing. "It might help to get a better idea of which missiles were fired and where the others are right now."

"You're already connected to Critter's computer. I'll see if he'll let us have the latest data his pilot came up with."

Lance walked back to Critter's station. Critter was busily talking on the radio, watching the Aurora's output. Lance couldn't tell if it was a replay of the previous flight or a brand-new mission. He tapped into the channel Critter was talking on.

". . . and glad to have you back. There have been at least four missiles launched already, and it'd sure help to find out which ones have been fired and where the rest are."

"Understood," Driscoll said. He was already exhausted, having quickly turned the Aurora for a repeat mission when the only other backup pilot remained grounded. Driscoll would even have sent young Major Killeen on this one, he was so tired, but Killeen was nowhere to be found. As far as Driscoll was concerned, the general's kid was Absent Without Leave—AWOL. General's kid or not, Driscoll had passed word to the Pentagon and requested that they alert the FBI. The normal rules of waiting twenty-four hours before reporting an officer AWOL were waived at his unit because of the highly classified nature of their work. Driscoll knew it wasn't going to make COMUSFORKOREA very happy when he found out his beloved son, whom he'd covered up for, was now running away from his responsibility.

That wasn't really relevant now, though. Driscoll forced his tired brain to walk through the mission, just as he always did. It was a repeat of the last mission, a quick pass over the missile farm, slow enough to get good pictures . . . and to draw the attention of a few surface-to-air missiles. Then a burst of speed to outrun them and return to the States. Piece of cake. "Feet dry."

"Heading is good," Critter informed his boss. "Altitude and speed are nominal."

"Can we get a feed on the data you get as soon as it comes in?" Lance asked.

"No problem. It's already geo-registered, so I can pass you a picture or I can mark the missiles and pass you the coordinates."

"I'll check with Adams, but I think the target coordinates would be best. It'd sure be quicker—we don't have a very high-speed connection rigged up between the machines."

Critter nodded, but his attention was on the display. It was turning into a Christmas tree of red lights. "Damn."

"What're those?" Lance asked.

"Aurora, this is Control. Be advised I am picking up massive search radar noise. They know you're there."

"Copy. I'm picking up warning hits on the radar warning receivers. They've never picked me up this far out before. Probably the wing damage."

"What wing damage?" Critter asked.

"There was some minor wing damage back at the base—not bad enough to ground the plane, but it probably screwed my signature." Driscoll kept a watchful eye on the display as radar from even farther away began to search for him. "I'd bet my radar cross section is about twice what it was before."

"And you came back? They were already picking you up with minimal signature. No wonder they're picking you up so easily on the search radar now."

"That doesn't really matter, as long as they can't get a track." The tone Driscoll had dreaded began blaring in his headset.

"Spoke too soon," Critter warned. "Try increasing altitude. Bump it up to thirty-five thousand feet."

Driscoll checked his flight plan. It had been computer-generated to keep him as far away from the SAM radar as possible. He was on the correct course, but his radar cross section had increased so drastically from the wing damage that the enemy was already getting a good lock. Driscoll gently pushed an electronic sensor embedded in his glove and the digital display changed from thirty thousand to thirty-five thousand. He pushed a similar electronic switch with his thumb to enter the new flight altitude. Almost immediately the nose of the flying dagger pitched sharply upward and his altitude increased. Would that put him clear of the radar?

"You are ten miles from the target zone," Critter

informed him. "Several target-tracking radar are still painting you. Suggest you boost speed to Mach two and engage camera wake filter."

"I'll hold here until I get a launch detection. The wake filter doesn't help that much."

"Understood," Critter said.

"What's a wake filter?" Lance asked.

"It's an electronic system inside the camera," Critter explained as he studiously monitored the display, leery of any SAM launches. "It's supposed to eliminate the distortion caused by running supersonic. You know, the shock wave—the sonic boom."

"Oh, like our own system that eliminates the atmospheric turbulence effects on our laser beam."

"I guess. I hope yours works better than . . . Aurora, I have multiple launch indications! Highly recommend you advance your speed."

"Copy, Control." The launch warnings were blaring in Driscoll's ears, new alerts sounding faster than he could shut them off. His video showed missiles coming from both his left and his right rear. Fortunately there were no alarms in front of him. He held the electronic throttle forward, pushing through the sound barrier and optimizing his speed at Mach two point one, the speed at which the video camera's wake filter performed best.

"I have you at Mach two point one. Video looks okay," Critter told Driscoll. "You're less than sixty seconds to the completion of the run. Looks like their radar is able to pick you up, but only when you fly directly over them. That means the missiles will have to chase you."

"They can close a lot of distance in sixty seconds,"

Driscoll reminded his controller. "Keep an eye on 'em for me."

Sergeant Adams had popped a small computer window open on his screen, and was watching the chase play out as he continued to search for the problem that was causing the sensor to work so poorly. "If you want, I can use our missile tracker to give you a better picture of how close they're getting."

Critter heard Adams over the intercom. "You can do that?"

"Sure. All the signals are geo-spatially located now. I'll use your system to locate the plane and our tracker to locate the missiles."

"I'll give you a hand," Captain Hawkins said. "The algorithm is already built into the tracker library. We just need to convert some of the data feeds. I can even give them a visual picture."

Both men worked furiously at their keyboards, and within seconds a small track appeared in the window with the Aurora. Then another, and another.

"I've got it," Critter told them when the signal was piped back over the cable Adams had connected between the two computers. Then he got back on the radio: "Aurora, this is Control. The closest missile is now eighteen kilometers to your rear. Closure is in fifty-two seconds. It's going to be close."

"Copy. Keep me posted. I'll stay on course and speed until either I've finished the run or the missile is within fifteen seconds. If the missile gets that close I'll have to initiate endgame maneuvers."

"He sounds tired," Lance said.

"He's probably exhausted. These flights are killers. Usually during one three-hour mission you spend at least half that time at an equivalent of one-fifth atmospheric pressure, which really depletes you. I usually sleep like a baby for a good twelve hours after a flight. This is Driscoll's second mission today."

"Don't you have any other pilots?"

"Besides myself we've got only two other qualified pilots, but both are grounded for a while. The squadron is about to be stood down. My guess is the Air Force has something better in the works. Anyway, we're pretty short of help."

"That's why Driscoll is pulling the back-to-back flights?"

Critter didn't answer. Instead he got back on the radio. "Thirty-two seconds. Video is still good. You've covered most of the missile field. Suggest accelerating to max speed now."

Driscoll pushed the electronic actuator within his glove. The indicator showed full throttle. Now it was just a race. "Full throttle."

"Can he outrun it?" Lance asked.

"No problem," Critter said. "He'll be at Mach seven in just a few seconds. As long as no missiles are fired from in front of him, he'll be okay."

"What's that?" Lance pointed at two small lights that had just appeared on the display. They looked the same as the other missile indicators, only directly in front of the Aurora's position.

"Trouble," Critter said, switching to the radio. "Aurora, this is Control—we have two missile indications, one dead ahead and the other ten degrees off your left wing. Recommend right turn to heading three six five."

Driscoll's flight suit squeezed monstrously tight, the tremendous G-forces trying to suck the blood from his brain as he pushed the flying dart to the right. He wanted to back off the turn, but he knew this one was going to be close. When the missile reached terminal velocity, it would be closing the gap at a blurring combined speed of Mach 16. Driscoll had to get on a vector that would lead him away from the deadly javelin. A black shadow began to form at the bottom of Driscoll's vision and crept slowly upward.

"Can he outrun these?" Lance sensed Critter's concern, could hear the tension rise in his terse recommendations to the exhausted pilot.

"The one on the left, yeah. The one on the right is going to get awfully close if Driscoll doesn't push it. He's already pulling more G's than I've ever pulled. His state of exhaustion could easily push him over the limit."

Lance thought quickly. The SAM was a much smaller target than what the laser was designed to find and kill. But it was worth a shot. "Target the SAM," he ordered Sergeant Adams.

"Searching."

"Laser ready." Once again, Captain Hawkins was ahead of the mission commander.

"Fire when you have a track." Lance felt like he was in the cockpit with the potentially doomed pilot, counting the remaining seconds.

The sensor temperature was higher than before, nearing its upper operational limit. The higher temperature meant lower sensitivity, making it that much tougher to find the target.

"There's not enough of a signal," Sergeant Adams said. "I can't find the missile."

"Keep trying," Lance said. The small light was rapidly closing on the Aurora's position.

Chapter 11

Sergeant Adams was frantically searching for the target.

"Can he bail out?" Lance asked as the missile loomed even closer.

"Not at this speed. It'd kill him for sure." Critter felt helpless as his friend pummeled his own body with the mighty G loads, trying desperately to escape the speeding missile.

"What was that?" Lance saw a small flash on the screen from their infrared sensor.

"Don't know, but I think it was the missile." Sergeant Adams put the cursor over the small blip that had appeared on the screen.

"Kill it," Lance ordered.

The area where the small blip had unexpectedly appeared meant it had to be the missile, according to the data coming from the Aurora's missile tracking system.

Sergeant Adams fired the laser at the blip's coordinates. The beam illuminated the space with its defocused beam, and the reflected energy from the missile's nose gave the computer good coordinates to close the track loop. In less than two seconds the warhead of the lightly built surface-to-air missile detonated, fried by the high-powered laser.

"Good kill." Lance slapped Adams on the back. His adrenaline was peaking.

"You are clear of the missile," Critter told his pilot.

"What the hell happened to it?" Driscoll backed off the turn, and the throttle. He also trimmed the nose of his plane skyward to evade the searching radar below him. He didn't want to go through that again. "Damn thing was almost to me when it just disintegrated."

"I'll let someone else explain." Critter took Lance's headset connector and plugged it into the radio at his own console.

"I think you owe one staff sergeant, the first laser jock, a beer when we get back to base. You have just witnessed a first—the destruction of a surface-to-air missile by a high-power laser," Lance told Driscoll.

"You tell your sergeant I'm going to throw a party in his honor." Driscoll didn't know what was going on, but he was definitely grateful to still be alive. He noted he was now back over the water and there were no missiles on his radar. He backed off the throttle to cruise setting. "Better find me some fuel, Control."

"Already have. Turn to heading zero niner seven and rendezvous with Albatross Six Niner in ten minutes."

"Take a look at the data, too. If I'm going to have to do this again today, I'd rather do it before I go back home."

"I'll let you know. By the way, good flying. Control out."

Lance watched as Adams and Hawkins returned the

laser and beam control system to its safely stored mode.

"I think I have an idea of what's wrong with the sensor," Adams said.

"I hope it's something easy to fix." Lance watched the screen as Adams brought up a series of data columns in a spreadsheet.

Adams pointed at the upper left corner of the screen. "This is a histogram of the sensor temperature. See how it's drifting around a good thirty degrees above nominal operating temp?"

Lance nodded.

"Now look at this." Adams pointed further down the screen. "Right here the temperature jumps another forty degrees."

"What caused that?"

"The laser."

"How?"

"Remember we said we might have taken some damage when that air-to-air missile was fired at us?"

Lance nodded.

"I think we've either gotten some shrapnel lodged in the beam director or have somehow damaged some of the mechanical structure. Whenever we fire the laser, something up there is heating up, like it's protruding into the beam. That's causing the inside of the beam director to heat up, in turn causing the background radiation to raise the sensor's thermal limit."

"But we haven't shown any pressure loss through the beam director," Hawkins said. "The beam director can't have been breached. We'd have seen a leak."

"True," Lance said. "What if we've only chipped the window? That might cause us to scatter energy back into the beam director when the laser is fired. That would also cause the unwanted heating."

"Yeah, that would do it," Adams said.

"You guys better figure out how to fix it," Critter said. "And fast."

"Can't fix it in the air," Lance said. "We have to land and replace the window."

"Then you better think of something else. The North Koreans are plenty ticked off now. They just issued another ultimatum, demanding we stand down all air forces within fifteen minutes and begin to withdraw all naval and land forces within twenty-four hours. If we don't, they're threatening massive retaliation of their entire missile fleet. I just finished looking at the video the Aurora captured. They aren't lying. Every one of their birds is now ready to fire."

"What do you think the answer will be?" Lance already knew what he thought it would be, and he wasn't sure he liked the implications.

"I already heard. We told them to take a flying leap, or words to that effect."

"Okay, let's think about this," Lance told his engineers. "We can't find the target at long ranges with the infrared tracker. If we can't find it, we can't use the laser to illuminate it and track it with the reflected energy. On the positive side, it doesn't look like the damage to the window, if that's really what the problem is, has put us in any danger. I don't think the energy that's getting fed back into the beam director is enough to do any damage to the plane. We'll have to keep an eye on the laser modules and make sure the return energy doesn't get fed back into any of them. That could be disastrous."

Hawkins nodded.

"Any ideas?"

They began throwing out ideas, evaluating them and discarding them as unworkable. Meanwhile, the mighty Airborne Laser, only partly functional, continued to fly circles in the airspace off the Korean shore.

Sergeant Adams was playing back the video from their shootdown of the surface-to-air missile that had threatened the Aurora. There had to be something there that would help them out of this tight spot. His mind wandered as he looked at the playback again. He was getting tired. Heck, he was plumb worn out. None of them had had more than a few hours' sleep in the last forty-eight. Lance had snapped at Hawkins just a few minutes earlier for trying to revisit an idea that they'd already decided wouldn't work. The strain they were now under was beginning to show.

Lance was scratching his head, watching the playback with Sergeant Adams. They were all racking their brains trying to figure out how to keep the North Koreans from bombarding the South Koreans or the Japanese with their missile warheads.

And the Americans. Couldn't forget about that Chinese long-range nuke they had down there. That was constantly weighing on his mind. That missile could reach the States. Lance thought about his loving wife and his two gorgeous little girls.

His crew would be safe, he was confident of that. Safe so long as they stayed out of Korean airspace, out of reach of their very capable surface-to-air missiles, and so long as the Japanese general remained committed to using his own air forces to protect the Airborne Laser. Lance knew he would return home safely no matter what the outcome of the fight. But if the Koreans chose to launch their long-range missile and it reached the States, it would surely turn the American public against this little war. The military would be forced to pull out, and the Koreans would be even bolder the next time. And if the Koreans got away with it, the Chinese would surely threaten the Americans the next time things got hot between those two countries. The future was riding on this fight.

"What's that?" Lance pointed to the sensor readout. There was a slight jiggle in the output.

"That's where we first detected the SAM that was after the Aurora. For some reason the sensor picked it up, and I used the very short track to fire the laser in that general direction. Once the laser hit the missile, the return energy was enough to close the targeting loop."

"Okay, but where did the signal come from?"

"I don't know," Adams said. "All at once the signal just jumped about two orders of magnitude. It didn't last long, though. See?"

The signal trailed off almost immediately after it peaked. Just long enough to find the missile. "You're right. But it peaks once again here later, almost identically."

"I hate intermittent electronic blips." Captain Hawkins was watching over Adams's shoulder as they tried desperately to understand what had happened. "They're the hardest to understand. This one isn't repeatable. Is it four hundred hertz noise from the generators?"

"I don't think it's electronic." Sergeant Adams typed in a command, and the plot magnified. "It lasts more than five hundred milliseconds, probably too long in duration to be caused by the electronics."

"What is it, then?" Lance asked.

"Can you plot the two spikes relative to the Aurora's position?" Critter had stood to look over their shoulders as well, since the Aurora was busy fueling for the return trip and there was little for him to do.

"Sure." Adams's fingers instructed the computer. The image they were viewing was quickly replaced by a low-quality image of the position of the Aurora and the position of the missile as identified by the first track. "Now, watch."

The image slowly moved as the Aurora tried to escape the missile's grasp.

"After the first blip—the spike in the tracker signal—I was able to get a lock by pointing the laser in the blip's general direction. With the reflected energy we began to track the missile. There's the second spike, almost hidden in the reflected laser energy. And there the missile blew up."

"I think I know what is causing your spikes," Critter said.

The three engineers looked at each other.

"Well, don't keep us in suspense," Lance said.

"It's flying through the Aurora's wake."

"What?"

"At that point the Aurora was supersonic." Critter pointed at the screen. "Here, the missile is behind the plane but closing on it. If you draw a cone from the tail of the plane centered on the vector of the Aurora's flight, it would intersect right about here, exactly where you saw the first blip."

"But you don't know what the angle of the wake would be," Sergeant Adams said.

"Right, but if you assume the first blip was caused

by the lower point on the wake, then the angle up to the second blip would be about the same, right?"

Critter pulled a government issue pen from his sleeve pocket and laid it against the screen, centered on the Aurora and pointed along its flight path. One blip was below and behind the plane, and the other was above and behind the plane. "I'd say those two signals were at about the same angle off the tail."

"But why would the missile fly through the upper half of the wake? Wouldn't it be homing in on the target?" Lance asked.

"Not necessarily. Sometimes they're designed to overshoot the target to compensate for countermeasures. The SA-6 has a significant counter-countermeasure capability. Lead tracking is one of them. That's a classic profile."

"He could be right," Sergeant Adams said. "I don't have a better explanation."

"I wouldn't give it a passing grade in a physics class," Lance said, "but I don't have a better explanation either. Can we use this information to help us target the other missiles?"

"Sure we can," Adams said. "All we need to know is about when they're going to launch, and to have someone who's willing to make a pass through there at just above Mach speed."

"But that's suicide," Critter said.

"Maybe not for someone who already knows his way through there," Lance said. "Someone who's already survived it."

"Driscoll? But he's exhausted. I can tell from his voice."

"Anyone else who tries it is going to be dead meat. We're going to need someone who's able to fly through there at just above Mach speed, to lay out a wake that the missiles will have to fly through. That plane is sure to attract a swarm of SAMs that he'll have to outrun. Driscoll's plane is the only one that stands a chance."

"I'm not sure even the Aurora can make it through that," Critter said.

"Why don't we give your pilot a chance to make that decision?" Lance said. "We'll lay it all out for him and let him make the choice."

"That pretty well sums it up." Critter had spelled out the plan proposed by the laser jocks. The only other thing he needed to do was give Driscoll an out. "I've told them that you have already pushed the envelope too long with back-to-back flights and that even the Aurora might not be able to survive that kind of mission. We already know the Koreans can pick you up on their radar."

Critter didn't think Driscoll would bite. He didn't.

"How fast can I go?"

"Not very," Lance answered. "Just above Mach one would be optimal. That puts you in the area long enough for us to track anything that's launched. If you go much faster, we could very easily miss some of the missiles."

"I gotta warn you, this thing sucks a ton of fuel running that slow. Very inefficient."

"Understood." Lance knew this was going to be tough to pull off.

"And if we don't do it at just the right time we'll miss the missiles. This is going to have to be precisely timed. What kind of tip-off can we use?" Driscoll asked.

"We can get one from DSP, the Defense Support Program satellites. They'll give us warning of the launch, and you'll be in position just off the coast. When we get the signal that a missile has been fired, you can head in as fast as you want, then slow down when you get to the missile field." Lance knew he was asking a lot.

"Slow down right over the top of all those SAMs? Not my favorite place to shut her down."

There was a short pause. Lance looked at Critter. What would Driscoll say? Critter was expressionless, returning Lance's gaze as if he were wondering why they would even ask the pilot—his friend—to take such a risk.

After almost ten seconds of silence, the radio cackled back to life. "Where do you want me?" Driscoll asked.

Critter gave Driscoll the coordinates for an orbit that would put him just off the Korean shore.

"The Aurora is full of fuel and can stay in orbit for about two hours. If we haven't moved by then, we'll have to refuel again. My guess is that Driscoll will be so drained by that time it would be fruitless to send him back to the hot zone."

"Understood." Lance had no way of knowing when, or even if, the Koreans might launch their missile assault. Was there some way they could pressure them into it? No way. That was ludicrous. Suppose they didn't have any plans to launch them in the first place—provoking them would be a reckless move. Besides, an effort like that would require the support of COMUSFORKOREA, and he was anything but on the Airborne Laser's side.

With very few options available, Lance set to work

to make sure everyone knew what was expected. Sergeant Adams had tied into Critter's console to get a better feed from the satellite missile warning system, and Captain Hawkins wrote a software script to ensure that the warning signal could be used to quickly verify the general location of the launch site within the boundaries of the missile field.

The laser was still running pretty well, but some problems with waste heat buildup from running it so long in standby mode were becoming a concern. Meanwhile, the aircrew was drained. Colonel Powers was still in the pilot's seat, and Aziz had just returned the copilot's seat to Captain Williams. Aziz took Powers's seat so she could stretch a bit.

"Pilot, this is Mission. What's the aircraft status?" Lance was still concerned about the number four engine.

"Aircraft is FMC—fully mission-capable."

Lance was glad to hear Captain Williams reply as pilot in command. That meant Colonel Powers was taking a break. And it gave Williams more of the responsibility he'd been ducking earlier in the mission. If there was one thing that seemed to be going well, it was Captain Williams's attitude. He no longer seemed to feel as if he was just flying passengers around. Perhaps his "Laser Jock" patch had something to do with his new enthusiasm, but more than likely it was the fact that they had probably saved countless lives by destroying the previous ballistic missile and had just saved a fellow pilot's life by taking out the SAM. Either way, they were doing some good, and though the odds seemed to be against them they were at least in a position to really make a difference.

"Better stand by," Critter said.

"What've you got?" Lance walked over to Critter's console. With his direct tie to the AWACS, Critter was continuing to monitor the situation, using a feed that provided him an identical display of the air and ground situation.

"Lots of ground movement on the north side of the border. Joint STARS radar shows both heavy and light armor moving south at a fairly rapid clip."

Lance looked at the screen, which showed thousands of tiny white tracks that were indeed moving south. What next?

"Here we go." Critter switched the display to check out the air picture. "We've got lots of strike birds on their way to engage. Eagles and A-10s were orbiting south of the border waiting on the Koreans to attack. We'll be in full battle in just over five minutes."

"Why would they attack now?" Lance asked.

"Think about it," Critter said. "But don't think too long. When you are fairly certain you will be attacked, the best option is to take the offensive. Especially if you've been preparing for this for years and now have an excellent card up your sleeve. Even if we take out half the advancing armor, the North Koreans can launch their missiles and press the attack with what armor they have left. The South may not capitulate right away, but the North will most certainly have won the initial battle, which will put them in an excellent position for negotiation. Assuming the South Korean populace even cares after the missiles rain down on their homes. The populace may force the South Korean government to kick the Americans out, which would really play into the communists' hands."

"So you think the missiles will go soon?"

"I'm almost positive."

"Better let the Aurora know it's almost showtime."

Lance turned back to his station beside Sergeant Adams. Both of his engineers were there, studying their displays. All the mods had been made, and they were viewing the output of the missile warning satellite directly. A tiny light appeared near the middle of the missile field. A warning tone went off in Lance's headset—the satellite was reporting a missile launch.

"Better send in our helper," Sergeant Adams said. "I'll try to get a lock on the missile, but without narrowing the search field I'll never track the target close enough to shoot at it."

"He's on his way," Critter reported.

"This is it," Lance told them. "Everyone stay on your toes."

The big plane banked sharply to get in position. Lance had to grab his chair to keep from falling.

All they could do was wait for Driscoll. Soon a small track appeared on the screen.

"That's the Aurora." Sergeant Adams had pulled the high-speed plane's telemetry into the display. "It's almost to the missile field."

"He'd better hurry," Lance said. "There won't be much time for us to tag that missile. Which way is it headed?"

"Telemetry from the satellite says south. We've got fifteen seconds to find it before it's too high in altitude to kill."

"It's not the Chinese bird, then?"

"No."

"Give me a vector, Control," Driscoll called over the radio.

"Turn to heading three seven five."

"Copy."

"He's turning," Adams said. "Level at twenty thousand feet. We should see the missile in a few seconds."

Colonel Powers staggered toward Lance. He didn't even notice her until she was right next to him. She was holding her right arm against her chest with her left hand. Her upper arm was bent at a disturbing angle.

"Colonel, what happened?"

"I was climbing back up the ladder when the plane pitched. I think my arm's broken."

"Sit here." Lance helped her into the seat behind his. He turned back to the console.

"Laser on-line," Lance ordered.

Captain Hawkins primed the device. "Laser ready."

The missile launch warning from the satellite went off again.

"We've got another missile," Lance said. "Where's the first one? We only have a few seconds left." If this didn't work, they would have placed Driscoll in unnecessary danger.

"There. Target." Adams pointed at the blip as the missile crossed Driscoll's wake.

The laser tracker locked onto the signal automatically and the laser pumped megawatts of energy into the small region of space where the missile had been detected, scanning the region in a conical pattern searching for the target. In milliseconds the laser beam bounced off the missile and its energy reflected back into the target-tracking sensor. From that point on, the missile was doomed.

"There's the other one," Adams said.

"Go to shared-track mode," Lance instructed. "Give me a total of six seconds on each bird." They were about to provide the tracking computer with a serious challenge. It would have to continue to estimate the trajectory of the first missile while panning back to the second missile before its actual location was lost.

"Got it," Adams said. "I'm sharing track between the first and second missiles at one-second intervals."

The missile launch warning blared again.

"Six seconds on first missile." Adams adjusted the joystick. "Targeting number two missile."

The computer estimated where the second missile should be based on the three target track positions that had been gathered during the shared-track algorithm. It quickly found its target. The warning system blared again.

"We've got another missile," Lance said. "I don't think it will cross the shock wave."

"Aurora, this is Control. Turn back to heading one six zero."

"Wilco," Driscoll answered. "Be advised I have two SAMs inbound. I don't think they'll reach me."

"Aurora is drawing fire—no danger yet," Critter informed the Airborne Laser crew.

"Keep me informed," Lance answered.

The missile warning system blared twice more. The display was beginning to look like it was covered with fireflies.

"Track on missile two terminated," Adams said.

"Did it get through?" Lance asked.

Adams was too busy looking for his next target to answer. Captain Hawkins had his laser working perfectly, and between brief checks of his own status displays he was helping Sergeant Adams find and kill the missiles. "It didn't get through. The computer lost the signal, so that probably means it blew up."

Lance watched as his sergeant manned the deadly

video game. There were three targets in the air, and Adams didn't have a lock on any of them yet. Then the missile warning system went off again—two more missiles. The Koreans were throwing everything they had into the air. But what about the Chinese bird?

"Got him. Firing," Adams said as he locked onto one of the missiles. The next missile disappeared after only two seconds and the next two broke the Aurora's shock wave almost simultaneously.

Could the computer track two missiles on such similar flight paths? The missiles were taxing the crew as well as the machinery—and there were still about six on the ground.

"I've got an intermittent track," Adams warned. "The tracker doesn't seem to be able to differentiate between such closely spaced targets."

"Keep it on target as long as you can," Lance said. "You're bound to hit at least one of them."

The tracker did settle down, no longer oscillating between the two missiles. After four seconds the missile exploded.

"One of them got through," Adams said.

"You did the best you could," Lance said. "Keep your eyes open."

The missile warning system blared yet again. In rapid succession the North Koreans fired five missiles.

"I've got a whole swarm of missiles coming up!" Adams said. "I need some help."

Captain Hawkins leaned over. "The laser is working fine. I'll give you a hand. You fire on them as they break the wake, and I'll manually plot the course of the others if you get behind."

"Thanks."

"You're doing a great job, Bryan," Lance assured

the sergeant. "Just hang in there." Lance checked the laser console. The laser fuel display wasn't on the screen. "How much laser fuel do we have left?"

Captain Hawkins was leaning over, monitoring Sergeant Adams's screen. "At least sixty seconds' worth. Target!"

The first missile broke through the wake and left its telltale blip.

"Got it!" Adams said. "Tracking."

"Give each target about four seconds," Lance said. "Then move to the next, even if you can't verify the first target is down."

"Target!" Captain Hawkins said again.

"Executing simultaneous-track mode," Adams said.

"Just keep track of total time on each target," Lance said. "Increase total time by one second for each simultaneous track you're executing. That'll compensate for the cooling effect when the laser isn't on the missile."

"Target!" Captain Hawkins found another one.

"Damn," Adams said. "They're launching everything they've got. First missile is down."

"Maybe if they launch everything we'll get this over with," Lance said.

"I may have a problem," Adams warned. "The gimbal doesn't want to push the beam all the way to port. I'm losing that last missile."

Lance checked the attitude and heading of the aircraft on his own console. They were at the eastern end of the orbit, turning back to the north.

Lance spoke into his mike: "Mission commander to pilot. Abort your turn. Continue on original course."

Pilot: "Returning to original heading. We can only sustain this course for thirty more seconds before entering North Korea's air defense zone. If we go in they'll send fighters after us first and I doubt if we can depend on help from the Japanese this time—there's a major fur ball building north of Seoul."

Adams: "Target down."

Captain Hawkins: "New target."

Lance: "Mission to pilot. Understand the situation. With any luck we won't have to go in."

Captain Hawkins: "Target. Damn—there can't be many more of them."

Lance: "Keep it up, guys. Looks to me like you're running a very high kill rate. Maybe even one hundred percent."

Critter: "Not quite. AWACS has tracked two missiles into the Seoul area."

Lance: "Damn, I didn't see you miss any."

Both of Sergeant Adams's hands were moving rapidly between the keyboard and the joystick. "If the missiles were out of the envelope of the shock wave, the tracker wouldn't have spotted them—target down."

Captain Hawkins: "Two missiles are still in the air."

Critter: "The Aurora cameras have been on while Driscoll made this last pass. According to my count there's only one missile left on the ground. It's the big one."

Lance: "The Chinese missile?"

Critter: "Yeah. But it looks like they're getting ready to light it off."

Adams: "Target down."

Driscoll: "Mayday! Mayday! Mayday! I have a SAM launch dead ahead!"

Critter: "Get the hell out of there, Aurora."

Driscoll: "Can't avoid it. Banking right and dropping. I'll try to get under it and make it go ballistic. Throttles to the stops—it's going to be close."

Critter: "You're fifty miles from the coast. Head east."

Driscoll: "Wilco. I'm under it, but throttles won't give me full speed. Mach three point two seems to be the limit—I can't outrun it at this speed."

Critter: "Prepare to bail out."

Lance: "I thought you said bailing out at that speed would kill him."

Critter: "The Aurora has a special pod that pops out and slows to allow the pilot to escape. It's supposed to work up to Mach four. But we haven't really tried it before."

Driscoll: "Feet wet, but missile's still closing. I'm going to have to blow this ride—better give the search-and-rescue folks a heads-up."

Critter: "They're already on their way."

Sergeant Adams: "Target down. That's the last one in the air."

Captain Hawkins: "Outstanding!" He and Sergeant Adams high-fived each other as the adrenaline began to abate.

Pilot: "We're ten seconds from the air defense zone."

Critter: "AWACS shows a flight of four MiGs diverting in this direction."

Driscoll: "Beacon activated. Autodestruct switch set. Will bail at three seconds to impact."

Critter: "That'll be too late. Bail out now! Bail out—bail out—bail out!"

Pilot: "We're entering the air defense zone. Do we proceed or turn? We've got inbound bogies—we need a decision now!"

"Orbit out of the air defense zone, but be prepared to head back in. With the gimbal problem we have to fly straight in to get the beam on the target." Lance was stalling, trying to figure out what to do. The nuclear-tipped missile was still there.

"Without something to lay a sonic boom across the missile field we can't even find the missile, much less track it and kill it," Adams said.

"Did the Aurora make it?" Lance asked.

"I'll try him again," Critter said. "Aurora, do you copy? Aurora, do you copy?"

Lance heard nothing but silence.

Critter shook his head. "I don't think the Aurora is an option. I just hope Driscoll got out in time."

"Sorry I couldn't get the missile off his tail. I was too busy with the ballistic missiles. There were just too many of them," Adams apologized.

"You did everything you could," Lance said. "But we've got one more target out there, and it could easily be headed for the United States. How can we kill it?"

"I'm out of ideas," Adams said.

"We've got another problem," Captain Williams called over the intercom. "Engine four is beginning to lose power. I'll have to shut it down in just a couple of minutes and trim back number one to compensate. We'll still be able to fly, but we won't be very agile. Not that we ever were."

Colonel Powers stood up and turned toward the front of the plane. "I'd better get back up there."

"Can you make it up the ladder?" Lance asked.

"Yeah, so long as hot shot up there doesn't make one of his daredevil turns while I'm going up."

Lance called Williams and told him about Colonel

Powers's situation, then turned back to his own problem. Lance wondered what else could go wrong. There was a missile out there with a nuclear warhead that was being prepped for launch, probably at the United States, most likely the West Coast. The Airborne Laser, broken as it was, was the only way to stop it. But they had to figure out how. Quickly.

Less than a minute later the missile warning signal went off. They were out of time.

"Let's head back in. We'll figure out how to stop it," Lance said, hoping they came up with something before he got them all killed.

Chapter 12

"We can't just head in," Captain Williams said from up front.

Colonel Powers took the jump seat and motioned to Aziz. "Just stay put, Aziz. You're copilot now."

"It's suicide," Williams continued. "If the MiGs don't get us, the SAMs certainly will."

"Something will come up, I know it." Lance was praying for a miracle.

"Shutting down four. Trimming back one."

Lance felt the nose of the plane pitch down slightly as power drained from the two engines. "Feet dry."

They were over the Korean landmass, less than a hundred miles from the missile they wanted to destroy.

"SAM site dead ahead," Critter warned. "Turn north twelve degrees to two eight five."

At least they had a good idea of what lay ahead of them. But that wasn't going to be nearly enough. Lance paced behind his two engineers. They were ready, but they had nothing to shoot at. The timer showed the missile had been airborne for ten seconds. They had only twenty seconds before it was completely out of range.

"AWACS indicates the missile is headed north. It's headed for the States!"

"NO!" Sergeant Adams slammed his fist down on the console.

Lance glanced at Critter's display and saw a dense nest of air defense weapons directly in front of them. There were also four distinct aircraft tracks headed their way. He'd have to turn back. It was just no use.

"What's that?" Critter pointed to a small spot coming up behind them at breakneck speed.

"Eagle Three Three, this is Reno. I hear you folks need some help."

"It's Turbo and the Strike Raptor!" Critter yelled.

"Affirmative," Lance answered. "We need a shock wave over the top of that missile. And we need it fast."

"Copy. One shock wave coming up."

"Caution, Reno. There are four MiGs dead ahead and SAMs all over the place. You've already found out your stealthy systems don't work."

"Understood. But you need a shock wave, and I've got one. Besides, I've got a couple of men on the deck down there and we're trying to get them out. A little diversion couldn't hurt. Is this a good heading?"

"Turn left ten to three three five."

"Turning."

"Two of the MiGs are turning to intercept you," Critter warned.

Lance felt the nose of the airplane pitch down. What was going on there? He'd have to wait to find out. "Sergeant Adams, we've got two MiGs headed this way. You can track them, can't you?"

"Yes, sir. I'm patched into the AWACS feed."

"That should give you a good coarse targeting solution. Light 'em up."

"Why didn't I think of that?" Sergeant Adams

asked himself. The AWACS told him where the MiGs were. He pointed the beam director in that direction and fingered the joystick.

"Firing." Captain Hawkins was keeping a close eye on the laser fuel level now. They were already down to less than twenty seconds. "Don't give 'em more than four seconds each after you get a lock."

"Locked and cooking," Sergeant Adams said.

"AWACS intercepted a Mayday call from one of the MiGs," Critter said. "They're breaking away."

"Cease fire," Lance said. He was still a little concerned about the legality of using the lasers to blind pilots, but that didn't drive him to cut the firing short—he was more concerned with saving the laser fuel.

"Can we attack the MiGs that are after Turbo?" Critter asked.

"Wouldn't do any good. They're heading away from us, and we'd have to rely on some chance reflections off of their canopy to get the energy into their eyes. Besides, we might pick up Turbo in error. We can't really tell who we're firing on if they're in such close proximity."

"We've got less than ten seconds before the missile is out of range," Sergeant Adams warned.

"He's almost there, running at Mach three."

"Eight seconds."

"The MiGs are firing on him," Critter said. "Air-to-air missiles."

"Six seconds."

"He's flying right at the ICBM. It's already at thirty thousand feet."

"Four seconds."

"I'm hit!" Turbo called. "I'll bail when you get a lock."

"Two seconds."

The blip on the screen was almost imperceptible. "I've got it. Firing."

"Get out of there, Turbo," Critter ordered.

Lance felt the nose of the plane pitch down again, more severely this time.

"Keep the nose up, the gimbals are at the stop. I'm losing the target!" Sergeant Adams's grip on the joystick was so tight his arm was shaking.

Lance felt the nose of the plane come up hard.

"I can't hold it this way for very long," Captain Williams called from the front. "It's going to stall."

"Solid track." Sergeant Adams relaxed his grip on the stick.

"How long should we burn it?" Captain Hawkins asked.

"There are only twelve seconds worth of fuel. I suggest we empty the beast." Lance knew this was the final confrontation.

"We're losing speed. Approaching stall," Captain Williams warned.

"You're the best pilot I've ever flown with, Williams. You can keep this bird in the air a few more seconds. Just do it," Colonel Powers said.

"If this were an F-15 I'd drop the left wing and use the rudder to stay on course. That'll keep the nose up a little longer."

"And how do you generally recover from a spin in your F-15?"

"Nose down and full power."

"And you really think that will work here?" Captain Williams quickly glanced at the fighter pilot sitting to his left.

Aziz shook his head, "Doubt it."

Williams grinned and dropped the wing. He'd show this fighter jock what real flying was all about.

The plane shuddered Lance knew they were about to fall out of the sky. The high angle of attack at such low thrust was rapidly bleeding their forward speed—and their lift.

"Three seconds."

The left wing tipped. They were going to fall. Williams was dropping the left wing to keep them pointed skyward and at their target. Lance could almost sense the pilot straining on the rudder to hold them in the right direction. There was danger in attempting the maneuver—risk of a flat spin when they stalled. He knew Williams was really pushing the limit for this big bird. Lance urged him on. They just needed a few more seconds.

"Six seconds."

Lance's stomach lifted into his throat as the plane dropped under his feet. She had spent all her forward momentum and gravity was taking over. The big plane didn't have anything left.

"Lost track," Sergeant Adams said. "I hope we got it." The cup of coffee he had forgotten about flew into the air as the plane fell from under it. It hit the console and the lid popped off, showering all three men with cold java.

Lance felt the tail of the plane spin around. "Hang on, guys. I think we're in for a ride now."

"Holy crap!" Aziz fought to help Williams get the big bird back under control. The controls were all dead, uselessly flopping around as the plane plunged downward and spun to the left as it fell.

"Take it easy," Williams said. "As long as we get it back under control before we get down to five thousand feet, we'll have plenty of altitude to regain speed and climb back out—even with only two engines. That gives us about twenty thousand feet before it gets serious."

"But it's not responding at all, and we're dropping at a thousand feet per second!" Aziz moved the controls through their entire range. There was no resistance at all.

"That's because we're in too much of a spin. In an airliner this is where you'd call a Mayday. Ain't it fun?"

Aziz looked over at the younger pilot. The nutcase was grinning from ear to ear. "You're crazy."

"Oh, don't worry. This is a pretty good plane. It should recover by itself if we can just finesse the power properly." Williams pulled power to engine number three and pushed power full forward on number two. "That should slow our spin and might help straighten us out. Just let go of the controls."

Aziz let go of the control yoke and looked back at the colonel. Was she going to sit there and watch while this crazy man let them drill a hole into the Korean mountains? She was watching silently, holding on to the side of her seat with her good arm.

Ten thousand feet passed. The mountains loomed closer. The plane's spin didn't seem to have abated. Aziz gripped the armrests of his seat. He urgently wanted to grab the controls and yank the plane out of its deadly spiral.

*   *   *

"We're losing altitude pretty fast," Sergeant Adams said as all four men watched the altitude indicator.

"And my stomach is still about to shoot out of my mouth," Captain Hawkins said.

"Don't worry," Lance said. "I'm sure they're going to pull it out of the spin soon." He hoped.

Seven thousand feet.

Aziz hadn't sensed any change in the plane's attitude. They were still spinning out of control. And they were almost at five thousand, the point of no return.

Six thousand feet. As the wings began to bite into the slightly thicker air, Captain Williams pushed on the rudder.

Five thousand feet. Aziz let out the breath he was holding when the plane seemed to respond.

Captain Williams pushed the yoke forward as the spin abated and the plane came back under his control. "That's a little closer than I'd have liked. We still have the mountains to deal with."

"Hell, I'm looking at trees." Aziz couldn't help. He didn't know what to do. Williams had waited long enough to grab onto a miracle. But he obviously hadn't planned on having to deal with the rugged Korean landscape as he brought the plane under control. They were still well below stall speed, so it was critical to keep the nose pointed downward. But that could be fatal, since the mountains loomed so close.

Aziz continued to strangle the armrests as the younger pilot pushed the throttle on engine number two forward. Now they had two engines at max thrust, but not enough power to pull them out of the dive.

"If I had more power, this would be a piece of cake," Williams said. This was the kind of flying that he had missed in all those years of drilling holes in the sky with the National Airborne Operations Center. It had felt good keeping the plane up long enough to try and destroy the missile—now he just had to save the plane and the crew. It was like back in the old days in the fields of southern Indiana. He had to rely more on his skill now than on his Air Force training. "You don't see any peaks over in that direction, do you?"

Aziz glanced left out his windows as the crazy captain used the newly responsive controls to force the plane to the left, heading into a steep river valley. He shook his head. "Nothing below us but a river about a thousand feet down."

"That might be just enough."

The big plane still shuddered, trying to find enough air under its wings to give it sufficient lift to pull out of its perilous attitude. More speed was needed before the air would provide the needed buoyancy.

"We're grazing the damn trees!" Aziz was pulling up on his armrests, trying to lift himself above the trees and rocks that were trying to scrape the paint off the underbelly of the plane.

"We're picking up speed," Williams said.

"I hope so, we're almost out of valley," Aziz told, him. "There's the river."

Captain Williams guided the bird into the river valley, finally leveling off a mere fifty feet above the water. "We're still just above stall speed. We'll have to stay straight and level for a little bit until our two good engines can build up enough speed to let us climb out."

"Have you looked in front of us lately?" Aziz's eyes were riveted forward, staring at an old bridge that spanned the wide river. They were headed right at it. He glanced at the pilot. The lunatic was smiling more broadly than before. "Pull up, for crying out loud!"

"Not enough airspeed. Besides, I've always wanted to try this."

"We'll never make it." Aziz scrunched down in his seat, as if that would help them make it through. The bridge was big, and there was quite a bit of room between it and the water below. But the pilings didn't seem all that far apart. An F-15 would pass through easily, but not this beast. Then he noticed motion on the bridge. There were a few vehicles on it—military vehicles.

Williams pushed the nose lower, the radar altimeter ticking off the distance to the water. He leveled off at twenty meters.

"Do you know how accurate that altimeter is at this low altitude?" Aziz asked.

"I'm not using the altimeter. This is called flying by the seat of your pants."

A bullet scattered off the windscreen, chipping it. "Now some idiot is shooting at us!" Aziz said. "There, on the bridge—soldiers!"

"Hang on back there," Williams warned the laser crew. "We're going to have to fly under a bridge. It's going to be pretty tight."

The owner of a small fishing boat in front of them shook his fist before diving into the murky water. The wake from the plane capsized the boat as they passed over it.

"That guy was so close I could read his lips," Aziz said.

"Here we go," Williams said.

The soldiers on the bridge began to pepper the plane's skin with small-arms fire.

"Hang on!"

The Koreans on the bridge realized the crazy pilot was going to try and fly beneath them. Most ran for their lives. One soldier defiantly continued to shoot at the plane.

"Aahhh!" Williams cried out in pain as a single bullet penetrated the windscreen and lodged in his left shoulder.

The massive flow of air over the plane lifted the Korean up and off the bridge as the big bird passed beneath it.

"Pull up," Williams told Aziz as they cleared the structure. "But take it slow."

Aziz took the controls and followed Williams's guidance.

"Are you all right?" Colonel Powers asked.

"I think so. I don't think the bullet hit anything too important. It's just bleeding a little."

There was a first-aid kit near the jump seat. Powers grabbed it with her good hand and dug out a gauze pad.

Williams pushed the bandage into the wound to stanch the flow of blood. He sat back in his seat as they reached one thousand feet. "You guys in the back have any idea which way we should go?"

"Turn due south," Critter said. "Looks like the good guys have scattered all the MiGs. We'll head for the commercial airport at Seoul. That's an alternate NAOC landing site, and they should have the right maintenance capabilities. Should be no problem at this point. Word is most of the air defense units have stood down. It appears we won this round."

"That's good to hear," Williams said. "I'd hate to think we had all this fun for nothing."

"Fun? You call this fun?" Aziz asked. "I don't know if you guys in the back have any idea what this guy just did, but he flew a 747 under a bridge! He's nuts!"

"But did you see those guys scatter?" Williams asked. "I haven't had that much fun since I was a kid."

"I didn't see anyone scatter," Aziz mumbled.

"What do you mean? They were right there in front of us. It was hilarious. Ouch!" The plane hit an air pocket and jostled his arm.

"I was busy—watching the instruments."

"Huh? Wait a minute. You didn't have your eyes closed, did you?"

"Hell, no, I didn't have my eyes closed!" Aziz wasn't about to admit it. He had never done anything like that before. This guy had scared him to death.

"Well, trust me. They scattered. It was hilarious."

"Let's just get this thing on the ground before you get us all killed."

"Any word on the Chinese missile?" Colonel Powers asked.

Lance was almost sick with worry. If they didn't get it there was no telling what the casualties might be.

"It appears we nailed it," Critter said. "North Korea is on CNN. They're claiming the South launched a weapon at them with nuclear materials on board. A dirty bomb. They obviously didn't think through the dangers of launching a nuclear weapon in the face of the Airborne Laser. We shot it down and it fell back on their property. Quite a mess to clean up, I suppose."

A flood of relief engulfed Lance. The United States was safe. His family was safe. This time. If the Pentagon didn't wake up after this battle and put some effort into a nuclear missile deterrent capability like the Airborne Laser, the next time they might not be so fortunate.

Why had Lance let Aziz talk them into going to the officers' club at the Korean air base where they'd been forced to land? Lance was exhausted after the mission, and knew Adams and Hawkins were beat too. But Aziz pressured them to join in, convinced them it was the only way to end such a successful mission, particularly after the North had capitulated so quickly. "Besides," Aziz had argued, "there's nothing else to do until they get our engine repaired and we can fly back to Japan." Lance would have preferred to stay with Colonel Powers and Captain Williams at the hospital. Critter had enough sense to bow out, but with a good reason. He needed to find out what had happened to Driscoll.

When the crew bus dropped them at the door, all Lance could see was pure pandemonium. Airmen were everywhere, officers and enlisted alike. The club was jammed full, and the warriors had spilled out into the parking lot. The club had accommodated the overflow by bringing a portable bar out onto the sidewalk. It was early morning, but everyone was holding a drink after the long night's war. Someone was standing at the entrance to the club, speaking through a megaphone, praising some young warrior's exploits over North Korean skies.

Aziz dragged them to the makeshift bar and bought the first round.

After a short wait, they all held a beer high and saluted the Airborne Laser. They had just started to join in the fun when a tall stranger in a flight suit appeared behind Sergeant Adams. "Are you Adams? Out of Eagle Three Three?" The man asked.

Adams turned. The man didn't wear a name tag or any unit patches, and his flight suit was wrinkled like it was right out of the bag. "Yes, sir."

"I thought so. Come with me, Sergeant." The man led Adams towards the club's front door, then climbed the half dozen steps to the entrance. Much to Adams's astonishment, the man grabbed the bullhorn.

Lance started to follow when Critter stepped up and stopped him.

"Where are you headed?"

"That guy's dragging my friend somewhere. I want to know what's up."

"Don't worry. Adams is in good hands. Very good hands."

"What? Who is that guy?"

"That would be an Aurora pilot. The search-and-rescue guys just fished him out of the ocean. First thing he wanted to do was find a guy named Adams. Something about thanking him for saving his butt."

"Ladies and gentlemen," Driscoll blasted over the bullhorn. The man's commanding presence caused the jubilant crowd to pause and listen.

"I want to introduce you to America's newest breed of warrior."

Adams's face shifted into panic mode, turning red as a beet.

"Sergeant Adams has used the most powerful laser ever employed in battle to disable more than ninety percent of North Korea's ballistic missiles, and while he was at it he shot down a SAM that was just about to terminate me and my aircraft." Driscoll lowered the bullhorn and turned to shake the deeply embarrassed sergeant's hand. "I'm Tom Driscoll, son, and I owe you my life."

"I'm glad to meet you, sir. And I'm glad I could help where I could. We owe you a big favor, too. Without you, most of those missiles would have gotten through."

"Whatever. Of course, I'm buying your drinks all day."

"That's not necessary, sir. But if it'll make you feel better I could use another Coke."

Driscoll grinned. He turned back to the crowd and raised the bullhorn again. "Drinks are on me!"

The crowd roared. At least a third of the people surged toward the bar. Two dozen others fought toward Adams to find out about this new weapon.

"Did you check on Turbo? Any word?" Aziz asked Critter.

"Not very good news there," Critter said over the din of the crowd. "Search and rescue is out, but they didn't get a beacon after his plane disappeared. Doesn't look good."

"He saved a lot of people. I hope he knows that, wherever he is."

"Yeah."

"Did anyone ever figure out why they finally let us into the fight with the laser?" Lance asked.

"Yeah, sort of," Critter said. "You remember your friend General Killeen? The guy who tried to shut the program down, then took over here in Korea and didn't want to see the Airborne Laser?"

"Never met him, but yeah, he sure didn't seem to want to give us a shot at first."

"The first missile that leaked through was very strategically targeted. It scored a direct hit on his command center. High explosive with some kind of penetrating warhead. Took him out. General Kang, the head of the Korean forces, stepped in and gave approval for us to weigh in."

"There's some irony in there somewhere," Lance said. He looked toward the front of the club, where Sergeant Adams was fielding questions from dozens of new fans. Lance caught Adams's eye, then raised his glass in congratulations.

Epilogue

"How's that arm of yours healing, Billie?"

"Fine, Bernie." She stood up as the Boeing vice president came out of his office. "The cast is supposed to come off in another week, then I'll be ready to fly again."

"You're sure I can't convince you to stay on the ground? I need someone full time to run the test program. We're meeting in the small conference room." He nodded at his secretary and led Billie down the narrow hallway.

"You're assuming there will be a test program. I haven't heard any commitment out of the Pentagon. I think they're still trying to figure out how to pay the bill for that little fight in Korea."

"Don't worry. I'm sure the program funding will come through in a couple of days. You'll see why in just a few minutes." He opened the door to the conference room. There were several men already inside. Almost half were wearing uniforms, but not American ones.

"I think you've already met Major General Nakano?" Bernie said.

The Japanese officer stood and bowed deeply to Billie. "It is once again my pleasure," Nakano said.

Billie bowed as well, remembering the way she had treated the general the first time she had met him. And how his fighter pilots had weighed in when Killeen wouldn't lift a finger to help.

"This time I believe it's my pleasure," Billie said. "I owe you an apology, and my thanks."

"Neither is necessary," Nakano said. "I hope you have changed your mind and will now accept these gifts for yourself and your crew."

A junior officer brought forward the same boxes Billie had been offered in Japan. "Gladly," she said. "On behalf of myself and my crew, we thank you for these gifts. They are received in honor."

Nakano bowed again. "And I also hope you will reconsider the opportunity to administer the flight test program for the laser weapon development. If my government is going to fund it, we would like to have a warrior such as yourself in charge. And when you visit Japan, I would be honored to have you as my personal guest."

Billie smiled. "I'll have to discuss this with Bernie, but I think you can count on me."

Jake Williams, newly selected for major, pulled up to the rusting hangar in his beat-up old Camaro. Even though it went against his plans, Jake had accepted the promotion to major gratefully. It had taken Colonel Powers a long time to teach him what she meant by what she kept calling the "extra pay" he was getting in the Air Force. At first he thought she meant his pilot bonus, but that wasn't it—not at all. The extra pay he had been getting was the opportunity to do something for someone else, to stand as the protector against aggression and preserve the liberty and freedom of a people—of an entire nation. He intended to draw on that extra pay for a few more years, as long as the Air Force would have him. He got out and the door creaked shut.

"Well, if it isn't our war hero," someone yelled from around the corner.

"Marv? Is that you?"

"Good to see you again, son." Jake's old flight instructor stepped toward his former student. "How's the shoulder?"

Williams stretched his arm. "You heard, huh? Good as new."

"I hope they at least gave you a Purple Heart." Another man, vaguely familiar to Williams, stepped out of the small airfield office and joined them.

"You remember John Montgomery, don't you, Jake?"

Jake shook his head.

"FAA?"

"For crying out loud," Jake stepped forward and shook Montgomery's hand. "It's good to see you again."

"Never thought I'd hear you say that, not after I threatened to ground you fifteen years ago."

"That little talk changed my life—for the better. I owe you."

"I knew you wouldn't mind if John joined us," Marv said.

"Not at all. The Chieftain ready?"

"Ready? Ready for what?" Montgomery asked.

"Thought you guys might like to go on a little ride."

The two men looked at each other.

"Why not?" Montgomery said. "It's not every day a fella gets to be flown around by a genuine war hero."

*   *   *

"She feels the same as she always did," Jake said as he pulled the Chieftain into a shallow descent.

"I keep her up pretty well, even though no one much wants to fly her anymore," Marv said from the back.

Jake pointed to the river below them. "See that bridge down there?" he asked John Montgomery, the former FAA inspector sitting on his right.

"Yeah."

"That's the one that got me introduced to you." The plane was still descending.

"I know."

Marv laughed from the backseat.

"You're not going to, are you?" Montgomery asked.

"No, I'm not," Jake answered. "*We* are. Hang on."

"Oh, for crying out loud." Montgomery pulled his seat belt tight, then grinned at the pilot. "Go for it, war hero!"

"This is it." Mandy opened the door of the two-story townhouse. She stepped over the mail that had been pushed through the slot in the door. "It's not the greatest place—not quite as nice as our house in Santa Barbara."

"I think it's terrific," Lance said. The twins shot past him, heading up to the rooms they had staked out earlier when they came with their mom to see the place. "It's close to Stanford, and the neighborhood looks so friendly."

"Several members of the faculty live nearby. I've met some of them already. You'll like Dr. Miller, just down the street. Teaches physics. He's a runner, too.

Said he'd show you the best places to jog around here."

"I'm so proud of you, Mandy. Just think, a professor in the family. Mandy Brandon, Department of Geology."

"Associate professor. First things first."

"Don't worry, you'll get tenure. I'm sure of it."

"We'll see how it works out." She picked up a small box. "This is for you. It's from Boeing."

Lance opened the box and pulled out the ascot with the rising sun emblazoned on the front. There was a note from Billie Powers, thanking him again for his help and urging him to accept the gift. She had.

"What is that?" Mandy asked.

"A gift. From the Japanese."

"Are you ever going to tell me what you did over there? I'm dying to know."

"Maybe. Someday. If the Navy gives you a security clearance like they said they would, then I'll be able to tell you some of it. Right now I'd rather just take a look around at this fantastic place you picked out. Then maybe you can take me over and show me your office."

Mandy beamed. "I'd be glad to."